Pearly Eye

Laurelle Rond

'Pearly Eye is a story about loneliness, relationships, and the desire to find a home both within ourselves and the world. We cannot help but turn the pages, guessing, thinking, and most crucially, feeling, and if I could define the whole book in a single word, it would be Serendipity.' ~ **Steven Foster, Lincoln, UK.**

'It is a time travel book with a twist, where the past bleeds into the present and the present struggles with memories of the past. The characters are well managed. They draw you into the drama of each time period. I read it once and loved it, then reread it again for the nuances of the story and enjoyed it even more the second time.'
~ **Donna Messick, Texas, USA**

'Laurelle Rond's storytelling fulfils one's senses in every way since it creates an illusion which stays with a reader for a long time. Rich, strong, and powerful language not only takes the reader on a journey through magnificently described landscapes, but also gives an insight into the human psyche and emotions. Once the reader is engrossed in the story, it's absolutely impossible to put the book down until the last page. To me, Laurelle's craftsmanship is superb and at its best.' ~ **Basja Cengiya, Novo Mesto, Slovenia, Europe**

'Pearly Eye is a fascinating read with a juxtaposition of two worlds millennia apart. Dialogue is simple, clear, and descriptive and I found myself drawn inexorably to the wondrous storytelling, vivid imagery, and other-worldly context. I honestly couldn't put it down and was in tears at the end. This is the first of a trilogy, so there is more to come. I'm looking forward to the next book and the continuing story.' ~ **Val Edson, Wheatley, UK**

'A gripping and fascinating novel with such interesting characters, you immediately feel connected to. This is a perfect 'lose yourself' read and needs to be up there with Diana Gabaldon in the category of beautifully written and absorbing books.' ~ **Jo Baldwin-Trott, Hove, UK**

'I absolutely loved it. I was totally absorbed with the characters and the story.' ~ **Louisa Cox, Woodstock, UK**

'From the first page Pearly Eye drew me into a rich story, expertly weaving past and present lives together. It is full of rich characters that took me on a roller coaster journey from darkness and cruelty to lightness and kindness in a superbly crafted, compelling read. I loved it!' ~ **Linda Aspey, Cotswolds, UK**

'Pearly Eye by Laurelle Rond is a beautifully crafted novel about love, betrayal and the invisible ties that bind us all through space and time. For anyone who loves the simple art of storytelling, it is a must-read. I absolutely loved it.' ~ **Tara Shaw, Shrewsbury, UK**

'It was one of those books I couldn't put down and when I did, couldn't wait to pick it up again and find out what happened next. The central character in the book was one I could believe in and the story I found both a compelling read at the time and very memorable afterwards – the sign of a really good book. I think this story is different and a very worthwhile read. I can't wait for Laurelle's next book as I love her unique style and ability to get you really involved in the characters and their journey.' ~ **Jackie Jarvis, Wallingford, UK**

'This novel should come with a health warning – it stopped me from sleeping because I couldn't put it down. Then it haunted me for months after I'd finished reading it. I can't wait for the next one!' ~ **Melinda Rond-Alliston, Bicester, UK**

'A cracking good story that draws you under its spell. The writing style was very descriptive, enabling me to visualise and inhabit both contemporary and prehistoric worlds. I wanted to know what was going to happen so much that I found it hard to put down at night. The story left me wanting more. I can't wait for the next instalment. I am a fan.' ~ **Dee Nunan, Great Milton, UK**

Published by Goldcrest Books International Ltd
www.goldcrestbooks.com
publish@goldcrestbooks.com

ISBN: 978-1-913719-56-2

Dedication

Sarah Colven
1955 – 1993

Your days were short but your dreams were big.
I will never forget your smile or the hope in your heart.
Be at peace.

Natasha Rond-Alliston

My first child, my friend, and my soul sister.
I am so grateful to have you in my life.
Enjoy your beautiful and precious time here.

Prologue

circa 2000 Before Christian Era

In the moonlight, Seela pushes a small child onto a low, snow-covered branch and swings herself up beside her. Quickly, she clambers higher and leans down to grab her little sister's hand so she can jerk her even further towards safety. They have been fleeing so long it seems as though they never had a home at all, but it would have meant death if they had stayed. It might still mean death. Running away in winter is dangerous. If the cold does not get them, starvation or hungry animals might.

Despite her stiffening limbs, she doesn't give up. As she pulls little Duna upwards for a third time, there's a low, vicious growl from the ground below just before the darkness is split by an agonised cry. Nostrils fill with the stench of wolf and she looks down into frenzied eyes yellow in the ghastly moon-glow. Horrified, she yanks her now sobbing sister still further up.

The next time the wolf hurls itself into the branches, it

misses. Again and again it tries to dislodge them yet somehow the quaking tree holds onto them with its freezing fingers and eventually a desperate howl signals the creature's defeat.

For a while, the only sound is panting and whimpering. As soon as the scent of wolf disappears, Seela becomes aware that something is oozing onto her foot. Wrapping her legs around the branch for purchase, she grips Duna with one hand and reaches down with the other. Sure enough, her fingers encounter a slick of something sticky on the little girl's thigh. Carefully lowering her head, she starts to lick the deep laceration, not stopping until there's a taste of salt.

When a clod of snow suddenly drops onto her face, she blinks rapidly before feeling for a strip of cloth from the bag around her waist. Once she has wound it tightly around Duna's small, thin leg, she rights herself and leans, panting, against the trunk. Then she pulls her sister close under her cloak to lull her to sleep. The five-stringed gitty on her back digs uncomfortably into her bones. She wishes she could reach round to take it off to play the instrument and comfort them both, but she does not dare move. Instead, she starts to shiver uncontrollably. Her breath falters and, as though the wolf has torn off her eyes and ears, all light and sound disappear.

It is a long time before she hears something. At first she thinks it is the whispering of bare branches trying to pluck at her hair with their dead fingers. But then she realises it is the voice of a woman singing far away. The voice becomes louder, joined by another and another, until a long line of grandmothers, mothers, and girls still to be born start to file past the tree.

When they draw to a halt in a huge half ring in front of her, the lead woman steps forward, her hair as strikingly red as Seela's own. One of her eyes is green while the other is as pale as a pearl from a shell. A chain of stones is in her hands, a glimpse of amber and white amongst the grey. As though Seela knows what she is supposed to do, she somehow reaches down from the tree to take it and slip it over her head. Once it is round her neck, a blissful heat begins to melt the ice from her bones, leaving her floating in a sea of comfort, warm as a cradle.

But the relief does not last for long. All too soon the rhythm of her heart resumes, air refills her lungs and she returns outside to the freezing world she has known all her life. As soon as she becomes aware of her sister once again solid in her arms, the women flee into the shadows, taking their song and the necklace with them. And yet Seela no longer feels alone. The woman with the red hair and pearly eye has not gone far. Trembling, Seela looks up through the snowy branches and sees that the moon has returned. Instinctively, she puts her hand on the place where the necklace had lain and feels strength where before there had only been fear. The wolf has gone and the tree is protecting them in its fist.

All she has to do is to hold on for the dawn.

Then they will continue their journey.

Somehow, the woman with the pearly eye will look after them.

Fehu – cattle and prosperity.
It is time to move forward

Chapter One

SELENA – Present Day

The song goes round and round in my head. I have never heard it before and yet it seems familiar. It spellbinds me with unintelligible words in a language from some ancient time, all the while burning an image of two green eyes into my mind. It is only when I realise that the bath has grown cold and I am shivering that I climb out of the water, wrap myself in one of the hotel's bath sheets, and return to the bedroom.

It's a mess; more like a floordrobe than a room. As I bend to tidy the tangle of clothes strewn across the carpet, it's hard to concentrate with the echoes of the song floating in and around me. If only I'd been able to sing something like that tonight, then maybe I wouldn't have failed in my last chance to be recognised as a singer-songwriter. When the organiser had said I could return for next year's Winter Festival as 'The Red Pirate', I'd briefly blazed with hope, quipping that he'd have to provide a parrot for my shoulder that wouldn't clash with my outrageously red hair. But then he'd added that he still wouldn't be able to pay me and my hopes had crashed to the floor.

So this is the end of the road for me. There's no money in music, at least not at my level. It takes too long to make a name and I don't have the luxury of time. Now I've been made redundant from my job at the library, I need to find paying work not only for myself but also to help Mum and Mara, my disabled sister and to keep our wreck of a house from falling down.

Despite my disappointment, the strange song refuses to leave me alone and I remember the girl in the dream. Unable to help myself, I reach for my Celtic harp and start to work out the music. Strangely, my fingers glide over the strings as though they already know the notes even though I only heard them for the first time tonight.

I'm in the middle of the last verse when the phone rings at the side of the bed. Annoyed at the interruption, I don't answer it at first, but when it continues I reluctantly pick it up. It is the night porter telling me that two policewomen are waiting for me downstairs. Alarmed, I wonder why they could possibly want to see me at nearly 2 o'clock in the morning.

When I reach the foyer, they all stare at me with fascinated revulsion and I realise that I have forgotten to cover my left eye with an eyepatch.

"Selena, would you like to sit down?" asks the blonde one in a hard Liverpudlian accent. She points to a sofa in the lobby.

"What's the matter?" I manage.

There is a long hesitation before she speaks. "I'm afraid there's been an accident."

"Your mother and your sister ..." says the black one in a soft Jamaican accent.

"We're so sorry," continues the first. "They wouldn't have known anything."

I stare at them, uncomprehending.

"Your mother was driving. I'm afraid the car wasn't road-worthy."

The words make no sense. Mum hasn't driven in years. I'm the one with the car and it is here with me. The only other car we own is Dad's and that is as dead as he is. Mum only keeps it as a reminder of happier times. My pearly eye goes cold. This must be a dream, like the one of the girl up the tree. I pinch my skin, expecting to wake up but the scene fails to change and I am left staring at the police women with my one green eye.

"Fortunately nobody else was involved. Otherwise …"

The voice fades and my mind starts to flip. I find myself wondering if the wolf will return to the girl and her sister. Mara would like that. She loves wolves. I must have told her every wolf story in every book. She doesn't like them portrayed as bad. She thinks they are good, and she often looks down as though one is sitting companionably beside her. I've often wished she could speak and tell me what she sees but although Mara is older than me, she has a mental condition meaning that her mind paused and stayed at about five years old.

About the same age as the little sister in the dream.

I feel a touch on my hand and see that one of the police women is now kneeling in front of me.

"Selena, here's some tea. It will help you to feel better."

She puts the mug into my hand. It turns my skin red; as red as the colour of the older sister's hair; as strikingly red as mine. But I barely notice. Instead I take a sip, not realising that it is burning me until it scalds my tongue. Quickly, I put it down on the table at my side. The liquid slops from the mug and drips over the edge; the same colour as dad's car, flecks of tea leaves floating like rust on the surface.

What was Mum thinking? Driving a car that could barely

start? Oh God, I should have been there to stop her. I should have saved them, not been chasing an impossible dream. Perhaps the wolf will come back and send me to the oblivion I deserve.

RAFF – Present Day

An exceptionally tall man sat at an old oak table in the kitchen of a ramshackle farmhouse. He could not get the song out of his head. It had been unearthly, like birdsong from another world. Unnerved, he tossed his long black hair over his shoulder and reached for his carving instruments; the best form of distraction that he knew. Carving took him into the zone and consumed most of his time when he was not looking for artefacts at some dig or other.

It was the dig that had brought him here to the Stennings although the project did not look very promising. For a start, it was the wrong time of year. But the owners of the land didn't seem to care about that. They just wanted the job done so that the land could be freed for planning permission. It was ridiculous: the land was part of a flood plain that was waterlogged for much of the year. That was a good thing for archaeology. It meant that the site would not have been wrecked by centuries of ploughing. But it was a disaster for building. Water from the stream would have to be diverted and that meant wrecking the delicate ecosystem.

As the song continued to worm its way through his mind, he touched the wood on the table so that he might feel rather than listen. He loved trees. Always careful to choose wood from a sustainable source, he had experimented to see what worked best, beginning with basswood, a malleable and inexpensive white wood without grain that grew throughout

Europe and the Americas. With his love of the flute, he had tried making simple musical instruments but getting the holes in the right place for perfect tuning had proved extremely difficult. He had then tried aspen which was good for carving animals. After that, he had experimented with butternut which worked well for making furniture. Black walnut had been next. More expensive and needing sharper tools and a mallet for working, the wood had proved wonderful for its rich colour and grain. Finally, oak had taught him how to use power carvers.

Now he was a master craftsman, able to carve anything from raised scenes and characters to letters and caricatures in both two and three dimensions. His favourite subjects were animals, and with his impressive set of tools, he could lose himself for hours. To date, his most impressive piece was the large wolf that sat outside by the front door like a guardian of the farmhouse.

This latest carving, however, was proving rather more elusive. His aim had been to carve a smaller wolf but this one was turning out to be more of a dog. He had used black walnut, a tree which could reach thirty or forty meters in height, and named for its dark, heavily ridged bark. Larger than the common walnut, it needed plenty of sun and perhaps that was why he liked it so much. The black walnut was an intriguing example of dark and light, rather like life, he thought, in which one was continually treading a path between the two. Nevertheless, why its inner shape was insisting on becoming a dog rather than a wolf, he had no idea. It was as though conviction was not only coming from deep inside the grain but also from deep inside him, carving a memory that he did not realise he had.

Frowning, he pushed his spectacles onto the top of his head and rubbed his eyes. For a split second, the light in the farmhouse faded as though it had gone behind a cloud. Unsettled, he stood and stretched, his impossibly tall body wavering like one of his beloved trees in the wind. Then he sat again and laid his hand on the unfinished head of the carving as though he might discover what was in its mind. The song grew louder and then, without warning, suddenly stopped.

He breathed a sigh of relief. Now it was quiet, he would be able to concentrate. Carefully, he picked up a chisel and began to search the wood for answers.

SELENA – Present Day

The funeral passes in a blur. Only a handful of people turn up and not just because of the snow. Mum became something of a recluse after Dad died and despite the fact that our family had lived there for generations, we were strangers to the community. Besides, they think I'm weird and refuse to look me in the eye.

As I arrive back at the house, I can't help but notice what a monster of a mansion it is. Highhill is like a mouth which needs constant feeding, haemorrhaging money faster than rats devour food. Mum only managed to keep it going by opening the house up as a bed and breakfast. According to the will, it is mine but I have no idea what I'm going to do with it.

Overwhelmed by guilt, I trudge to the back door. As though the house doesn't want me here anymore, the heavy key refuses to turn in the lock. It takes three attempts to open it and the moment I step inside I wish it had never let me in. Mara's haphazard scribblings on the walls call out to me as though she were still here and my heart feels as though it will break all over again. In the living room I draw the curtains and switch on the lamps, but the light does nothing to dispel the silence. So I lift the lid of the piano to play a chord and then run my hand across the strings of the harp, but the sounds die away as though they too are weeping.

It's no better upstairs. Mum's room yawns emptily, the only colour the faded pink bedspread that she crocheted so painstakingly many years ago. Old toys lie on Mara's floor as though, rather than being a woman of nearly thirty, she was still a child. I pass the guest rooms and arrive at my bedroom at the end of the corridor. Inside is an iron-framed bed with an enormous black chest at its foot. Two trunks occupy one wall and an old oak wardrobe another. The single picture on the wall is of a Pre-Raphaelite girl sitting by water, her Titian hair flowing in a ripple down her back. I chose it when I was eleven because it seemed full of promise. Now I can only see tragedy.

Too agitated to lie down, I make my way to the bathroom. A mistake. Above the sink is a mirror that shows me my reflection all too clearly; one green eye pink from crying, and a black eyepatch over the other one to match my dress. I pull it off and gaze hatefully into my pearly orb, so pale that it appears to be inside out. My hair is the opposite, its colour an impossible red. I look a fright. No wonder the people at the funeral gave me a wide berth. I wouldn't want to talk to me, either.

Grief-stricken, I run downstairs and escape into the garden. The February sky is dark with the brooding clouds of winter waiting to vomit more snow. I don't stop till I reach the lake and climb into the little boat moored up at the side. Then I row across to the island in the middle and the treehouse that Dad built for me before he died. It sits between two sturdy oaks with a ladder hanging down from a doorway at the top. Inside, it is almost completely round with a platform for sleeping on and a duvet wrapped in a plastic bag to keep it from the damp. Above, several curved shelves are fixed on the wall for food and books. This used to be my refuge. When

I couldn't stand the name-calling or bullying any longer, I would hide here and pretend I'd entered another world where everyone was kind and a pearly eye didn't turn you into a freak. A great sob rushes up from my belly and threatens to strangle me. Turning tail, I run back to the boat, row across the lake and scramble back up to the house. Then I grab my bag, put on my coat, lock up the house and start walking.

I have to get out of here. I have no idea where to but I don't care. For now, the house will just have to stay empty.

Nowhere can be as painful as this.

BERTIE – Present Day

Bertie woke from the nightmare, his thick greying hair damp with sweat. There had been a girl with red hair. And his sister had been cowering. Impossible; Hester was never afraid of anything. As for the song, he had never heard anything like it before. Part melody and part unintelligible words, it had pulled at something inside him, something he hadn't known existed and something he most definitely didn't want to feel. With a shudder, he straightened in the chair. For heaven's sake, this was no way to take an afternoon nap.

Stiffly, he pushed himself to his feet, walked to the kitchen, switched on the kettle and made himself a pot of tea. For the first time in ages, he wished that their mother had not walked out on them when they'd been so young. Had she still been here, perhaps she would have known how to handle Hester. Now he was dreaming about his sister when they hadn't spoken in years. To change your gender was hard enough; to lose your family as well was devastating. Hester had broken his heart when she had refused to call him Bertie rather than Beatrice and banned him from seeing any of her family again.

Taking his tea into the sitting room, Bertie returned to his favourite armchair and tried to push the dream out of his mind. He should be thinking about the deadline his agent had set for a new book proposal, not weird warnings about his sister. His last book might have sold well and all five of his books and his name, Bertie Fratton, might have their rightful place in the British Library, but that meant little these days. If he were to stay a leading light in popular psychology, he needed a new idea. But Bertie always thought better when discussing his thoughts out loud. Fortunately, he had the perfect friend for this in Larna. She had supported him during his transgender surgery and was a very good listener. They had met quite by accident one day when he, as Beatrice, had been about to buy too many pills to put an end to the misery. Larna had talked him round in the chemist into becoming Bertie and they had been best friends ever since.

Two weeks ago and some twenty years after they had met, Larna had just moored her narrowboat on the river in the Stennings in Oxfordshire to be near to him. He was thrilled. Although he had many other friends now, she had always remained the closest, and in many ways, the most interesting. It was time he showed her around Oxford so he wondered if she would like to go to a concert. There was one coming up on Thursday lunchtime in one of the colleges at the university.

She would love the rarefied atmosphere of the chapel and he would use the opportunity to run through some ideas.

SELENA – Present Day

The departures board is covered by cancellation notices. That's England for you. One sniff of snow and everything grinds to a halt. There is a train running to Paddington and that is as good a place as any. It is also far away from Norfolk. But when we arrive in London, I panic. There are too many people. So I choose another train, this time to Oxford which is reputed to be beautiful.

After sleeping most of the way, I wake up hungry for the first time since the funeral. I follow a gaggle of women into Oxford town centre and find a café whose front is decorated in a lovely shade of duck egg blue. Inside, it appears to be teeming with life. On one side is a group of foreign tourists with expensive cameras, seemingly unperturbed by the foul weather. On the other side, two women, surrounded by shopping bags, are discussing their purchases. Next to the window a group of students, fashionably scruffy in jeans and thick jumpers, are arguing animatedly with each other. I find a seat at the back and order some food. Once I've devoured eggs on toast and two mugs of tea, I start to relax. There's a strange kind of freedom in being away from home and somehow I don't care about occasional stares. Nobody knows me here or realises that my eyepatch covers a bizarre, pearly eye.

It is only when the tables begin to empty and the clock on the wall approaches five o'clock, that I realise I'm going to have to leave. Wrapping my scarf around my head and turning up my collar, I step out into the whirling snow ready to look for a place to stay. There's a little money in my bank account but not much, so I'm going to have to be careful.

The city centre seems to be sewn together by a crossroads where Aldgate, the High Street, Cornmarket, and Queen Street meet, like thoughts going off on different tangents. Down medieval-looking side lanes the accommodation is too expensive, so I ask a couple of people where I might find somewhere cheaper to stay and am pointed in the direction of Cowley, a suburb just outside the city centre.

After a long, cold walk I eventually find a sign for a bed

and breakfast and knock on the door. A woman answers. She stares at my eyepatch for a moment longer than necessary and asks for £40 upfront. Once she's led me upstairs to a small room with a single bed and plain chest of drawers, she quickly tells me that breakfast is between 7 and 9 o'clock. Then she bids me goodnight and closes the door behind her as though she can't get away fast enough.

Alone again, I stare around the room, looking for something to distract me from the images of Mum and Mara which flit painfully round my mind. There's nothing worth watching on the television and I didn't think to bring a book. Tired as I am, I'm too anxious to sleep so I put my phone on charge, peel off the eyepatch and have a shower. By the time I am done, there's enough juice in the phone to check my bank account. I still have some savings left but after paying for the return train ticket and food at the café, the balance is alarmingly low.

I'm going to have to go back to Highhill tomorrow.

It feels like yet another failure.

LARNA – Present Day

Larna put down her phone and smiled. A concert. How wonderful. Delighted that she'd made the decision to move into a narrowboat on the Thames, she felt like the luckiest person in the world. *Water Haven* was beautiful, and it was hers. She would have to get used to living on the water, but it was the best decision she had ever made. A podcast about travelling the waterways of England had given her the idea and, as she had no dependants, and enough money from her inheritance, she could roam wherever she wanted to.

Now she couldn't wait for the spring. Apparently river folk were a sociable bunch in the sunshine and she was eager to make some new friends. Spring would make nature erupt with colour again and the world would stop looking so drab. Her dislike of sadness had turned her into something of a rescuer and this had got her into trouble more than once. After one too many glasses of wine, Bertie had made her promise not to save anyone else, but if he thought she would stick to that he didn't know her well enough. For now, she couldn't wait to explore Oxford, even if the winter was hanging on and the weather was abnormally cold. As far as she had seen, it was a magnificent town, full of history and character. With a broad smile of sheer happiness, she went to her wardrobe at the back of the boat so that she could choose something bright to wear for the concert.

How thrilling life was.

SELENA – Present Day

The next day I slip on some ice and only just prevent a nasty fall. In air chill enough to freeze skin to bones, I reluctantly make my way back to the train station for the return journeys to Paddington and Norfolk. Once I've thawed my hands under the hot tap of the ladies' loo, I sit on one of the red chairs in the waiting area. The idea of going back to an empty house is almost beyond me. If only I'd saved harder when I'd worked in the library rather than spending my money on the harp and a dream of earning my living with music, I might not be in such a precarious position. Besides, I'm not ready to face estate agents and listen to what I already know: that Highhill is run down to the point of dilapidation and won't be easy to sell.

A voice alerts me to the arrival of the first train. Wearily, I push myself to my feet and make my way to the platform.

I'm just about to put my ticket in the machine when a girl steps out in front of me. She has astonishingly red hair like mine and is carrying a small child who seems to be asleep on her shoulder. She stares at me with her intense green eyes and refuses to budge. Embarrassed, I try to move round her but my hand starts to shake and the ticket falls to the floor. At the same time, we both reach down to pick it up and, for a split second, our hands touch. Her skin is icy cold and a smell of old rotting fruit fills my nostrils. At the same time, a shock, like electricity, jolts my hand back and I shoot to my feet. Blinking hard, I prepare to challenge her but she and the child have vanished. I look back down at the ground. There is no sign of the ticket either.

It is only when someone nudges me aside and swears under their breath, that I realise I am in the way of the other passengers who are trying to get to the train. Bewildered, I walk away. I don't know what else to do. Without enough money to buy another ticket, I return to the red chairs in the waiting area, trying to work out what has just happened. The ticket was in my hand. I was about to put it into the machine when the girl blocked my way. We reached for the ticket at the same time. It dropped to the floor and girl and ticket disappeared into thin air.

Am I going mad?

In the end, all I can do is try to look as though I'm waiting to catch another train. I stay there all day. Lunch is the cheapest sandwich I can find, and I miss dinner altogether. Eventually it grows dark again. I loiter for as long as I dare but when a member of staff approaches, stares suspiciously at my eyepatch and then at me, I trudge over to the door.

Outside, the sky has cleared. The temperature on a nearby display says it is minus two. Jamming my hands into my pockets, I start walking again. I must keep moving. If I stop,

I'll freeze where I stand. Time slows to a crawl. I trudge round and round this way. Then that way. Finally in a wonky figure of eight around the centre.

By 4 o'clock, my eyelids are so heavy that my face is falling onto my chin. My legs are dragging along the ground. My spine is collapsing into itself. Too weary to continue, I stop in a doorway where there's a large piece of discarded cardboard. I drop my bag onto it and kneel down. Then I curl up where I am, face first into the cold ground and close my eyes.

circa 2000 B.C.E.

It was hard going trudging through the snow. The air was frigid with cold, and Seela wondered how much longer she would be able to carry Duna. In the whiteness, everything looked the same and with the sun hidden behind heavy yellow clouds, she was no longer sure where she should go. She was starting to lose all sense of direction now that the red-headed woman with the pearly eye had gone.

Desperate to find shelter before night and the wolf returned to claim them, she kept her head down until she heard a rustling. Nearby, a little brown bird with a yellow beak was perched upon a branch, a crest of feathers raised on the top of its head above its twinkly black eyes. Forgetting how tired she was, Seela pursed her lips and whistled back. The little brown bird cocked its head, looked at her before answering, and then took off from the branch, causing great clumps of snow to fall to the ground.

As Duna moaned in her arms, Seela sighed and shifted the weight of her sister before walking on. After a while, the little bird found them again, this time singing more urgently as though it was trying to tell her something. Curious, Seela

23

whistled back and watched as the bird listened. This time, when it flew off, she followed. When the bird finally alighted on an oak tree, Seela sniffed the air and caught the scent of smoke. Clutching Duna closely, she walked for a while longer, not stopping until she heard a woman's voice. Hoping that it was the woman with the pearly eye, she began to move forward but when the voice was joined by a man's, she quickly hid behind the massive trunk of an oak tree, trying to control her breathing. Not daring to move, she clutched Duna tighter, praying that her little sister would not wake yet.

When a third voice joined, she mustered the courage to peer around the trunk. A man, a woman and a youth were talking animatedly around a fire, the flames flickering over their faces, lending them colours of red, orange and yellow. They were the first people she had seen since she had run away, and she only just stopped herself from crying out loud in relief.

Watching carefully, she tried to judge whether they would harm her and her sister or offer them shelter. In the end, hunger made her decide to trust them. Praying to The Mother to keep them safe, she took a deep breath and raised her foot ready to step out and ask for help, but before she could move forward, an image of the woman with the pearly eye flashed in front of her, holding up her hand and telling her to stop.

Seela put her foot carefully down again and slid back behind the tree.

The woman with the pearly eye had spoken.

It was time to wait.

Fehu reversed – loss of money

Chapter Two

SELENA – Present Day

I am woken by a shout and my eyes fly open into stiletto-sharp air.

"Move, we don't want your sort here. Scarper!"

A man is glaring down at me, his fist raised. In my haste to struggle to my feet, the cardboard rips in two. At the same time, something moves at my back.

"Now fuck off, both of you, and don't come back!" the man shouts, his breath white and venomous in the cold dawn air.

Shivering uncontrollably, I glimpse a tan-coloured mongrel disappearing round the nearest street corner. Clutching my bag, I begin to hobble away on the icy pavement, my neck on fire from having lain so awkwardly.

Soon, I smell fresh coffee. A nearby café is filled with early commuters sitting at clusters of tables eating breakfast. With my mouth watering, I spy a half uneaten baguette on an empty table nearest the door. Quickly, I pull my eyepatch back in place. As casually as I can, I sneak in, snatch the food and stuff it into my pocket. Before anyone can stop me, I grab a barely touched beaker of coffee from another table. Then I run. Once I am out of sight, I gulp down the cold coffee and cram the baguette into my mouth. It's not enough. Still ravenous, I go to open the door of the café again for a second helping, but the waitress must have spotted me before. Her fierce glare is a warning, so turning swiftly away, I start walking again. Not for the first time, I curse the way I look. With my fiery red hair and eyepatch, I am far too recognisable.

After a while, the dog returns. Unfazed by my weird appearance, he doesn't draw back, and this time he allows me to stroke him. Little more than skin and bone, he's trembling as though he's trying to shake himself out of his skin. I don't need to look inside his mind to know how he feels. Squatting down, I'm careful not to look into his eyes in case I frighten him away.

"I'd better give you a name," I say gently. "What about Buddy? I need a friend and you look as though you could do with one as well."

He wags his tail and licks his lips. Pushing myself slowly to my feet, I spy a nearby street food van. Urging him to come with me, I try to beg for some food for the dog, but the vendor is hard-faced and refuses to give me anything. I argue with him. Can't he see that the poor creature is starving? He looks at me sideways and I fix him with my pearly eye. Despite the eyepatch, it does the trick. He hands over a sausage and a plastic cup of lukewarm coffee.

Once I've thrown the food to the dog and drunk the coffee, I reach out to stroke the animal's head. "Come on, let's get going, Buddy," I say. "We need to find somewhere to spend the night." Wondering if there might be a cheap hostel somewhere outside the city, I take out my phone, but it is old and although I recharged it at the B and B, the cold seems to be sapping whatever energy it had left.

We spend the day looking for somewhere to stay but by nightfall, we have still found nothing. I turn down yet another lane but, instead of more houses, I find myself in a field away from the street lights. Moonlight casts eerie shadows all around while above, the stars are glassy bright. Despite the snow, the ground has turned so dark that it seems to have disappeared altogether. I bend down to reassure Buddy who has started to whine but when I touch him, he takes off, fleeing back towards the light.

I go to follow him but a silver glint in the distance stops me. Unable to resist the pull, I step towards it, not stopping until I reach the edge of a river, its surface bubbling as though someone beneath is trying to breathe. Fascinated and afraid in equal measure, I crouch down and see a face in the depths. It's thin, crumpled and young, with long, bedraggled hair.

It's the girl from the dreams; the girl at the station.

But this time there's no sign of her sister.

A great surge of grief rushes up into my throat and when one of her hands extends towards me, I can't stop myself from leaning nearer her. My pearly eye explodes with pain and I draw back. Just in time. Something brushes the top of my head. Terrified, I look up, but there is only Orion's belt high in the sky, bright and uncompromising in its clarity.

When I look down again, the face has gone. For a moment, I freeze, the grief of losing Mum and Mara so intense that I wonder if I will ever breathe again. But then an owl calls nearby and I am forced back into the world.

It's my turn to flee.

Once I reach the orange glow of the city centre, I search frantically for Buddy, but there's no sign of him. I'm shivering so hard that I don't know what to do with myself. In the end, I track a circuit around the centre, counting how many laps I can walk. I must keep myself from sleeping because if I close my eyes again, the girl will return to pull me into herself and not even my pearly eye will be able to stop me from falling in.

Eventually, my body starts to give up and my legs threaten to give way. I wait till I'm by a dark place in the doorway of the Covered Market. Then I huddle into it and, using my bag for a pillow again, allow my sore eyes to close.

As I descend into oblivion, the cold and darkness are so complete that I wonder if I will ever wake up again, but the smell of smoke in the air distracts me and, before I can rise back to the surface, I find myself watching three figures arguing by a fire.

circa 2000 B.C.E.

"Priestess, why have you banished Hogan into the forest?" the first figure, a big man, demanded angrily. "In snow like this, he will die."

"That is his punishment, Mevin," the second figure, an upright woman, replied. "He committed the most evil of acts against The Mother herself."

"Mana did not deserve to die," said the third figure, a tall, gangly youth.

"Riadd, keep out of this. Mana was just another weakling girl," Mevin retorted, shaking the snow off his shoulders like a great bear. "Go back to the women and children where you belong. You may be tall as a weed but wait until you have grown some muscle before you challenge me. Besides, you know as well as I do that the girl babbled nonsense. She was nothing. Hogan was our leader."

"Mana was our SeeSayer," countered the priestess. "She spoke wisely. She predicted that New Bloods would arrive who would change everything. You should have listened to her more closely."

"I was not allowed to do so," retorted Mevin. "None of us were."

"That is because she spoke through The Mother," said the priestess, "and only I could be told what she said."

"You think too much of yourself, woman. If Mana had known something, she should have told us herself."

"You know full well that she couldn't speak properly. She needed my voice to communicate her messages."

"Pah," he spat. "Admit that our children are weaklings and do something about it!"

"Mevin," she cried in despair, "we are about to erect a giant Stone to bring travellers to us. When they see our fertile land, they will stay. Our bloods will mix and our children will be born strong again."

"Even if it does work, that will take an age," Mevin declared bitterly. "It would be far quicker to raid other camps, but you have banished the one man who could help us do that. Hogan knows where the other clans are. We need his knowledge if we are ever to become strong again. Let me go and find him in the forest and bring him back. Let me …"

"No!" Lanalla cried. "Hogan angered The Mother and he must be punished. He is no longer worthy to live with us." She straightened her shoulders and glared at him. "Guard your tongue carefully, Mevin, if you do not want to call The Mother's anger down on you as well."

"Still your threats, priestess. Your rule is over. It is time for a man to lead us. We have had enough of women."

"But…" Riadd began to protest.

Mevin slapped him hard across the face. "Stop your pestering, boy. You follow this woman like a lovelorn puppy and she is not even your real mother. It's about time you learned how to be a man." He reached out and grabbed him by the scruff of the neck and began to drag him away. "I have had enough of women's talk. Come, we have men's work to do."

"Don't hurt him," pleaded the priestess, but Mevin ignored her and in moments man and boy had disappeared out of the clearing.

Once they had gone, the priestess slumped dejectedly by the fire and closed her eyes, looking as though all the life had drained out of her into the snow.

Behind the tree where she was hidden, Seela took a deep breath and gently laid the still sleeping Duna down on the ground. Then she removed the small harp from her back and, with it in her hand, stepped out into the clearing. Noiselessly, she moved across to where the woman was sitting and knelt on the ground in front of her. Then she began to play the tiny instrument.

At the sound of the music, the priestess opened her eyes and raised her head. The girl's hair was the colour of the sun on fire, music flowing out of her hands like birds flocking across the sky.

As their feathers floated around her, her despair began to recede.

Perhaps The Mother had not deserted her after all.

SELENA – PRESENT DAY

This time I wake to something hitting my face. Buddy flees as a laughing teenager disappears down the road leaving an empty beer can rolling in the gutter. With my eyepatch somewhere around my chin, I try calling his name, but my throat is too sore to make much sound and he doesn't reappear. Aching from head to toe, I force myself to my feet, put the eyepatch back in place and jam my frozen hands into my pockets.

At least I have survived another night outside. Belly concave with hunger, I trawl the cafés looking for half-eaten food, but this time I am worried that the police will be called. I don't want to be charged with vagrancy or whatever they do to people who are out of luck and have no home to sleep in. Despite the cold, several buskers have already started to perform. At the top of Cornmarket, there's the unmistakable sound of panpipes, guitars and drums from a group of Peruvian musicians, whilst further down, a classical guitarist with an amplifier and fingerless gloves is managing to pick out a melody.

As I trudge along, an idea begins to form. Checking that my eyepatch is firmly in place, I walk towards a doorway and remove the scarf from around my neck. Once it's folded into a hopeful square, I lay it down on the ground and sit cross-legged behind it. Then I clear my throat and start to sing an easy folk song. My voice cracks and threatens to run out altogether but I keep going. Something about the singing begins to calm me and gradually my voice strengthens. After a few minutes, a couple of coins land on my scarf. Encouraged, I try another folk song. More coins, then, a two-pound coin from a passing American who whispers to her companion that I am a poor, one-eyed thing with a lovely voice who must be desperate to be singing in weather like this.

I stop when my tongue is too sticky with thirst to continue. Bending to retrieve the money, I count £8.23 plus a couple of unusable euros. Added to the change I have, that's still not enough for another train ticket, let alone a night's accommodation, but if I sing for the whole day then perhaps I'll have enough by the end. First however, I need to warm up with some food and find something to drink, so promising myself that I will return once I've eaten, I clamber to my feet and start walking again, fantasising about breakfast.

As I turn into Queen Street, I cry out with delight as Buddy reappears. Crouching down, I offer him my hand as though he is my best friend returning after a long trip away. He wags his tail uncertainly and allows me to scratch him behind his ears, but he's still wary. Determined to earn his trust, I watch the string of saliva oozing from his black lips and realise that he needs food as much as I do.

At the fast-food stall on the next street, I order food, two cups of water and coffee. I hold out one beaker of water to Buddy, and he laps greedily while I down the other. Then I throw him half of the food and gobble down the rest. Finally, I wrap my fingers around the hot plastic beaker and take a blissful sip. I never knew coffee could taste so good.

All too soon everything has gone, yet we are still hungry. Throwing caution to the wind, I order a toasted sandwich, reassuring myself that, in a minute, I'll go back and earn enough to stay the night somewhere. When the food comes, I tear off a large chunk, crouch down and hold it out to him. Gently, he takes it from my fingers. "Thank you for keeping me warm last night," I whisper to him. "Now, shall we go and earn some more money?"

This time he comes with me. With Buddy lying down by my side, I start to feel more confident but without warning, he suddenly growls, leaps to his feet and flees.

"What the fuck d'ya think ya doin'?"

The voice comes from my blind side. Turning my head, I see a man in front of me, his face covered in piercings, head roughly shaved and a cigarette dangling from his lips. He reaches out, grabs my eyepatch and pulls it down. Fuck," he says. "You look like something from outer space."

I try to turn away, but I can't move.

"Where the hell are you from?" he snarls, blowing smoke into my face, "another planet?"

When I don't answer, he spits something onto the ground just in front of me. My stomach heaves.

"Look, Wall Eye, this is my spot." He crouches down to peer closely into my face. His breath is so rank that I flinch.

"So piss off and don't come back."

I don't need telling twice. Struggling to my feet, I grab my bag and the empty scarf and flee.

Once I'm safely round the corner, I stop and lean against the wall, panting. My breakfast threatens to come up, but I force it down. There will be no more food today.

"Are you all right?"

A woman in her forties dressed in vividly bright colours is standing in front of me, her eyes full of concern. "Did that nasty man upset you?" she asks, her eyebrows rising in surprise when she sees my pearly eye.

Humiliated, I pull the eyepatch back up into position and turn to walk away.

Seeing my discomfort, she reaches out a hand to stop me. "Look, I'm sorry but I can't stop now." She takes her hand away to rummage in her bag and then holds something out to me. "Here's my card. If I can do anything to help, just call me." She hesitates. "And have this." She opens her purse and pulls out a £10 note. "Look after yourself, dear," she says, handing it to me. "I heard you singing earlier. You have such a beautiful voice."

LARNA – Present Day

Larna hurried away, perturbed by what she'd witnessed. The poor girl had been frightened by that awful man. She wasn't surprised. She'd have been frightened too. And that eye; it looked like a pearl. She'd never seen anything like it before.

The poor thing must be recovering from an eye operation. The dreadful man should have known better. Hastily, she looked again at her watch. Bother, she really was going to be horribly late for lunch. Bertie would raise his eyebrows at her behaviour and not for the first time. He might have made her vow to stop rescuing people but much good it had done him. She was quite simply incapable of walking by and ignoring someone in distress.

With a sigh, she started walking briskly towards the college. When she arrived ten minutes later, Bertie was waiting for her outside. "I'm so sorry, Bertie," she apologised. "I got caught up."

He smiled. "Well, as long as you're here, dear girl."

"You look very dashing with your pink bow tie and matching carnation."

Gallantly, he inclined his head. "Thank you. You look rather lovely too in all your incandescent colours." He held out his arm. "Shall we go?"

The chapel was a beautiful building and entering it was like stepping back in time. The organ pipes were unique, painted by pupils of William Morris, and the wood carvings on the pews were exquisite. The audience for this concert was in keeping with the atmosphere; not a pair of jeans in sight, average age of well over forty, and a preponderance of conservative greens, browns and plaids.

Unperturbed by the stares at their flamboyant clothes, Bertie led her to a seat near the front as though they were a couple of exotically plumed birds. Almost as soon as they had sat down, the musicians processed down the aisle to their places. There was a brief introduction by one of the college Fellows and then the music began.

At last Larna could relax and, with a deep sigh of contentment, she closed her eyes. At first, the music was soothing, and she found her tension beginning to ease, but then her mind conjured up the girl from the streets again and the organ was replaced with the plaintive sound of a harp. Suddenly, trees began to spring up all around her as though she was in a dense forest. At the same time, there was a feeling of intense heaviness across her shoulders as though she was carrying an enormous burden. Despite the smell of fire coming from somewhere close, she started to feel horribly cold and began to shiver, the smoke in the air making it difficult to breathe.

circa 2000 B.C.E.

The silence felt thick as the snow on the ground and, for a long time, neither girl nor woman spoke. Then the air breathed again, and the priestess found the courage that had begun to desert her. "What is your name, child?"

"Seela," came the hesitant reply.

"Then welcome, Seela. I am Lanalla, priestess of this clan. Are you alone?"

A hesitation preceded a slight shake of the head.

"Is there someone else with you?"

A nod.

The priestess watched the girl carefully. While she had been playing her beautiful music, she had seemed older. Now she was shrinking into herself as though she was trying to disappear and looked more like a child. "How old are you, Seela?"

Another long pause. "Eleven summers."

"A woman, then." Lanalla waited for a moment. "Who is with you?"

"My sister," Seela replied at last.

"And how old is she?"

"Six summers."

"Is that all? Where is she now?"

"She is hidden."

"Why?"

"She was attacked by a wolf."

The priestess frowned. "She is hurt?"

Another nod. "Do you know which plants I could use to stop the bleeding?"

"I would need to see her to tell you that."

Seela didn't move. "First tell me who Mana was."

"Ah, you heard our conversation." Lanalla folded her hands. "She was our SeeSayer."

"What's a SeeSayer?"

"You do not have a SeeSayer in your own clan?"

Seela shook her head.

"A SeeSayer tells the future."

"The future? How could she do that?"

"The Mother told her."

The girl looked relieved. "You have The Mother too?"

"Of course. She is the giver of all life."

For the first time, Seela met Lanalla's gaze. "What happened to Mana?" she asked again.

Lanalla found herself drawn into the extraordinary green of the girl's eyes. They were deep and asking for help. Yet there was a strength in them that showed great intelligence. "She was killed," she replied, steadying her breathing. "She was different, you see."

"Different?"

"Many of our children are different. Mana had one foot in this world and one in the other. That meant that she could see things that we could not."

It was a long time before Seela responded. Then it was in a voice thin with fatigue." My sister is different, too."

The priestess straightened. "Your sister is different?" she asked hopefully. "Then bring her here by the fire."

Seela hesitated.

"She will be cold in the snow."

The girl still did not move.

Lanalla rubbed her hands together and blew on them before laying them back in her lap. "Seela, I promise will not harm the child. Let me see where she is hurt and try to help her."

Slowly, Seela stood and walked away. Moments later she reappeared carrying her sister. The tiny girl's head was a strange shape. The top left of the skull seemed to have been crushed inwards slightly and one of her legs was roughly bandaged and hanging at an awkward angle.

The priestess let out a long-held breath. "What is her name?" she asked.

"Duna."

"Well, you must be exhausted," she said, and without waiting a moment longer, she bent to scoop the child into her arms. "Come with me out of the snow. We will go to my hut and I will look after you both."

LARNA – PRESENT DAY

Larna was jerked back into the moment by the sound of applause. For a moment she sat dazed and shivering, wondering where she was. She looked down into her arms, but they were empty. Where was the child? A great grief began to rise up from deep inside, but she swallowed it down hard.

"Darling girl, are you all right?"

As Bertie put his hand on hers, warmth flowed back into her and she was able to breathe more easily again.

"You should have told me how tired you are."

"I'm fine," she said, trying to sit straighter on the unyielding pew. "I wasn't sleeping. I just find it easier to listen with my eyes closed, that's all." She cleared her throat. "The music was beautiful."

He didn't look convinced, but he rose and offered his arm. "The janitor wants to lock up the chapel. We left you alone for as long as I could, but ..." He cleared his throat. "Shall we go, dear heart?"

She looked around. They were alone apart from a man at the back. Embarrassed, she pushed herself stiffly to her feet, took Bertie's arm and they made their way back out of the college.

"Lunch, I think," he said. "I know the perfect place: warm, secluded and cosy."

He took her to a café that served food throughout the afternoon. Once inside, he ordered and paid for both of them while she found a table that looked out over one of the quaint narrow streets of the city.

As Larna sat down heavily on a cushioned bench, she wondered what was happening to her but was no clearer as Bertie put down a laden tray on the table. She could still feel the child in her arms. Hoping that the scent of the coffee would revive her, she slowly picked up the coffee cup and held it to her nose but when an image of the strange pearl-like eye of the woman on the street flashed into her mind, she hesitated and looked down dubiously at the plate in front of her. Something seemed to shift in her stomach. Taking an experimental sip of the coffee, she quickly put it down again. It tasted all wrong in her mouth.

Bertie reached over and put his hand on top of hers. "Larna, dear girl, what is the matter?"

Larna looked up at him, wondering if she should say anything. If she told him about the dream she'd had during the concert he would smile courteously and tell her that she'd been asleep and she couldn't bear that.

"Actually, I saw a disturbing scene on the way here," she confessed reluctantly. "A girl, well woman really, was about to busk. A perfectly horrid man frightened her off." She stopped. "The thing was, one of her eyes was white. It was like a pearl set into her face. Later, when I spoke to her, and before she put her eyepatch back, I could feel it looking right through me."

The look on his face told her everything she needed to know. Heat rose into her face and wished she had not said anything. She waited for him to tell her she should have walked on by. Then she hardened her resolve. "Bertie, she was in desperate need of help. It wouldn't be right to pass someone like that and not do anything." She closed her eyes and waited for the reprimand.

"But you promised."

Opening her eyes again, she looked at him. "I didn't promise to stop being myself. I gave her some money to go and buy some food, that's all. She looked half starved."

"Well," he sighed. "I suppose that's reasonable enough, but …"

"No buts," she said, wondering why she always felt the need to justify herself. Picking up the coffee cup again, she managed a sip and then a second. This time, it tasted surprisingly good. She looked at the plate of food he had put in front of her. Perhaps she could try to eat something now.

"So, how are you finding the Stennings?" he asked once they were both tucking in.

"I love them," she replied, wiping her mouth with a paper napkin, "especially Little Stenning."

"Ah, my sister's Queendom."

Finally a subject she felt confident about. "Actually, I went to a coffee morning in the village hall there this week to meet some of the locals. Your sister was there. I bit the bullet and invited her round for tea next week."

It was his turn to feel nervous. "For tea?" he spluttered. "Next week? But Hester hates boats."

"She'll love mine. *Water Haven* is beautiful," she said, relieved at the strength which had started to pour back into her.

"Yes, but if she finds out that you know me ..."

"Bertie, surely it's about time you forgot your little feud."

"It's not a little feud," he protested, "and it's not mine. As you well know, I have tried to speak to her but she won't have anything to do with me."

"But you became a man years ago. Surely she's had chance to accept it by now."

"It seems not."

It was her turn to reach her hand over to his. "Then you're going to need me, aren't you?"

He frowned. "What do you mean?"

"To put everything right." With her free hand, she tucked a strand of her silky brown hair behind her ear. "You've always said that I have a gift for bringing people together. Well, now we can use it to reunite the two of you. I'll soon have you speaking to each other again."

He groaned. "Hester is a stickler for convention. She'll think you're a gypsy."

"No she won't. My narrowboat is an asset to any environment, especially one like the Stennings."

"I doubt she'll see it that way. She's probably planning to have you evicted as we speak."

Larna's face hardened. "Bertie, don't be mean."

He sighed. "Darling girl, I'm just trying to warn you. Hester hates anything that is different, including bright colours. By definition that means she'll loath the boat and she won't approve of you. *Water Haven* is decorated with castles and roses and you dress to rival peacocks." He moved his hand away from hers and put it on his lap. "Look, why don't you bring your boat just a little further down river into Oxford. People love eccentrics there. You'll fit right in."

Larna threw her hands up in mock outrage.

"Besides, if you moved to Oxford you'd be nearer to me," he coaxed.

She snorted defiantly. "You know very well that I need the peace and quiet of the countryside. The Stennings are perfect for me. Besides, that bit of river is already starting to feel like my own piece of paradise. Everyone who passes smiles and waves. They love the boat."

"I bet they don't love the caravan," he said suddenly.

Her head shot up. "That caravan is very precious to me," she said, squaring her shoulders. "As you very well know, the boat is too small for guests so it's perfect for the odd occasion when I have a visitor who wants to stay." She lowered her voice and aimed for a more conciliatory tone. "Look, what if I promise not to wear anything too outlandish when your sister comes? I'm sure I can dumb myself down a little."

"You shouldn't have to," he replied, splaying his hands helplessly into the air. "You know full well that everything you wear is outlandish. You look like a rainbow in heels."

She laughed, breaking the tension. "I do declare you're jealous, Bertie Fratton."

"Me? Never."

Larna's eyes began to twinkle. "You never know, your sister might even fancy a new wardrobe once she realises that I was a designer. Still a designer if asked."

He groaned. "Larna, darling girl, if you insist on seeing her, just make sure that you get rid of all the insects first. Hester is an entomophobe. She has an insect phobia and rivers teem with insects of every kind. She only lives near water because she inherited the manor after I was disowned."

Larna inhaled sharply. "Well, I'll just have to make sure that there's no sign of my winged friends when she visits, won't I? I'm sure we'll get on famously."

"No, you won't. Do you realise that she went through a phase of reading Karl Marx and named her two sons Karl and Marcus as a result?"

"Good Lord, an insect-hating communist. What fun."

"Hardly," Bertie replied sourly. "She decided she hated communism in any form along with being a mother."

Larna looked horrified. "What, she doesn't like her children? You never told me that before."

"She can't stand them. The elder boy is something of a recluse while the younger left the family firm in the lurch. *Frattons* used to be Oxford's biggest printing company. Now the rumour is that it's going downhill fast. To be honest, I'm relieved to have been severed from any connection with it."

Seeing the opportunity to change the subject, she pounced. "You said on the phone that you wanted to ask me something."

It took a moment but eventually his expression cleared. "Ah yes. I need a subject for my new book. I rather hoped you might be able to help me."

"Me?" she questioned, surprised. "I know nothing about psychology and you know I'm too dyslexic to be able to read."

"Don't do yourself down. You're one of the most intelligent people I know. Besides, you've listened to my books on Audible. You should be an expert by now."

"Why thank you, kind sir," she said.

He sighed. "The truth is that my agent has given me a deadline to come up with a new book proposal."

"That's odd. She doesn't usually do that, does she? Besides, your last book was a bestseller. Surely that counts for something."

"Apparently not. She says that if I don't follow my success with another book quickly, I'll drop off the radar and become a has-been."

"But that doesn't make any sense. It sounds as though you need to change your agent."

"I wish it were as easy as that but she is top in the business. No-one else could get me such good publishing deals. What I need is to come up with an idea that will rock the world of neuropsychology." He paused. "Larna, you're a free thinker. What does the pseudo-scientific world need now, do you think?"

"I've got absolutely no idea."

"Well what kind of things do you think about?"

"Dreams," she said before she could stop herself.

He frowned. "That's odd. I've been thinking about dreams, too."

"Have you?" she said, relieved not to have been asked to explain. "What kind of dreams?"

"Um, I had a nasty dream the other day. More of a nightmare, really."

"What about?"

"It was about Hester. She was being attacked by a necklace."

Larna stared at him. "A necklace? How on earth could your sister be attacked by a necklace?"

He shook his head. "I have no idea. A red-headed girl was dangling it in front of her. Hester looked terrified. I've never seen her looking so scared. It was as though I was being warned that something awful was about to happen to her."

Larna shuddered. "How horrible." For a while, they both lapsed into silence. Then Larna looked back at him. "Well, what about using dreams as the basis for your next book?"

"What?"

"I know that plenty has been written on dreams, at least on their possible meanings, and I think I'm right in saying that dreams are the only link we have between the unconscious and the conscious minds, but what about a book on the potential of dreams as warnings? I remember listening to a podcast in which it was revealed that several people dreamed about 9/11 before the attack. They tried to tell the police but were all dismissed as cranks."

Two vertical lines appeared between his eyebrows. He looked into the distance over her shoulder, evidently considering the idea.

"It would be like building a bridge between psychology, science and spirituality," she continued. "And everyone dreams, whether they are Nobel prize winners or Joe Bloggs."

"Wow," he said, stroking his chin thoughtfully, "I knew you were the right person to ask."

"And if you started with the dream you had about your sister, perhaps you could also use it for research and speak to her again."

Suddenly, he shot a suspicious look at her. "Larna, is this idea just a ploy to rescue Hester and me?"

She grinned. "Why can't it be both? Bestseller and reconciler all in one? Tell you what, when I meet her next week, I'll tell her that you're the best person I know."

"Don't you dare! If you tell her that you know me, she'll have you off that mooring before you can blink."

"Of course she won't. Having a sister that has turned into a brother is exciting." Larna tapped the side of her nose conspiratorially. "Bertie, you may as well give up now. I'm determined to get the two of you talking again."

He shook his head mournfully. "Dear girl, she will eat you alive."

"Oh ye of little faith. Look, why don't you just concentrate on your new book and leave your sister to me?" She looked at her watch. "Now, thank you for lunch; it was delicious, but I have to go. There's a Meet and Greet in Little Stenning Village Hall that I'd rather like to attend." She fluttered her eyelashes mischievously. "I don't suppose you would consider driving me back in *Marigold*? I'll never get back in time if I catch the bus and you know how much I love your Aston Martin."

At first he pretended to look outraged. Then his face broke out into the smile she loved so much. "Larna Avery, you are incorrigible!" Standing up, he reached for the keys in his pocket. "Come on, then," he said, holding out his hand. "Let's go. But I warn you, I'm going to drive fast, so be prepared for the ride of your life!"

HESTER – Present Day

Hester Knebworth, a statuesque woman in her fifties, stood staring in horror at the old shabby caravan parked on the bank of the river and pulled the fox fur mantle more closely around her neck. Then she turned to face the boat. Painted gaudily with roses and castles, it was enormous; utterly inappropriate for the tranquil, respectable haven of Little Stenning. Heaven only knew how the Avery woman had managed to secure a licence for it. The council would just have to be told to revoke it. But first, she would pay the horrible woman a surprise visit. She certainly would not be coming here for tea next week. She preferred to catch the harridan off-guard.

She was just listing the details of the mooring in her mind when a woman dressed in appallingly bright colours began to walk towards her from the direction of the village. She blinked hard. Larna Avery was an outrage and as tasteless as her boat. Barely managing to repress a shudder of disgust, Hester stepped back from the bank and waited for her to approach.

"Mrs Knebworth," the Avery woman said brightly as she stopped in front of her.

For a horrible moment, Hester thought she was going to try to give her a hug. Quickly, she stepped back.

"I wasn't expecting you until next week."

Hester pursed her lips into a tight line.

"I don't suppose you could wait to see the boat," the woman continued with an over eager smile.

Hester turned her look into a glare.

"Please do come in," Larna Avery continued. "As it happens, I baked a cake this morning."

Reluctantly, Hester followed the hideous woman onto the deck and from there through a door into a small kitchen.

"Welcome to my humble abode. I must say that it is a privilege to have you visit me. Have you been on a narrowboat before?"

Hester did not move.

"I see. Well, I er … Um, let's go through into the snug."

Grimacing, Hester followed her through the beaded curtain which served as a kitchen door. There was a strange scent in the air as though the woman burned incense. Sweat broke out on her neck and she threw off the fox fur as though it was trying to strangle her. She cleared her throat and finally spoke. "I haven't got long," she said, looking pointedly at her watch. "Things to do; people to see."

"Of course, Mrs Knebworth. You're an important person; I understand that. I'll put the kettle on."

"No thank you."

"Oh, then how about some cake?"

Hester felt a wave of disgust rise up from her stomach. "I don't eat cake."

"But I thought I saw you…" She stopped herself. "At least take a seat."

Hester looked around and wrinkled her nose. Sit down? The woman must be crazy. This end of the room looked clean enough but was bound to be a haven for horrible, crawling things. As for the far end, it was hideously draped with scarves in a scene more in keeping with the Arabian Nights than a British home. God knew what could be lurking in those folds. She walked over to the window and, remaining on her feet, turned her back to the obscene greenness of the river.

"I, er, am so pleased to meet you properly at last," Larna tried, sounding flustered now. "Have you been on a narrowboat before?"

Hester groaned inwardly. She was used to small talk but not when she was on a mission. She was just about to bring the conversation round to the inappropriate nature of the mooring when the telephone rang. Unfortunately the woman only apologised, ignored it and began to drone on about the history of narrowboats. Refusing to be delayed any longer, she opened her mouth to begin her scolding but noticed something high up on the wall above one of the pictures. Suddenly, she tensed. What if it was a spider, and what if that spider had an entire family hidden behind the curtains? Her mouth closed as panic started to push heat up into her face. Damn it. A hot flush: how she cursed the wretched things. They turned one such a frightful colour. "Mrs Avery…" she said, her voice coming out as a squeak rather than the rich alto she had spent years cultivating.

"Ms actually, but please call me Larna."

Hester cleared her throat and continued. "Ms Avery, is that your caravan on the bank?"

"Um, yes. I use it for…"

"It needs to go. And so does your boat. Little Stenning does not welcome gypsies. I understand you have a licence. It should not have been granted." She waited until Larna Avery was staring at her in disbelief, before walking to the bead curtain, pushing it aside and flouncing out of the boat.

As soon as she was back on dry land, Hester smiled slightly, careful not to create too many lines on her cheeks. It had felt good to have put the dreadful woman back in her place, almost comical as the woman had turned from enthusiastic to flustered in a few short sentences.

With her back ramrod straight, she began to walk back to the manor. It was a long time since she had felt such a sense of power. She was the Lady of the Manor and it was about time that everybody knew it.

Uruz – courage

Chapter Three

SELENA – Present Day

The woman's card is in my pocket. She said something about calling her. And she gave me a £10 note. But she's long gone, and my phone is dead. Buddy has disappeared, too. Loneliness washes over me like a tide and I think I'm going to drown. If only I hadn't lost my return ticket to Norwich, at least I could have been in my own house even if it had fallen down on my head and buried me.

I don't know what to do. I dare not busk again. When that awful man had grabbed my eyepatch, pulled it down, and looked disgustedly at my pearly eye, I'd felt so humiliated that I'd wanted to die. But I can't tramp these streets much longer. I need to get away from here. Escape to somewhere else.

My pearly eye is just starting to go numb when something nudges my leg. It's Buddy; he's come back. He wags his tail hesitantly and licks my hand. He must be hungry. Beyond hunger. I'm starting to feel sick. I put my hand in my pocket to pull out the money. Instead, I find myself staring at the woman's card. Her address swims through the tears along with her telephone number. My phone might be dead but perhaps I could find a phone box. Ask her if I can come and stay. But where to look? Everyone has their own mobile these days.

I start walking, my bones creaking like a rusty door. It takes hours. I keep forgetting what I'm looking for. And I can't control the shivering. It's starting to shake me out of my body. I force myself to think. Phone box. I need a phone box. I push myself forward and manage to find a couple, but one only takes cards, and I've no more money left in my bank account. The other phone box has been vandalised.

At last, I find one that works and accepts coins. I've never used a telephone box before, so I have to follow the instructions, but my green eye refuses to work properly so I have to concentrate really hard. Eventually, I manage to drop my one remaining 20p piece into the slot. Then I push the numbers on the keypad and wait. There's a ringing sound and I let my breath out in a gasp. But the sound goes on and on until it clicks off. She's not there. How can she not be there? The 20p piece falls out so I try again. This time, I can't get my fingers to work properly. They're shaking so hard that they keep on pressing the wrong buttons. I try again, again and again.

I'm just about to cry when I try one last time and at last, someone picks up.

"Larna Avery," says a sing-songy voice.

I open my mouth to reply when a great sob suddenly rises up. Horrified, I choke it down.

"Hello?" she tries again. "Is anyone there?"

"I er…" I swallow again. "You kindly…" It's no good. My voice has tangled itself up into a knot and I can't undo it.

"I'm sorry; I don't understand what…"

"I'm the busker," I try. Then my voice breaks, and I start to weep.

There's a moment of silence on the other end. Then: "The busker? Oh good heavens? Are you the one that horrid man threatened? The one with the...?"

The one with the hideous eye. That's what she was about to say, wasn't it? My voice rises as though I'm going to be sick. "Yes, I..." I try to breathe. "I don't think I can spend another night outside..."

This time the silence is appalled. "You are sleeping *outside*? In weather like *this*?"

"Yes, I..."

"But what about your family? Can't you go home?"

"I h...haven't... I can't..."

She breathes in sharply. "Oh my goodness, this is terrible. Look, you'd better come and stay with me for a night or two until we can get you sorted out. My address is on the card. All you need to do is to catch the bus to..."

The phone starts to bleep ominously. The 20p is about to run out. I scrabble in my pocket for more change but there are only a few pennies left. As the line goes dead, I stare at the receiver in my hand in disbelief. Desperate, I push the button several times. Nothing happens. The line is dead. I stare at it for several moments, trying to will it back into life. Then I push the buttons randomly, anger rising that I had got so close.

There's a whine outside and I turn to see Buddy looking pathetically at me through the glass. What am I thinking? He's hungry. The door is so heavy that it feels as though it is made of lead and I have to fight to open it.

Outside the air is frigid and wet. When Buddy jabs his nose into my leg, I fall to my knees and this time he lets me bury my face in his neck. The snow has turned to rain and it's soaking my coat. I can either die right here or I can stand up and do something for the dog. I have the woman's card. I have her address. I have her offer. All I need is a map. It won't be long before the shops close, so I push my feet towards a stationers. The man at the door shakes his head when I try to enter and tells me that he's about to close, but I manage to plead my way in.

It doesn't take me long to find what I'm looking for. Quickly, I open out the map and find that Great Stenning is about ten miles away.

"You'll have to take that to the till now. We're about to cash up," the man says harshly.

Ignoring him, I carefully fold it back up, replace it on the shelf and leave. Relieved to discover that Buddy is still waiting for me outside, I find a length of discarded rope to form a makeshift lead and put it around his neck. Then we go in search of a bus stop. It doesn't take long for one to arrive. The driver doesn't look pleased when I hand her the £10 note, but reluctantly counts out the change. With the bus virtually empty, I sink into a seat at the back with Buddy at my feet. God, it's so warm. The seat is so soft. Perhaps I'll just stay here and never get off.

"Approaching the Stennings."

I wake in a panic. Pushing myself to my feet, I lurch down the bus, pulling Buddy with me, and drag us both back out into the cold. It's growing dark again and the shapes of the landscape loom like silhouettes in a horror film. We are on a road with a hill ahead which is topped by a strange looking monument. It is too dangerous to walk along the road in the twilight and, with no sign of the Stennings, I turn down a track at the side of the road. By now, the rain has turned to stinging sleet.

In need of directions, and desperately thirsty, I spy a ramshackle farmhouse up ahead with a light on downstairs. The sleet has turned into snow by the time we reach the front door. There's an enormous dog in the porch so Buddy starts to growl. But when I realise it's only a wooden carving of a wolf, I step forward and tap with the knocker.

After a few moments, the door starts to creak open and an exceptionally tall man with long, black hair ducks under the lintel and steps out into the light. Although I have never met him before, he seems oddly familiar, and beneath the patch, my pearly eye starts to tingle. Hunching into my coat, I move further into the porch, trying to move away from the weather. "I'm sorry to disturb you," I rasp, "but please could you tell us the way to the river in Great Stenning?"

The man's eyes widen in curiosity as they take in my eyepatch. Conscious of his scrutiny, he looks down and smiles at Buddy who immediately starts to lick his lips.

"And please may I have a drink of water?" I ask, my voice so faint I can barely hear it myself.

He looks back at me. "You look frozen. Why don't you come in for a minute? I was about to make some tea."

I can't afford not to trust him with snow falling down my collar. I may not know this man, but if he is offering a warm room and tea, I'm not going to say no. Nervously, I step over the threshold and follow him down a narrow hall to a doorway with the date 1723 carved into a wooden beam. Beyond, a cosy fire burns in the enormous grate of a kitchen decorated with brass horse heads hanging on leather. Old farming implements are propped up in the corner. Snuffers and reed holders are stacked against the wall and there's a huge oak table in the middle surrounded by rickety wooden chairs. By the window is a cracked red leather armchair that has seen better days. And by that is a full-sized pedal harp. I have to stop myself crying out with relief. It's like coming home.

The man walks over to the sink and fills the kettle before turning it on. Then he puts some water in a bowl which he places on the stone flags for Buddy to lap up greedily. Finally, he pulls out one of the chairs. "Sit down and warm up. Tea won't be long."

Once Buddy has drunk his fill, he slumps onto the floor by my feet and lays his head on his paws. The warmth of the kitchen wraps round me like a blanket and, without realising it, I too close my eyes.

The next thing I know, the man is putting a mug of steaming tea in front of me on the table. Embarrassed at having been caught napping, I sit up and cradle the mug to my chest as though it's a hot water bottle.

"Have you come far?"

"From Oxford," I reply, sipping the tea and relishing the way it flows hot and strong into my stomach. I'm not going to tell him that really I've come from Norfolk. "I'm trying to find Great Stenning."

"Well, you're almost there. It's only a mile further along the road."

He might as well have said fifty. "Your harp is beautiful," I say, unable to help myself. "It looks very old."

"It is," he replies, pleased by my interest. "I found her abandoned here and have been doing some restoration."

"Can you play, then?"

"No, my instrument is the flute, but I'd love to learn how to play this old girl. I've had her restrung but something's wrong with the tuning and I can't work out how to make it right."

"Have you been using a chromatic tuner?" I ask him.

His eyebrows rise in surprise. "A chromatic tuner?"

"Yes. That won't work with the harp."

"Do you play then?"

I nod. "Yes. All you need is one fundamental note and the rest you can do by ear in fifths."

"Good Lord. Would you mind showing me how?"

I should say no and leave, but Buddy is starting to snore and looks so comfortable by the fire. Besides, I can't face the thought of going back out into the snow. I finish my tea, walk over to the harp and sit on the chair behind it. It's a beautiful instrument with the head of a goddess carved into the wood at the top, but as soon as I lower the harp onto my shoulder, I have to grit my teeth to stop myself from crying. My instruments are my best friends and I miss them terribly.

Stilling my body, I reach out to pluck one of the strings and a rich, resonant sound fills the room. Breathing deeply to steady myself, I begin to tune, starting with the C in the middle and pitching the octaves and then the fifths until I have worked my way both up and down the instrument. Enthralled by the sounds, I then play a simple folk tune to check that all is well.

"That was beautiful," says the man eventually from what seems a long way away.

"Thank you." Remembering how tired I am, I stifle a yawn, reluctantly push the harp away. "I must go," I say.

"I'd love to hear some more," he coaxes. "I knew the harp would sound wonderful but not as wonderful as that."

There's nothing I would like more than to stay in the warmth and play music but if I don't move soon I will fall asleep on the chair. "How do I get to the river?" I ask, pushing myself unsteadily to my feet.

He looks disappointed but stands too. "Go back to the road, turn left and you'll find Great Stenning. The river is at the far end before you reach Little Stenning." He hesitates. "What's at the river?"

"A friend. She's on a boat."

He thinks for a moment. "Do you mean the narrowboat that's moored there?"

I nod uncertainly.

"It's beautiful," he says. "It only arrived a couple of weeks ago."

Picking up my bag, I call Buddy and walk through the archway into the corridor beyond.

"Here," he says from behind me, "let me open the front door. It's stiff." He reaches past me and, with a big wrench, the cold air rushes in and hits me like a punch. Buddy steps backwards. He doesn't want to leave, either.

"Are you sure you're going to be all right?" he asks, rubbing his hands together before blowing on them.

"Yes," I say, bending down to pick up Buddy's rope lead. "Thank you for the tea."

"Thank you for tuning my harp."

"Bye then," I say, screwing my face up against the cold.

"Bye. Maybe see you around."

As soon as the door closes, the night folds black, silent and freezing around us. Suddenly, exhaustion hits me and I'm not sure how to lift my foot, let alone take a step, but when Buddy starts to whine with fear, I force myself to move forward into the dark.

We reach Great Stenning soon enough but the walk through it and on towards the river seems interminable and by the time we reach the water I am staggering with fatigue. There's a caravan on the bank with a narrowboat behind it, lit up with a string of coloured lights and the name 'Water Haven' painted on the side. Relieved to have found it, I step onto the deck and knock the door. A head covered with a vivid bandana appears at one of the small, curtained windows, a radio is silenced, and moments later the door opens.

"You're here," she says. Then she looks at Buddy. "Oh, I didn't realise you had a dog."

My heart sinks. I should have warned her. What if she turns us away?

"Have you really been sleeping outside? In weather like this?"

Ashamed, I look at my feet.

"Well, you must be frozen. You can stay in the caravan. It's a bit rusty on the outside but it is good enough inside and has everything you need. I spent months travelling in this before I bought the boat. It might be small but it's adequate. Now I use it for friends when they come to stay. Fortunately, the heater is rather good. I've had it on since you phoned. It should be nice and toasty in there by now. Follow me."

She opens the door and the three of us step into a blissful wall of warmth.

She turns to face us. "I'm Larna," she says. "Larna Avery. But of course, you know that from my card. What's your name?"

"Selena."

"How lovely. And your dog?"

"Buddy."

"A perfect name for a best friend," she grins. Then she grows serious again. "I didn't see him when you were busking."

"He didn't like the nasty man."

She grimaces. "I don't blame him; I didn't either. Now, are you hungry? I've got some soup in the boat. I can bring you out a nice big bowl and a chunk of my homemade bread. Will that do till breakfast?" Then she frowns. "But I haven't got any dog food." She thinks for a moment. "Do you think he would eat some Weetabix? I can get some proper food for him tomorrow."

I nod gratefully. I think he would eat her hand if she gave it to him.

"Terrific. Now, let me show you around. There's a toilet and a shower at the back and the couch here folds out into a bed with bedding in the space underneath. Just pull the catch and…"

My hands are so cold that I can't release it. She moves over to do it for me, and before I know it, she's unfolded the couch, made it into a bed and covered it with a sheet and what looks like a very warm duvet.

"Right, I'll go and fetch you some food."

Once she's left, I sink onto the bed and my eyes start to close. What seems like seconds later, she is opening the door again holding a tray laden with two bowls.

"There are some tracksuits in the wardrobe," she tells me. "Feel free to use them."

My reply is a yawn and she retreats with a smile, closing the door behind her.

The soup tastes like heaven in a bowl. Buddy, too, devours his meal. Once we have finished, I put the tray down by the sink and lie down on the bed, too tired to undress. Buddy leaps up beside me and within seconds we are both asleep.

FALALA – Present Day

Dr Falala Sefu stood looking at the dig. The air might be as dark as her ebony skin, but it wasn't as smooth or lustrous. Instead there was a cloying quality about it as though whatever light it contained had been swallowed up long ago by tragedy. This wasn't how it should be, she thought anxiously. She should never have left her successful university lecturing career for a dig that was months too early. Excavations took place in the summer when the ground was soft, not now when winter was refusing to allow spring to arrive and the ground was frozen under an unexpected mantle of snow.

She had to find a way of turning this catastrophe into a success.

But it wasn't easy being a black woman in a white man's

world. Yet again, she would have to use every resource available to prove that she had a right to be here. And that was not all. There were more problems than her skin colour and the weather. Marcus's family were turning out to be a nightmare. According to the County Archaeologist, Clem Hardwick, the Knebworths were now trying to wriggle out of all but a fortnight of excavations so that they could apply immediately for planning permission. It was ludicrous. This field was a flood plain, waterlogged for much of the year, and not remotely suitable for housing. The only part that was safe was the hill, and that was far too steep for building on. Two weeks was all they had been given. After that there would be no job and they would all be officially unemployed.

It was time to have a chat with Marcus.

Wondering how he would take her news, she climbed into her car. *Molly* was her ancient but beloved Volkswagen Beetle that had served her faithfully for far too long. These days, the engine didn't always start. She had been saving up for a new vehicle but now she had taken this unpromising job, she doubted that she would be able to afford anything else anytime soon. Gritting her teeth, she turned the key in the ignition. No response. After four more unsuccessful attempts, she sighed, climbed back out, opened the bonnet and tightened some loose wires.

Next time she turned the key, the engine sprang reluctantly into life and the car chugged jerkily down the lane away from the field and back into the village. Marcus's flat was on the left hand side of the road, but on the right side of the Stennings, socio-economically speaking. Falala wouldn't have expected anything else. Despite the family's lack of communication, apparently his mother Hester had arranged it and, according to Marcus, Hester Knebworth was a stickler for status. Parking *Molly* at the side of the road, she walked to his front door and pressed the bell.

Marcus opened the door looking like a crumpled bed sheet that needed a good iron. There were dark circles under his haunted eyes. "Fally? What are you doing here?"

"We need to talk."

"Talk? Why? What's happened? Can't it wait until tomorrow?"

"No."

"But I was about to go to sleep," he protested.

She checked her watch. "But it's only just gone nine."

"Is it?" He looked surprised for a moment. "I'm tired."

"Good God, old man, you're not yet thirty. What's the matter with you? You need coffee, not sleep."

Shamed, he groaned and let her in.

Once inside, she looked round in dismay at all the boxes which still littered the floor of the hall. "Bloody hell, I thought you were going to have a tidy-up. This place is beginning to look as bad as the flat you rented at university."

"That wasn't a flat," he retorted. "It was a hovel."

"It was certainly unfit for human habitation when you were in it. I do hope your living room is better." It wasn't. Piles of books and laundry littered the floor. The only piece of furniture not draped with something was the enormous television, which sat in the corner. "You are hopeless, Marcus Knebworth. This flat could be wonderful. It's five times the size of the pokey place I'm renting."

"As I've told you many times before, if God had wanted me to be tidy, he'd have given me a vacuum cleaner for legs."

"*She'd* have made you tidy up first," Falala retorted harshly. "I hate to imagine what the kitchen is like."

"Er, I haven't done the washing up yet," he admitted.

"Well, don't expect me to do it. Forget the coffee. I don't want food poisoning."

He shrugged. "So why did you come?"

"To tell you that I've invited your brother to the dig tomorrow morning."

"What?"

"Show me where I can sit and I'll explain."

He walked over to the sofa, clearing the clothes in one practised stroke.

Shaking her head wryly, she sat. "Look, I'd hoped that, as leader of the dig and the younger son of the Knebworths, you would have had some sway with your family, but as you are refusing to talk to them, I've decided to act on my own. We need to get your family onside. As neither of your parents seems available to talk, I've decided to approach your brother instead. I want to pick his brains and find out why they are so keen to stop the dig."

Marcus nearly choked. "My brother? Please tell me you are joking. I don't want Karl anywhere near the dig. He's an idiot and doesn't know anything about archaeology. Besides, I've told you everything you need to know. They want to apply for planning permission. It's as simple as that."

"So why give us the job in the first place if they are only going to give us two weeks? It doesn't make sense."

"They're all fools."

"Oh come on, Marcus, give them some credit. The field is really promising. The fact that it is a floodplain means that ploughing won't have disturbed the land beneath. Who knows what might be waiting there for us to discover?"

"Yes, I know, but ..."

"So," Falala interrupted, "I'm going to ask your brother to persuade your family to delay seeking planning permission until the summer when the ground will be warmer. Then we might have something exciting on our hands."

He shook his head and sighed. "Fally, you do know that you are sticking your nose in where it's not wanted, don't you?"

She sat up straighter. "I beg your pardon? I gave up a good job for this, Marcus, and I don't intend to throw my career away by being told not to poke my nose in. That sounds like …"

It was his turn to interrupt. "Sorry, sorry, sorry," he apologised, putting his hand up to stop her. "I know how hard you've had to fight for your position. I promise you, I would have said the same to anyone, regardless of their skin colour." He wiped a bead of sweat off his forehead. "It's just that my family is a nightmare. Mother is greedy beyond belief and Father is stuck in the twentieth, if not the nineteenth century."

"Good job I'm speaking to your brother, then," Falala said wryly.

"Karl is no better," Marcus protested. "He's an idiot. The only thing he likes is art. He pretends to be a business man but he hasn't got a clue."

"Then it sounds as though your family need your brains."

Marcus looked at her, misery in his eyes. "I tried to help them, I really did, but Mother made it impossible so I left and she's never forgiven me."

Falala refused to give up. "So use this opportunity to build some bridges."

Marcus shuddered. "No thank you. Look, I'm happy to do the dig if they'll let us, but then I want to get as far away from here as I can. I thought I could cope being back here but the truth is, this place makes me feel sick." He put his hand up to his hair. "Just look at what it's done to me. Before I came here I was blond. Now my hair is snowy white."

"Well, your hair matches the weather," she quipped, but then bit her tongue, seeing the look of distress on his face. Sitting back, she considered him and frowned. This vulnerable Marcus was not the student she had so nearly fallen in love with at university. What had happened to change him so quickly? "Actually, your hair looks rather distinguished like that," she said rather more gently.

"But, as you kindly reminded me, I'm not thirty yet. People will think I'm an old man."

"No they won't. There are plenty of men with white hair and women love them." When he failed to respond, she continued. "Look, remember how excited you were when you received the initial letter from your father."

"That was only because there weren't any other job offers."

"Then let's try to make the most of this one. All your family need to do is agree to delay the excavation until the summer."

"And what makes you think they will do that?"

"Because they've gone to the expense of erecting a Portakabin in the field. Surely that means they want the dig to go ahead."

"That was probably Father trying to do the right thing. I doubt he ever got permission from Mother."

"Why on earth would he need permission?"

"Because she runs everything behind the scenes. As soon as she discovered that he had offered me a job, she would have done everything possible to shut us down."

"No, Marcus, you're wrong. She got you this flat and, from what you said the other day, had it furnished too. Can't you see that she wants you here?"

He turned away, now small boy rather than man.

"So please try to think differently about this. Why don't you go and see her and use your infamous charm to bring her round? I've never known you to fail in that department yet." She put a comforting hand on his shoulder. "Meanwhile, I'll have a word with your brother. Just you wait, we'll soon have your family eating out of our hands."

"I don't know ..."

"Well I do," she said, running her fingers across her tight black crop. "Just don't come in tomorrow until your brother has gone. I'll try to get permission to delay this whole thing until the summer. Failing that, I'll see if I can persuade him to extend the two weeks they've given us to at least two months." She stood up, eyeing the mess of clothes on the floor and was just about to reprimand him for his untidiness when she saw the look of uncertainty on his face. Deftly, she stepped over the pile and turned towards the door.

"Be careful, Fally," he murmured.

She forced herself to smile. "I'm Dr Falala Sefu, remember? I'm always careful. Now, go to bed and be grateful that you can have the morning off tomorrow. I'll phone you as soon as the coast is clear."

Uruz reversed – illness

Chapter Four

SELENA – Present Day

I wake to rain hammering somewhere above my head, but it is not until Buddy jumps off the bed and starts to scratch at the door that I remember that I am in the caravan by the river. Grateful that he seems to be house-trained, I let him out into the field, wondering what his story is. He must have been part of a family once, so what happened? Why did he become a stray? Is he lost or was he abandoned?

It's freezing outside, in marked contrast to inside the caravan which is toastie warm. Guilty that I must have fallen asleep with the heater on, I quickly switch it off. Once Buddy is back inside, I peel the grubby clothes from my body and head for the shower. The water pressure is weak, but the spray is just about warm enough. It's bliss to feel clean and I promise that I will never again take hot water for granted.

Once I am dressed in one of the tracksuits from the wardrobe, we go outside. There's a note pinned to the door of the boat to say that Larna has gone out shopping. Time for a walk, then. Heading out towards the footbridge that leads into Little Stenning, we come to an old and picturesque village full of thatched cottages and climbing trellises all arranged round a manor house that has seen better days. In some ways it reminds me of Highhill, but I refuse to dwell on that now.

We keep walking until we arrive in dense woodland at the bottom of a second hill. Following the wiggly track upwards, we climb to a tiny church on the top flanked by an enormous yew tree and the most incredible view over the rolling countryside of Oxfordshire. It is different from the flat Norfolk fields and broads. Both are beautiful in their own way. Oxfordshire is more idyllic, but I miss the sea and the huge Norfolk skies.

It is only when my stomach growls with hunger and Buddy looks up at me with imploring eyes, that I tear my gaze away. Both of us are famished again. I may have found us a bed for the night, but I have no money left to buy us any food. Larna's note said she had gone out shopping so I'm hopeful that she will bring something for us to eat today, but I can't rely on her kindness even if she did say we could stay for a few days. I'm just going to have to find a way of earning enough money to buy another train ticket so I can return to Norfolk. But what will I do when I get back to Highhill? My job at the library in Norwich is long gone so I'll have to find something else. But then I think of Buddy. How can I take him back with me if I have to go out to work all day? As for singing, any gigs for folk harp and voice are likely to be unpaid. Besides, there's too much grief in me to sing.

Tears are beginning to prick behind both of my eyes when Buddy suddenly barks and runs off back down the track. Desperate not to lose him, I run down to the bottom and find him jumping up and down at a blackbird thrashing in the frame of a trap, one of its wings caught and broken. Quickly,

I fix Buddy's makeshift lead around his neck and tie him to a tree further away before returning to the poor creature.

The bird's yellow eyes are glazed with pain, its beak open and panting and its feathers drenched. Very carefully, I kneel and explore the device with my fingers to see how to open it. The trap has been tethered to the ground; the netted frame spring loaded. Placing my thumbs at the edges, I try to prise it apart, but it won't move. As the bird starts to struggle, I will it to stay still and pull again, but the metal refuses to budge. Not prepared to leave the poor bird here to die alone, I summon every ounce of strength and try again. This time, it springs apart.

Terrified, the blackbird stares up at me before it begins to flutter its good wing in a pathetic effort to right itself. Cradling my hands round its small body, I set it on its feet, but it is pulled over by the broken wing that hangs down heavy and useless. Supporting it with one hand, I gently remove the trap with the other so the bird can't hurt itself further. For a moment, the little bird raises its head and looks up at me. Then its eyes close and its head droops back, lifeless.

All the tears I had suppressed for Mum and Mara suddenly rush upwards. At the same time, my pearly eye starts to throb in warning. Looking up, I see a shine of red hair and green eyes. A young, painfully thin girl is standing behind an enormous oak staring at something on the ground by her feet. My heart stops. It's the girl from the dream; the same girl whose face stared into mine from beneath the surface of the river in Oxford at night. She is the same girl I saw at the train station, the one who stopped me from catching the train back to Norwich. As a stray ray of sun suddenly hits her, there's an overpowering smell of rotting earth. Then she seems to gasp and disappear.

Where her shadow should have been, something glints

among the roots. Curious, I start to dig and eventually pull out a long, rusty chain with lots of stone pendants attached to it and, at the bottom, two grubby crystals: an orange oblong at the top and a white, slightly luminous crystal beneath. In between them is a larger, grey stone. As I hold the chain up to investigate further, it quivers in my hands as though it's alive.

Before I can stop myself, I hurl it away into the undergrowth. As soon as it lands, I hear Buddy barking again and remember that I have left him tied to a tree. Rushing over to him, I untie the leash and he bolts. Moments later he returns with the rusty chain in his mouth and, tail wagging, drops it at my feet as though he wants me to play. Relieved that he hasn't run off, I give in and pick up the chain, but as soon as I touch it my pearly eye burns again and I start to feel dizzy.

Then I remember the poor blackbird lying discarded on the cold ground. Already the poor thing is growing cold as though it had died long before I had found it in the trap. With a shudder, I drop the chain back onto the ground and gently pick up the bird. Once I have buried the body in the hole where I found the chain, I carefully cover it up with soil and dead leaves so it won't be dug up by a fox. Buddy is once again staring hopefully at the chain as though it's part of some elaborate game. With a shake of my head, I pick it up again and put it in my pocket. Then I carefully lift the trap, holding it as far away from me as I can, and return to the village, dropping it into the only litter bin on the main street.

By now I'm feeling very strange indeed, as though my insides have been taken out and replaced in the wrong order. Oblivious, Buddy darts between my legs as I walk, nearly tripping me up several times. In the end, I have to laugh but only because if I do not, I will cry and then I will be lost altogether.

When we reach the boat there is still no sign of Larna, so

we retreat back into the caravan and turn on the heater. When I take off my coat, the chain jingles as though it wants to be let out. Careful not to loosen too much dirt, I remove it from my pocket and put it on the table. Flakes of rust fall onto the floor, and there are stains on Larna's tracksuit top from where I held the dying blackbird. Peeling off the tracksuit, I wash the stains off the top and hang it on the back of a chair. Then I change into one of the others that is hanging in the wardrobe.

Once I am done, I pick up the chain again and, holding it carefully away from me, angle it up to the light so I can study it. There's a strange glimmer coming from the twenty-three pendants that hang unequally down from the central chain. The stone at the bottom has an X carved into it. The orange and white crystals are attached to it by what looks like wire. Some of the carved signs on the pendants look like letters, while others seem more random. Most confusing of all is the fact that while the stones are freezing cold to the touch, the crystals are warm.

Despite the heater, the air has turned frigid and I have a sudden urge to sit down. There's a feeling of grit in my pearly eye so I start to rub it gently with a finger but as soon as I touch it, both of my eyes stream with tears as though I'm peeling onions and I have to close them against the sting. Behind my eyelids, heaviness starts to pull me downwards as though a blanket is being lowered over my head. The chain starts to rustle in my hands as a feeling of snow builds up around me.

It may be morning but I can't stay awake.

circa 2000 B.C.E.

The priestess came out of the snow into the shelter of her hut carrying a pail of icy water. Seela and Duna had been here for several days now, and she was at least making some progress with the smaller girl. Her primary task was to tend the little girl's scratched leg. Judging by the depth of the rake of claws, the wolf had been enormous. She had wrapped the girl's leg with poultices soaked in infusions of calendula and elder. Now all she could do was pray to The Mother to grant a healing.

The older girl was proving more difficult. She supposed that it was no surprise that Seela did not trust her. They must have travelled some distance to be so bedraggled, dirty and hungry, but now they were clean, fed and rested, she was concerned by the way that Seela continued to hover over Duna as though she suspected that her younger sister was in danger. It must be because of the argument they had overheard. Learning that the previous Leader of the clan had killed Mana, a child, must be unsettling.

Somehow, she had to find a way of earning the girl's trust. As priestess, she was in the best position to do this. Now the village was without either a Leader or a SeeSayer, she was the only person with any real power, but she would have to be clever to hold onto it. Every time she went outside, Mevin seemed to be watching her, as if he was looking for a way to oust her from her position. If only she had the Amulet she would have used it to cow the big man into submission, but she hadn't seen it since Mana's death, and she had no idea where it might be.

Once she had poured some of the water into the pot that hung over the small fire in the centre of the hut, she dropped in two more handfuls of herbs. Then she turned to look at the two sisters huddling together in the shadows. A plan was forming in the back of her mind, but she would have to tread carefully for it to have any chance of success. Curious to discover what had brought the girls here, and why they had been travelling alone in the forest, she waited until the air was filled with a comforting aroma before she attempted a conversation, hoping that the differences in their accents would not prove an obstacle.

"The wound on your sister's leg is looking much better, Seela," she tried at last, enunciating each word slowly and clearly.

At first Seela looked as though she would continue with her silence, but eventually she opened her mouth to speak and pointed to her sister's leg. "What are you using as a binding?"

Lanalla breathed out a breath she didn't realise she'd been holding. "Plantain, chickweed, dandelion and burdock root in a poultice. It will help her skin heal from the wolf's scratch." She hesitated. "Did your mother not teach you how to make a poultice?" It was a daring question.

Seela looked away and then up at the priestess. "Yes, but I didn't know where to find the plants in the snow."

"You have to collect them in the spring and summer and then dry them for use in the winter," Lanalla said quietly.

"Our mother did that, too," Seela mumbled.

"She did not give you herbs to take with you on your journey?"

Seela tensed.

"Where is she now, your mother?"

It was a while before the girl answered. "We had to leave her behind."

"Why?"

"Duna was in danger. Folk do not like the way she looks."

"You ran away?"

"Folk in our clan wanted to kill her. The big man said that you kill children too."

Lanalla shook her head fiercely. "No, Seela, I look after children. There was a man, it is true, who hurt Mana, but he has been banished. You do not need to be afraid. He will not survive long all alone." She clasped her hands in front of her. "And you do not need to fear me. I am the priestess of this clan. I will keep you safe." When Seela failed to respond, she continued. "Where does your family live?"

"Near the Great Stones," the girl eventually said reluctantly, as though she was giving away a great secret.

"The Henge to the south west which grows up into the sky?" Seela nodded.

They fell back into silence and put their attention on Duna. The little girl was pale as she slept and, despite the pungency of the herbs, there was a cloying smell of infection in the air.

"Why are you helping us?" Seela suddenly asked.

"Because I love children."

"Do you not have any of your own?"

"No, although I have taken Riadd under my wing."

"Riadd?" Seela queried.

"The tall youth you saw arguing with Mevin."

"The young one who looks like a tree that has grown too tall?"

Lanalla allowed herself a brief smile. "Yes. He is like a son to me." She paused again. "Tell me about your sister."

Seela wrung her hands nervously. "She cannot speak but I understand what she needs. I am her voice."

"I see." She looked closely at Duna, lying on the pallet. The girl was indeed odd to look at, but no odder than Mana had been. Mana had been older by several turnings of the sun and she hadn't been able to talk either. At least not outwardly. She had spoken to Lanalla clearly enough in her mind. Her face also had been shaped strangely and she had found it hard to walk. Before she had been killed, Mana had communicated to her that New Bloods would arrive and that one of them would have the mark of The Mother.

Could this tiny girl be the new SeeSayer, then? Would Duna

be able to learn how to project her thoughts as Mana had done? Would the child be able to help her retain her power as priestess?

A draught from the door flap suddenly stopped her train of thought and she looked up to see Riadd stride in. As always, her heart leapt to see the youth who had become like a son to her since his parents had both been killed. He was so tall and gangly that he could barely stand upright in her hut so she had allowed him to build his own dwelling even though he was not yet a man.

"Mevin wants to know…" he began, stepping forward with a limp.

"Have you hurt your leg?" Lanalla asked anxiously.

He winced. "Mevin is trying to teach me how to fight. I am all over bruises from having fallen so many times."

"Mevin's nothing but a brute."

Riadd frowned. "He's the only strong man we have left."

"I know, but I do not trust him."

Riadd shrugged. "My Ceremony of Manhood is approaching. If I am to become a strong man too, I must learn from him. You must not worry about me. I am…" Suddenly his eyes caught a movement in the shadows and he saw the two girls. He looked questioningly at Lanalla. It was the first time he had been in the priestess's hut since the argument outside by the fire. He had realised that she was collecting water more often but had not known why.

As soon as Lanalla realised he had seen the sisters, she stepped protectively towards them. "These are the New Bloods that Mana predicted would arrive," she whispered. "I am keeping them safe. Mevin must not hear about them. The little one has been injured by a wolf and needs time to heal. Please promise me that you won't tell anyone."

Riadd went to step closer but the older girl put her hands

protectively over her sister and shrank even further back into the shadows. "I promise," he murmured, "but how do you know they are the predicted New Bloods?"

"I would check with the Amulet if I could," Lanalla admitted, "but I don't know where it is."

He paled. "It can't be lost. It is sacred to our clan."

"I know," she winced. "It disappeared when Mana was killed. Everything has gone wrong since then. The Mother is angry." She put her hand on her heart. "I can feel it."

"Then we must find it."

"I agree, but Mevin is watching me closely and I dare not let him discover that it has gone. He would blame the disappearance on me and look for it himself. He must not hold it. He is a man. He would take The Mother's power for himself and destroy us all."

Riadd nodded gravely. "Have you any idea where to look?"

"Yes, but we would have to search for it at night time when he is asleep and I cannot leave the girls here by themselves. What if they ran away? I need to keep them here. They are Mana's prediction and all I have left."

"Then we will take them with us when we look," he said simply.

Lanalla looked at him for a moment. "You will help me?"

"Of course. There will be no moon tonight."

"Tonight?" she said, astonished.

"Why not? The sooner you find the Amulet, the sooner we will all be safe again."

SELENA – PRESENT DAY

A knock on the door wakes me.

"I'm back," calls Larna from outside.

As I push myself to my feet, something clatters to the floor.

Picking up the rusty chain, I slide it under the couch before opening the caravan door.

Larna is standing on the step. "Sorry I was so long. I got carried away as usual. Are you hungry?" she asks eagerly. "Would you like to come and join me in the boat?"

Flustered, I block the sight of the wet tracksuit top drying on the back of a chair and smile weakly. "Thanks," I splutter. "I'll be with you in a minute."

"Bring Buddy with you. I've got a treat for him."

Hurriedly I close the door, retrieve the chain, wrap it in my scarf and hide it in the wardrobe out of sight. Once I have brushed more flakes of rust into the sink and washed them down the drain, I call to Buddy and we head over to the boat.

Larna is visibly excited as she lets us in. "I hope you don't mind, but I've bought Buddy a couple of bowls: one for water, one for food; a bed and also some shampoo. I thought we could give him a groom and a bath after breakfast so that he feels nice and clean and comfortable," she adds diplomatically. "But let's eat first. Here, boy, I've got you some proper dog food." She bends down, full bowl in hand. "There you are."

Buddy dives for his share and it is gone in moments. He doesn't ask for more however because he sees the bed in the corner. Curling up inside it he looks as though he has at last found home.

Larna beams as she turns to face me. "The tracksuit suits you," she says. "Feel free to use my washing machine for your own clothes. It has a built-in tumble dryer. Now, time for food."

My breakfast disappears almost as quickly as Buddy's. While I am eating, Larna explains that *Water Haven* is a wide-beam 80 foot narrowboat, and that most of Britain's canals were built to carry cargo in the nineteenth century. I don't listen to all she says. The dream is still too vivid in my mind and I can't help wondering what the Amulet is and why it is so important.

"Shall we go into the snug for our coffee?" she asks once I have finished eating. "I've lit the fire in there. It should be really cosy by now."

Although Buddy seemed asleep, the moment we move he wakes and all three of us push through the beaded curtain that divides the two areas. The snug is well named, cosy and inviting. At the near end is a living space complete with a blazing stove, two sofas, an armchair, two vases of fresh flowers on tiny tables and a bookcase. Further down, three brightly coloured paintings hang on the wall. Beyond them, the second area is draped with scarves and veils around a rug with two seats and cushions on the floor. At the very bottom is a table of different coloured crystals lit from beneath by a lamp so that rainbows spill out in all directions. It looks like a combination of the Arabian nights and a Swami tent.

"Here you are," Larna says, putting two mugs of coffee on a small table. "Now, why don't you sit in that armchair over there? It looks out over the river and is wonderfully comfortable."

Grateful, I take one of the mugs and sit down. She's right. It's like sitting in a hug, and the view out of the window is gorgeous. Larna disappears briefly back into the kitchen, calls Buddy, and returns with the new dog bed. As soon as she has put it in front of the fire, Buddy climbs into it and immediately falls back to sleep as though he's finally found heaven.

For a while, we simply sit and enjoy the warmth of the stove. I am just beginning to think about the tall, gangly youth named Riadd from the dream, when she starts speaking again.

"Now," she says, "I expect you're worrying about the next few days."

I look up sharply.

"Well, don't. I'm very happy for you both to stay until you're back on your feet."

Stunned, I stare at her, all thoughts of the dream chased away. "Are you sure?" I ask.

She smiles kindly. "You've fallen on hard times. That can happen to anyone. Actually, if you could help me carrying water, fuel, shopping and sorting out the loo, I'd be really grateful. I hadn't realised how far I would have to walk or how hard I would have to work to live on a boat."

"Of course," I say. "And do you think that I might also be able to find some work round here? Then I could pay you some rent and earn enough money for a train ticket."

"Where to?" she queries, a look of surprise on her face.

"Back to Norfolk."

"Norfolk? Oh, that's a lovely part of the world. I used to go there on holiday when I was a child."

I try to smile but a wave of grief catches me unawares and I have to look away.

"What kind of work do you do?" she asks.

There's no point in telling her I was a librarian until I was made redundant, a casualty of the digital age. Nor is it worth telling her that I was an emerging singer-songwriter because there isn't any money in that. However, I often kept house while Mum was looking after Mara so I suggest cleaning.

She considers me for a long moment. "Well, I suppose you could try the manor, just over the footbridge in Little Stenning. Hester Knebworth can be a little... er... reserved but I'm sure she'd be happy to help if she can."

KARL – PRESENT DAY

Anxious not to disturb his mother, Karl Knebworth tiptoed silently across his bedroom floor. When one of the floorboards

77

squeaked, he stopped with one foot hovering in the air but there was no shout from downstairs, so he cautiously continued over to his bed and pulled out the sketch books from underneath, where they were hidden from his mother's eyes.

Of late, he had started to see things; images coming into his mind that made no sense at all. Vague to start with, they only began to take shape when he put them on paper. It was near impossible to quell the feeling once it started, and one was beginning now, like a headache turning into a migraine. As his brain shifted to one side to give the picture more space to form, he reached for the paper in front of him, picked up the pencil and took a long, deep breath.

To his surprise, he drew a boy, long black hair tied back with twine, dark eyes staring out towards an invisible horizon. Once the pencil had finished its frantic dance, he stopped, closed his eyes, and tried to calm his breathing. But already another image was appearing. He moved back into his deeper mind to see what was forming. When he could make out that it was another figure, he turned to a fresh sheet and allowed his pencil to dive onto the paper. In moments, he could see that it was a girl and that she was weeping, her hand stretched out as if in a plea, her grief so marked that, once he had finished, he had to push the drawing slightly away from him lest she contaminate him with it.

It wasn't until a third image began to manifest that he remembered to check the time. Horrified, he saw that he'd been drawing for much longer than he'd thought and he was due at Marcus's dig in half an hour. Closing the sketchbook, he pushed it and the pencil back under the bed. If only he could do the same with his mind, or whatever it was that was fashioning the images, he would be able to obtain some relief. Instead he stood up and struggled into his suit, all the while trying to block any more pictures from entering his vision.

Outside, it was raining heavily. Shrugging on his anorak, he secured the bottoms of his trousers with rubber bands and, quiet as a mouse, left the manor and climbed onto his bicycle. At least the air was slightly warmer than it had been yesterday, and everything smelled fresh, new, and full of promise.

As he began to pedal, he wondered what it would be like seeing his brother again. While he had always admired Marcus for his outstanding sportsmanship, good looks and academic brain, he had never been jealous. Secretly, he had been awed when his younger brother had abandoned *Frattons* to live his own life and wished he had the courage to do the same. Instead, he had been reeled into the family firm to take Marcus's place, proving to be a poor substitute and no more cut out for business than flying to the moon. He saw the world in colour and paint and images, not numbers and calculations, and it hadn't taken long for him to become a colossal disappointment both to his parents and himself. Now there was little to show for his thirty-one years. He didn't drive, still lived at home and his one passion was banned to him. Reconnecting with his brother would be the one highlight in a life gone rusty with failure.

The top of the lane that led down to the Knebworth field was rutted and puddle water splattered his trousers as he bounced through the potholes. Once he had reached the Portakabin at the bottom, he climbed off his bike and wiped the rain from his eyes. A black woman with a sculpted face, cat-like amber eyes and glowing ebony skin appeared at the door, looking surprised as though she had expected to see somebody who looked like Marcus. Embarrassed, he lowered his head. His short stature, thinning brown hair and intense, protruding blue eyes were never anything but a disappointment.

"You're drenched," she said. "Come on in. I'll find you a towel."

As he stepped inside, he removed his anorak, sending drops of rain flying in all directions, and tried to look through her and find his brother but he couldn't see anyone else.

She held out her hand to him. "Give me your coat. I'll hang it over the back of a chair."

For a moment, they both watched it dripping onto the floor. Then she handed him a towel and watched him mop at his head. Once he was a little drier, he bent down to slide the rubber bands off the bottoms of his trousers but snagged them on the laces of his shoes. As he straightened, she held out her hand to introduce herself.

"I am Dr Sefu," she said.

"P...p...pleased to m...meet you, D...D...D..."

"But you can call me Falala," she offered. "Now, would you like a hot drink?" she asked. "You must be cold after your cycle."

Ashamed that she had noticed his mode of transport, he nodded gratefully.

"Tea or coffee?"

"T...t....t..." He looked away, unable to continue.

"Right you are then," she said after a moment. "Tea it is." She turned to the small area designated to be a kitchen. "I'm afraid that Marcus has been called away," she said chattily, "so you've just got me. The other member of the team, Raff, will be in soon. Now, do sit down. Do you know much about the dig?"

Karl shook his head.

Falala ran a hand over her crop, obviously discomforted by his unease. "The three of us formed an archaeological team back at university. I was a lecturer there and asked Marcus and Raff to run a project with me. They were both very bright and dedicated and it turned out that the three of us worked well together. So we ended up here, on your parents' field."

The kettle boiled and she turned away to pour water over two tea-bags. "Milk?" she asked, turning back to look at him.

He nodded.

"Sugar?"

He shook his head.

"Right, here you are then. This should warm you up." She handed him the mug.

They both sipped in silence for a while. All he could think of was why was Marcus was not here to meet him?

"Do you know why the C.A. has only given us a fortnight to excavate the land?" she said, breaking his train of thought.

His face fell. What was a C.A.?

"Sorry, that's jargon," she apologised as though she had read his confusion. "I mean the County Archaeologist." She cleared her throat. "Look, I invited you here to ask if your family might reconsider their time frame. Digs normally happen in the summer you see, when the ground is softer. With the earth so hard and cold, we can't do much at the moment. So we either need to put the dig back till May or, if they can't wait that long, we need to extend the two week deadline by at least a couple of months."

Karl began to panic. Even had he been able to find his voice, he would have had no idea how to reply. No-one had briefed him about the dig. All he had been told was that Marcus was returning to look at the field at the bottom of the hill.

He was just thinking that he would look even more stupid than usual when the door opened and a very tall man walked in, almost knocking his head on the frame. Karl's heart began to beat fast like a metronome wound too tight.

"Ah, Raff, this is Karl, Marcus's brother," Falala said. "Karl, this is Raff, the other team member I told you about."

Karl couldn't tear his eyes away from the planes of the man's face and the angles of his cheekbones. Then there was the straight nose, the full mouth, the hair and the way it hung in a ponytail over his shoulder. They were the same, just on a man rather than a youth. It was the image he had drawn just before coming here.

Desperate for fresh air, he pushed himself to his feet, scraped the chair backwards, grabbed his anorak, and fled.

RAFF – PRESENT DAY

Raff stared at the open door in amazement. "What did I do?"

Falala shook her head. "I've no idea. The poor thing looked as though he'd seen a ghost. Do you think we should go after him?"

Raff walked across to the window. Karl was pedalling frantically down the lane. "He'll get soaked in this bloody rain." He shook his head, baffled.

"Surely that can't be Marcus's brother. They look nothing like each other." Raff turned back to face her. "Why didn't you warn me he was coming?"

"I wasn't sure what he would be like," Falala said sheepishly. "I just wanted some time alone with him to try to persuade him, as a representative of his family, to give us more time."

Raff's eyebrows rose. "But that's Marcus's job"

"I told him to take the morning off."

Raff frowned. "Fally, what the hell are you up to?"

"I was trying to help."

"Help? How?"

She opened her palms in a pleading gesture. "By getting Marcus back with his family. So we could persuade them to give us more time."

"Well that's hardly likely to happen if Marcus isn't even here."

"You know how he feels about his family."

"But you said you wanted to get them together?"

"I know. I'm sorry." She reached for her phone. "Look, I'll call him now."

He tried to throw off his annoyance, but it was just another thing that felt wrong about this whole wretched situation. "You do that. I'm going outside."

"But you've only just arrived. And it's pouring with rain. At least have a cuppa before you go back out again."

"We don't have time to waste," he replied tersely. "Not unless you managed to persuade Marcus's brother to extend the two weeks before he ran out."

"No, I..."

Trying to push away the image of Karl's shocked face, Raff climbed into his overalls and focused on what needed to be done. They needed to plan where to start excavating. The digger would arrive tomorrow and it was a big field.

Grateful for the cold spikes of rain on his face, he stopped at the bottom of the field where the stream divided it from Stone Clump and gazed up at the monument on top of the hill. Ever since he had come back here it had looked menacing, as though it was a strangely curved finger beckoning to him rather than upwards towards the sky. He was just turning away, trying to block it from his mind, when he heard a call. Looking back up the field to the Portakabin, he expected to see Falala, but there was no sign of her. Frowning, he turned back to face the stream where the sound had appeared to come from.

The next call came from below his feet. This time he could tell that it was a girl's voice. He looked down as though he had X-ray eyes and could see beneath the layers of soil and history. A face rose up in his mind. Red hair. Green eyes. Elfin face. But then, as though it had been a dream, the glimpse vanished.

His first thought was that this must be a sign as to where

they were supposed to start digging, but logic told him that could not be true. The ground would be waterlogged so close to the stream. On the other hand, water could preserve organic material in ways that dry conditions could not. The land here wouldn't have been ploughed and that meant far better preservation of any archaeological remains. Intrigued, he crouched down to feel the condition of the ground. Only two days ago it had been frozen and the stream had become partially iced over, but now the rain was thawing the soil, and there was a slight give to the surface.

Perhaps things weren't quite as hopeless as they seemed.

Motivation renewed, he strode back up to the Portakabin, forgetting to duck as he entered and bumping his head hard on the frame.

"Ouch!" said Falala.

"Shut the door, Raff," Marcus muttered, running his hand through his newly turned white hair. "It's bloody cold in here. That heater is so old that I'm thinking of labelling it as one of the finds."

Raff rubbed his head and swore under his breath as he pulled the door to. "You're here already Marcus. I didn't see you arrive."

"That's because your eyes were closed."

"What?"

"You were standing down by the stream looking like a statue. Are you tired, or something?"

Raff snapped. "It's the middle of the day. Don't be an idiot."

He noticed the surprised look that Fally gave him. It wasn't like him to be rude but the call had got under his skin. Turning back to Marcus, he made an effort to gentle his tone. "Don't mind me. I'm just wet. Throw me that old towel, will you?"

"So what did Karl say?" Marcus asked Falala as Raff wiped the rain off his glasses and from his ponytail.

She shrugged. "Not much. As you warned, he has a nasty stammer, but with any luck he will have been impressed by what we've set up in here. I just hope that he manages to persuade them to give us more time."

Raff looked round at the set-up. There was a long table for finds, some old easy chairs, and an unopened cardboard box full of archaeological equipment, including a microscope, so they could set up a mobile restoration unit. "We'd be better to delay until the summer," he said.

"That might be true but what would we do until then?"

Raff shook himself. "Good point. Okay, let's just concentrate on the digger coming tomorrow."

"Any ideas yet about where we should start?" asked Falala.

Raff nodded. "Yes, at the bottom of the field by the stream."

"But the ground will be waterlogged there," protested Marcus.

"Precisely; it won't have been ploughed so any remains may well have been preserved."

"Why do you think we should start there?" asked Fally curiously.

"Just a hunch," Raff replied. He wasn't prepared to say anymore. Not yet. Suddenly he felt desperate for the dig to succeed. If there was a young girl with red hair and green eyes buried underneath this field, why was she so desperate to be unearthed?

Thurisaz – danger ahead

Chapter Five

SELENA – Present Day

The manor reminds me uncomfortably of Highhill. Once I have skirted around the worst of the slush-filled potholes in the drive, I have to force myself to pull hard on the old-fashioned bell at the front door. After a moment, an elegant, large-boned woman in her fifties opens the door. Dressed in a yellow and black striped dress, she looks like a giant wasp with an expression sour enough to curdle milk.

"Yes?" she hisses. "What do you want?"

Behind the eyemask, my pearly eye flares into life, causing me to step back so awkwardly that I nearly lose my footing down the step. "Mrs Knebworth?" I say quickly, before I can lose my courage. "I'm staying with Larna Avery. She suggested that I come to see you."

Her face screws up in distaste. "Larna Avery? Why on earth would that woman send you to me?" Then she glares at my eyepatch and smirks. "Please don't tell me that she is consorting with pirates now."

All my instincts tell me to run. For the briefest moment I wonder if I could ditch the idea of finding some work and simply ask Larna to lend me the money to buy a train ticket back to Norfolk, but I dismiss the notion almost immediately. I am twenty-five years old and must stand on my own two feet. Taking a deep breath, I raise my head and look back at her with my one green eye. "Do you have any cleaning work available?"

She flinches at my stare and then tries to laugh the question off. It is not a pleasant sound. "*Cleaning* work?" she retorts, her voice so snake-like that I find myself looking to see if a tongue is flicking out of her mouth. "Is this some kind of joke?"

"No, I am perfectly serious."

"But surely you have to be able to *see* dust before you can remove it."

A spark of anger flares in my gut and for the first time since Mum's accident I feel my hands tighten into fists. My shoulders pull back, and I stand straighter. "I can see perfectly well, thank you."

"Really?" she says suspiciously. "I don't see how."

My stare at her seems to do the trick and she briefly breaks eye contact with my single green eye.

"What's your name?" she barks.

I hesitate, unsure that I want to give her any personal details.

She cocks an eyebrow.

"Selena," I mumble eventually.

She sniffs and looks me up and down. "Your surname?"

Revealing my surname is one step too far, so I choose the name of my favourite place to give me confidence. "Birdinghall," I declare.

"Birdinghall?" she sneers. "How peculiar. Well, Selena Birdinghall, do you have any references?"

The question takes me by surprise, forcing me to look down. I hadn't realised I would need references. "Not with me," I hedge. Determined not to be cowed, I look back at her.

Her eyes have narrowed. "How convenient." She considers me for a while. "Are you any good at cleaning?"

"Yes," I say, giving her a challenging look.

She doesn't look convinced. As we glare at each other again, my pearly eye starts to warm and I decide that this is a battle worth winning. "How much are you willing to pay me?"

At first she looks affronted by the very mention of money as though I have dirtied the air. Then she starts to laugh. "You've got courage, girl," she says. "I'll give you that. I suppose you'd better come inside. I'll see what I can find for you to do."

For a moment I don't move, wondering why she hasn't answered my question, but I dare not lose the opportunity so I follow her into the hall, assuming that she will tell me in a moment. She doesn't. Instead, she walks around the house making no comment, looking even more like an insect from behind. I try to make conversation but she refuses to respond so I too fall silent.

The ground floor appears to consist of three reception rooms, a large kitchen with a laundry room on one side, and a cloakroom. Most of the furniture looks antique. There is a considerable amount of silver in the cabinets as well as an extensive porcelain collection and a large number of decorative paperweights. Oddly, there are no photographs to give an indication whether or not she has a family.

It is only when we end up back in the enormous hall at the foot of a magnificent staircase that she deigns to speak again. "Go on up," she orders stiffly.

By now my pearly eye is starting to burn. Ignoring it, I force my foot onto the first tread and keep going. When we reach the landing, I step back so she can pass. As she wafts across me I flinch away at the smell of her. It's not that she's unwashed; rather there's something bad lurking around her edges. She stops at one of the doors. "This is Karl's room," she says.

"Karl?" I query.

"My elder, rather incompetent son," she explains. "You can clean this after you've finished downstairs. I dare not even look. God knows what creepy crawlies lurk inside," she adds with a dramatic shudder.

As I follow her back downstairs to the kitchen, I wonder how I'm going to ask her about payment again, but the moment never comes. She shows me the tools I am meant to use. The mop is ordinary enough, but the vacuum cleaner is far more expensive than anything Mum and I ever used and the cleaning products would look at home in Buckingham Palace. As I begin to work, I cannot help wondering why the manor is so grubby. There's dirt beneath the surface layer of dust that doesn't seem to want to budge and a sour taste starts to develop in my mouth that feels as ingrained as the grime.

By the time I have cleaned, washed, and polished for an hour downstairs, my whole body is aching and the burning in my pearly eye has translated into a crashing headache and an uncomfortably dry mouth. Wearily, I return to the kitchen and reach for a glass to pour myself a drink of water.

"What are you doing?"

I spin round to see Hester Knebworth in the doorway.

"I'm thirsty."

"Then you should have brought your own drink." She points to the vacuum cleaner with a hand sore and swollen as though it is covered with insect bites. When she sees me staring at it, she snatches her hand away. "Upstairs. Now."

"I need a drink of water, first," I insist.

She looks horrified and grimaces as though I am the bad

smell, but I refuse to budge. "Very well," she concedes, "but make sure you wash the glass properly when you've finished and don't leave any finger-marks."

If it weren't for my desperate need for money, I would tell her where to go. Instead, I drink as slowly as I can, trying to control my breathing. Then I wash up the glass and put it back in the cabinet as though I have all the time in the world. She doesn't take her eyes off me for a second. I don't think she even blinks. Discomfited, I finally pick up a duster and the vacuum cleaner and head for the stairs.

Entering Karl's room feels like an escape and, once I close the door behind me, I discover that, despite all my attempts to remain calm, I am panting. Determined to get out of this house as soon as possible, I look round and see a room devoid of personality as though nobody sleeps here. As I start to dust, tiny specks rise up into the air and float down again back to their resting places. This is going to be hopeless.

When I have at least attempted to touch every available surface, I attach the hose of the vacuum cleaner and put it under the bed. Immediately it snags on an obstruction. Kneeling down, I spy a pile of sketch books. I pull them out and, to my amazement, see an extraordinary drawing of an oak tree on the top. Unable to help myself, I run my hands over the trunk as though I can actually feel the bark. On the next page is a painting of a red rose so real that I can smell its scent. After that the image of fruit that is so lifelike it makes my mouth water. Curious, I keep on turning. There's a dog whose tail seems to be wagging. Next is a boy with an oddly familiar face, his long, black hair draped over the shoulder of what looks like skins.

But it's the next sketch that makes me gasp out loud. Although the charcoal drawing is in black and white, I see it in colour. It is a girl with red hair and green eyes. As my pearly eye flares, intensifying the headache, I squint through the pain and bring the sketch closer so I can see it more clearly. I expect it to show me something different, something in black and white, but the strong impression of colour remains. Flummoxed, I close my green eye and open it again, thinking I must be imagining the impossible. But no, there it is still. A picture of the girl I saw at the railway station when I dropped my ticket. The same face that I saw reflected back to me beneath the surface of the river. The figure in the woods staring at the ground where the chain was buried. The girl I keep dreaming about.

Panic is just starting to rise up into my chest, threatening to choke me, when the sound of the front door slamming downstairs jolts me back into myself. Hands shaking, I shove the sketchbooks back under the bed and rise back up to my feet.

I've got to get out of here.

"Keep your voice down. The cleaner's upstairs." says Hester Knebworth from down below.

I freeze.

"The *cleaner*?" says a man. "I thought you'd got rid of Mrs Hooper?"

"This is someone else. She came looking for work."

"But we can't afford a cleaner. That's why we got rid of Mrs Hooper. I thought we'd agreed."

"As I've told you on countless occasions, I refuse to be reduced to living in a pigsty."

"But…"

"Let me remind you, Alan, this is *my* house. You've already given Marcus *my* field to destroy. At least let me make the decisions for the manor which is, as you very well know, *my* family home."

"But…"

"It's your fault that we're in this financial mess. You haven't made it any easier by allowing Marcus to crawl back into our lives and giving him the field. We could have secured planning permission much sooner and sold the land for a fortune."

"I…"

"We are not duty-bound to help him just because he is our son. You may be a pompous do-gooder, Alan Knebworth, but I'm not. If I want a cleaner, then I shall have a cleaner."

"Hester, calm down. You'll make yourself ill."

"I've never been ill in my life."

"Well you might be when you hear this."

"Hear what?"

There's a brief silence. Then: "The County Archaeologist phoned this morning. Apparently Marcus and his team want a time extension on the dig."

"Well they can't have one," she says, her voice venomous.

"They say that the ground is too hard for them to start."

"Precisely." She cackles. "They'll just have to give up, won't they? Now, what's the County Archaeologist's telephone number? I'll soon give him a piece of my mind."

"Hester, stop it. We need him on our side if he's to sign them off. No-one reacts well to being bullied."

There was a charged silence.

"Wouldn't it be fairer to Marcus to give them a little more time?" he continued after a pause. "This late winter can't last forever. Spring is bound to come soon and then the ground will soften. He'll realise that there is nothing to find and we'll be able to sign off the land and put it in a planning application. We just need to be a little patient, that's all."

"Patient?" she spat. "We don't have time to be patient. We've only got twelve days left to find the money."

"Don't worry about that. I've put an advertisement in the paper to sell your car. That should give us some time."

Another silence.

"I beg your pardon?"

"I've put…"

"Yes, I heard you the first time. You've done what with *my* car?"

"I've…"

"You have no right to touch anything of mine."

"We're married, Hester, whether you like it or not. What is yours is mine."

"Oh rubbish, this is the twenty-first century, not the Middle Ages."

"I…"

"Of course, if you sell my car, I'll have to drive your Rolls."

"Don't you dare…"

She laughs nastily and then everything goes quiet again until the front door slams for a second time.

I force myself to move, inching open the door so I can head for the stairs. I have just reached the bottom when there is a scream. Hester Knebworth is rooted to the spot in the hallway, gazing in horror at something hanging down from a ceiling lampshade. It's a tiny money spider dangling inches from her face. Catching the little creature in my hand, I deposit it outside. When I return, Hester Knebworth is still white as a sheet and has barely moved.

"You *touched* it," she moans. "Go and wash your hands. Now!"

"But it was only miniscule," I protest.

"It was a *spider*," she whimpers. Clenching her jaw, she slowly straightens, her face changing back to a ferocious glare as though she is creeping from the body of one person into another.

I run to the cloakroom, give my hands a cursory wash and escape to the front door.

"Have you finished the cleaning?" she says, her voice still shaky.

"Yes."

"Then I'll see you again at the same time tomorrow."

"Tomorrow?"

"Indeed."

I clear my throat. It's now or never. "You didn't answer me about payment."

She looks away as though she's hunting for more spiders.

I take a deep breath, trying to quell the uneasy hammering in my chest. "I would really appreciate it if you could pay me for my work today."

She looks back at me as though I have just asked for the moon. "Pay you? Don't be ridiculous. I don't keep money in the house. Any stranger could steal it."

Outraged, I stare back at her. Is she calling me a potential thief?

Then her shoulders fall as though she knows she's going to lose this one. "Look, I'll give you some money at the end of the week. Two hours a day should be adequate."

"But…"

Suddenly her eyes are hard as flint again. "Take it or leave it." Without waiting for a reply, she opens the front door and gestures for me to leave.

Unable to bear the weirdness any longer, I run, not stopping until I'm back over the footbridge across the river. Larna is out on the deck of the boat, checking the frost coverings on her plant pots. Buddy rushes to greet me, wagging his tail like a propeller. Larna straightens and rubs her back. "How did you get on with Mrs Knebworth?"

I wipe my hand across my forehead to clear the sweat, wondering how to reply. I want to say that Hester Knebworth is hideous, that I'd rather have spent the morning with the Addams' Family, and that the manor is a Hammer House of Horrors, but I don't want to seem ungrateful so I take a deep breath, grit my teeth and try to ignore the fact that the vile woman still hasn't told me how much she'll pay me. "She gave me some work and wants me to go back again tomorrow. She says she will pay me at the end of the week. I should be able to give you some rent then. Next week I'll earn enough for a train ticket back to Norfolk. Is that all right?"

She smiles. "Of course. She obviously liked you, then."

"I wouldn't go that far," I say wryly.

Larna grimaced slightly. "I've only met her a couple of times and, to be honest, I did get the impression that she can be a little tricky, but she gave you some work and that is the important thing. Now, how about some lunch? You must be hungry after all that cleaning."

"You really don't have to feed me," I protest.

"Of course I do, especially if she isn't going to pay you until the end of the week. Besides, I'm enjoying having someone to cook for. I've made a quiche. It's already in the oven."

At last the heat in my pearly eye starts to fade, along with the headache. "Is there time for me to have a shower, first?" I ask, desperate to wash the whole ghastly morning off my skin.

"Of course. It won't be ready for half an hour at least. Let yourself into the boat when you're ready."

Back in the caravan, I let the water flow over me for longer than usual despite the tepid temperature. The grime from the manor seems to stick like clay and I wonder how on earth I will be able to stand cleaning there long enough to return to Norfolk. But eventually I feel better, and by the time I am dressed in the third of Larna's tracksuits, I am ravenous.

As soon as I'm back in the boat, I bend down to nuzzle Buddy who smells rather gorgeously of alpine flowers.

"I hope you don't mind," Larna grins. "I gave him a bath."

"He smells wonderful. Thank you. I can't believe how much you're doing for us."

Her reply is to put two plates of delicious food on the

table. We chat inconsequentially until we have finished. Then she leans back in her chair and looks at me. "You said you were a librarian. I assume, therefore, that you like reading?"

"Love it."

"Then would you mind having a look at my books in the snug? There's something I need help me with."

"Of course. Let me do the washing up first though."

Delighted to be able to do something for her, I make sure everything is tidy in the kitchen before going through the bead curtain into the snug. Buddy pushes past me and goes straight to the rug in front of the fire, curling up happily in front of it as though he's lived here all his life. Larna follows on behind him with a chuckle. The bookcase is along one of the walls and filled with all sorts of odd titles from gardening to poetry, history to boats, photos to cartoons. Unlike the tomes I'm used to handling, they all look new and unread. I am just about to look more closely when my eye is drawn to a black pouch lying on the second shelf down and I reach out to touch it.

"Those are my runes," Larna says with a smile, "a rather beautiful version of the early Germanic/Scandinavian form of letters. Why don't you tip them out into your hand and pick one?"

Intrigued, I upend the bag and watch as black pebbles with a single marking on each fall into my palm. In moments I have chosen the one with an X on it because it reminds me of the sign carved into the stone at the bottom of the rusty chain.

"That's clever," she tells me when I hold it out to her. "You've picked *Gebo*. It means a gift and suggests your luck is about to change."

"That would be nice," I admit, mentally crossing my fingers that it's true. Carefully, I tip the runes back into the bag and replace the pouch onto the bookshelf. "Now, what did you want to ask me?"

She hesitates before she speaks again. "You are probably wondering why all my books look so new. I'm afraid that all these books are a testament to wishful thinking. The truth is that I'm dyslexic and can barely read a word apart from the titles. Of course it's easier these days with so much audible information, but I'm still saddened that I can't read any of my books properly. When I look at the printed page, words jumble up and dance in front of my eyes in circles and spirals until I feel sick." She grimaces. "Anyway, a friend of mine has asked me to help him come up with an idea. He's a successful writer of popular psychology who wants to write another bestseller. We have come up with a subject but I want to make sure that it is doable. There are a couple of books here on dreams. Would you have a look at the indices for me?"

"Of course. Give me a moment." I run a practised eye over the titles and pull out two books. "Here you are." Putting one aside, I open the first to the table of contents and run my finger down the headings. "What exactly are you looking for?"

She shakes her head. "I'm not sure. What is popular now with readers?"

"That's easy," I tell her. "Anything to do with neuroscience. It's the new buzz word."

"Do you think there could be a neuroscience of dreams?"

"I don't see why not," I reply. "Dreams are always popular but there still isn't much written about them, apart from possible meanings."

She claps her hands together. "Then that's perfect. Leave the two books out, will you? I'll give Bertie a call and tell him the good news."

"Bertie?" I query.

"Bertie Fratton: you might have heard of him."

I nod slowly. "Yes, the library was often asked for his work."

Her face grows lighter. "Actually, he's my best friend. And you'll never believe it, but he is also Hester Knebworth's brother."

Suddenly I'm on alert.

She sees my expression change. "That isn't a problem, is it?"

"It's fine."

"Well, don't worry. I promise you that they're nothing like each other. In fact they're far beyond chalk and cheese. Now, would you like some coffee?"

My head has started to ache again. "Actually, would you mind if I went back to the caravan for a while? I'm rather tired after this morning." It's a feeble excuse. After all, I'm only twenty-five, but she seems to accept it easily enough.

As soon as I'm back in the caravan I take off my shoes and lie down on the couch, weary to the bone. But it's a mistake. My pearly eye is throbbing again and the mention of Hester Knebworth has curdled my stomach. In an attempt to put her out of my mind, I reach for the chain on the table and clutch it to my chest as though it will somehow take away the memory of the vile woman and her miserable manor house.

To my relief her image does start to fade, but it is replaced by flickering flames as though I am by a fire. Blinking rapidly, I try to clear my sight but shadows are drawing closer.

Then I start to shiver as snow begins to fall.

circa 2000 B.C.E.

"If we go now, Riadd, we can be back before dawn," Lanalla said as she took a large stick and plunged the bound end into the flames of the fire in the hut. "Pick up the child. Seela, follow me."

Outside, light from the torch cast sinister shadows through heavily falling snow, haunted by the ghost of a sickle moon.

Moving as quietly as possible, the priestess led Riadd and Seela westwards through the forest towards the hill where the Stone would soon be erected. It was a long, hard walk but eventually they arrived at a rocky escarpment. Lanalla started to count her footsteps out loud while following the contours of the rock with her free hand. When she reached a long strand of plants, the darkness seemed to blink and she disappeared.

"Lanalla, where are you?" Riadd called out. The only answers to his question were the animal noises of the night and, after a while, even they faded away.

Despite the fur that the priestess had fastened round her shoulders, Seela stood shivering in the heavy stillness, unsure what to do. She was just reaching out a hand to check that her sister was warm enough when there was a muffled cry from inside the hill. Moments later, a disembodied face appeared through a tangle of branches, lit beneath by the dimming glow of the torch. There was a final splutter and then the light died.

"Seela, come in here," the priestess urged.

Riadd stepped forward to help but she held up her hand to stop him. "No, Riadd, this is women's work. Stay outside with your dog and keep Duna warm. Seela," she continued, extending her outstretched hand towards the girl, "come with me."

Reluctant to leave her sister's side, Seela looked at Riadd. When he nodded, she warily took the priestess's hand and allowed herself to be led into the cave. Away from the flickering light of the torch, the darkness was total.

"This is where we must look for the Amulet," Lanalla explained. Holding on tightly to Seela's hand, she placed it on a ledge of rock. "It is the sacred home of the SeeSayer. Feel your way along the ledge until you find something. I cannot do it. My hands are no longer as supple as they used to be."

Heart in mouth, Seela felt cautiously along the narrow shelf. Old, dried-up leaves and twigs scratched her skin, whilst strands of web began to wind their way around her hands until they were covered with stickiness. With a shudder of revulsion, she snatched her hand free. "There is nothing here," Seela exclaimed quickly. "I want to go back outside."

Despite the darkness, the priestess managed to grab her arm and wouldn't let go. "We cannot leave until we have found the Amulet. It must have fallen to the floor." Despite the tremor, the woman's grip was strong as she forced Seela to her knees. "Feel along the ground, girl. It must be here, somewhere."

Seela started to feel sick and her head began to pound. In the darkness she could see nothing. It was like being up in the tree, waiting for the wolf to pounce. As panic started to rise, the image of the woman with the pearl eye flooded her mind, giving her strength. Pulling hard, she managed to wrench her arm free and fled outside, colliding with Riadd who was standing by the cave's entrance. Careful not to disturb the sleeping child in his arms, he steadied her with his body. It was snowing again, and the flakes were like light crystals in the blackness. As she looked up at him, all she could see were his eyes glinting back at her, flint sharp in the darkness. Springing away from him, she leapt backwards into the cold. "How is Duna?" she demanded, trying to keep her voice calm.

"She's still asleep," Riadd said, his face once again vanishing into the dark. He looked up at the sky where a streak of light was appearing from the east, cresting the forest with the promise of colour. He stepped into the entrance of the cave. "Lanalla," he called, "it will soon be first light. We must go."

It took several moments for Lanalla to appear, looking like an old woman as she trudged out of the cave. Riadd didn't have to ask if she had found the Amulet. The answer was there in her shrinking. Slowly, she raised her head, and looked over at them both. "It's not there," she said, her voice shaking with loss. "The Amulet has gone." She looked up at the sky as if to cry to The Mother, but the falling snow stung her eyes and she had to look down again.

Seela expected harsh words of reproach but instead the priestess held out her hand for support. Relieved, she reached out and took it again. This time the hand felt like ice in a storm, trembling and about to break.

"At least the snow will cover our tracks," Riadd tried.

But the priestess could only smother a sob as they began to trudge away from the cave.

Without the Amulet, she was lost.

LARNA – Present Day

Excited, Larna dialled Bertie's number.

"Dear girl," he said as soon as he heard her voice. "How lovely to hear from you again so soon. Have you changed your mind about seeing Hester next week?" he asked, suddenly sounding worried.

"She came round yesterday instead. A surprise visit, she called it. Bertie, she was horrible. She told me to get rid of the caravan and the boat. Said we weren't welcome."

Bertie sighed. "Dear heart, I did warn you."

"I know, but she was so rude." She took a deep breath and cleared her throat. "At least something good came out of it. She's given Selena some work."

"Selena? Who's Selena?"

"She's the woman I told you about who I saw busking on the way to the concert in your college."

"The one who was threatened by the horrid man?"

"That's the one. But..."

"Do you mean you have seen her again?"

"Yes, she's staying in my caravan. But listen, she..."

"*What?*"

"Bertie, she's lovely and so is her dog."

"She's got a dog, too?"

"She needs him, poor love. Do you remember I told you she is half blind? She has this extraordinary white eye. She usually covers it with an eyepatch. Oh, Bertie, it's such a relief to have someone to cook for. We sit in front of the fire in the boat and..."

"No, no, no, no, *no*," he groaned. "Please don't tell me that you've let her into your lovely boat?"

"Stop it, Bertie. She absolutely loves it in here and I'm enjoying the company."

"Larna, dear girl, for heaven's sake get rid of her."

"I'm hardly going to turf her back out onto the street," she replied, starting to get cross. "Have you seen the weather?"

"Surely there are hostels."

She thought about putting the phone down on him, but just managed to restrain herself. "You may be my dearest friend, Bertie, but where is your compassion?"

"I have lots of compassion, as you well know."

"Well show some to Selena."

There was a long pause. "How old is this Selena?" he asked suspiciously.

"I don't know. In her mid-twenties."

"And you say that my sister has given her some work?"

"Yes. Selena wants to pay me some rent."

"Rent?" he cried in alarm. "For heaven's sake, old thing, how long is she planning on staying?"

"I don't know. She just needs a little bit of help. We all do, remember?" she snapped.

"Okay, okay. Don't bite my head off. At least let me come to the boat and give her the once-over. I just want to check that she's all right and isn't going to rob you."

She sniffed. "Only if you're nice to her."

"I'll be nice once I know she's genuine." He cleared his throat. "Now, what is it you were phoning to tell me?"

SELENA – Present Day

When I wake up, I find that I am clutching the chain to my chest as though it is some kind of talisman. The dream about the cave and something called the Amulet is still sharp in my mind and there's no sign of it going away like a normal dream. As I put the chain back onto the table, I feel a sense of loss and a shiver runs through my body. Puzzled, I pick it up again and immediately feel warmer. Once again I put it down. The air feels suddenly icy again and there's a strange, numb feeling in my pearly eye. When I pick it up again, the air grows warmer and my eye comes back to life. As though this is some kind of crazy experiment, I repeat the action several more times and get the same result. With the chain in my fingers I feel warmer; without it, I feel colder. And that is not all. With the warmth I feel stronger while with the cold, I feel weaker. Without the chain, my eye feels numb; with it, it feels alive.

What is this thing that I have dug up?

Bemused, I lay the chain on the table but put my fingers on it to keep the connection. The rune on the bottom pendant shines more brightly than the others, perhaps because of the amber and selenite crystals. According to the runes in Larna's boat, the X carved into it means *Gebo*: a gift. But what does that mean? And what kind of gift?

The chain is long enough to be a necklace so, wondering

what might happen if I lay it directly on my skin, I brush off as much of the rust as I can and slip the chain over my head. The moment that the bottom stone is sitting snugly over my heart, a song starts playing in my head. It's the song from the dream, sung by Seela, the girl with red hair. Quickly, I reach for a notebook and notate the melody. Perhaps one day I'll be able to add words and turn it into a song.

By the time I have finished scribbling, my eye is positively glowing. I'm feeling light-headed now, and there's a sensation of rocking as though I'm in the boat rather than the caravan. But when I put my pencil down and close the notebook, everything changes and goes dark. Then I start to feel as though I'm being pulled slowly through an opening into another place.

Suddenly afraid, I rip off the necklace and throw it back onto the table where it quivers like a snake before rolling in a heap onto the floor. As I stand and step towards the door, my feet refuse to move forward. Turning back, I pick up the necklace and put it in my pocket. Able to move properly again, I retreat outside. It's bitterly cold again and there's no sign of Buddy. He's probably still fast asleep by the fire in the boat.

Hoping he'll forgive me if I go for a walk without him, I head out across the field and cross the footbridge over into Little Stenning. Once I am past the manor, I walk towards Stenning Woods, not stopping until I reach the old oak again where I dug up the necklace and buried the blackbird. The atmosphere is strange, as though the air is waiting for permission to breathe. The only sign that I was here before is a small mound. Two stones lie on top of it as though someone has marked the place. But who? No-one, apart from me and the girl with the red hair, knew what happened.

I touch the necklace in my pocket, wondering if I should bury it back in the ground. It might make me feel strong when

I hold it, but I never want to feel that dizzying sensation of hurtling through space again. I go to pull it out but it refuses to budge. I try again, but it acts as though it has been glued onto the fabric. Irritated, I turn the pocket inside out and attempt to shake the contents onto the ground, but the necklace still stays put and refuses to fall.

Unable to rid myself of it, I warily continue my walk up the path to the church at the top of the hill. It is a quaint, chapel-like building with a small, square wooden Saxon tower and thick stone Norman walls. Wondering why it might have been built in such an unlikely location, I am just reaching out to open the gate into the graveyard when I hear the sound of a car door slamming. At the same time, there's a cold sensation at the back of my neck as though I am being watched. Moments later, a middle-aged woman strides purposefully round to the side of the church and lets herself in with a large key.

Hastily, I make my way between the gravestones towards the door where faint strains of organ music are already floating through the air. She must have come here to practise. Opening the heavy door as quietly as I can, I wait to hear the fearful groan of old hinges, but the reedy timbre of the organ cloaks all other sounds.

Inside, the church is even tinier. There are three pews on either side of a nave with a simple altar at the top. A few unlit candles and a beautiful white marble statue of the Virgin Mary are the only decorations, apart from a simple stained-glass window at the top in which Mary's face is full of grief as though the world has become too painful for her to bear.

Choosing one of the lower pews, I sit down to listen to the music. The air in here is frigid so I huddle into my coat and put my hands in my pockets. As soon as my fingers close round the necklace, I feel its warmth as though it is forgiving me for having tried to bury it back in the earth.

Without warning, my pearly eye starts to tingle into life. At the same time, the vision at the edges of my green eye starts to blur. Then, as though I can't bear the heaviness any longer, my eyes close and before I know what's happening, the sound of the organ is fading and I am drifting inwards towards a place I once knew long, long ago.

circa 2000 B.C.E.

"Take this, Riadd, and this."

There was the sound of a dog yelping.

"If your filthy cur ever attacks me again, I'll crush its skull with my foot. Now get up and tell me what you and the priestess have been doing all night. I've been waiting for you since dawn. Where have you been?"

Inside her hut, Lanalla spun round to face Seela. "Quickly, hide yourselves in the shadows."

Seela grabbed her little sister and ran to the pallet at the back of the hut just as Mevin opened the door flap and barged into the hut, dragging Riadd behind him by his long black hair.

"Let go of him," cried Lanalla as she rushed over to the youth and knelt down beside him, putting her hand on his head. "Riadd, are you all right? Speak to me." When the youth groaned, she heaved a huge sigh of relief and stood up. "Mevin, you are nothing but a brute. Now get out. You have no right to barge in here without permission."

Mevin didn't move. "I will go," he said in a low voice, "when you tell me where you have been all night."

"That is none of your concern."

"Everything concerns me if I am to be the new Leader."

She glared at him. "You are no Leader."

"I will be if you do not let Hogan come back."

"You think too much of yourself."

"Then it seems that, at last, we have something in common."

Lanalla flinched.

"Besides, there is nobody else," Mevin continued harshly. "Kurt is a fool and Bannan is too weak. We are decimated, priestess. This is the mess that you have made."

"There are other candidates," she said, recovering herself. "Alanis and Fellana…"

He spat on the floor. "They are women, and I have had enough of you all. The Folk need a man to guide them in the right direction."

"But women have the ear of The Mother," she protested. "It is women who bring new life into the world."

"Are you so sure?"

Lanalla stared at him in bewilderment. "What do you mean?"

"Haven't you noticed that women only have children after they have shared pleasures with a man?"

She paled.

"It's not only women who bring new life into the world," he continued. "Men also play their part by providing the seed."

"That is ridiculous. You make no sense."

"What makes no sense is that most of the new life you women are bringing into the world only survives for a short time and when it does, you turn the girls into SeeSayers and hide them away. What we need is New Blood to strengthen our children. You said that Mana predicted that some New Bloods would arrive soon, but where are they? You say that raising a stone into the sky will bring them to us, but how can that be? We have to become strong again if we are to survive. Your time is over. My time has arrived."

"No," came a voice. "You are wrong, Mevin."

Mevin looked at the floor where Riadd was struggling to his feet.

"Riadd," said Lanalla, "are you..."

"He is not your son," barked Mevin.

"But his parents..."

"...made you promise. Yes, we've all heard the story many times before. Look at him, woman, swaying like an overgrown flower. You do him no favours by bringing him up in your ways. I am trying to teach him to be a man. You must let him go. I ..."

From behind him was the sudden sound of a whimper. Surprised, Mevin peered into the dark. "What is that?"

"Your imagination," said Lanalla quickly. "There is no-one but the three of us in this hut."

He looked at her suspiciously. "Are you hiding someone?" Instead, of waiting for a reply, he strode to the back of the hut, picked up a handful of furs from a pallet and threw them to one side. For a moment, he was stunned into silence. Then suddenly, he roared angrily. "What is this? Two girls?" Reaching for the smaller one, he yanked her up by her arm, making her scream. As he pulled her out into the dim light and saw her head, he spat in disgust and threw her back to the ground. Then he grabbed the older girl's hair and held her fast. She wriggled like a fish so he grabbed her chin and pulled back her head so he could see her face.

Riadd went to spring at him but Mevin pulled Seela's head so far back that she cried out. "If you come any nearer, boy, I shall really hurt her."

Duna had begun to cry. Lanalla went to comfort her but Mevin yanked Seela's hair viciously again. "Don't move," he hissed; "either of you." He pointed to the smaller girl with his foot. "You were going to put this cripple forward as the new

SeeSayer, weren't you? Oh, priestess, how desperate you must be to cling onto your power. She is even more pathetic than the last one."

"Mevin, stop," pleaded Lanalla. "You insult The Mother with your words."

"I insult no one but you," he bellowed. Then he pulled Seela's abundant red hair upwards again so he could look at her white face. She spat at him like a cat, hitting him in the eye with her spittle. "Ah," he said, wiping his face with his free hand, "this one is more promising. She will heat the blood of every male in the settlement."

At the words, Riadd leapt forward but Mevin kicked him so hard in the back of his knees that the youth fell to the ground. Then he pinned Seela's arms to her sides. Desperately, she struggled to free herself but he only laughed. Riadd lashed out with his feet and caught Mevin behind one of his ankles. "Ouch! That's better, boy," he flinched. "You're learning how to fight, at last. Now take this." He freed one of his hands and struck Riadd across his face.

"Stop it, Mevin," cried Lanalla. "You're hurting him."

Leaving Riadd on the floor, Mevin began to drag Seela to the entrance but Riadd struggled to his feet and leapt onto his back. At the same time, Seela managed to free one of her hands and scratch the big man down the length of his face with her nails. Cursing, Mevin released his grip. Riadd jumped down, grabbed her and pulled her to the back of the hut.

"You bitch," hissed Mevin as he wiped his face with the back of his hand. "I'll ..."

But he didn't have time to finish as Bika launched himself at Mevin and bit him savagely on his arm. Mevin threw off the dog and sent him sprawling. There was an agonised yelp and, once again, the dog lay still.

Panting, Mevin turned to Riadd. Then he grinned. "Perhaps

there is hope for you after all, boy. Leave the skirts of this woman and learn to fight like a man or I will kill you and your cur." Then he turned to Lanalla, his eyes bitter with hatred. "Guard your wild cat well while you can, for once I am the new Leader, I will take her into my hut and give her my seed. She is strong, will give good sport and at last, the Folk may begin to renew themselves again."

ᚦ

Thurisaz reversed - end of good fortune

Chapter Six

SELENA – Present Day

"You shouldn't be in here," says the organist harshly. "How did you get in? Please leave."

I open my eyes. Her gaze widens in alarm and she steps back. Realising that my eyepatch must have slipped down, I hastily pull it back up and try to stand up but I am so cold that I can barely feel my body and have to hold the back of the pew for support. I close my eyes again in an attempt to block out both the world and the dream.

"Oh no you don't, young lady," she declares. "The bishop will have a fit if he hears that you've been sleeping in the church. Now come on. It's late. I've finished practising and I want to lock up."

Only then do I realise that my free hand is still clutching the necklace in my pocket. Freeing my fingers, I let it fall down into the fabric. Then I follow her unsteadily towards the door. Outside it is dark and, although there are no flakes in the air, a fresh layer of snow is lying on the ground. My pearly eye is stinging as though there is smoke from a fire trapped inside, and I have to blink rapidly to clear my vision. Wishing that Buddy was here with me to bark away the shadows, I make my way slowly to the gate in the churchyard. The trees are creaking and groaning as if they, too, are frightened that Mevin will hurt Seela and her sister.

As the dream continues to invade my mind, I am not surprised when I detect the scent of rotting apples and stale talcum powder. Seela is close. I can feel her near me. For the first time I welcome her visitation. I need to warn this lost soul from the station, the river, and Karl Knebworth's sketches. She showed me where the necklace was buried and I must help her in any way I can. So I wait in the surreal shadows as the air stills like an animal preparing to pounce.

And then there she is, her shape suddenly twitching between branches, an unearthly glow illuminating her pale face, her long red hair clogged and matted with despair. Stealing myself, I do not jump back. Instead I step forward and open my hands towards her in unconscious supplication. For a long moment, we stare at each other. Her mouth begins to move. I think she is trying to speak to me but her voice sounds like the creaking of an old gate.

"Seela?" I try.

Her throat begins to work even harder but already she is fading as though someone is dragging her backwards through time, not allowing her to be here.

"Seela," I implore, "don't go. Tell me what it is that you need."

For a long moment I fancy that I hear the song singing her reply but the melody is wrapped in words I cannot understand and, as she vanishes, I am left with the impression that somehow I have failed her.

THE TEAM – Present Day

"I can't believe that it has snowed, again," said Marcus. "I thought global warming was supposed to make things hotter."

"Climate change is playing havoc with the weather," said Raff. "This is just one of the extremes we're going to have to get used to."

"Well, I refuse to give up," said Falala, looking at the flotation tank which had been set up to sort finds from debris. "It might have been a long day and the earth that the digger uncovered yesterday might have been covered with snow, but we've been surprisingly successful. I didn't expect to find a hand-axe, and your discovery of a posthole is off the scale. It's almost as if this field wants to be excavated."

Raff shook his head. "I can't believe it, either. I've dreamed about finding one and here it is: a clear, circular patch of dark earth. Now perhaps we can deduce a possible layout of the post that used to hold up the wall. I'm going to try to plot the corners and sides of the building. Marcus, you're the genius with numbers. How about calculating where we might find a second, a third and even a fourth posthole?"

Marcus shrugged. "I can make a calculated guess." He bent his head and tapped away at his calculator. Then he looked at the diagram they had drawn of the site. "Here," he said, pointing with his finger. "One should be here."

"Brilliant," said Falala. "Now we've got a good case for ringing the C.A. and demanding a time extension." She looked at them both, excitement shining from her eyes. "I was beginning to think that we'd be out of here before we'd even started." She pointed to some pottery fragments which appeared to have rims. "I've come across some like these before. Let's upload the photos to the computer. We might be able to find some matches. If we can come up with an approximate date, we're laughing."

Raff had started to tap on the keyboard almost before she had finished speaking. He had specialised in dendrochronology, the science of dating tree growth rings, at university and was eager to try out his skills. It only took a few minutes. "Got it," he called out. "Here's a table of narrow ring events showing how the rings found in ancient trees can be used to date preserved wood."

Falala and Marcus leaned over his shoulder to look at the screen. "Any possible dates?" asked Marcus.

"Yes. 3195 BCE, 2345 BCE, 1628 BCE, 1159 BCE, 207 BCE, 44 BCE and 540 CE," Raff replied, continuing to alternately peer at the screen and scribble notes. "I'd say either 2345 or 1628 BCE, but we'll only know for sure when we get some more evidence."

"The early Bronze Age," Falala whispered, almost too thrilled to speak. "I can't believe it."

Marcus returned to his own laptop and uploaded some more photographs. Then he sat back on his chair and laughed out loud. "My family are going to have a fit when they realise that their precious field is an archaeologist's dream. Mother will go berserk!" He raised his hands to the ceiling and stretched. "Guys, this calls for a drink. But first, I'm going back to the flat to have a long, hot bath. It's been a long day."

"Lucky sod, I've only got a shower," Falala scoffed.

Marcus turned to her and grinned. "You can always come and share mine. There's enough room for two."

"Fun-ny," quipped Falala. "How about dinner tonight in the village pub now we have something to celebrate? It's about time we went out and ate together."

They agreed to meet at eight. After her shower, Falala made the mistake of looking something up and became oblivious to the time. When she finally looked up at the clock, she realised that she would be late if she walked so she grabbed her keys and headed out to her beloved vintage Volkswagen, *Molly*.

As usual, the engine failed to respond when she switched on the ignition. Hungry, tired, and cold, she swore again under her breath before reaching out to stroke the walnut dashboard in apology. Promising herself that she would book a service tomorrow, she tried again but when there was still no response, Falala climbed back out into the chilly air, opened the bonnet, and tapped the starter motor sharply. It worked and the next time she attempted ignition, the engine roared to life.

The pub was on the outskirts of Great Stenning so, rather than weave through the busy streets, she decided to take the faster route and turned out onto the main Oxford road. To her surprise, it was deserted. As she switched her headlamps to full beam, huge flakes of snow started to fall and within moments the windscreen was covered with white. Cursing, she switched on the windscreen wipers, but they were too slow and couldn't cope with the sheer quantity of snow. Realising that it would be dangerous to continue driving, she pulled over to the side of the road and decided to wait it out.

All of a sudden, there was a frantic knocking on the passenger window. Leaning over to wind down the window, she came face to face with a girl, snow covering her long, red, bedraggled hair.

"Are you in trouble?" Falala asked. "Do you need a lift somewhere?" When the girl failed to answer, she leaned across, grabbed the door handle, and pushed it open. "Get in," she yelled. "You'll freeze out there."

As the girl fell into the seat, the car was filled with an unpleasant, musty smell. Despite the snow that was now driving into the car, the girl made no effort to shut the window, so Falala had to reach across her to wind it up. The smell was overpowering, as if she hadn't showered in weeks.

"Where are your parents?" Falala asked quickly.

The girl's eyes were closed and she was trembling violently.

Falala knew enough about hypothermia to see that she needed urgent medical attention so, wrinkling her nose, she reached round her and put the seat belt into its dock. Then she straightened up and turned back to face the steering wheel, praying the car would start and that Marcus and Raff would forgive her failure to turn up at the pub.

After four nerve-wracking attempts, *Molly* finally spluttered back into life. With her nose virtually pressed up against the windscreen, Falala indicated to pull back out into the road. Fortunately there was still no traffic. The snow was falling so heavily that she could only crawl along at barely ten miles an hour.

It wasn't long before the temperature inside the car began to plummet. She reached across for the heater button but, at her nearness, the girl started to panic and knocked Falala's arm. "Be careful," Falala warned, only just managing to regain control and turn the car back onto a straight line. The girl took no notice and started lashing out at the door. Grasping the steering wheel with one hand, Falala tried to restrain her with the other, but the girl was now lurching from side to side, her sodden red hair whipping wildly against the glass. "Calm down," Falala shouted. "You'll make the car skid."

Either the girl didn't understand, or she was too panicked to respond sensibly, because all of a sudden the passenger door flew open.

"No!" screamed Falala, but it was too late and the girl fell out. Horrified, Falala jammed on the brakes and jumped out of the car, running round to the passenger side whilst trying not to slip on the snow. Afraid that the girl had hurt herself even more and that she would be lying somewhere in the road, she searched frantically but there was no sign of her anywhere. Horrified, she peered through the trees at the side that were thick and covered with white, offering a myriad of hiding places. Surely there would be footprints showing where she had gone, but there was no sign of any of those either.

By now Falala was so cold she could barely think. Frantically, she called out into the silence but there was no response. In the end, all she could do was to brush off as much snow from her clothes as she could and climb back into the car to get warm. She wondered if she should call the police and tell them that there was a girl out here somewhere who had fallen out of a car and disappeared, but even as she rehearsed what she would say in her mind, she knew it sounded ridiculous. Instead, she closed her eyes for a moment, trying to calm herself.

When she opened them again she stared in surprise. Not only was the windscreen clear, but the snow had disappeared. She blinked rapidly and then rubbed her eyes but it made no difference. It was only when a car hooted its horn at her and overtook her at an alarming speed, that she realised she was in the middle of the road. Hastily, she crossed the fingers of her left hand and turned the key in the ignition. To her surprise *Molly* started first time and before she realised what was happening, she was chugging forward slowly back towards the pub.

It didn't take her long to arrive.

Raff jumped to his feet the moment he saw her.

"Sorry I'm late," she spluttered.

"What happened?" he asked. "You're soaking."

"One hell of a snowstorm," she retorted, looking dazed. "I need a brandy."

"A snowstorm?" queried Raff as he helped her out of her dripping coat and hung it to dry over the back of a chair. "But the sun was shining when I left."

"Hardly," she said, running a hand over her wiry, black hair, "Look at the state of me. I can barely see for the snow in my eyes."

Barely noticing the puzzled look between the men, she gratefully accepted the freshly washed handkerchief that Raff held out to her. Then she sat down and wiped her face while Raff piled more logs on the fire. She couldn't stop thinking about the girl. What could have happened to her? What if she was lying injured in a ditch somewhere, with nobody to help her? Angry with herself for not having called the police earlier, she reached into her pocket and pulled out her phone, her hands shaking so badly that it took several goes for her to press 999 accurately. When she was finally put through to the right department, the conversation was all too brief. She recounted what had happened with the girl in the storm but was told that there hadn't been any snow. Treated like a prankster, she finally ended the call. Moments later, her stomach gurgled audibly.

Relieved, Marcus leapt to his feet. "Time for food, I think. I'll go and get some menus and a brandy for you, Fally."

As soon as Marcus had left, Raff put his hand on her arm. "Are you okay?"

She hugged her arms around herself. "There was a girl," she tried to explain. "I think she was hurt. I was just trying to take her to hospital but she jumped out of the car. I'm really worried that she was hurt. But the police didn't even ask my name. I might have expected that sort of treatment if they'd seen me," she said bitterly, touching her black skin, "but I sound as white as anyone else on the phone." She looked up imploringly at him. "Raff, there's something wrong with this place. None of us has been the same since we arrived in the Stennings."

Raff didn't comment. He didn't like being back here either, but that didn't mean that he imagined weather that didn't exist. Marcus's newfound melancholia was one thing, but this was different. Falala had never shown any indications of oddness before. Puzzled, he wondered what was happening.

They should be heady with excitement about the dig. Instead, they were all on edge.

Hoping that food would help to settle them, they all tucked in with relish once their meal had arrived and as soon as they began discussing the field, the conversation began to ease. "Clem Hardwick is looking forward to the meeting tomorrow afternoon," Raff commented. "You have quite a fan there, Fally. He's read some of your papers."

"Really? Which ones?" she asked, relieved to think about something other than the girl.

Raff smiled. "You'll have to ask him."

"He'll have you pegged as one of those academics with thick glasses," Marcus quipped, reaching into his pocket to pull out a piece of paper. "He's going to be in for a shock when he sees how gorgeous you are."

Falala kicked him playfully under the table. "Idiot."

And suddenly, the world fell back into place and all that mattered was the dig, the three of them and the fact that they had managed to land a job which, at last, looked promising.

"What do you think of this?" asked Marcus, pulling a piece of paper out of his pocket.

It was a sketch. Falala spent several seconds studying it before handing it to Raff. "It's good," she said. "When did you draw this?"

"The idea came to me while I was in the bath. It's a representation of what the settlement might have looked like. Put this with a few of your photos, Raff, and Clem Hardwick will begin to get an idea of the site."

"Well done," said Raff appreciatively. "This will really help our case."

"Good," said Marcus, looking pleased. "I think this calls for a proper drink. I'll get some more beers, then we can work out how to tell my family that they need to give us more time."

It was a productive discussion during which they came up with a plan, but after an hour, Raff looked at his watch and stretched. "I'm going to call it a day. It's getting late and I want to do a little more work before the meeting tomorrow."

Marcus looked disappointed. "Don't be such a light-weight. It's only ten o'clock. Surely you don't need to do anymore work tonight. The evidence we've uncovered speaks for itself. Clem can't fail to be impressed by what we've done."

"I know," Raff retorted. "The drawing you've done is excellent and will undoubtedly help, but I want to make sure that all our finds are collated accurately so that he can do nothing but give us what we want."

"Geek."

Raff put his hands up in mock surrender. "Guilty as charged."

"Bugger off, then," Marcus said. "I'm sure that Fally and I will find something else to do while you're being boring."

"Hey," protested Falala. "Work isn't boring." She turned to Raff. "Thanks. You're right. We need to have everything documented for the meeting tomorrow. I was going to arrive early to do it, but if you're happy to do it then I won't have to. Thanks for coming this evening and don't stay up too late." She smiled before turning back to Marcus and giving him a playful cuff on his arm. "If you twist my arm, I might stay with you for a bit."

Once Raff had left, Marcus went to the bar. When he returned with two more beers, she frowned. "I hope one of those isn't for me. I'm driving, remember?"

"Well, I'll just have to drink both of them myself, then." He completely emptied the first glass. "Anyway," he said, wiping the froth from his mouth with a practised sweep of his sleeve, "I'm just doing what all decent archaeologists do."

"And what's that?"

"Getting drunk, of course."

"And where did you learn that in your university degree?"

"Freshers' Week, I believe."

"Fool," she said, punching him again. This time he caught her hand. "Are you feeling better, now?" he asked in an unusually compassionate tone.

She went very still. "The snowstorm you mean; the one which apparently didn't happen?" She shrugged. "Well, I'm either losing my marbles or the police were tightly tucked up in bed and didn't see it. But it was real, Marcus, I promise you," she shivered. "I just hope that the girl is okay."

He slid over to sit beside her and put an arm around her shoulders. "As long as you're all right," he murmured.

"I'm fine. How about you? You're going to have a hangover if you carry on drinking like that."

"I need some Dutch courage. I took your advice and arranged to see my mother tomorrow morning."

"Really?" she said in surprise. "But that's wonderful."

"To be honest, I'm dreading it. The woman's a nightmare."

"Let's hope she's changed. People do, you know. After all, it's been a long time since you saw her."

He almost laughed. "I doubt it. She's mad, my brother's a fool, and all father wants to do is to escape. Can't say I blame him."

"Marcus, you have to improve your attitude. You've got to decide that change is possible or it'll be a disaster before you even go. I've met your brother and he seems fine, if rather anxious. He was really disappointed that you weren't there, you know. Couldn't you at least try to give him some brotherly support?"

Marcus groaned. "We've got nothing in common."

"He's family. Doesn't that count for something?"

Suddenly, the lights flickered on and off three times.

Falala looked up. "Looks like it's time to go."

Marcus took another swig of beer from his almost full second glass. "Well I'm not ready to go yet. Let's wait until the landlord is glaring at us."

"He already is. You'll just have to leave what you haven't drunk."

"No chance." He picked it up and drained it completely dry.

"Bloody hell, Marcus," protested Falala. "You'll be in no fit state to meet anyone tomorrow, let alone your mother. And don't forget that Clem Hardwick is coming in the afternoon. You need to be on form for that meeting, too. The lights flashed again and she held out her hand. "Come on, I'll drive you back to your flat."

He groaned. "You're such a bully."

She sighed. "Someone needs to sort you out." She lead him to the car park.

"I'm surprised this old banger's still going," he said as he climbed in.

"Be nice to *Molly* or she won't take you home."

"Why's this seat all wet?"

"I told you, that girl was soaked when I picked her up."

"What girl?"

"For God's sake, Marcus, just put your seat belt on and shut up."

Fortunately, *Molly* started on the third attempt. When they arrived at Marcus's flat, he made no attempt to open the car door. Instead, he reached out and touched her arm. "I don't want to go back to my flat, Fally," he slurred. "I'm lonely there. Can I come to yours? I could always sleep on your sofa."

"It isn't big enough."

"Your floor then. I'll behave myself. Honest."

"Yeah, right; like you did last time."

"That was a one-off."

"Exactly."

"I mean it, Fally. I'll sober up and sleep like a baby. Promise."

She hesitated, trying to push away the thought that she was lonely too and that she didn't want to have to think about the girl any longer. Suddenly, she found herself switching on the indicator and checking the rear view mirror to see if anyone was behind her. It was all clear so she pulled out into the road and began to chug towards her own flat, wondering what kind of state she had left it in. She hoped she wasn't being naïve. Their night together at university had been a mistake but she knew how she felt underneath her bravado. She would just have to ensure that he slept on the sofa.

When they arrived, they had to climb two flights of stairs to get to her flat. It was the first time Marcus had seen it. "Bloody hell," he said with a shake of his head as they went in the front door. "You weren't joking were you when you said this was small."

"I told you it was cosy. Stop complaining unless you want me to drive you back to yours."

He slumped into a chair like a sack of potatoes. "I could go to sleep right here."

"Bathroom first," she said rather more harshly than she intended.

"But…"

"Use it."

He groaned but levered himself up.

"I'll make up a bed for you while you're gone."

He turned and grinned. "I'd rather snuggle up with you."

"Don't be ridiculous. Go pee. And use my toothbrush."

He had the grace to look surprised.

"Go!"

While he was gone, she looked for sheets, but she'd just

changed her bed. They were in the wash and she didn't have a second set. There should be a sleeping bag somewhere but she couldn't remember where. Perhaps she should drive him back to his flat, but there was no guarantee that *Molly* would start again. Telling herself to stop taking everything so seriously, she reminded herself that at university people slept together platonically all the time, so when he returned and yawned, she held out her hand to him. "Bed," she said quietly.

"What?"

"You heard me."

He didn't argue as she led him into the best room of the flat. Unlike the living room, it was a decent size, with a bed large enough for both of them. As long as he stayed on his side and she stayed on hers, there would be no harm done.

Once he had undressed down to his underpants and slid into bed, Falala disappeared into the bathroom and changed into the one nightdress she owned. By the time she returned, Marcus was already fast asleep. Breathing in a sigh of relief, she slid between the sheets. But it was cold, and she could still feel the freezing snow of the storm as it had lashed her face. With a shiver, she edged closer to his warm body. *Black meets white*, she thought with a frisson of excitement. *Night meets day*. If she kissed him, he would never remember. The kiss turned into stroking, and Marcus responding in a half sleep. Afterwards, she wondered how she had forgotten how good it felt being so close to him and at last allowed herself to smile.

She wasn't prepared for what happened next. What should have been sleep felt as strange as picking up the girl on the road. She tried to quell the dream but it was too strong and, as she fell downwards into blackness, the nightmare began.

circa 2000 B.C.E.

In a desperate plea to The Mother to call in New Blood, nineteen men and women gathered for the final raising of the Stone. Double the number would have been preferable but there was no-one else. Mevin put himself in charge with Bannan, Kurt and Faolan as his deputies. He insisted that Riadd come with him, although he doubted that the youth's ever-growing bones would lend much strength.

As they all strode together up the hill, Mevin began to grumble. "If only the priestess had not banished Hogan, this task would have been so much easier."

"Hogan should not have killed Mana," muttered Riadd.

"Be quiet, boy," retorted Mevin. "You know nothing of these things."

"Then teach me. I am to become a man in a few moons. Surely being a man means more than just fighting? Tell me what else I need to know."

Mevin glared at him and then turned away. "Not now. We have work to do. You are not yet strong enough to do the heaving but you will be able to help prop up the Stone with wood as we raise it."

Riadd was quiet until they reached the massive monolith lying on the ground. Broad at the base and tapered at the top, it had been dragged here from the mountains in the west before he was born. "Why is it so pitted with holes?" he asked.

Fellana, one of the women, answered. "The Mother has been spitting on it for millennia with Her frost, rain and wind. Her breath is so harsh that it turns mountains into stone. She needs the holes to breathe through."

"A monster indeed," added Mevin sarcastically.

There was an uncomfortable silence until Raff asked a second question. "How will it point up to the sky when it is raised? It is too crooked."

"Have you never seen swollen bone disease before, boy?" scowled Mevin. "The Mother is an old, old woman. It's about time we laid her to rest."

Alanis, another of the women, ignored the comment and turned to Riadd. "The Stone is crooked because it is one of Her back teeth."

There was a ripple of nervous laughter followed by someone dramatically chomping their jaws.

"How was it brought here?" asked Riadd curiously.

"My father told me that a giant sled was built made of rollers tied to longitudinally placed logs," Kurt replied. "Once the Stone had been manoeuvred onto it, the earth in front was soaked with water. That way the sled was able to slide and be pulled and pushed along the ground."

"The story goes that the sled kept breaking when they reached this hill," continued Bannan. "They had to build five more sleds just to haul the Stone's colossal weight up here."

"They must have had the strength of twenty cave lions," said Fellana. "If this was one of Her back teeth, then how heavy would the Stone have been had they brough Her whole mouth?"

"Save your strength for what we have to do," snapped Mevin. "I will hear no more of The Mother. From now on, we worship The Father."

"You sound as though you are already the new Leader," grumbled Fellana. "What if The Mother doesn't choose you at the Ordeal?"

Mevin swore under his breath. "Hold your tongue, woman. I told you: The Mother is dead. I've had enough of women. Leave us. You should never have come up here in the first place. From now on, this hill is for men only."

"But …"

Mevin raised his hand and struck Fellana across the face so hard that she fell.

"Wait till Lanalla hears about this," said Alanis defiantly as she helped Fellana to her feet. "She will ask The Mother to curse you for your brutishness."

Mevin's reply was to send her sprawling as well. As she fell, there was a resounding crack when she hit her head on the Stone. Then she lay still. Frightened, the other women moved forward to pick her up. Without further protest, they carried her down the hill back to the settlement.

Left alone, the men stared stunned at the blood that now spotted the massive monolith lying on the ground in front of them. It was not a good omen. Alanis was one of their strongest women. What if Mevin had killed her? Would he be banished too?

"Now," said Mevin, his voice edged with threat, "let us stop wasting time and complete our task." He pointed to the pile of ropes in front of them and the mass of timbers that had been cut from the forest and hauled up to the top of the hill for the purpose. "Once we have dug a hole for the base, we will secure the ropes around the tapering top of the Stone and, as we raise it, prop it into position with the wood."

Reluctantly, the men began to follow Mevin's orders. Once a hole had been made, the strongest of them formed a long line one behind the other while Riadd was directed to hand them the ropes. As they began to heave the Stone into the hole, solid pieces of timber were used as supports. Once it was in place, levers were then used to rock the monolith from side to side, so that larger, tied pieces of wood could be inserted to form a prop tower. Little by little the Stone rose towards the sky, looking like an accusing finger. Progress was slow but eventually it was standing in as upright a position as its crooked shape would allow.

Lungs heaving, they let go of the ropes.

"Curse anyone who tries to move this Stone," panted

Mevin. "May they be crushed to death beneath it and rot forever."

Exhausted, several of the men sank onto the ground, clutching their backs.

"Oh no you don't," Mevin warned. "We are not finished yet. Now we must carve two holes at head height to represent the eyes of The Father, that He may ever look outwards and see who is coming." Ignoring several challenging looks, he pointed to two of the larger pits which stood roughly at equal eye level. "Enlarge these holes with the stone flakes brought from the flintknapper but don't carve right through. Imagine you were carving eye sockets." When nobody moved, he growled: "Stop idling and get on with it."

It was long, arduous work and the holes they increased were uneven, but the rock was still visible at the back and so Mevin was satisfied.

"Next," he continued, "let's carve our names into the base so that time will remember our effort to welcome in The Father."

"And the New Blood that will save us," added Riadd.

Mevin glared at him before taking a bone hammer out of a bag and setting about inscribing his name into the bottom of the monument. One by one, the other men followed. Then finally, when they had all finished, they stepped back to survey their handiwork.

"You've added Hogan's name," Riadd protested. "But he does not belong here any longer."

"Hold your tongue, boy. Hogan will return, I promise you." He turned to face the others. "Now, we have to bury The Mother, once and for all."

"How will we do that?" Bannan asked.

"We will hold the Ordeal. Once I have won, we will sacrifice a child."

There was a collective gasp of horror. The men were used to sacrifice but not of children. Children were precious; even those that were born deformed.

Mevin waited for someone to argue but they were all too shocked to protest. Satisfied that everyone seemed to be in agreement, he continued. "There is a child who is hiding here and she will do very well. We will bury her cremated remains in an urn and dig the urn into a small pit close to the foot of the monument. That way The Mother will be dead and The Father will take her place."

Suddenly, Riadd let out a gasp of understanding. He opened his mouth to protest but Mevin's hand came up, ready to silence him. This time the boy saw what was about to happen and stepped back neatly before he could be hit.

Furious, Mevin's hand fell. Then he tried to smile, an expression which turned his face ugly with menace. "We follow The Father's way now. Go back down the hill. Eat and rest. Tomorrow we prepare for the Ordeal."

ᚠ

Ansuz – wisdom

Chapter Seven

SELENA – Present Day

This time when I wake up I know exactly where I am. After a
hearty, delicious breakfast, I help Larna with the chores. Then
Buddy and I set out for a walk. This time we head away from
Little Stenning and back towards the first hill, Stone Clump.
It's the first time I have been in this direction since I arrived
here.

The monument on the top of the Clump reminds me of
my long dead grandmother's arthritic finger, all knobbly and
gnarled, as though it is trying to point up to the sky but not
quite managing to choose a specific direction. At the top of the
hill, the view is breath-taking. Beneath the rise, the Oxfordshire
countryside rolls out like a beautiful patchwork quilt stunningly
sewn in different shades of green. On one side nestles the valley
with its farmhouse, where the tall man gave me water and tea
and showed me his harp. On the other side is the wood-covered
second hill with its little church at the top and the oak tree at
the bottom where I found the chain. In between the hills snakes

the river, separating the two Stenning villages. Two bridges span it, one for pedestrians, the other for cars.

The stone monument is roughly triangular in shape. At head height, two cup-shaped holes are carved into the centre. When I put my hand into one I find an old, chipped, bronze threepenny bit tucked into a groove at the bottom. Inside the other is an old silver sixpence, put there decades ago presumably either as an offering or a wish. As I hold each coin in my palm, my pearly eye tingles in alarm so I hastily replace them in the holes lest I disturb the guardian spirits of this primeval place.

It is a gorgeous day, and with the world spread out at my feet, the desire to shake off the feeling of heaviness makes me feel mischievous. Impulsively, I begin to run down the hill. Buddy looks up and, catching on to the game, chases me down the steep descent. As we arrive at the bottom, Buddy dances excitedly round me, no doubt hoping to repeat the fun. Laughing, I glance back up at the hill and shake my head merrily. Running down the hill is one thing. Running up it, something else entirely.

Once I've caught my breath, we make our way down a barely-used track that leads down the back of Stone Clump. On the far side of a stream, three people are working on the land, digging what appears to be a rectangular trench. A prefabricated cabin stands at the top of the incline behind them. A handwritten sign is tied to a gate.

Do not enter – dig in progress

One of the figures is a black woman wearing overalls. On the other side of the field, a white man with a shock of bleached hair is digging energetically. In between them, a third figure crouches, studying something on the ground. As he stands up, his height and black hair reveal him to be the man from the farmhouse.

When the woman looks up and sees me staring, she puts down her spade and comes over to the fence. "Can I help you?" she calls across the stream.

"Hello," I say. "This looks interesting."

"Do you like archaeology?" she asks, her face lighting up with a smile.

"I don't know," I say truthfully. "I've never seen a dig before but I've always wondered what one was like."

She hesitates for a moment and then looks at her watch. "I could do with a break. Would you like to have a closer look at what we're doing?"

Buddy has begun to wag his tail at the man from the farmhouse.

"You'll need to put your dog on a lead," she says. "Then you can cross the stream over there," she continues, pointing a little further away. "Use the large stepping-stones."

Buddy doesn't need telling twice. He's getting used to a lead now and is eager to see the man again.

"I'm Falala," says the woman as she holds out her hand. "Fally for short."

I take it, strangely grateful for the warmth of her grip. "Selena," I reply.

Her face lights up with another smile. "Right then, Selena, come with me and I'll show you the workings."

She takes me up the field where the tall man from the farmhouse is now standing, watching our approach.

"Hello again," he says.

"Do you two know each other?" Fally asks in surprise.

"Yes, we met at my farmhouse a couple of days ago," he explains. "This lady is a very accomplished harp player. My name's Raff," he continues with a smile, while holding out his hand. "We never did introduce ourselves."

"Selena," I say. His grasp is firm and, yet again, I find

myself grateful for the touch of a hand. "And this is Buddy," I say, pointing to the dog. "He evidently remembers you."

Raff bends down to scratch the dog's ears and for several seconds Buddy closes his eyes in sheer pleasure. Then, all of a sudden, Buddy's eyes fly open, his entire posture changes and he starts to growl. At the same time, my pearly eye starts to zing in warning, as the hairs on the back of my neck rise and my body clenches, readying itself for a blow. I turn to see the man with bleached hair walking towards us.

"I'm Marcus," he says, holding out his hand. "Who are you?"

As though the proffered fingers might grab rather than grasp, I shrink back and clench my teeth in a reaction so visceral that it's as much as I can do to stop myself from running away.

There's an awkward moment before Fally steps in. "Marcus, this is Selena. She's never seen a dig before and has come to have a look." Frowning, she turns to me and tries to smile again but she looks uncertain now. "Would you like a cuppa?" she asks.

I'm no longer sure what to say.

"Do I know you from somewhere?" asks the white-haired man, stepping closer.

Looking down at my feet, I shake my head.

"Marcus, it's nearly ten o'clock," says Raff, noticing my discomfort. "Shouldn't you be off now? You don't want to be late for your mother."

Marcus's face falls. "Shit," he says. He hesitates, wipes his hands on his work clothes, and then runs up towards the Portakabin.

We all breathe out an audible sigh of relief as he leaves. "Don't mind him," Fally says after a pause. "The weather's been lousy and we're all a bit tense. Digs usually take place in the summer when the ground is warm but we're stuck here trying to work ground that is hard as iron." She rubs her hands and blows on them as if to make her point.

"Fally's right," says Raff. "Where's global warming when you need it?" They both try to laugh but don't quite manage it.

"Now, how about that cuppa?" Fally asks again.

Desperate not to bump back into Marcus, I shake my head. "That's kind of you but I really need to get going."

"Oh, that's a shame," she says with a look of genuine disappointment. "Another time then."

I have to stop myself from bolting in the opposite direction from the Portakabin, back down to the stream at the bottom of the hill. Just as we are about to cross the stepping-stones across the stream, Buddy whines and stops. Scared that the white-haired man has followed me, I freeze to the spot.

"Did you manage to find your friend at the river all right?"

The voice is Raff's. Relieved, I turn back to look at him. Up so close he seems even taller. "Yes, thank you."

"What is it like, staying on a narrowboat? I've always wondered."

"I don't know. I'm in the caravan."

He looks concerned. "Are you warm enough? It's hardly caravan weather."

"There's a good heater in there."

He smiles. "That's a relief."

For a moment, we fall into silence. To my surprise, my pearly eye is feeling comfortable again and the hairs on the back of my neck have flattened. Nevertheless, I don't want to be on this field any longer than necessary. "I'd better get going and leave you to your work."

He looks disappointed and a flush of red creeps awkwardly up my neck. When he reaches out and strokes Buddy again, I wonder why I still feel so uneasy. If Buddy likes him, then he must be all right.

"See you around then."

Already he is turning away. Feeling strangely abandoned, I start walking towards the stepping-stones. Once we've crossed them and are back on the track, we both turn back to look, but the tall man is already half way up the field.

I begin to retrace my steps to Stone Clump but the surroundings no longer look like a green patchwork quilt.

Instead they are grey with the threat of shadows and the face of a man with white hair.

FALALA – Present Day

Falala walked hurriedly into the Portakabin hoping to catch Marcus before he left. He had barely looked at her since last night and she didn't understand why he was being so distant. When they had slept together before it had not made one iota of difference to his behaviour. Now he was acting as though she was a pariah.

He was already putting on his coat when she walked in. "Hi," she said, trying to sound light and cheerful. "I'm glad I caught you. Got a second to discuss this before you go?" She grabbed something from the table and held it out to him.

"It's nearly ten o'clock," he mumbled, refusing to look at her. "I don't want to be late for her ladyship."

"It's just that Raff has come up with another diagram. It's really interesting, and…"

"It will have to wait," he interrupted bluntly.

"Please, Marcus."

Clenching his teeth, he turned slowly and faced her.

Grabbing the chance, she walked over to him, holding

out the drawing. "Look, he's come up with a detailed representation of what an early Bronze Age settlement might have looked like here in the Stennings. Here are some animal enclosures on either side of two roundhouses." She moved her finger. "And here is a drove-way leading down to the river." She held out the diagram, hoping to close the distance between them. "Please look. It's brilliant. I'm only asking for a couple of minutes. I'm sure your mother won't mind."

"You don't know her," he said curling his lip. He tossed the drawing the briefest of glances. "Raff has just copied what I showed him last night," he snorted with disgust.

Opening the door, he stepped out and slammed it behind him.

HESTER – Present Day

Hester stood in front of the mirror, violently brushing her chestnut hair until the bristles caught a tangle and a clump of hair came away. Horrified, she looked at her brush. Her hair was thick and glossy. There was no reason for it to tear out like this. Yet it wasn't the first time it had happened and she knew whose fault it was. Ever since she had been on Larna Avery's appalling boat, her hair had begun to come out. Had the harpy somehow hexed her? Horrified, she promised herself that, once she had got this meeting over with Marcus, she would find a way of letting the community know what they had in their midst.

Grimacing, she flushed the hair down the lavatory, replaced the hairbrush in the drawer and thoroughly washed her hands twice. Then she returned to the mirror and dispassionately assessed her face. Unable to deny what she saw in the reflection, she frowned. Flesh was starting to sag around her jaw line, and numerous lines had appeared around her eyes.

Two deep furrows creased the flesh between her eyebrows into deep exclamation marks. Worst of all, tramlines were etched down towards her mouth as though it was starting to turn in on itself after years of presenting a quintessentially English stiff upper lip.

Putting her hands up to her temples, she pulled back the skin. Immediately, her face sprang back into a temporary semblance of her youth, but as soon as she let it go again, the frowns reappeared deeper than ever. *Blast*, she thought. Unlike lesser mortals, she had expected to be exempt from the ravages of time. When she was younger, she had watched people grow old and, despising their weakness, had promised herself that she would never age. Why then, when she had been able to control everything else in her life, had she not been able to control this? Aghast, she began to run more water to wash her hands again. Once the future had been secured with the sale of the land to the developers, she would enquire about facial surgery.

She was just about to pick up the soap when something dark caught her attention. In the corner, between the two walls, was a smudge. For a moment she stared at it. The breath snagged in her throat and she felt her stomach clench. It was an insect. Oh God, what if it started flying towards her? Feeling sick, she turned off the tap.

Then it moved.

She fled.

MARCUS – Present Day

Furious, Marcus strode fiercely towards the manor. He needed this meeting with his mother like a hole in the head. How could he have got so drunk last night and woken up this morning in Fally's bed? He had no idea whether or not anything had happened between them but now he couldn't look her in the face, let alone talk to her. It didn't help that the red-haired woman with an eyepatch had suddenly appeared in the field. One look at her and his guts had turned to water. He'd had to clench his hands behind his back to stop himself from grabbing her there and then.

And now he was going to be late for his mother as well.

Ever since he had arrived back in the Stennings, everything had felt wrong. He suspected that it was partly because he was spending time with Raff again. A decade earlier, they had been the best of friends, but after Marcus had slept with Raff's girlfriend, nothing had been the same.

Straightening his shoulders, he began to walk up the drive to the house that had once been his home. He was surprised to see just how shabby the manor had become. The last time he had seen it had been when he had deserted the sinking ship of the family firm. No doubt his mother would still be angry with him. Seeing her again would be akin to putting his head into an alligator's mouth. Nevertheless, Fally was right. They needed more time to progress with the dig.

Taking the final few steps, he steeled himself to ring the bell pull. After a long few moments, the door opened and his mother appeared. Gone was the immaculately dressed lady of the manor. Her skin had become lined, her hair was askew and she looked wary. For a moment, they simply stared at each other.

"Good God, Marcus, what have you done to your hair?"

The last time she had seen him, he had been blond. All too aware of his premature whiteness, he instinctively put his hand up to touch it. When she unconsciously mirrored him, reaching up to smooth her own awry coiffure, he noticed that her fingers were red raw. "Good God, mother," he countered, "what have you done to your hands?"

It wasn't a good start. Hester pursed her lips, turned, and walked into the hall.

Marcus wondered what he should do. He wanted to turn away and never return, but he had to find a way of persuading his horrible mother to give them more time. If he returned to Fally having failed, he would feel more of a heel than he already did.

"Well, are you coming in?" Hester said, turning back to face him.

Refusing to give her the satisfaction of seeing him unnerved, he stepped into the house and followed her into the dining room. To his surprise, there was a cake in the middle of the table along with a coffee pot, a jug of milk and two china cups and saucers. There was no sign of a sugar bowl. Shame, she could have done with a bit of sweetening. However, he had to admit that it was the most effort she had ever made for him.

"Sit," she commanded.

Resisting the urge to refuse, he did as she asked.

"Coffee?"

He nodded.

"Cake?"

"Yes please."

Neither of them said anything while she poured and cut. Once the cup and plate were in front of him, he found he could not stomach anything at all.

She noticed and frowned. "So you decided to become an archaeologist," she said, using a statement rather than a question. "Barely a step up from playing sandcastles on the beach." She paused, sipped her coffee and wiped her mouth with a napkin. "I see that you couldn't find any decent work. How fortunate for you that your father gave you a job. Not that he should have done, of course. Yet another stupid mistake on his part."

Angrily, he clenched his jaw. No olive branch then. He took a deep breath to steady himself. "I didn't come here to argue."

"Then what did you come here for?"

"I thought we should meet, now I'm back in the Stennings."

Her eyebrows rose sardonically. "I don't see why."

All the signs told him to leave, but he had to find a way of getting her back on side. "I wanted to thank you for organising the flat for me," he tried.

"You could have thanked me over the telephone."

He tightened his jaw still further.

She narrowed her eyes. "Shall we forget the platitudes, Marcus, and say what we really mean?"

The blood drained from his face.

"You made your feelings quite clear when you abandoned *Frattons*."

"That's ancient history," he murmured.

"Not to me, it isn't."

"I went to university, Mother, that's all. That's what eighteen-year-olds do."

"Eighteen year olds do not leave their family in the lurch."

He swallowed hard. Somehow, he had to find a way of turning this around. "Well I'm very grateful to Father for giving us a chance."

"Us? Who's us?"

"My team. Dr Falala Sefu is a well-known archaeologist who lectured at University."

"That doesn't sound like a very English name."

Marcus bit his lip. "And Raff McGuinley you know."

Hester looked surprised. "That boy you used to play with when you were younger?"

"The same."

"The one whose mother died when he was doing his A Levels?"

140

Marcus nodded.

"And the one whose girlfriend killed herself by driving into a tree?"

Marcus went very still.

"Well, it sounds like a team made in heaven," she said, her voice heavy with sarcasm. "How fortunate you will be leaving in a few days. Put all of you out of your misery."

Marcus felt his heart start to hammer uncomfortably. Taking a deep breath, he forced himself to smile. "You have gone to a lot of effort this morning," he said, trying to sound appreciative.

At first she didn't seem to know what he meant. Then she saw that he was looking at the table. "My cleaner prepared it," she said dismissively.

"So, how have you been?"

"As if you care," she huffed.

He cleared his throat. "How's Father?"

She clenched her jaw and refused to answer.

"Karl?"

Still nothing.

"Then how's *Frattons*?"

She glared at him. "Marcus, just say what you have come here to say and then we can end this ridiculous charade."

"I ... I ..."

"Oh, for God's sake, please don't tell me that both of my sons stammer."

Something in him snapped and he could keep up the pretence no longer. Pushing his chair back so quickly that it nearly toppled over, he stood. "You know, I was really hoping that you'd changed after all this time but quite obviously, you have not. You're as much of a snake as ever."

She flushed a dull red. "Marcus, I'm warning you..."

"Oh, fuck off!"

Before she had a chance to reprimand him for his language or anything else, he turned and bolted.

SELENA – Present Day

I can't sleep. My mind is turning over and over like a wheel spinning in mud. Burying my head under the pillow, I force myself to close my eyes. It would help if Buddy was in here with me but he's decided to stay in the boat with Larna tonight. I can't say that I blame him. I'd rather be there, too. The truth is that I'm scared. If I sleep I'll dream. Mevin has found Seela and her sister and he's threatened to sacrifice Duna. I want to know what happens next but everything is pointing to a tragedy and I've had enough sadness to last me for a lifetime.

In the end I give up on sleep, climb out of bed and open the door to see a full moon in an utterly black sky. After hurriedly throwing on some warm clothes, I grab a torch and head for the door. Before I can grasp the handle, my pearly eye shoots pain right through my head and an image of the necklace comes vividly into my mind. When I try to step forward, more pain jams into my head. After several unsuccessful attempts to leave the caravan, I pick up the necklace and put it in my pocket. Immediately the pain recedes.

Outside it is so cold that even the moon is shivering. As the river blinks back at me, brittle as a black sheet of ice, I try to persuade myself to return to the safety of the caravan, but I cannot. Suddenly anywhere inside four walls feels like a trap.

With no idea where I am going, I start walking. Despite the brilliance of the moon, the darkness is so profound that all life seems to have been obliterated. I find myself passing Stone Clump and then Raff's farmhouse in the valley, all the time feeling as though I am being drawn forward by an invisible thread. It's not until I smell the water of a lake that the darkness intensifies still further and I look upwards to see that clouds are wrapping themselves around the moon as though they are trying to strangle it. Moments later, a great flash of lightning cracks open the silhouette of a craggy escarpment up ahead. There is an enormous crash of thunder. Then the heavens open and it begins to rain hard.

I run, sprinting towards the rock, hoping that there might be a ledge I can shelter under. When the second flash of lightning comes, I am ready for it, but instead of the rock face, I see the silhouette of a girl standing by the edge of a lake. Wondering if I have conjured her up through sheer force of will, I stop and switch on the torch.

Forcing my limbs to move, I edge forward. As soon as I am close enough, I catch the scent of an animal that has been dead for too long. And then I see it; the likeness; the similarity. The red hair. The cleft in the chin. The high cheekbones. We are the same and yet we are not. She is dry where I am drenched. Her hair is still where mine is frantic in the wind. There's a little bird on her shoulder whereas I am alone.

As my pearly eye screams, I step still closer so I can warn her that her sister is in danger from Mevin, but as the beam of light catches the red of her hair and the mottled purple and yellow of bruises on her face, I realise I am too late. Mevin has already found her. Doing the only thing I can, I hold the necklace out to her as though it will somehow save us both. For a moment I see a glint of recognition in her eyes and think that she is going to reach out to take it, but the air starts to thicken between us. My hand starts to tremble violently, scattering the light from the torch in a myriad of different directions. Then the bird on her shoulder tries to open its wings to fly away but one of them is broken and hangs down uselessly. Finally her face begins to blur in the white cloud of my breath and, as a new thunderclap rents the air, she disappears.

The emptiness left behind is appalling. Never have I felt so alone as though part of me has been snuffed out and yet it is still there. My pearly eye begins to cry, a solitary tear forcing its way out to mingle with the rain on my face, making me shiver uncontrollably.

I shove the necklace back into my pocket and point the torch at the heavy hill of rock beyond the lake in the hope that it will offer shelter. Although my bones feel as though they are crumbling, I force myself to walk forward into the muddy earth. Time and time again I slip as my shoes squelch and slide through tiny rivulets weaving through the ground like worms. Finally I reach the escarpment, only just saving myself as I lurch onto the rock.

To my surprise, I find my hand plunging through a thick curtain of leaves into empty space. There's a squeaking sound and a bat flies out, just missing my head. Lungs heaving for breath, I swing the failing torch beam into the shadows of a low ceiling, a hard and uneven floor, and dank walls dark with patches of faded colour as though traces of ancient paintings decorate the stone.

I am in a cave.

Only then does the light start to flicker and finally extinguish itself, leaving me in a terrifying darkness. There's a rank stench of rotting fruit and the vile taste of decaying mushrooms. Ancient voices start to rumble in the air and I feel, rather than see, the impression of woman lying on a filthy bed of straw in the corner.

As thousands of tiny feet start to crawl over my skin, my mind begins to fragment. The necklace in my pocket starts to burn the skin of my hand, bringing me back into myself. I have to get out of this hideous dark. Heart clamouring, I put the fingers of my free hand outwards into the gluey air, inching out a bit at a time, and shuffling my feet forwards as though I am decrepit with age. When my hand snags in a sticky cobweb, I snatch it back in revulsion lest the decay eat my skin.

There are monsters here waiting to devour me. My legs buckle and I sink to the cold ground, still clutching the necklace in my pocket. My fingers start to trace the pendants until I find the carving at the bottom between the amber and selenite. It's a gift, Larna told me. A present. Something to unwrap.

I no longer know whether my eyes are open or closed. I can only hope that as long as I keep holding the gift rune, I will be safe.

circa 2000 B.C.E

Seela crouched at the back of the hut and put the small basket on her lap. It was still dark outside and dawn was still sleeping beyond the sky. Placing three tiny worms inside, she took some water from a beaker and poured it into the palm of her hand. As the little bird opened its eyes to look at her, she angled her hand so that he could reach the water. Once he had drunk his fill, she put the basket back on the ground and left him to his meal. Then she put on her cloak and tip-toed out of the hut. She didn't have long. By the time the sun was peeping over the horizon she would have to be back inside the fusty hut again. Picking up the empty bucket she began to walk stealthily through the snow, past the circular huts of the settlement, passing dwellings, stables and places for work and weaving. She must not be seen. Lanalla had been clear about that. If Mevin found her outside alone, she would be lost.

In the forest the snow was at last beginning to melt but the air was still bitingly cold and her skin was prickling. As soon as she arrived at the river bank she looked back, warily checking that nobody had followed her. When she was sure she was alone, she studied her surroundings. The river stood between two hills. On the eastern hill the silhouette of the newly erected Stone looked ridiculous in its attempt to point up at the sky and yet it had a presence that defied its crooked shape. Further away, the western hill looked like a smudge in the darkness. Her eyes settled on the rickety bridge over the river where stakes had been set into the bed and long tree trunks tied onto multiple spearheads driven into each bank. She shivered and promised herself that she would never cross it lest it wash her away to the ends of the world.

Dawn was already beginning to streak the sky. She would have to hurry if she wanted to avoid being seen. Breaking the thin ice on the surface of the water, she hastily lowered the bucket into the freezing water but as the bucket filled, something peered at her from the mud at the bottom. Instantly, she was transported back to the time when she had been hiding in the tree trying to avoid the wolf. She would never forget the way the night had split with Duna's cry as the creature had raked her sister's leg with its claws, or the way its starving, frenzied eyes had been yellow in the ghastly moon glow. Most of all, she remembered the song. It had been sung by a woman who had the same red hair that she had, but instead of two green eyes, one of hers had been white like the pearl from a shell. It was this eye that was staring at her now from the surface of the river. In an attempt to see the image more clearly, she leaned closer to the water and, before she could stop herself, she toppled into the water. A fierce winter current was flowing downstream and in moments she was being dragged spluttering into the deep centre of the river.

Unbeknown to her, Riadd had been watching nearby. Commanding his dog to stay by the bank, he yanked off his cloak and dived in. He managed to grab Seela's arm before she was pulled away still further. Then he hauled her back to the bank and up onto dry land. He had just begun to wrap his dry cloak around her when Bika started to bark ferociously. Riadd looked up and saw Mevin striding towards them. Quickly, he let go of the cloak and grabbed Bika.

"What do you think you're doing, boy?" shouted Mevin. "Take your hands off her. She's mine."

Riadd began to shiver uncontrollably. "No, she isn't."

"You can barely stand. She needs a man to save her. Give her to me."

"I will be a man soon. I..."

"Then prove it. Fight me for her. If you win, she's yours. If I win..."

Still holding on to Bika by the scruff of his neck, Riadd turned to Seela who was at last beginning to revive. "Run back to the safety of Lanalla's hut," he whispered through chattering teeth. "You need to get warm."

Seela didn't wait to argue but pushed herself unsteadily to her feet and fled, her long red hair flying out behind her like a broken wing. By now the sun had risen above the horizon and several villagers were already outside. Oblivious to her need to stay undiscovered, she ran past them all.

"Lanalla," she cried, as soon as she entered the hut, "you must send help!"

The priestess looked up in surprise from her place by the fire where she was cutting some herbs.

"By the river. Riadd ..."

"Sshh, calm yourself," interrupted Lanalla. "You are making no sense."

"They are f... fighting."

"Fighting?"

"Yes, I fell into the river while collecting water. Riadd jumped in to save me."

Lanalla walked over to Seela and put both of her hands on her shoulders. "You are freezing and wet, girl. Take off these wet clothes and change into something dry."

"But there is no time," Seela spluttered. "They …" Her voice died away as a long shudder of cold stopped her breath.

Lanalla looked closely at her and shook her head. "Seela, Riadd is young and lithe. Besides, Mevin will not hurt him. He is just trying to teach him to become a man." She held out a woollen garment. "Now take off your wet clothes and put this on."

Seela could barely move her hands so Lanalla dried her and dressed her in a clean tunic. Then she ladled an infusion of herbs from the pot by the fire into a clay cup which she placed in the girl's shaking hands. "Now, sit down and drink this. It will warm you."

It was a while before colour returned to Seela's face. "Lanella, tell me what I can do."

Lanalla thought for a long moment. "Where is your gitty?" she asked eventually. "Folk will have seen you run back here. We must tell them who you are. I will say that the Stone has already brought us a New Blood, just as Mana said it would."

"But …"

The priestess did not allow her to finish. "Wrap yourself in my cloak and go outside and play by the door for everyone to hear. It is time for you to introduce yourself. Play to The Mother and play for your sister to overcome the wolf's spirit. Play for Riadd to become a man at last so that he may protect you from Mevin. Most of all, play for yourself."

Ansuz reversed – deceit

Chapter Eight

LARNA – Present Day

It was a beautiful morning, the sky washed clear by last night's storm. An unremarkable brown bird with a reddish-brown tail landed on the boat, its throat pale, underbelly grey, and pale eye-rings enormous above the yellow bill. As it began to sing, its voice soared in a mixture of warbles, trills and melodies exhibiting a superb vocal range. Transfixed by this strangest of blackbirds, Larna jumped when Buddy began to bark from inside the kitchen. No, she cried silently, *you'll frighten it away.* But it was too late. The blackbird stopped its oratorio, twitched its head and flew up, dropping a feather as it rose into the sky. Larna tried to reach for the plume but already it was drifting away from her fingers down onto the water.

Disappointed, Larna let Buddy out into the field but, as his tail began to dance, she couldn't help but smile. Despite his frightening away of the bird, she wondered why she had never had a dog before. Buddy was such a loving companion. Along with Selena, she was beginning to feel that she was finally building a family of her own. Of course, Selena could never make up for the daughter she had lost, but the excruciating loneliness had gone and she was finally starting to feel a genuine happiness.

Her stomach rumbled, reminding her that it was time for breakfast. Wondering if Selena might like something other than porridge this morning, she walked over to the caravan and tapped on the door. "Selena," she called enthusiastically. "How about one of my special cappuccinos before breakfast?" She waited for a sleepy reply but there was no response. "I can put on an extra sprinkling of chocolate," she added enticingly.

When there was still no reply she felt a frisson of alarm. It was most unlike Selena still to be asleep at this hour. "Are you okay?" she tried again, knocking harder this time, hoping that she was not intruding.

She was about to step away when something made her turn back. Climbing the three steps again, she banged on the door. When there was still no reply, she grasped the handle and pulled it open. The caravan was empty. Incredulous, she looked around. The bed was still rumpled. Selena's bag was still here. Her scarf, too. The toothbrush she had given her was by the sink. But her coat was missing.

Selena had gone.

A wave of grief rose up like a wave, taking her completely by surprise. Stunned, she sat down hard on the bed and put her head in her hands. She couldn't lose another daughter, not again. The image she had tried to push down rushed up to choke her. Angela being peeled from her arms. Her baby, named as the gift of angels, who had looked as though she was sleeping, dreaming of another world. Angela, who had forgotten to enter this one.

Some of the questions that she had refused to ask now threw themselves at her like missiles. What if she had never gone to that party when she'd been fifteen? What if she hadn't lost her virginity to a boy whose name she didn't even know? What if her parents hadn't felt shame about her pregnancy and both since died?

For the first time, she realised why she had become such a rescuer. All along she had been trying to save her child. She had tried to protect Selena from the streets but now Selena had left. She had only managed to borrow her for a few days just as she'd only been able to borrow the idea of her own baby for such a short time. Her body began to tremble violently as if all the pain wanted to gush out but couldn't find an exit. How was she going to continue living if everything she tried to love was taken away from her so precipitously?

It wasn't until Buddy came to find her that the world returned. Her arms felt like lead but she managed to put them around his shaggy body and hug him tight. Then she pulled away slightly to allow him to lick her tears dry. Reminding herself that he had not had his breakfast, she returned to the boat, dragging her feet like an old woman.

After she had fed him, she lit a fire in the snug, made herself a cup of herbal tea and sat looking out over the river with Buddy at her feet. She had everything, didn't she? A beautiful place to live. The work needed to keep a boat was more than she had expected but now that Selena was helping, she could cope easily enough. But what if Selena had gone? Loneliness was crushing. It chewed you up, spat you out and tore you apart. It refused to let you put yourself back together again and make something of your life. It killed you even as you lived.

As if she wasn't already in enough pain, her head began to pound with the warning signs of a migraine. Reassuring Buddy that he could stay in front of the fire, she left her drink untouched and retreated to the far end of the living area. Then she put on some gentle music, lay down on the cushions and slid on an eyemask.

At first, the darkness behind her eyes soothed the throbbing. Ice was dripping into her brain and bones just as a clamp was being tightened around her skull. Without opening her eyes, she reached for a blanket and covered herself, but it didn't help. There was the peculiar sensation of something being lowered over her head. A chain, all gold, bronze, amber and white in disembodied light was so heavy that it was crushing the breath from her body.

This was the reason that everything had gone so wrong.

She was being punished.

This hell was of her own making and there was no escape.

SELENA – Present Day

I wake up to find myself lying in total darkness, the necklace still entwined round my fingers. I am so cold that I think I must have turned to frost, and so blind that I have to feel my eyelids with my fingers to discover whether my eyes are open or shut. My hearing is not so compromised. A woman is panting in the corner, trying desperately not to give birth.

A silent scream begins to rise upwards from my own belly up into my throat. I have to get out. Holding the necklace in front of me, I follow the glow of the white crystal and manage to glimpse one of the walls of the cave. Cautiously, I inch towards it, feeling every speck of air with my outstretched fingers until I reach the wall. There is a darker grey in the blackness in front of me. As I move to the side, my hands touch a plant. Then, as if by magic, I am grasping a leaf and pulling myself back into the world.

Outside, the lake is shining with early light. Ducks, grebes, moorhens, geese and swans are swimming on the water as though spring has finally arrived. With a sob of relief, I run headlong towards them, turning the lake into a frenzied whoosh of scrambling wings until only a solitary bird is left in the sky. Gasping from the shock of the cold water, I roar my relief up to him. *I have escaped. I am free. I am alive.* Our gazes lock for an instant before he too flies away.

Thirsty, I bend to scoop great handfuls of water into my parched mouth. Diving headlong into the water, I wash the dream and the fear from my body, desperate to become myself again.

RAFF – Present Day

Disturbed by a cry, Raff opened his eyes into rivulets of sweat. He couldn't get Marion out of his mind nor the argument which had sent her running off into the night. Honesty was cruel. She should never have admitted that she had slept with Marcus and he should never have told her to get out. He would never forget the way that tears had drenched her face as she had looked at him with her pleading eyes.

Sitting up, he tried to blot out her confession and ignore how cruel and judgemental he had been. Marcus was correct. He hadn't been in his right mind. His mother had been dying and he had been unable to face more pain. But if only he had comforted Marion rather than telling her to leave, then perhaps she would still be alive today. For God's sake, she had only just passed her driving test. No wonder she had crashed into a tree and died on impact.

Unable to bear the memories any longer, he was just climbing out of bed when he heard the cry again. Suddenly alert, he walked to the window and opened it wide, allowing the fresh air to cool his heated skin. Outside it was light and the air was full of birdsong. Reminding himself that he had to be on top form for this morning's meeting with Clem Hardwick, he hurriedly dressed and made coffee. Eager to see if spring had perhaps finally arrived at last, he stepped outside into the garden.

This time the cry was quite clear.

It seemed to be coming from the lake.

Coffee forgotten, he started to run.

SELENA – Present Day

My pearly eye screams as arms close around me. Mevin has come to kidnap me. I try to wriggle free but his arms are too strong and now he's carrying me away from the lake. *Riadd,* I cry deliriously, *Riadd, you've got to save me.* But he doesn't come to the rescue and before I know what is happening, I am being dumped unceremoniously into a chair.

"What were you thinking of, out there in the rain? You're drenched."

The pain in my pearly eye starts to fade and my green eye comes fuzzily back to life. I am in a room that I recognise. But then I recognised the inside of the cave and I hadn't been there before.

"You need to get out of your wet clothes. I'll fetch you a blanket."

My mind reels. Mevin has fought Riadd and won and it's my fault. I should never have gone down to the river to collect water. Now the white-haired man is going to claim me as his own. I am lost.

It is only when I see the huge inglenook fireplace decorated with polished brass horse ornaments, that I realise this is no Bronze Age shack. Sitting up straighter, I peer over my shoulder. The kitchen is enormous with old farming implements propped up in the corner and snuffers and reed holders stacked against the wall. I try to push myself to my feet, but my head swims and I have to sit down again.

"Talk to me. Are you all right? What on earth were you thinking, going for a swim in the lake fully clothed at dawn?"

Finally, I look at the man behind the voice. Instead of an overgrown youth, he has long, black hair and a look of utter shock on his face. It's Riadd not Mevin who has carried me here. But why is he wearing glasses?

"There was a storm," I bleat.

He frowns uncertainly. "What storm? There hasn't been any storm. The ground is completely dry."

"I sheltered in a cave."

He looks even more puzzled. "There aren't any caves round here."

"There are ancient paintings on the walls. I saw them before the torch died."

"Selena, what are you talking about?"

His use of my name finally puts me back where I should be and I realise this is Raff. Shuffling forward to the edge of my chair, I shake my head to clear my mind, but instead of clarity, the image of a woman with chestnut brown hair rises up to glare at me, her hands pink with sores. I am due to clean for Hester Knebworth this morning. If I don't go, she'll refuse to pay me anything, and then I won't be able to stay with Larna and help her with the boat and all the heavy chores. "What time is it?"

"Nearly nine."

"I need to go," I croak, trying to get to my feet.

"But your clothes are still wet."

"It doesn't matter."

"Yes, it does. Wait there while I get you something to wear."

Moments later he returns with a shirt and very thick jumper. How he thinks they're going to be any better than a blanket, I don't know.

"They'll be enormous on you but at least they're dry," he says. "I've got nothing that will fit you trouser-wise so you'll have to put your own wet ones back on. Let me wring them out first."

Raff disappears while I pull his shirt and jumper over my head. He's right. They're so long you could fit three of me into them. When he comes back he hands me the jeans that tear my skin uncomfortably as I pull them back on.

"You're not in any fit state to walk. I'll take you back on the motor bike."

I go to shake my head but he insists and leads me outside. It's strange climbing on to a motorbike; I've never ridden one before. To my surprise, the sensation of the cold air, the movement of the wheels and the way we have to lean to turn corners, helps to bring me back into my body and, by the time he drops me at the edge of the field I am beginning to feel more myself.

As soon as he has turned off the engine, I hear Buddy barking. Seconds later, Larna appears. Her face is white, her eyes are huge and she looks terrified. Then colour suddenly infuses her cheeks and she runs towards me and hugs me so tightly I can't breathe.

"I thought you had left," she cries shakily as she finally holds me away from her so she can look at me. "Where have you been? You look dreadful. And what on earth are you wearing? Please tell me you haven't been sleeping outside again."

I don't have the chance to reply because Raff is stepping forward to introduce himself.

"I'm Raff McGuinley," he says. "I work at the dig at the bottom of Stone Clump. Selena went for an early morning swim in the lake. She was very cold so I've lent her some of my clothes." He hands her a carrier bag. "Here are her coat and top."

He's talking to her as though she's my mother.

Grief suddenly overwhelms me and I am back in the lake, drowning.

THE TEAM – Present Day

"Mr Hardwick," said Falala with false brightness, "how nice to meet you at last. I'm Dr Sefu. Do come in."

Clem grasped her hand warmly. "I understand you're the brains behind this little team of yours."

Marcus stepped out from the shadows where he had been lurking and thrust out his hand in front of her, causing her to take a step backwards. "I'm the team leader, Marcus Knebworth."

Clem studied him for a moment. "Ah, the heir to the Fratton millions," he said dismissively. Then he turned to Raff. "Good to see you again, Raff. I do hope you've been busy since we last met. I'm intrigued to see if you've made any more discoveries."

"We certainly have," replied Raff. "All the finds, graphs and analyses are laid out here on the table. But we thought we'd show you the workings first."

Marcus stepped forward. "Allow me to take you outside and show you what we've been doing. Raff, make us all some coffee, will you?"

Before either Raff or Fally could argue, Marcus led Clem out into the field. "That puts me in my place," Raff murmured under his breath.

Fally didn't reply but a glance at her face showed him that she too was surprised.

As he busied himself with the kettle, Raff thought of the object he had found in Selena's coat pocket that morning when he had tried to wring out the water from the lake. It had been a rusty chain with stone pendants and two crystals. To get a better idea of the metal beneath, he had rubbed the chain with his thumb to see what might lurk underneath the grime. When a suggestion of bronze and gold had glinted up at him, he had become excited. As for the amber and selenite, they were in remarkably good condition. Perhaps he would ask her if he could do some restoration and try to discover exactly what this chain, with its pendants and crystals, was.

Coffee made, he turned to Fally to give her a mug. Unusually, she hadn't said a word. "Are you all right? You're very quiet."

She turned away and pretended to fiddle with some papers. "I'm fine," she muttered.

Raff was about to question her further when Marcus and Clem burst back through the door.

"It's bloody cold out there," said Marcus, rubbing his hands together and blowing on them. "Is the coffee ready yet?"

Raff handed them each a mug and for a moment everyone looked awkward. Then Raff sat down and the others followed.

"So, what would you like to know first?" he asked Clem.

"Tell me from the beginning."

"Circles," Marcus said before anyone else could answer.

Clem frowned. "Circles?"

"That's what we're finding and that's why we think this site is so old," Marcus went on. "In the Bronze Age, circles were used to describe the return of seasons and new growth and as a result they built everything in the round: burial chambers, henges, earthworks, monuments, roundhouses…the lot. As you know, straight lines were introduced much later by the Romans."

"Apart from enclosures and fields, of course," Raff interjected. "Cattle, sheep, goats and pigs were the common farm animals in the early Bronze Age, and differentiation of ownership meant that they had to be enclosed by rectangular fields, walls, fences and ditches. Fields in the Bronze Age were larger and cut in patterns that followed the lie of the land. Hence the field that we have here."

Clem turned to Falala. "And what about you, Dr Sefu? What do you think? You're the expert on the Bronze Age. Do you think that is what you are unearthing?"

She cleared her throat. "Call me Falala, please. And yes, I do think that this field contains the boundaries of a Bronze Age site. Come and have a look at the finds, and I'll show you what I mean."

Clem put down his mug, removed the glasses from the top pocket of his shirt, placed them on his nose and followed her over to the table. She handed out some gloves, pulled on a pair herself, and then picked up a fragment of pottery which she held out to Clem. "Look at the shape of this. If it is a bell beaker, then it could help us to date the settlement. As you know that particular pottery method was brought across from Southern Germany around 2750 BC, along with copper and then bronze."

Clem studied it carefully before replacing it on the table.

Raff picked up the hand-axe and gave it to him. "This is almost certainly made of bronze."

Clem nodded. "Have you any paper work to flesh this out?"

Marcus reached for the sketch he had made and thrust it into Clem's hand. "This should explain everything," he said eagerly.

"And there's this one, too," said Raff, walking over to the

computer and fetching the piece of paper he had printed out earlier.

Clem regarded each of the diagrams in turn before folding them and putting them in his pocket. "I'll take these away with me and read them later, if you don't mind."

"Of course," both men said in unison.

"What about the flood plain?" Clem asked.

"Let's sit down again?" suggested Fally.

"By all means."

Once they had pulled off their gloves and returned to their seats and coffee, Fally continued. "The flood plain helps. It means that the land here hasn't been ploughed so the artefacts are likely to be in better condition. The stream and the river would have given immediate access to fresh water for both people and animals. In fact I suspect that, given enough time, we will discover a droveway leading down to the water."

"This is all looking very promising," said Clem. Then he turned to Marcus. "What I don't understand is why your parents are insisting on a dig at this time of year, Mr Knebworth? Surely they could have waited until the summer."

"I believe that they want planning permission for the land," replied Marcus, sounding less sure of himself now.

"But, as we have already said, this is a flood plain. Planning permission for housing is out of the question."

Marcus shook his head. "Not necessarily. Planning permission is increasingly being granted on land prone to flooding because of the constant need for new developments."

Clem shook his head disapprovingly. "There will be a huge outcry from the villagers if planning permission is granted. I thought the Knebworths were supposed to be the pillars of the community? How will they live that down?"

Embarrassed, Marcus flushed. "You'll have to ask them."

Clem's eyebrows rose in surprise.

"Unfortunately Marcus doesn't have a relationship with his family," explained Falala quietly.

"So they haven't told you why they have asked you to start a dig and now want you to stop it?"

"I'm afraid not," said Raff.

"Can't you just order them to extend the dig, Mr Hardwick?" Marcus bristled. "Surely part of your job is to tell people what to do.

Fally winced. "What Marcus means," she said, calmly crossing her fingers in her pocket, "is that we would like you to ask his family to extend the dig into the summer so that we can make a real go of what could be an extraordinary dig. You know how important timing is. Now it is just too cold and the earth too hard." She smiled. "But despite the coldness of the ground, we've already made some interesting finds. Think of what we might discover when the earth warms up."

Clem considered her again. "You really think that you have found enough to warrant that long?"

Falala fetched her iPad and found a picture on the screen. Then she handed it to Clem. "Look at this," she said enthusiastically. "Here are the positions of the finds. The first roundhouse is plotted exactly where we've found the postholes. Over here is the boundary line. If we are given time to excavate this entire area, I think we will find the evidence for an important site. Please ask the Knebworths to give us more time. You are the expert here, Clem. They will listen to you."

He handed back the iPad to Falala and then looked thoughtfully at the three of them. "Well, I have to admit that I am impressed. You're big thinkers and have demonstrated a good depth of knowledge. He looked at Falala. "It also helps that you have such excellent academic credentials." He hesitated and stroked his chin. "I'll have that chat with the family, and meanwhile give you a permit for four more weeks.

If you can come up with more evidence then I'll consider a further extension after that."

"Thank you," said Falala. "We will do our very best to discover all we can. Thank you for your time," she said, holding out her hand.

Once he had shaken it he turned to Raff and then Marcus. "I'll go and give Alan Knebworth the good news. Or would you like to do it?"

"Be my guest," Marcus said through gritted teeth.

"Very well," Clem replied. "I'll be in touch."

SELENA – Present Day

"You're late. I'd given up on you," Hester Knebworth hisses. "And what on earth are you wearing?" she snaps crossly.

I glare at her. Larna's poncho is rather garish but my coat is still wet and, besides, this woman has no right to quiz me about my clothes.

"Well, you'd better come in. Better late than never, I suppose."

I set about my duties with as much energy as I can muster but after a night spent in the cave, I am too tired to do more than the bare minimum. As soon as I have finished, I go in search of the odious woman, anxious to claim my money and leave. She is in the living room reading a magazine and doesn't even bother to look up but turns a page as though I'm not there.

"I've done everything you asked me to do," I say. "It is Friday and you promised to pay me."

"I have decided that I shall not pay you until you have worked for a month."

I can't help gasping. "But that's not fair," I protest.

"You were unpardonably late today. Now, take this dirty

cup and saucer. Once you've washed it up and put it away, you may go. I'll see you on Monday."

All this without looking at me once. Speechless, I stare at her as she holds out the crockery. I go to protest again but she puts the cup and saucer down on the table to her side and makes a batting motion with one of her hands as though I am one of her loathsome insects. "Now off you go, and don't be late tomorrow."

Cursing her in my mind, I leave and slam the front door behind me.

Larna emerges from the boat as soon as I arrive back. She takes one look at my furious face and shakes her head sadly. "Oh dear, that didn't go well, then. Didn't she like you being late?"

"She doesn't like me, full stop."

"Oh, I'm sure that has nothing to do with it. She just sees you as staff, rather than a person in your own right."

"Charming. She didn't even pay me, despite her promise. I wish I'd never gone to work for her," I add petulantly.

"Then don't go back. I told you I don't need any rent."

"And let her get away with not paying me? No way. I've worked hard for that money."

Larna sighs. "Why don't you come inside the boat? You'll feel much better when you've had some food and a nap. I've made you some late lunch. Come and sit by the fire and you can have it on your lap."

There's no point in arguing. Besides, she's right. I am starving. I do as she says and soon I am tucking into another of her delicious meals as if I haven't eaten for a fortnight.

"What were you doing swimming in the lake so early in the morning?" she asks me once I have finished.

"I couldn't sleep," I confess.

"But cold-water swimming. That's a bit extreme, isn't it?"

"I was being spontaneous," I lied.

She laughs. "The lake is a long way to go to be spontaneous. I didn't think you even knew about it."

"I didn't. I just needed some fresh air and found it by mistake. Do you know much about its history?"

"It was created in the seventeenth century to fill up the hole made by a stone quarry."

"Is that the stone used to build the Stennings?"

"That's right. It's not quite the colour of Cotswold stone but not that dissimilar. That's why these villages are sometimes called the Little Cotswolds. We'll have to take Buddy there sometime for a walk. He'll love it." She pauses. "Raff seems vaguely familiar. Do I know him?"

"Perhaps you've seen him at the dig or walking around town," I suggest.

"He said he is an archaeologist. As far as I know, the Stennings haven't had a dig before. Gita in the shop seems quite excited."

"The friendly Indian lady who also runs the post office?"

"Yes. She was really kind to me when I arrived, so I pop in frequently to find out what is happening in the Stennings. She said yesterday that everyone's starting to talk about the dig. They've never had an excavation here before, at least not since the quarry in the seventeenth century. Anyway, she also says that one of the archaeologists is exceptionally handsome. That must be your Raff."

"He's not my Raff," I cut in quickly.

She quirks an eyebrow. "Well apparently there are three archaeologists: your Raff, Marcus Knebworth and a woman." She scratches the side of her nose. "What's he like, Hester Knebworth's younger son? Have you met him?"

"Marcus? He gives me the creeps."

"Why?"

I shrug. "I don't know. All that white hair on a young face. He's like a character out of the Addams Family." I go to grimace but find myself yawning instead. Embarrassed, I hastily cover my mouth with my hand.

"Time for a nap, young lady. You go and get some rest."

After I have washed up my dish, I'm just about to leave when a car horn honks from somewhere outside the boat. Larna claps her hands together in delight. "It's Bertie," she cries. Surreptitiously I step back and glance out of the window. There's an outrageous yellow sports car in the field.

"That's *Marigold*," she tells me.

"*Marigold?*"

"Yes, she's Bertie's car. I asked him here to meet you."

Horrified, I start to protest, but she puts up her hand to stop me.

"Look, I know you're tired, but I'll make some coffee and you can at least say hello before you go and have a rest. Bertie is a writer and delightfully eccentric. You'll love him."

"But..."

"Do you know, he used to be called Beatrice. He's the bravest person I know."

"Beatrice?" I query.

"I know. Wonderful, isn't it? Now, I'll just go and let him in."

THE KNEBWORTHS – Present Day

Alan Knebworth was sitting in his office, head in hands, when the phone rang. He didn't move. If it was somebody else demanding money, there was nothing more he could say to them. There was no money. They were as good as bankrupt. The ringing ceased and he sighed with relief. Then it started again. And again. The fourth time it rang, he gave in and picked it up with a trembling hand.

"Mr Knebworth? It's Clem Hardwick, the County Archaeologist."

Alan sighed with relief. At last. He could do with some good news. "Does this mean that we have the go-ahead? Can I proceed with the planning application?"

"I'm afraid not, Mr Knebworth. You'll remember that I warned you that this is not the right time of year for a dig. You should have waited until the summer."

"So it can't be done? Phew, what a relief. I'll get onto the Planning Officer's department and start the process."

"I'm afraid that won't be possible. Despite the hardness of the ground, somehow your son and his team have managed to discover enough to convince me to extend the dig for a further month."

Alan felt his chest tighten. "Please tell me that you're joking."

"You should be pleased. Your land is yielding invaluable archaeological material."

"But I need to sell the land. I only gave Marcus permission to work on that field to tide him over until he found proper archaeological work."

"Well, it seems that your field is providing him with exactly that. And I have to warn you that if they continue finding material of importance, I will be obliged to extend the permit still further into the summer itself, so that the real work can begin."

Alan felt the blood drain from his face. "Hester will go berserk," he whispered.

"Hester?"

"My wife. She simply won't accept anything less than an immediate planning application."

"Well, I'm afraid she's going to have to wait."

"Hester doesn't wait for anyone or anything. Look, off the record, is there some kind of a deal we could strike? Just between the two of us, I mean. We're both men of the world. There must be..." His throat began to restrict.

"This is not helpful, Mr Knebworth."

"Look, I only said Marcus could do a little digging, just to help him out a bit." He went quiet before he continued. "Mr Hardwick, I'm begging you..."

"I'm afraid there is nothing else I can do," replied Clem. "Now, if you'll forgive me, I have another meeting in five minutes. I'll be in touch in a few days to let you know how we're intending to proceed. Goodbye, Mr Knebworth."

As the line went dead, Alan stared disbelievingly into the receiver and a band of numbness started to squeeze his chest. Heart pounding, he picked up the telephone and dialled the manor.

"Hester?" As usual he was greeted by silence. "I'm afraid I've just had some...some..." Afraid of her reaction, he stopped.

"Spit it out, Alan."

He tried to take a deep breath, but his lungs refused to expand properly. "I'm afraid I've just had some bad news," he tried again. "Hester, we can't sell the land yet."

There was a sharp intake of breath at the other end of the line. "What do you mean?"

"Clem Hardwick is refusing to terminate the dig. Apparently, Marcus and his friends have found something. They need to continue excavating."

"Don't be ridiculous, Alan. What are you talking about? I thought he warned us that the ground would be too hard to find anything at this time of year? You know as well as I do that giving Marcus the job was just a ruse to tell the authorities that we had tried. What did you say to this archaeology chap?"

"I explained that..."

"Well you can't have explained very well," she interrupted. "How long do they want us to hold off for?"

"Four weeks. Indefinitely if the site proves important." He screwed up his face and waited for the explosion.

"A month is out of the question and I hope you told him so," Hester bellowed. "This is my land, Alan, and if I want to sell it then nobody is going to stop me."

He sighed and then winced at the pain that shot up into his jaw.

"Give me his number, Alan. I'll sort him out."

"I er…"

"Oh, for God's sake, I'll find it myself."

Hester slammed down the receiver and retrieved her address book. Clem Hardwick, indeed. What kind of a name was that? Furiously, she punched in the number. She'd give him a piece of her mind. How dare he think he could dictate to her what she could do or could not do with her own land?

The wretched number was engaged. She tried several times before she gave up. 'Stupid, *stupid* man,' she muttered, unsure whether she was referring to Clem Hardwick, her husband, her sons or the entire male species. Fortunately, there was more than one way to skin a cat. She would just have to persuade Marcus to pull out of the dig. Without him, the whole ludicrous project would crumble.

Of course, it should never have come to this. Had her father entrusted *Frattons* to her rather than given it to her idiot of a husband, they would never have been in this mess. Thank God she'd had the foresight to open a Swiss bank account and regularly transfer money from the company. At least she had managed to amass quite a reasonable sum. But it was too soon to put her plan into place yet. There were still insufficient funds to secure her for the rest of her life.

In the cloakroom, she filled the basin full of hot water, picked up a nail brush and began to scrub her nails. In her mind, the cleaner's face appeared: that red hair, and that ghastly eyepatch. She clenched her teeth and rubbed harder. Damn. Damn. *Damn.* As she pulled out the plug and dried her hands, she left a smear of blood on the towel. Angrily, she threw it into the linen basket. Then, she grabbed her coat and gloves, picked up her keys, and marched out of the manor, determined to find someone to punish.

It didn't take long to drive to the offices of *Frattons*. She shuddered at the sight of Karl's bicycle chained to the railings of the office car park. When was he going to become a real man and learn to drive a car? Inside the building, the front desk was unmanned. She marched straight through to Karl's office and found him sitting gazing out of the window. "Karl," she barked.

He jumped and turned to face her. "M... M... M..."

"Oh, for God's sake," she cut him short. Sitting down in the upright chair opposite the desk, she placed her Louis Vuitton bag on her knee and absent-mindedly touched the desk, trying to remove a slight mark with her gloved finger. How had she managed to produce such an ineffectual, hairless man? He was an abomination. "What's the position with this land deal? I assume they've still come up with nothing?"

Karl looked at her, terrified.

"Your brother. The field. The land I want to sell for housing. "You went there, didn't you?"

Sheepishly, he nodded.

"Well, have they come up with any evidence?"

Karl's mouth worked frantically. "I ... I ... I ..."

"I'll take that as a no. What did they say when you paid them a visit?"

"I ... I ..."

"Did you tell them that we were terminating the agreement?"

When he made no further attempt to reply, she grasped the handles of her bag angrily and stood up. "Phone and make another appointment," she instructed, picking up the telephone and holding it out to him. "Now."

He stared at her incredulously.

"Oh, forget it," she snapped. She marched over to the door, but before she left, she turned back to Karl, her eyes blazing. "You Knebworth men are hopeless. You should all be put down."

Furiously, she slammed shut the office door and drove straight over to the site of the dig. The field had been her father's wedding present to her and she intended to milk every last drop of money that she could out of the bastard.

As soon as she turned down the track, she had to slow the car to navigate the bumps. Cursing the mud, she reminded herself to instruct Selena to give the car a good wash next time.

Incensed by the ugly prefabricated building that now squatted on the edge of her land, she stopped the car and beeped the horn loudly. Eventually, a man and woman appeared. The woman was black and the man was too tall, his long hair tied back in a ponytail. She watched in distaste as they approached the car.

"May we help you?" asked the woman.

Hester lowered her window but refused to look at the woman and her filthy dungarees. "I've come to speak to my son," she declared haughtily.

"Your son?" said the man. "Ah, you must be Mrs Knebworth." He held out his hand and smiled. "I'm Raff McGinley and this is Dr Falala Sefu. We're Marcus's colleagues. We've been looking forward to meeting you."

Hester shrank away from his outstretched hand, lest she be contaminated. "Tell Marcus I want to see him."

Raff lowered his hand back to his side.

"I'm afraid he isn't here," Falala said, "but we'll ask him to call you as soon as he arrives."

Hester narrowed her eyes. "That isn't good enough. He should be here. I am his employer and I wish to speak to him. No*w*."

Falala's gaze did not waver. "He's gone to visit someone," Falala lied again, "on a business matter."

"Typical," spat Hester. "Then I'll wait."

"He may be quite a while," cut in Raff. "Perhaps you could make an appointment for another time, Mrs Knebworth? We'd be delighted to show you around the site then."

"Make an appointment to see my own land? Don't be so ridiculous."

"We've got some spare overalls that you could put on," Raff continued smoothly, "but I'm afraid we don't have any more boots and, I must warn you, the mud in the field is quite atrocious."

Horrified, Hester glanced down at her highly polished designer shoes. Without replying, she swound up the window, released the hand-brake and drove off. Marcus had been there; she'd been sure of it. She could smell him. Determined that he wouldn't get away with lying to her, she phoned his flat the moment she had returned to the manor and left a voice message instructing him to meet her tomorrow night at seven at the restaurant, *Chez Nous*.

Anxious for someone else to blame, her mind turned to Larna Avery. She was done with having a harpy living on a boat in between her villages. It was time to hound her out. Switching on her iPad, she began to type an email, wincing as the movement of her fingers pulled at the scabs on her hands. When she was done, she read the message and smiled. It was perfect: low-key, undramatic and believable. She pressed send.

The vicar would be horrified to think that he had a witch in his midst.

Raido – travel

Chapter Nine

SELENA – Present Day

"Bertie, this is Selena. Selena, this is Bertie Fratton, Hester Knebworth's brother."

With his immaculate thatch of thick grey hair, freshly laundered suit, yellow silk tie matched with the handkerchief in his top pocket, and yellow sports car parked outside on the grass, he is impressive. My mouth goes dry. Adrenaline rushes into me and suddenly I am wide awake.

"And this is Buddy," she continues.

I have always thought that you can tell a lot about someone from the way they are with animals. As he looks at the dog, his nose twitches as though he expects him to be smelly, but when he sees that Buddy is in fact rather well groomed, he seems relieved. Silently, I thank Larna for the bath she gave him.

He turns back to me. "Who exactly are you?" he asks in a mellifluous voice that is somewhat at odds with his appearance. "Larna tells me that she found you in Oxford."

"Bertie," Larna says sharply, "you promised to be gentle."

He holds up a hand to stop her. "It's all right, my dear. I know what I'm doing."

"Well, behave. It won't take me long to make the tea."

As soon as she disappears into the kitchen, he turns back to me. "Why were you busking?"

It sounds more like a threat than a question. "Busking isn't a crime," I reply, holding my head up defiantly.

He raises an eyebrow. "That depends on why you were doing it. What's your story?"

I glare at him with as much energy as I can muster, hoping that he will at least flinch at the sight of my eyepatch. He doesn't. "It's complicated."

"Stories usually are," he replies. "Larna tells me that a man threatened you. Was he trying to sell you drugs?"

"No."

"Are you sure?"

"I've never taken drugs in my life."

"Well that's something, I suppose."

"Mr Fratton, I'm not a bad person," I protest.

He doesn't look convinced. "I didn't say you were, but you need to know that I won't let you take advantage of Larna."

"I have no intention of taking advantage of her," I insist. "I'm doing everything I can to pay her some rent."

He quirks up an eyebrow. "Oh yes? How?"

I'm about to answer when Larna appears with a laden tray. "Now, how are you two getting on?"

Neither of us replies. She sighs, pours three cups of tea and hands them out. Bertie takes his and sits down on the chair by the bookcase. I take mine and sit in the seat by the window. Unsure how to handle the situation, my brain starts to work quickly. Bertie is Larna's best friend so I don't want to antagonise him, but he's trying to catch me out as though I've done something wrong. Somehow, I need to bring him onside.

"How about some cake?" Larna offers. "Bertie, it's lemon drizzle, your favourite."

He takes a slice but I decline.

"Where do you come from?" he asks after he has swallowed a mouthful of cake and said how delicious it is.

"She comes from Norfolk," Larna answers for me.

He doesn't take his eyes away from my face. "What brought you to Oxford?"

"She..."

"Larna, dear girl, please let her speak for herself."

She turns to me and shrugs almost apologetically.

"I needed a break," I tell him.

"From what?"

It's a question too far and suddenly I am lost for words.

Seeing my distress, Larna speaks for me again. "Selena's a musician, aren't you, love? She sings beautifully."

"Selena," Bertie tries again, this time a little more gently, "did something happen to make you leave Norfolk?"

I take a deep breath and say the words I never wanted to hear. "My mum and sister were killed in a car accident. I just had to get away."

They both gasp. "Oh, you poor thing," says Larna, "I had no idea. That's absolutely awful."

"I'm sorry I didn't explain before."

"I understand," she says. "Grief can take your tongue."

Suddenly, a yawn erupts from me before I can stop it. "Oh, I'm so sorry. Last night must be catching up with me."

"Last night?" he queries.

I look helplessly at Larna, trying to convey to her how desperately I need to end this conversation and return to the caravan.

She turns to Bertie. "Selena didn't sleep well last night." Then she looks at me. "Off you go, love and have a nap. I'll call you for dinner later."

It's a relief to return to the caravan and lie down on the couch but the heater is off and I'm cold. Grabbing a blanket from somewhere near my head, I close my eyes. It's a mistake. My pearly eye flares in warning and I hear a dog whining. Strange, I think. Buddy stayed in the boat by the fire, didn't he?

But I don't have time to answer myself, because I'm walking in the snow again, my feet only covered by thin strips of fur-lined leather.

As though in greeting, my hand rises upwards and everything goes black.

circa 2000 B.C.E.

"Riadd, may I come in?" said Seela. "I have brought you something."

The youth struggled to his feet and limped to the doorway of his hut that was decorated with wooden carvings of birds and animals. Gratefully, he took the beaker from her outstretched hand, but was unable to stop himself from wincing with pain.

"Lanalla said you were only bruised," Seela murmured, shocked at his pallor, visible even in the dim firelight. "Did Mevin hurt you badly?"

"It is nothing."

Seela wondered if she should go, but she was too concerned to leave. "Did you carve the animals and birds on the posts outside?" she tried.

He nodded.

"They are beautiful. How did you make such likenesses?"

"I have been carving all of my life."

"What do you use to make the carvings?"

"The tools over there in the corner."

"May I look?"

He stepped back slowly to let her in.

She walked over and picked one up. "What is this?" she asked, holding it up to him.

"A stone polisher."

"And next to it?"

"A bronze awl."

"These?"

"Antler spatulas to work leather."

"What about these?"

"Beaver tooth engravers."

She held up a flint knife.

"I used that to carve the animals into the wood."

She hesitated before picking up a long piece of bone with holes carved into it and held it out to him. "What is this?"

"A flute."

She smiled. "There was a flute player back in my own village. I loved to hear him play."

Despite his soreness, he took the flute from her hands, put it to his lips and reluctantly blew a run of notes. In moments, he had run out of breath.

"Where do you hurt?"

"My side."

"Will you let me look?"

He frowned uncertainly.

"My mother always used to put her hands on any hurts and they went away," she said. "Would you like me to try?"

He nodded. Shifting slightly, he pointed first to his side and then the top of his leg. Seela knelt beside him and placed one hand on each. He sighed, closed his eyes and started to relax.

"Was Mevin very angry?" she murmured.

"He's just trying to teach me to fight."

"Don't you like fighting?"

He shook his head. "I'm too tall. Good fighters are broad and squat." Colour had returned to his face and the pain around his eyes and mouth was beginning to recede. "Your mother taught you well. I don't hurt so much anymore. You have magic in your hands. Perhaps Lanalla will make you the new SeeSayer."

She frowned. "I'm still not sure what a SeeSayer is. My village does not have one."

"The SeeSayer tells the priestess what's going to happen and warns us if we are going to be attacked. She keeps us safe."

"She?" Seela queried. "Is she always a girl?"

"Of course, it is girls and women who talk to The Mother."

"What is a SeeSayer like?"

"SeeSayers are different from others. They have been touched by The Mother."

Seela shook her head with sudden and unwelcomed understanding. "Then I think that Lanalla plans to make my sister Duna the SeeSayer, not me."

"Does Duna have magic in her hands too, then?"

"I don't think so. And she has never warned me about anything. She can barely speak." Suddenly frightened, Seela looked up at him. "Is that the only reason Lanalla is giving us shelter?"

"She has always wanted a daughter, as well."

"Has she no children of her own?"

"She did have one but the baby died. Now she pretends that I am her son." He tried to straighten his back despite the pain in his side. "She wants me to become the new Leader but I will never be strong enough to be able to win the Ordeal."

"The Ordeal?" she queried. "What is that?"

"Don't you have an Ordeal where you come from, either?"

She shook her head.

"An Ordeal chooses the next Leader," he explained slowly. "The contenders go into the forest for the night and try to survive alone. With nobody to protect them against attacks from wild animals and each other, they do not always return."

She remembered the wolf and shivered. "When will it be held?"

"In three days' time," he replied miserably. "Mevin is bound to become the New Leader. There is no one strong enough to challenge him."

"Then Duna and I must leave tonight."

Riadd looked at her and shook his head. "You can't. It's not safe out in the forest."

"It's not safe here. We'll just have to find somewhere else to shelter."

"There isn't anywhere else." He lowered his head in thought and then looked up again, his eyes now gleaming. "Seela, I've got an idea."

"What?" she asked.

He smiled and tapped the side of his nose. "You'll see."

SELENA – Present Day

Curious about what Riadd had dreamed up, it takes me several moments to realise that I am back in the caravan and not in a hut filled with carved animals. A glance outside shows me that Bertie's car is still there. Anxious to avoid returning to the boat, I decide to go for a walk. My coat is still damp, so I grab the colourful poncho from the wardrobe and head for the door. At the last moment I hesitate and scoop the necklace into a small shoulder bag.

Like Seela, I don't know where to go. The walks from here centre on the two hills. Stone Clump is wilder and more forbidding, while Stenning Hill with its church on the top is gentler yet more eerie. At first, my feet don't know which way to turn, so I decide to do a little experiment. Taking a step in each direction, I concentrate on my pearly eye to see if there is any response. Sure enough, it tingles slightly when I step towards Stone Clump and so I decide to walk in that direction. After that I simply follow my feet.

They take me to the dig. Hoping that Fally meant it when she said I could call in whenever I liked, I find myself approaching the door of the Portakabin at the top of the field.

"Selena," says Fally from the open doorway. "How lovely to see you. Come in. I was just about to put the kettle on. Would you like a cuppa?"

Gratefully, I step inside. Raff is sitting at a table in the corner. As soon he sees me, he stands up and comes striding over.

"Are you feeling better?" he whispers.

Memory of the cave shoots into my mind. Doing my best to block it off, I nod.

"I'm glad you're here," he continues. "I wanted to speak to you."

But before he has the chance to finish, my pearly eye starts to zing in warning, and Marcus appears in the doorway. Unnerved, I turn away.

"Sugar?" calls out Fally.

"No thanks," I manage.

"Sweet enough already, eh?"

The comment comes from Marcus who is now close behind me. I tense and instinctively move closer to Raff.

"Hold the tea for a few minutes, will you, Fally?" Raff calls. "Selena and I are just going outside for a chat. Won't be long." Then he turns to Marcus. "I've left some charts on the table over there for you to look at. Will you see if you want me to change anything?"

Before Marcus can object, Raff has put a hand on my back and is guiding me to the door.

Once we are outside, I breathe an audible sigh of relief.

"You don't like him much, do you?" Raff says as soon as he has closed the door behind us. It's more of a statement than a question, so I don't bother to reply as he leads me down to the stream at the bottom of the field.

"Have you recovered from this morning?" he asks.

"Yes. Thanks for helping me."

"Just promise me that you won't go cold-water swimming again at this time of year unless you're wearing a wetsuit."

I shudder. "I promise."

"Good." He hesitates. "Look, I hope you don't mind, but while I was hanging up your coat to dry, I found an old chain in one of the pockets. I'm not sure what it is, but as you know from the harp, I love restoring things. I wondered if you'd like me to polish it up a bit and see if I can get rid of the rust. It wouldn't take long; just a week or so."

I stare at him, horrified. Knowing that someone else has touched the necklace makes me feel naked, yet the other part of me is relieved at the thought that at last I can tell someone what has been happening. Slowly, I reach into the little bag and draw it out.

"This, you mean?"

"Oh, you've got it with you," he says in surprise. "May I?" he asks, pulling a handkerchief out of his pocket. I nod, and he carefully takes the necklace from me and examines it, turning it around to study it from different angles.

"Where did you get it?"

"Here in the Stennings."

He looks up in shock. "Really? Where?"

"I dug it up in the woods at the bottom of Stenning Hill."

"Good heavens. When was this?"

"The day after I arrived."

He looks down at the chain.

"What do you think it is?" I ask.

Sucking in his breath, he turns it over in the handkerchief. "I've no idea. I've never seen anything like it before."

"Could it be a necklace?" I ask. "It's long enough to slip over someone's head."

"I suppose so." He holds it up to the light. "The pendants are interesting. There's something carved into all of the stones."

"Yes. Larna says they're runes."

He looks at me in surprise. "Who's Larna?"

"Larna Avery. I'm staying in her caravan by the river."

"Ah, of course. Have you shown it to her then?"

"The necklace? No. But she says that this X on the bottom stone means a gift."

He studies it again. "How extraordinary."

"Have you any idea how old it might be?" I ask him.

He shakes his head. "I've got a friend down in London who specialises in these kinds of things. He might be able to give us an idea."

Suddenly I feel cold. "I couldn't possibly let you send it away."

He looks surprised. "Really, why not?"

"I ..." I think quickly. "I like having it with me."

He frowns.

I try again. "It helps me to feel better."

He frowns again. "What if I only took it for one night and don't send it to London? While I give it a polish to get rid of the rust, I could have a proper look."

"What the hell is that?" hisses a voice behind us.

We both jump.

"Marcus," says Raff, putting the necklace behind his back and stepping in front of me like a shield. "I thought you were looking at the charts?"

"What have you got there?"

"It's none of your…"

"It most certainly is. This is my dig, remember? If you've found an artefact…"

"It belongs to Selena, not us. And it's not from this field."

The man with the white hair turns his gaze onto me. "What is it?" he demands. "How long have you had it? Where did you get it from?"

"Marcus," says Raff, rescuing me, "you're firing questions like bullets. Lay off, will you?"

Ignoring him, Marcus peers closer. "How old is it?"

"Marcus, I said stop badgering her."

The white-haired man tries to snatch the necklace from Raff's hand but as soon as he touches the metal, he pulls his fingers back, rubbing his hand as though he's been burned. "That hurt. What the fuck is it? The bloody thing stung me."

Raff laughs uncertainly. "It's a chunk of metal, stone and crystal, Marcus, not a snake."

"I need to know where it was found," he splutters.

"I told you," says Raff, an edge in his voice. "It's not from the dig. We don't know what it is. I'm going to take it away and look at it, all right?" He looks at me and I glare back. "If Selena says that's OK, that is," he adds.

Marcus goes to say something else but changes his mind, and with a last look at the necklace, he stomps off back up the field, leaving a dark hole in the air behind him.

Once he has disappeared into the Portakabin, Raff turns round to face me. "I'm so sorry about that. I don't know what's got into him. He's been moody ever since we arrived here." He looks down at his hand again. "So, what do you think? Will you let me take it for a day or so?"

I don't move.

"By the way, you shouldn't touch this directly. Acid from your skin will corrode the metal."

"Okay," I say, knowing that I will ignore the instruction. "You can keep it overnight, but I want it back tomorrow morning."

"Deal," he says, already wrapping up the necklace in the handkerchief and putting it in his pocket.

THE TEAM – Present Day

Marcus slammed the door as soon as he got back into the Portakabin. "Who the hell does Raff think he is?" he shouted to Falala. "I'm sick to death of him throwing his weight around as if he owns this field. This is my team and my family's land and he would do well to remember that."

She stared at him in surprise. "What on earth are you talking about?"

"Raff bloody McGuinley has taken that girl down into the field and they're talking artefacts. They've no right. This is my project. Anyway who is she? You seem to be very friendly with her."

"Selena's staying round here, I think. Raff said something about her living on the narrowboat."

"That gaudy one on the river by the foot bridge?"

"I suppose so."

"That's where the woman who is a designer lives, isn't it? I saw one of her cards in the post office. It should be easy enough to get her telephone number."

"Why do you want her number?" Falala asked, trying to push away the sudden stab of jealousy.

"So I can find out about this artefact."

"What artefact?"

He glared at her, a fire raging through him that he couldn't control. Then all of a sudden, the rage died down and he looked around as if he didn't quite know where he was. He ran one of his hands distractedly though his white hair before snatching it away in disgust. What was happening to him? He was growing old before his time.

"Marcus?" she tried again. When he didn't respond, she walked over to him and put her hand tentatively on his shoulder. It was the first time she had touched him since they had slept together, and she wasn't sure how he would react.

For an excruciating moment, Marcus wanted to turn round and accept her comfort, but he remembered himself in time and shook her off. Then he walked to the computer and rebooted it. He would work on Raff's drawings and make them his own.

"Oh for God's sake," she erupted bitterly. "Why won't you talk to me, Marcus? You can't go on ignoring me forever."

He was saved from having to reply by the sound of the door opening.

"Selena's gone," Raff growled.

"Gone?" said Falala in surprise. "But why? What about the tea?"

"Marcus scared her off."

"I did not," Marcus spat from his seat at the computer.

"Yes you did."

Marcus rose to his feet. "How come you and this Selena woman are suddenly old friends?"

"We're not old friends."

"Then why does she want to talk to you and not me?"

"Probably because you're being so bloody rude. Leave her alone, Marcus."

"Why, what is she to you?"

Raff glared at him with barely suppressed fury. "Do you always have to take what belongs to someone else?"

There was a horrible silence.

"So she belongs to you now, does she?" Marcus sneered.

"I didn't mean that. I…"

"So what did you mean?"

"Sod off, Marcus. It's none of your business."

"Everything that happens on this dig is my business. I want to see that artefact again."

"And have it bite you? No way. Besides, it has nothing whatsoever to do with this dig. There are millions of artefacts in the world and they don't all belong to you."

"Has she given it to you, then? Are you both plotting something behind my back?"

Raff strode over, forcing Marcus to look upwards. "What the hell's got into you?"

Marcus glared back, fury sparking from his eyes. "You've always worked by yourself, haven't you? You can't bear being part of a team."

"What are you talking about?" hissed Raff.

"When Marion…"

"Don't you dare talk about Marion," Raff warned.

"When Marion came to me she was desperate for help, for some support. But you were so tied up in your own shit that you couldn't give it to her."

"My mother was dying, for Chrissake."

"You could have included Marion in your pathetic little pity party. Instead you drove her to…"

"You took advantage of someone who just needed a shoulder to cry on."

"That shoulder should have been yours. You were her boyfriend."

"Couldn't you have offered her some comfort without taking her to bed?"

Marcus laughed. "She wanted some action, Raff, and you were too wrapped up in your tiny little world to give her any. So, as your friend, I gave it to her for you."

Raff struck him across his face.

Marcus's eyes flew open in shock. "You bastard."

"You're the bastard. She died because of you."

"No, she died because of you." Marcus hurled the words like javelins. "She came to you for forgiveness, and you threw her out. You let her down, Raff. God knows what state she was in by the time you'd finished with her when she got in her car. You knew she had only just passed her driving test but you still ..."

"*Enough!*" Falala screamed at the top of her voice, slamming her hand down on one of the tables. The finds juddered dangerously but she stood her ground.

Marcus glared at her and then at Raff. "Oh, just piss off, both of you," he erupted before storming out and slamming the door behind him.

Raff sank into the nearest chair and put his head in his hands. "I should never have come back here."

"But you were friends for such a long time."

"When we were children."

Falala pulled up a chair beside him and put a hand on his arm. "Look, what happened to Marion was an absolute tragedy. I can't begin to imagine what it must have been like for you. Marcus was wrong to do what he did but you've got to stop carrying Marion's death on your shoulders. You were only seventeen and we all do things at seventeen that we regret."

Raff didn't move.

"Look," she continued, "when he invited you to be part of this team, I'm pretty sure that it was his way of apologising, but you've got to find a way of forgiving him and yourself, or none of this is ever going to work."

At last Raff raised his head.

"I'm going to make you some strong tea," Fally continued. "That will help. Then I'll go and talk to Marcus and persuade him to apologise." She stood up and walked over to the kettle.

"Now, tell me what this artefact is that has got Marcus so worked up."

"It's some kind of chain with stone pendants and a couple of crystals. Selena called it a necklace."

"You make it sound like some kind of New Age trinket."

"Well, it's not."

"Can I see it?"

He shook his head. "Not yet. I want to clean it up first. It may be nothing, but I'll let you know. Look, forget the tea. What I need is fresh air and a ride on the bike."

She turned to him in concern. "Are you sure that's wise while you're in this state?"

"I'm not Marion," he said, rising to his feet and picking up his rucksack.

"No, I know," she said, appalled at the ravaged tone of his voice, "but..."

"Just leave it, Fally. I'll be fine."

SELENA – Present Day

Bertie's car is still on the field when I get back so I retreat to the caravan, in no mood for another grilling. Besides, I no longer have the necklace to give me courage.

Within moments, Larna is knocking on the door. "Selena?"

I go very still.

"Selena, I know you're in there."

Still I don't move.

"Selena, please; we need to talk."

Realising that she isn't going to go away, I reluctantly open the door.

"Are you all right, love?" she asks me, her voice full of concern. "Did you have a nice sleep?"

I nod.

"Well, you must be hungry."

I bite my lip.

She takes a deep breath. "If it's Bertie you're worried about, he says he'll go after he's had a brief word with you. He says he's had an idea and he thinks you'll like it. He won't stay for dinner, I promise. Once he's gone, it'll be just you and me. How does that sound?"

I don't move.

"Look, I think he wants to apologise," she continues, her face full of concern.

I don't know what to do. The idea of seeing Bertie again makes me want to run. On the other hand, he is Larna's best friend and I have to find a way of persuading him that I'm not out to take advantage of her.

"Besides, Buddy's missing you," she adds.

I flush guiltily. I am leaving him with her too often, and even though she seems to love having him with her, I must not prey on her kindness. Giving in, I follow her into the boat. I'm going to have to face Bertie sometime and may as well get it over and done with.

Bertie rises to his feet as I enter the snug. At the same time, the phone rings. Larna sighs and picks it up from the table, looking at the number. "I've no idea who this is," she says. "I'll go and take it in the kitchen." She turns briefly. "Bertie, be nice," she warns. Then she clicks the green button to answer the call and disappears back through the beaded curtain.

When Bertie motions me to sit, I don't move.

He sighs. "Very well." There's an awkward silence before he speaks again. "Larna tells me that you have been cleaning my sister's house so that you can give her some rent. She also tells me that, so far, Hester has refused to pay you. Is that true?"

188

I nod, uncomfortable that they have been talking about me behind my back.

"It seems to me, therefore, that you need to find a more reliable source of income."

Puzzled, I wonder what his game is. I thought he wanted me to leave because he didn't trust me. Is he now suggesting that I find a way of earning enough money to stay?

"Do you dream much?" he asks next.

Shocked, I stare at him. Nobody knows about the dreams apart from me. Why is he asking about them?

Undeterred by my expression, he continues. "As Larna told you," he explains, "I'm a writer. I'm thinking of exploring the subject of dreams for my next book and need a volunteer."

"I don't dream," I lie.

He shrugs. "Everybody dreams. It's just a case of whether they remember the dreams or not. You can tell whether somebody is dreaming by their brainwaves. It's simple enough, but if you don't wake up when you're actually dreaming, you won't remember what you've dreamed."

I frown at him. "Why are you asking me when you patently don't trust me?"

He looks at me warily. "Larna likes you and so I'm willing to have myself proved wrong. Besides, this could help us both."

"How?"

"If you prove to be a reliable subject, then I will pay your rent for you."

Stunned, I stare at him. "To stay in the caravan?"

"For a short while, yes. The experiment shouldn't take long."

"I see."

Something about this doesn't make sense. "Haven't you got anyone else you could ask?"

"Yes, but I'd rather ask you." He rubs his nose thoughtfully before looking at me again. "Dreaming will be a lot easier than cleaning Hester's house," he says with a half-smile. "We can do the first experiment at my house. If it goes well, I'll hire a portable lab with some equipment. What do you say?"

For a long moment, I stare at him. The hostility in his face has been replaced by enthusiasm. I tune into my pearly eye for advice. This man is offering me a lifeline, giving me a chance to stay legitimately in the caravan for a while longer. But do I dare trust him? When my eye does not zing in warning, I nod slowly. "Okay."

"Good." He takes a card out of his inside pocket and hands it to me. "Here's my address and telephone number. Shall we say tonight?"

"Tonight?" I protest.

"I'm keen to get started as soon as possible."

I'm about to argue when Larna suddenly bursts into the snug. "It's happened again," she cries. "That was the vicar. He's just spent the last five minutes accusing me of being evil." She runs her hand over her colourful bandana. "What on earth am I going to do? And where has this all come from? I thought everyone here loved having such a beautiful boat on the river?"

She's about to say more when the phone starts ringing again. Flinching, she straightens. "I'll just have to persuade him that he's wrong," she says, pressing the green button again. As though she will somehow be protected from malice, she stays in the snug when she puts the receiver to her ear. She waits for a moment, looks surprised and then covers the mouthpiece with her hand. "It isn't the vicar. Selena, it's for you."

"For me?" I say surprised. "Who is it?"

"I don't know. He didn't say."

She hands me the phone. Bewildered, I take it and turn away from them. Perhaps it's Raff with some news about the necklace. He's the only one who knows I'm here but that doesn't make sense because I didn't give him Larna's telephone number.

"Selena?" comes a man's voice. "It's Marcus, Marcus Knebworth from the dig. I wanted to ask you if you might like to meet for a drink somewhere? There's a nice little pub..."

Horrified, my stomach clenches. Marcus Knebworth? The man with the white hair? Heart thudding, I press the red button to end the call.

If he has discovered where I am staying, then I am no longer safe.

RAFF – Present Day

Despite being on the Honda there was little sense of relief. Raff thought he had put Marion's death behind him. But Marcus had just proved that was not true. He was glad he had hit him. The bastard deserved it not only for what he had done to Marion, but also for the way he was treating Selena as though she was scum under his feet.

Desperate to free his mind from the pain, he pushed the starter pedal down hard with his foot and revved the engine. It was a mistake. The track was muddy after the snow and rain and the wheels began to clag and then slide in the ruts. A good thing. He would have to empty his mind of all else and concentrate.

By the time he reached the London road, his wheels were covered in mud. There was no way he should continue with the motorbike like this, but he didn't care. Unusually, the road was empty, and this was a rare opportunity to ride hard and fast. Pulling out in the opposite direction from the Stennings, he began to accelerate. It wasn't long before he was able push the speed dial up. As the thrill of the ride overtook him, his mind cleared. Now all he could see was the road, feel the vibration of the bike on his body, and hear the roar of the accelerating engine.

He was just beginning to feel better when the muddy wheels began to swerve and he realised he was going too fast. Fighting to get the bike under control, he saw someone on the road up ahead. "Move," he yelled into his helmet, but the figure stayed where it was. Then quite suddenly he saw a girl with blood on her clothes flagging him down. Slamming on his brakes, he veered violently off to the side, narrowly missing her. The wheels spun out of control and he was flung over the handlebars into a hedge.

Stunned, he lay sprawled on the ground a few feet away from the bike. As soon as he could move, he looked around for the girl, terrified that he had hit her. Ignoring the bruises on his flesh, he pushed himself to his feet. Relieved that he could walk and had not broken any bones, he began to search, scouring the road for a sign of her, but it was empty. His blood turned cold. What if he'd knocked her into the ditch? Calling out, he stumbled up and down the roadside trying to find her, but there was nothing. Frantic, he reached inside his jacket pocket for his mobile phone but it wasn't there. Damn, he must have left it on the table in the Portakabin.

Promising himself that he'd call an ambulance as soon as he returned, he glanced over at the bike. It was lying at the edge of the road on its side. Walking over to it, he carefully inspected it. Unbelievably, neither wheel was buckled nor did there appear to be any damage apart from a few scratches. Pulling it upright, he climbed back on, his hands trembling so much that he could barely grip the handlebars.

It roared into life as though nothing had happened. Briefly squeezing his eyes shut, he bit back the fear of the road.

Deeply shocked by his own recklessness and how close he had come to killing himself, he opened his eyes again to find that the road was suddenly teeming with traffic. Taken aback, he very slowly eased the bike into the inside lane to look for somewhere to turn round. Trying to calm his thumping heart, he wondered if this was how Marion had felt in the moments before she had careered headlong into the tree.

Sickened, he started to move towards the dig to fetch his phone, oblivious to the drops of blood in the middle of the road, and the quiet, muffled sobbing from the woods behind him.

MARCUS – Present Day

As Marcus closed the door of his flat behind him and broke into a jog, he felt another surge of anger rise inside him. The redhead had put the phone down on him. Who did she think he was? Didn't she realise that he was a Knebworth and from one of the most important families in Oxfordshire?

But as the muscles in his legs stretched, he told himself he was overreacting. With good reason. He was due to see his mother at the restaurant in a couple of hours. God knows why she wanted to see him again. He hoped that her choice of somewhere as expensive as *Chez Nous* meant that it was to apologise for her rudeness when he had gone to the manor.

Hoping that running might make him feel better, he sped up and thought about the narrowboat by the footbridge between the Stennings. It hadn't been hard to find out the Avery woman's telephone number. If she was as colourful as her boat, his mother must be throwing a fit. She had always been ruthless about how things should look and, to be honest, he was surprised that she had allowed it to stay. However, he was rather glad. Its prominence had helped him to locate the Selena woman who, with her outrageously red hair and weird eyepatch, fitted in perfectly with the eccentricity of the boat. If his mother ever met her, she would go crazy.

As he ran, sweat began to run off his face. He didn't see the raised pavement slab and, without warning, fell heavily. For a moment he lay stunned upon the ground, unable to move. Then, hauling himself up to his feet with the aid of several curses, he forced himself into a jog again, ignoring the blood dripping down his leg from a nasty graze.

For a while the stinging in his hands and knees was a distraction, but then Selena's face reappeared in his mind, clearer than ever, as though it was beckoning him towards it. He started to sprint, pushing his body to the limit until all there was left was the pounding of his feet on the pavement and Selena's face. As though he knew her from somewhere, desperation began to rise in him. He had to get to her before Raff did and claim her for himself.

As he approached the river, he began to slow down. An enormous boat was moored on the opposite side of the bank, a shabby caravan not far from it in the field beyond. Crossing the bridge, he slowed to a walk, wiping the sweat from his face. Then he saw a yellow Aston Martin parked in the field. It was magnificent in every detail. He loved cars and longed for the day when he had enough money to replace his old Fiat. He was unlikely to achieve the heights that his father had with the Silver Shadow but the Rolls was not his style. He would prefer something classier like this.

It wasn't until a dog started barking that the longing and envy was replaced by another surge of anger. It must be the red-head's dog, a mangy thing that hung around her like a protector. Telling himself to calm down, he walked away from the car and towards the boat. He had never liked dogs.

If this one rushed out and tried to bite him, he would give it a good kicking.

With gritted teeth, he put a foot on the deck and walked to the door. A woman appeared, holding Selena's snarling dog by the collar. Although she was wearing a colourful bandana around her head, she was more ordinary to look at than he had expected for a designer. "Is Selena in?" he demanded harshly. "I phoned earlier." He took a proprietorial step closer but the dog barked furiously and bared his teeth, forcing him backwards.

Without answering, the woman picked up the snarling animal. "I'm afraid that Selena isn't in. Can I help you?"

He had hidden from his mother enough times to recognise a lie when he saw it. "I only want to say hello."

"As I said …"

He narrowed his eyes. "I don't believe that she isn't here."

Her eyes widened with shock. She went to close the door but he put out a hand to stop her.

As soon as he saw the fear in her face, he smiled. "Now, shall we start again? I would like to see …"

"Good God," said a man's voice from behind the woman. "Is that you, Marcus?"

Marcus stared at the suit. He seemed vaguely familiar but he had no idea where from.

"Dear boy, I heard you were back in the Stennings."

Marcus shook his head. "I'm afraid that I …"

"It's me. Your uncle."

Marcus felt the power drain out of him. Uncle? He didn't have an uncle."

The man's lips pursed. "Good Lord, she didn't tell you, did she?" He sighed dramatically. "I used to be your aunt Beatrice."

Aunt Bea? What was he talking about?

The man smiled. "It's wonderful to see you again, dear boy." He turned to the woman. "Larna, this is my nephew Marcus, Hester's younger son. May he come in?"

Larna stared at him in horror. "Sorry, no. There isn't room for all of us. It's a small boat, as you know."

The man looked at her questioningly but she shook her head vigorously.

"Very well. We will have to continue this conversation somewhere else. Fancy a drink sometime, old chap? We've got years to catch up on." He reached into his inside pocket. "Here's my card. Ring me when you fancy catching up."

Reluctantly, Marcus took it. Then with a nod, he turned on his heel and ran back to his flat.

Once he was inside, he leaned against the door. What was Aunt Bea doing posing as a man? And why had she disappeared from their lives? He looked at the card. The name on it made no sense: Bertie Fratton. There was no Bertie, only Beatrice. Bertie Fratton. Wasn't he a writer? Quickly, he dived for his phone and searched for the name. It came up straight away. And the face was the same face that he had seen at the boat. Only then did he begin to see the resemblance. The thick hair, the patrician nose, the full mouth, the immaculate sense of dress. Oh God, surely not.

Dry-mouthed, he turned to pour himself a glass of water. Wincing at a sudden pain in his leg, he stripped off his joggers to find a nasty graze shaped like a dog bite from where he had fallen. Confused, he stepped into the shower and tried to wash himself clean, only too aware that he would be meeting his mother soon at the restaurant.

It didn't take him long to get ready and all too soon he was on his way to the restaurant. A waiter showed him to the table where his stony-faced mother was already seated.

"You are limping," she stated.

Annoyed that she had noticed, he clenched his jaw but refused to comment.

"Well, sit down," she said tartly, "and stop making a spectacle of yourself. I want an explanation. Why has your father been told to delay submitting the planning application for the field?"

It was as much as Marcus could do not to turn round and walk straight out again, but he forced himself into the chair, if only to question her about his aunt Beatrice. "There's more excavation work to do," he rasped.

"What could you possibly find under a muddy field?" she demanded.

"We're not sure."

"Not sure?" she uttered, her voice rising with anger. "You are delaying our planning application because you're *not sure*? That field was given to me as a wedding present. Your father had no right to hand it over to you without my say so."

Fuelled by her hostility, he went for the jugular. "Why did Aunt Bea disappear all those years ago?" he asked, gratified when she looked shocked.

For a long moment he thought she wasn't going to reply. Then she called to the waiter and asked for a bottle of chilled white wine. "We're eating Dover sole this evening," she informed him.

It was his turn to be surprised. "You've already ordered?"

"Of course. You were late."

"But I don't like fish," he protested. "I never have. You know that."

"Fish is wonderfully nutritious and virtually fat free," she replied. "You need to make something of yourself. Look at you. All the money we spent on your education. It's come to nothing and now you're developing a paunch."

Speechless, he could only stare at her.

"Don't look so surprised, Marcus. It's about time you heard some home truths."

"Home truths?" he retorted bitterly. "What about your failure with *Frattons*? It's the talk of the town."

She grew pale under her make-up.

Pleased to have hit his mark, he continued. "Everyone's saying that the company is in serious financial trouble."

"Keep your voice down," she hissed.

"Well? Is it?"

"There are certain ... problems," she admitted with a quick glance to check that nobody was watching them.

"What kind of problems?"

"Why do you care?" she demanded.

"Why do you care about whether or not I have a paunch?" he countered.

She narrowed her eyes at him.

"Well?"

She sniffed huffily. "The printing business is in dire straits," she admitted. "Computers; everyone does their own printing now. Small businesses don't need us anymore and large companies are cutting back."

"So what is *Frattons* doing to move into the future?"

"What do you mean?"

"How is it developing to cope with the changing market?"

"You were supposed to do that for us. It's your fault that it's gone wrong. Had you done the decent thing and stayed in the company, none of this would have been a problem. Instead of that, you just walked away."

He almost laughed. "You mean that the changes in the twenty-first century are all down to me? I'm flattered. I never realised I was that important."

"Don't be so ridiculous," she said crossly. "You should

have realised that your father couldn't cope. He's useless and has no idea about the current market."

"Well what about Karl?"

"He's useless as well."

"Well what about you, then?"

"As you very well know, I'm a woman and not allowed an opinion."

"Oh, spare me the dramatics," he said vehemently. "Everyone knows you run the company behind the scenes. Anyway, has nobody told you about feminism? Women are equal now, haven't you heard? You've had ample opportunity to bring in new ideas if that's what was needed. If the company's going down Mother, then it's as much your fault as anyone else's. You've got the best business brain I know. Why haven't *you* gone in and sorted out the mess?"

She flushed. "I wouldn't be so smug if I were you. If *Frattons* goes under, there will be nothing to pass on to either of you when we die."

"As if I wanted anything," Marcus bit back. "The days of inheritance are long gone. You'll probably both live till you're a hundred, and by then I won't care."

"There's no need to be rude, Marcus." As she took a sip of wine, some of it spilled because of the shaking of her scabbed hand. "You need to realise that the piece of land you're so inconveniently sitting on is our escape route. If we can obtain planning permission for a housing development, then there's a good chance we will be able to buy our way out of trouble."

"But the land is on the edge of the flood plain," he protested. "There's a stream running right through it at the bottom. You'll never get permission to build on it."

"I have connections in the planning department," she said. "They'll agree."

"I hope not. I checked the stats before I got here. That

field has already flooded three times in the last two years. Going for planning permission there is both underhand and unethical."

"It's not like you to care about other people, Marcus. Besides, if the government doesn't give a fig, I don't see why we should."

He sighed. "Then perhaps it's good that the decision is out of your hands."

"What do you mean?"

"As you delighted in telling me, the County Archaeologist has decided to give us more time excavating."

"Well, we will see about that. I am telling you here and now that I need that land, and if you don't give it back to me I will find another way."

He glared at her, preparing to argue some more, but the waiter was approaching carrying two plates covered by ornate silver lids, and he was prevented from replying. After placing the plates elegantly in front of Hester and Marcus, the waiter removed both covers with a flourish. Marcus wrinkled his nose distastefully at the smell of the fish and pushed his plate away. Hester, however, inhaled the scent of the sole with relish and licked her lips. Then she looked up at him and smiled guilelessly. "Eat up, Marcus. Some nutritious food will go a long way to improving your mood."

He ground his teeth. "So tell me, how bad is it? How much money does the company need?"

She finished her mouthful and dabbed her mouth delicately with the edge of the linen napkin before replying. "Thousands."

"How many thousands?"

"A hundred."

Had he been eating he would have choked. "A *hundred thousand pounds*? Why on earth have we come to *Chez Nous* if things are that bad?"

Her face hardened as she looked at him straight in the eye. "I have standards, Marcus, as should you. People expect certain things from the Knebworths. Now eat up your dinner before it gets cold."

"I would rather hear about what happened to Aunt Bea."

She flinched. "Aunt Bea, as you call her, no longer exists."

"So I discovered today," he said wryly. "It would appear that I now have an Uncle Bertie instead." He shook his head in disbelief. "Is that why she disappeared all those years ago, Mother? Did you chase her away because she decided to change her sex?"

Hester slowly put her fork back into the sole. "I don't want to talk about it."

"Well, you're just going to have to."

"No, Marcus, I'm not."

"You are. I want the truth. Why didn't you tell us what had happened? Why didn't you say that she was transgender?"

Hester went pale and then red. A bead of sweat oozed out of the flawless make-up on her forehead, making it smudge.

"Well?" he demanded. "Are you going to explain or am I going to leave and embarrass you in front of everyone here at the restaurant?"

She put down her fork and opened her mouth but no words emerged.

He stood up.

"What are you doing?" she spluttered.

He smiled grimly. "Until you are ready to tell me, it seems that we have nothing more to say to each other."

"But what about your dinner?" she tried, her voice miraculously recovered. "If you're going to pay for it you might as well enjoy it."

"If I'm going to pay for it?" he repeated incredulously.

"It's the least you can do under the circumstances."

An unpleasant laugh burst out of him, causing people at nearby tables to turn and look. Oblivious, he scraped back his chair. "You are ridiculous, do you know that?" he spat.

Then he strode out of the restaurant without the trace of a limp.

HESTER – Present Day

Furious, Hester let herself into the manor and picked up the phone to dial a code that would make it impossible for the recipient to trace her. The phone rang at the other end several times before it was answered.

"Yeah?"

"Jimmy, it's me."

There was no answer.

"You owe me a favour," she continued sharply.

When the line went dead, she redialled. Nobody answered. She made herself a cup of coffee and tried again. And again. And again. Eventually, he gave in and answered.

"What the fuck are you playing at? Leave me alone."

"Oh Jimmy, you have such a short memory. Please don't try to evade me. You can't escape. You know I'll find you wherever you are. Now then, let's be civilised and talk business."

"I don't do civilised, lady."

"Now that's a real shame. I find it hard to believe that you would like the police to hear all about your little secret after all this time." She listened carefully for the sharp intake of breath and then inhaled with a pleasurable flutter of her eyelids. "Oh, Jimmy, you are in a pickle, aren't you?"

"Bitch," he cursed. "What do you want me to do?"

"There's a piece of land I need bulldozing. And please don't try any funny business. I've lodged a letter with my solicitor containing details of places, people, dates, times; you know the kind of thing I mean. If anything should happen to me, he's under strict instructions to take it straight to the police. There's enough evidence in there to put you away for life."

He gulped. "When?"

"Tonight."

"*Tonight?*" he said, in astonishment. "Where the fuck am I going to get a bulldozer tonight?"

"You'll find a way. You have to find a way. Because if you don't…"

Raido reversed – fear

Chapter Ten

RAFF – Present Day

Raff had been working for hours on the artefact. Twenty-three pendants were attached to a chain in two rows of eleven on each side with the final one at the bottom. Two crystals were attached by wire to the bottom stone. The upper one appeared to be an amber bead, while the lower was almost certainly a selenite wand. The metal was a mixture of bronze and gold, and because gold does not tarnish or rust, this probably explained its excellent condition. As for the stones, each had a rune carved into it, an early Germanic/Scandinavian form of letters from pre-Latin days. It was impossible to say whether these letters were meant to be read or were purely for decoration. All Selena had told him was that, according to her friend, the rune carved between the amber and selenite on the bottom stone meant a gift.

The crystals particularly fascinated him. Amber was usually found in the Baltic but was also occasionally discovered in the south of the British Isles. It began as resin that oozed from a diseased or damaged tree that provided protection to the wood from insects, small animals, and pathogens. In order to determine whether this piece of amber was real or fake, he rubbed it vigorously with a cloth, and held it up to his nose where he was indeed able to detect a scent of tree resin. Encouraged, he looked at the cloth and found an oily residue. The static charge between the amber and his hair was the final confirmation that the amber was almost certainly genuine. The shape inside the amber looked like the remains of an insect that had crawled onto the thick, sticky resin of the tree and become stuck. Carefully, he inserted the amber under his portable microscope and was able to identify part of a wasp-like creature with a striped coat of yellow and black.

Awestruck, he sat back. He was holding an extraordinary example of pre-history, far older than anything he had ever dealt with before. The creature inside this stone could be anything up to 100 million years old which made the 4,000-year-old Bronze Age site look positively modern.

Fascinated, he turned to the selenite. The white crystal was a transparent version of gypsum comprising the crystallisation of calcium sulphate. Usually found in granular, tabular, and prismatic shards, it was a rather soft stone and unlikely to be as old as the amber. Suspecting that it might be a later addition made of glass, he held it against his cheek, but it was warm whereas glass would have been cold. When he carefully inserted it under the microscope, he was excited to see countless air bubbles and speckles of impurities. Finally, he held it up above his face. It looked like liquid light. Genuine selenite, then.

Whatever this necklace, or whatever it was, turned out to be, this was no piece of junk.

A yawn took him by surprise. Looking at his watch, he discovered that it was nearly 2am. Disappointed that he would have to give what was increasingly looking like a genuine artefact back to Selena in only a few hours time, he carefully wrapped up the chain and its crystals in some brown paper, put the microscope back in its box, and tidied up. Unable to face going upstairs to a cold bed, he decided to rest in the kitchen for what was left of the night. Fetching his jacket from the back of the door, he shrugged it on and sank back into the old and rather cracked red leather armchair by the window.

In seconds he had closed his eyes. At first, the silence was comforting, but just as he was starting to drift off to sleep, he became aware of the sound of crackling flames and a strong scent of wood being burned. Trying to remember whether he had lit the dying embers in the fireplace, he was just about to force his eyes back open when he became aware of a pain in his leg and ribs. Uncomfortable, he shifted his weight. It didn't help. He wondered if he was hungry. After all, he had eaten nothing since breakfast. Maybe it would help him to relax if he made himself a cup of tea and tried to find a biscuit.

Reluctantly, he prepared to move, but before he could put his foot to the ground he felt the sensation of plummeting downwards. He tried to fight against the feeling but smoke began to choke his lungs and before he could stop himself, he was falling into a deep, dark hole.

circa 2000 B.C.E.

As Riadd reached out to tend the fire in his hut, he barely noticed the wound that Mevin had inflicted on him in the fight. Now that Seela was in his hut with him, the pain barely seemed to matter. Instead, he felt an overwhelming protectiveness towards her, rather than the usual need to protect himself.

He stopped poking the logs with a stick and turned to face her, surprised that she had stayed away from her injured sister for so long. Her response to his work had been unexpected, her green eyes lighting up in surprise and pleasure at his skill in both carving and music. Now she was sitting on one of the benches he had carved, stroking the smooth wood under her hands, looking at him eagerly.

"So," she said, "are you going to tell me what your idea is?"

Summoning the confidence to tell her, he looked around the hut, feeling a surge of pride in his dwelling with its tools and animal carvings. He had not expected to be allowed to build his own hut after the death of his parents, but Lanalla had shown him favour and now treated him as her own son. This status had helped him within the community, and in his own way, he was seen as important.

Limping over to the table, he picked up a stone polisher and rubbed it with his fingers. Then he straightened his shoulders and stood tall, making the most of his gangly height. "I would like to keep you safe," he said rather clumsily as his voice broke on the words. "I am the most skilled carver in the settlement and I would like to offer you my protection." When she said nothing but only looked confused, he started to feel stupid. What was he thinking? She needed a fighter, not a carver. He was of no use to her at all with his body growing in the wrong direction, upwards rather than outwards. Feeling himself beginning to slouch, he forced himself to straighten. "If you were handfasted, Mevin would not be able to touch you," he continued bravely. "My Ceremony of Manhood will be held in three moons."

At last she responded by shaking her head. "Mevin won't wait for three moons."

"I will make him promise not to take you until I can fight for you."

"You would fight for me? But you could never beat Mevin."

"I won't have to. We will trick him. We will be handfasted before the fight. All you have to do is to choose me. Then, as my mate, he can have no claim on you." Before she could protest further, he put his fingers to his lips and whistled. The dog appeared as though he had been waiting for a summons and sat by his feet. "Go and fetch Lanalla," he ordered. Bika seemed to understand and ran out of the hut.

What seemed like only moments later, there was a rustling at the door, and the priestess arrived. "You wanted me?" she asked, blowing on her hands to warm them.

"Yes," Riadd said, his voice still wavering up and down. "I want you to bring forward my Ceremony of Manhood. Seela and I want to be handfasted."

Lanalla looked as though she was about to laugh. Then she became serious. "Riadd, my son, what are you talking about?"

"I want to protect Seela from Mevin," he said earnestly.

Lanalla shook her head and then smiled indulgently. "You are a sweet boy but I have taken her under my protection. You need not worry. I will look after her."

Riadd tried to quell his rising frustration. "But Seela has agreed. She wants to be handfasted to me, don't you Seela?"

"But she hardly knows you," said Lanella. As annoyance passed over Riadd's face, she spread her hands in an attempt to calm him. "Riadd, what is this all about?"

He sniffed and held his head high. "Mevin has called for an Ordeal to decide the next Leader, and he is bound to win. He cannot claim Seela for himself if she and I have been handfasted."

The priestess's eyes widened with surprise. "Ah, I see. That is clever. But it will not work. You do not have the power of manhood, yet."

"Then make me a man now," he pleaded. "Afterwards you can bind us, so that no matter what happens in the Ordeal, he will not be able to take her."

Lanalla reached out to touch him on the arm but Riadd flinched and she stepped back. "You know I cannot perform any ceremonies without the Amulet," she continued after a few moments of silence.

His eyes widened. He had not thought about that.

"The Amulet gives me the ear of The Mother," Lanalla continued. "Without it, She cannot hear me and I have no power."

Riadd thought fast. "Then perform the ceremonies without the Amulet. You are priestess. That is power enough."

"Are you saying that you want me to deceive The Mother?" She asked shocked.

"Of course not. You would not be deceiving Her. You've always said that you talk to Her all the time. You do not need the Amulet to make me a man and to handfast Seela and me. Just do it and Seela will be saved."

RAFF – Present Day

Heart hammering, Raff woke with a start as a feeling of foreboding rushed up into his throat. He felt like a teenager again, as though he had just heard that his mother had cancer. Tears pricked the back of his eyes. He forced the grief down until his eyes had cleared. Then he saw something glinting in the darkness. Swallowing hard, he pushed himself to his feet and searched for the light switch.

Only then did he remember that he was in the kitchen. Back aching from where he had sat awkwardly, he stretched. Apart from the glint, it was pitch black and the light switch was on the other side of the room. Reaching his hands out so that he could avoid bumping into any obstacles, he carefully he made his way past the table to the wall by the door. The glint was turning into a glow. Selena's necklace was on the table, wasn't it? But surely he had wrapped it up. The strange light must be coming from something else.

As soon as he found the switch and could see again, he looked at the table. As he had known it would be, the necklace was carefully wrapped up in brown paper. His tools were in a pouch and the microscope was in its box. There was no sign of a torch or anything else that could have emitted any sort of glimmer. And yet he remembered thinking that the selenite was like liquid light.

And liquid light glowed, didn't it?

With a shiver, he looked at his watch. It was still only 2.30 am. Cold to his core, he stood and filled the kettle, but as he reached for a tea bag the dream started to replay in his mind. Something was terribly wrong. For a moment, he stood stock still, trying to work out if this was tiredness playing on his mind or a warning.

Suddenly restless and desperate for fresh air, he switched off the kettle, picked up a torch, put his phone in his pocket, and left the farmhouse.

Outside the night was clear but the wind was strong. Too strong. He began to worry. Had he fixed the tarp securely enough over the workings before leaving the dig yesterday? He had been so eager to look at the necklace that he couldn't be sure.

Cursing himself for being careless, he began to run, not bothering to switch on the torch even though there was little moonlight. Occasionally he tripped over stones and roots that lay hidden in the dark on the valley's track, but his feet seemed to know the way as though he had run the track a thousand times before in the dark.

Using the silhouette of the massive, crooked monument on Stone Clump to guide his way, it wasn't long before he arrived at the field. As soon as he reached the covered workings, he heard the sound of flapping. Hastily he pulled the torch from his pocket and shone its light onto the tarp, but bizarrely it was still in place. Mystified, he bent down to check that the covering really was securely fixed and was just pulling at one of the ropes when he became aware of a strange trembling beneath his feet. Straightening, he looked around. Not only was there the unexpected sound of an engine in the quiet of the night, but a strange light appeared to be approaching from behind the Portakabin at the top of the rise, throwing the structure into sharp relief. In moments two bright lights were moving towards him, bouncing up and down as though they were travelling over rutted ground.

It was a tractor and it was driving straight towards him.

Hastily he rose to his full height and placed himself squarely in front of the workings. Then he waved his arms wildly in warning. For a moment, he thought that the large vehicle was not going to stop, but it suddenly ground to a halt only feet away.

The driver jumped out, yelling over the noise of the engine. "Move. Get out of the way!"

The lights were blinding. "What are you doing?" shouted Raff. "This is an archaeological site." The driver shouted something back but Raff couldn't make out the words above the noise. "Turn off the engine. I can't hear you." Raff held his breath to see what would happen. After several moments, the sound lessened to the dull whirring of the engine turning over.

"Get out of the bloody way," the tractor driver yelled. "I've got a job to do."

"What do you mean you've got a job to do?" Raff shouted back.

"I've been told to plough up the field."

"In the middle of the night?"

"Just move."

"Who has told you to do this?"

"Mind your own fucking business. Move or I'll plough you into the ground as well."

Raff took the mobile phone out of his pocket and held it up for the driver to see. "I wouldn't if I were you. I've already telephoned the police," he bluffed, "and they should be here any minute. Perhaps you'd like to explain to them what exactly it is that you're trying to do and who wants you to do it."

For a moment, he thought the driver was going to lunge at him, but the man evidently changed his mind because, while shouting expletives, he jumped back into the cab, revved the engine and began reversing back up the field.

Raff let out the breath he had been holding and fumbled with his phone, trying to switch it on. Blast, it was out of battery. He had been so keen to start the restoration work on the necklace that he had forgotten to charge it. A good job that the driver hadn't realised he was bluffing about having called the police. As soon as he could no longer see the tractor, he ran up to the Portakabin and turned on every light he could find in an attempt to prove that he was not alone. Shocked that someone had tried to destroy the dig, he paced around the cabin, wondering what he should do, but as the adrenaline drained away he began to falter. By now it was 4 am. He needed to sleep but he didn't dare leave the place in case a second attempt was made.

In the end, the only sensible decision was to spend the rest of the night outside by the workings. Taking an old but warm sleeping bag that Falala had stuffed inside a cupboard for emergencies, he trudged back down the field again, making himself as comfortable as he could in the cold of the damp night air. For a long time, he gazed up into the night, still too wired to sleep, but eventually, when he had given up any hope of rest, his eyes began to close.

In moments he found himself falling again.

circa 2000 B.C.E.

"I tell you, I don't care that you don't have the Amulet," cried Riadd. "The Mother will hear you. Forget the Ceremony of Manhood. Just handfast us. Make Seela safe."

Lanalla looked from one to the other, thinking fast. She wanted to keep Riadd onside but an idea was beginning to shape itself inside her head. If she was to remain priestess, she needed a SeeSayer. She had thought to choose Duna as her next prophetess but the little girl was dying. As soon as the inevitable happened, Seela would flee and she would have lost her first chance of keeping New Blood for the settlement. She had been racking her brains in an attempt to work out how she could keep the girl but it was possible that Riadd had just presented her with a solution.

Sliding her ceremonial knife out from its pouch on her belt, she reached out her free hand. "Very well. Seela, hold out your left arm." Before the girl had a chance to object, she cut the inside of Seela's wrist with a long stroke of the blade. "Now you, Riadd."

For a moment he was too shocked to respond. There had been no prayers, no entreaties to The Mother, no solemn promises between them. He looked at Seela to see what he should do. The girl's eyes were huge and frightened and she was gasping from the pain of the cut. Quickly he rolled up the sleeves of his skins and held out his arm.

But Lanalla did not make a similar cut on the boy. Instead she said: "Seela, do you promise that you will follow the Mother in all Her ways?"

Scared, the girl stared at her.

"Seela, I need to hear your voice," said the priestess.

Seela did not understand what was happening. Riadd was frowning. She didn't know what to do.

Quickly, Lanalla closed her eyes as though she was at last praying. She conjured up a picture of the Amulet in her mind. Had she been holding it, she would have put it round Seela's neck. "Riadd, step away from Seela," she demanded suddenly. Carefully, she reached into her pouch again and this time, pulled out a clump of wool and a long piece of material. "Seela, give me your arm."

By now Seela was shaking. Warily, she held out her wounded arm to the priestess.

Lanalla placed the wool on the cut and then wound the cloth around it three times. The little bird on Seela's shoulder blinked but did not move. Finally, Lanalla began to chant in a low, sing-song voice:

I bind you from Behind,
I bind you from Before,
I bind you in the Midst,
I bind you to the Floor.

I bind you from Above,
I bind you from Below,
I bind you to the Centre,
That you may never Go.

I bind you from the Left,
 I bind you from the Right,
I bind you by the Day,
I bind you by the Night.

I bind you to this Place,
I bind you to this Kin,
I bind you to this Magick,
Let it unfold and Spin...

Riadd cried out in alarm. "What are you doing, Lanalla? Those are not the words for handfasting."

"I am sorry, Riadd, I had no choice. I have to keep the village safe."

"I do not understand..."

"I have made Seela our new SeeSayer," she said quietly.

"You have what?"

"I have made S..."

"But a SeeSayer cannot be handfasted. Undo it."

"I cannot, Riadd, son of my heart. Seela cannot be your mate. She belongs to The Mother now."

Stunned, Riadd's jaw dropped open. "What do you mean, you have given her to The Mother?"

"She can be with no man."

"But how will I be able to protect her from Mevin?"

Lanalla stood as tall as she could and spoke in her most authoritative voice. "I will be the one to protect her. She cannot be your mate."

Dumbfounded, he stared at her. "But you said you could do nothing without the Amulet."

"I saw it in my mind. It was enough."

He stepped very close to her. "Are you telling me that you have tricked us?"

Lanalla had never seen Riadd so angry before. Suddenly frightened, she tried to smile but the corners of her mouth refused to move. "I'm telling you that I have saved Seela," she managed to protest. "Now she is the SeeSayer, Mevin cannot touch her."

Riadd stared at her in disbelief. "Are you mad? Have you forgotten that Mana was killed by Hogan?" He slammed his hand into his fist. "Being the SeeSayer didn't protect her at all. What have you done?"

Lanalla turned ashen white. "I …"

"You have betrayed us both."

"No, I …"

"I will never forgive you for this."

SELENA – Present Day

My pearly eye is going crazy. I should never have agreed to stay the night at Bertie's house.

"Dear girl, you're the perfect dream subject," he says excitedly. "Just look at this picture of your brain-waves."

I struggle up into a sitting position. "I don't care," I splutter. "I just want to go."

"But don't you want to see what happened?"

"No," I protest. "I want to leave."

"But it's the middle of the night. At least have some more sleep. You can go after breakfast."

"I want to go now," I insist sharply.

"You're not thinking clearly, dear girl. Let me tell you about your dream before you…"

"Sorry," I say. "Another time."

He doesn't give up. "Then how about a nice cup of tea? I've got some of Larna's cake here, too. She gave it to me especially. Perfect for a post-midnight feast. Then, if you still want to leave, I'll drive you back in *Marigold*."

I feel for the necklace in my pocket. It isn't there. Of course, I have lent it to Raff. "Okay," I lie. "Thank you."

As soon as he's in his kitchen, I bolt. Outside, it is a clear pitch black apart from a crescent moon in the sky. The Stennings are ten miles from Oxford, and there are no buses at this time of night. I've never been much of an athlete, but when fear is driving you, it's surprising how far you can run without stopping. Once I've got my second wind, my body falls into a soothing rhythm that not only propels me forward along the empty roads but also starts to settle me after the dream. Lanalla tricked Riadd and me. She was supposed to handfast us, and instead, she made me the SeeSayer. I don't even know what a SeeSayer is. She had no right to do that without my consent. She... I stop myself. What am I thinking? It wasn't me she betrayed, it was Seela. I doubt they even had the word consent in those times. Pushing myself harder, I run faster but it's a mistake and soon I have to slow down to a fast walk.

By the time I see Stone Clump in the distance, I am almost crawling. Dawn is beginning to streak the sky and birds have started to sing. All I want now is to get the necklace back. Panting, I rap at the farmhouse door but there is no response. I shouldn't be surprised, of course. Raff must be asleep. I knock harder, but there is still nothing. Focussing my pearly eye inside the house, I detect something, but it's not Raff. Alarm bells start ringing in my head. What if he has broken his promise and taken the necklace to his friend in London as he wanted to?

Stung by the possibility of another betrayal, I tune into my pearly eye as though it can tell me where Raff is. To my surprise, a clear image of the dig comes into my mind from my pearly eye. Turning away from the farmhouse, I start running again.

It doesn't take long to skirt Stone Clump. Once I reach the stream, I stop and follow the line of the field up towards the Portakabin. A grey shroud of mist covers the field like a blanket and I start to shiver as I begin to walk again, if only to keep my legs from seizing up. With no idea why I have come here, my gaze is suddenly caught by movement. There is something lying on the ground by the workings.

"Seela?"

The disembodied voice stops me in my tracks. For a moment, it stops my breath, too. My green eye focuses on the ground where something is beginning to rise out of the mist.

"Seela, is that you?"

It's not a person. How can it be? Is it a ghost, then? My mind frantically tries to rationalise what I am hearing. Seela has called to me before. She has even appeared in front of me, where I can see her properly. But this is different.

"Seela?"

The voice is more frantic this time. The shape is rising higher now. It seems to go on forever, upwards and upwards and up...

"Riadd?" I reply. Suddenly I feel sick. Are Seela and Riadd both able to appear in front of me now, or am I dreaming again? Despite the fatigue, I can't stop my legs from taking me to him in the field. I don't know what I'll discover, only that he needs me, and that Lanalla is no longer on our side. As I enter the mist, it parts like the Red Sea, and I find myself looking at a tall man, not a youth. My brain seems to shift. He is too old to be Riadd. Perhaps I'm not dreaming after all. "Raff," I correct myself, as though I am trying the name on my tongue to see if it sounds right. "It's me, Selena."

His forehead furrows as he is torn from one world into another.

Stepping closer, I reach my hand out towards him. It is shaking. "Here, let me help you stand." His hand is freezing cold as though he had been dead for centuries. "You need to warm up," I say quickly. "Come on. Let's go up to the

Portakabin." I grasp his arm and pull. As he tries to walk, he sways so uncertainly on his feet that I have to reach round his waist to steady him.

Once we're safely inside, I sit him down and find a blanket to drape around his shoulders. Then I fill the kettle. While I am waiting for it to boil, I search for his glasses. They are on the table, so I put them in his hands. Turning back to the makeshift kitchen, I make some coffee for us both, pouring some cold water into his so that he will be able to drink it and not scald his tongue. Then I hold my hands around his as he cradles the mug.

After several sips, he blinks hard, and colour starts to come back into his face. Finally, he looks at me. "Selena, have you got a mobile phone on you?"

It's not a question I was expecting. I shake my head.

"Mine's dead," he continues. "I need to phone the police."

"The police? Why, what's happened?"

"There was a tractor. It tried to destroy the workings. I had to stay in case another attempt was made."

"What?"

"If I give you his address, will you go and fetch Marcus for me?"

At the thought of the white-haired man, something in me falters. "I'd rather get Fally," I say quickly. "Where does she live?" He gives me her address and I turn to go. "Are you going to be all right while I'm gone?"

For a split second, he looks at me with something like pain in his eyes. Then, slowly he nods.

Tired as I am, it doesn't take me long to get to Fally's flat. To my surprise, she answers my ring at her bell straight away as though she also hasn't been able to sleep. As soon as I tell her what has happened, we jump into her battered old car. For a while, I don't think it's going to start but eventually we are able to chug down the street back to the dig.

"Thank God you're here," Raff calls as soon as we arrive. "Has Selena explained to you what happened?"

"She's told me that a tractor tried to sabotage the dig last night, and that you slept outside in case another attempt was made." She reaches into her pocket. "Here's my phone. You can call the police."

He shakes his head and frowns uncertainly. "Actually, I'm not so sure that we should anymore. Apart from some tractor marks, there's not enough to report."

"Won't they be able to identify the tractor from the tyre tracks?"

"Oxfordshire is full of farms with tractors. They're hardly likely to come and check it out when no actual crime has been committed."

"Oh, I see what you mean" Falala says. "When did the tractor appear?"

"In the early hours."

"What on earth were you doing here then?"

He's shaking his head. "I don't know. Call it a premonition."

"Bloody hell," she says with feeling. Then she shakes her head with disbelief. "Who would want to sabotage the dig? It doesn't make sense."

He shrugs. "I've no idea. I suppose it could have been a mistake. Perhaps he got the wrong field."

"But the only time farmers plough their fields in the middle of the night is at harvest and that's six months away." She spoons coffee granules into three mugs and pours on hot water.

"How are we going to make the field safe?" Raff asks, still looking pale, and with dark, haunted rings under his eyes. "I can't sleep outside here every night in case it happens again."

"No, you can't," says Falala as she adds milk and stirs. "I wonder what Marcus is going to say."

"It'll doubtless make him feel even more paranoid," Raff mutters under his breath.

Falala hands a mug to each of us. "Have a little compassion."

"Sorry. I'm just tired, that's all."

"Of course you are. Look, I'll call Clem and see what he suggests. His number's in my phone. It'll be too early for him to be at work but I'll leave a message." She sits down and looks at me, realising that I haven't said a word. "Selena, you look just as pale as Raff. Are you okay?"

"Yes," I mutter. I'm not about to tell her that I spent half the night being experimented on, or that I have half run, half walked more than ten miles and am dead on my feet.

"Well, you both look dreadful. Go home. I'll stay here, guard the fort, tell Marcus what happened and then phone Clem."

"Are you sure?" Raff yawns.

"Absolutely. Now bugger off, both of you."

He looks gratefully towards the door. "Thanks, Fally. You're a brick. Come on, Selena, let's go."

It's a relief to be outside in full daylight again. I follow Raff down the field, past the workings to the stream at the bottom, and over the stepping stones, wondering if I dare ask him about the necklace. Once we're over, he stops. "Well, this is where we part ways," he says, "but before you go, tell me why you are out here so early. Have you been walking again through the night?"

"Sort of."

"That's becoming a bit of a habit, isn't it?"

His tone is kind enough, but I don't want to explain any further, so I decide to take the plunge. "Did you have a chance to look at the necklace last night?"

He takes off his glasses and puts them in his pocket. "Yes, I did."

"And?"

"It's looking much better than it did."

"May I come with you and get it now?"

He looks surprised, but nods. "Of course."

We walk together in silence to the back door of the farmhouse where he lets us in with an old key. "Tea?" he asks.

I shake my head. I've already drunk more caffeine this morning than I would in a week.

"Okay," he says. Then he walks over to the oak table, puts on some plastic gloves and unwraps the brown paper from a package. "Here, what do you think?" he asks, holding it out to me.

The transformation is astonishing. The necklace is almost unrecognisable from the chain I found in the ground. Where the necklace was rusty before, the metal chain is now gleaming and the stone pendants look as though they have only just been carved. As for the amber and selenite, they look like eyes of different colours, with the grey stone in between. They call to me and, for the first time, I see a reflection of my pearly eye in the white of the selenite. I go to take it from him, but he holds it back.

"Oh no you don't," he warns. "First you must put some gloves on. Remember, the acid from your skin will damage it."

Reluctantly I put on the gloves he hands me. Then I pick up the necklace. Despite the latex, there is still enough of a buzz for a connection to be made. Strength begins to seep into me and, relieved, finally I begin to relax. "Did you discover anything about it while you were working?" I ask.

He shakes his head. "Not much, I'm afraid," he yawns. "The metal is a mixture of bronze and gold, and as you already suspected, the crystals are indeed amber and selenite. The insect inside the amber looks as though it's a prehistoric wasp. I've no idea how old the necklace is, how long it's been in the ground, or what it is exactly, but I do think you should get it looked at properly. If it's as extraordinary as I think it might be, you should send it away to be analysed."

"Sorry," I murmur, "but I'm not letting it go again."

Despite his obvious weariness, he suddenly looks surprised. "Why not?" he asks. "It could be worth a small fortune." Puzzled, he searches my face as though he might find an answer in it. "It would only take a week or so. And I'd send it to my friend. He's completely trustworthy."

"No," I repeat.

Bemused, he shakes his head. "Then at least promise me that you'll keep it wrapped up and out of the rain, and that you'll always wear gloves when you handle it. It could be important. And digging it up here in the Stennings, so close to whatever we are unearthing … well, it could be valuable to the dig."

"But I didn't find it anywhere near your field," I say defensively. This necklace is mine; no-one else's.

"Maybe not, but it wasn't so very far away." He reaches for a box of gloves. "Here, take these."

Reluctantly, I take them, but if he thinks I'm going to put them on, he's kidding himself. Still, he won't ever know that I've continued to touch it with my bare hands so I try to smile. "Thank you."

He looks at me again. "Before you go, tell me why this necklace, if that's what it is, is so important to you."

It's a reasonable enough question but I have no wish to answer it. Changing the subject, I point to the sheet music on the music stand in the corner of the kitchen. "What have you been playing?"

"Bach," he says, following my gaze.

"Oh, I love Bach," I say. "Will you play for me?"

He looks at me in surprise. "To be honest, I am rather tired."

"I know. Me too. But some music might help to calm us both."

Almost reluctantly, he nods and picks the flute up from the oak table. Then he walks over to the music stand, turns the music back to the first page, straightens, and lifts the instrument to his lips. As though he is pausing to kiss the mouthpiece, he changes the shape of his lips to create the embouchure.

From the first sound, it is obvious that he is a superb musician. The initial long, low note is so pure that it seems to hover in the air like a bird. It begins to soar as the music opens up into a melody as if the bird has taken flight. I want to sing and allow the music to take me to a place where there is no pain.

Once he has finished he gazes at me for a long moment until I have to look away. "Your turn," he says quietly.

"My turn?" I query.

"Yes, will you play the harp for me?"

Suddenly I feel vulnerable. Music may transport you to a different place, but it also reveals who you really are. Before I can find an excuse, he takes the cover off the harp and reveals the magnificent instrument. Glorious as a Viking ship and complete with goddess prow, her strings are pristine in cream, red and black, the wood shiny from carefully polishing. Placing one of the chairs behind the harp, he beckons me over.

The feeling that courses through me as I touch her is nearly as powerful as the necklace, and I inhale the sound deeply into me as though I might drink in her magic. Slowly, I once again set about checking the strings for tuning. When each is vibrating with its fifth in perfect harmony, I allow my fingers to start moving across them in running arpeggios. As I begin to play, her sound spreads out like a flower opening its petals as music erupts from my fingers. It's the song that Seela heard while she was up in the tree trying to save her sister. Reminded of the deaths of Mum and Mara, I have to force myself to continue until I rise upwards out of grief into something yet to be discovered.

Raff must feel it too because he picks up his flute again, puts it to his lips and improvises with me. To start with we dance around each other hesitantly but it's not long till we are weaving a colourful tapestry of sound together. Sometimes we run away from each other in dissonance, while at other times we come together in harmony. Finally, we dare to tease each other, as though we are rediscovering the playful children we once were.

When the music eventually draws to a close, the echoes of the notes die away to sleep within the walls. Then we look at each other. Scared that he has seen who I truly am, I push the harp away from my shoulder and stand.

He strides over and stands so close that I can smell his scent of cinnamon and apples. Unable to help myself, I stare into his deep black eyes, the pupils so big that they threaten to drown whoever looks into them.

As though he might find the answer to one of life's great questions in my skin, he asks me to show him how to play.

The question makes my breath snag before I realise that he is asking for a harp lesson. Part of me is desperate to run away but the other part of me wants to stay. In the end, my body decides for me and I find myself stepping away from the chair so that he can take my place. Once I have moved to stand at his back, I begin to explain. "There are forty-seven strings on this harp. Each is pitched high from the short ones at the top, to the low long ones at the bottom. The red strings are Cs, the blacks are Fs."

He holds out his hand to me. "Show me."

His fingers are long and beautifully honed like a Rodin

225

sculpture. In order to touch them, I have to lean forward and put my arms around him. As our hands momentarily rest together, skin tasting skin, it is as much as I can do not to gasp out loud. I've never felt anything like this before and the feeling is so intense that it almost hurts. "Curl your fingers in towards each other when they're not playing," I instruct. "Every time you play a note, each finger must return here, as though it's coming home. Take your first finger and put it like this. When you pull, you'll make a sound like a bell…"

As my voice falls away, he plucks a string, making the whole room quiver. The second time he plucks, the vibrations shudder me through to the core. My legs start to feel weak but there is nowhere for me to sit unless I peal myself away from him and break the connection and I cannot bear to do that.

But then he is pushing the harp away and turning to face me, his eyes now cave-deep. As he takes my trembling hands in his, the touch of his skin becomes unbearable. I crave it and yet want to push it away. My eyes fall to his mouth. It is quivering like a bee waiting to land on a scented, pollen-rich flower. Weakened, my eyes fall closed and I feel the touch of his lips on mine.

The kiss takes me away from myself. At the same time, it carves me into something entirely real. An electric current runs through me, causing the hairs on my body to rise, sweet as apple blossom, yet deadly as though they are full of poison.

As he pulls away, he looks deeply into my green eye.

"May I?" he whispers.

I freeze. He is gazing at my eyepatch. Terrified that his look of longing will turn to one of disgust, I shake my head.

"Please."

Before I can stop my treacherous fingers, they reach up and pull the mask down. I wait for revulsion to mar his face. Instead there's a look of wonder. My pearly eye stills. It has not been looked at this deeply since doctors peered and prodded me when I was a child, finally agreeing that there was nothing they could do. Fizzing with expectation, it throbs with warning. Yet it feels gentled and stares back at him, as though it has nothing to do with me at all.

Then something shifts, and I find myself looking out of it at him. It is a strange kind of gazing. It doesn't see his outside appearance but inside him. Different rainbow colours are flowing in and out of each other, merging and yet remaining distinct like oil on water.

It's like looking into his soul.

There's a buzzing in my ears and a swirling in my chest and my pearly eye smiles.

RAFF – Present Day

As Raff stared into the pearly eye, he felt himself sinking. At first, the feeling was not unpleasant. He was a good swimmer, and this felt like a dive into a pool that took him the entire length underwater. But when it was time for him to raise his head and breathe, he found that he could not. Panic hit him like a fist in the face as his lungs began to heat up, demanding release. In moments they were on fire, consuming him, catapulting him into space and a blackness that threatened to eat him alive. Beyond fear, he could only watch as images sped past him too fast for him to be able to comprehend. Then, without warning, it was all over and he was breathing again; the blackness turned back into colours, and everything around him still.

Where he had been tired before, now he was exhausted. With effort, he peeled himself away from Selena's eye and sat back in the chair.

"Are you all right, Raff?" Selena asked. "You have gone very pale."

He didn't know how to answer "I'll be fine," he muttered. "I just need to sleep." He didn't want her to go, but that was what he was saying, wasn't it? That he wanted to be left alone to rest.

"Me too," she said, suddenly looking vulnerable as she raised her eyepatch back into place.

And before he had realised it, she had gone. For a long moment, he felt stunned, as though there was no more air to breathe. He began to shiver. It was like being outside at the dig all over again with no protection, no safety, no sanctuary.

He was at the mercy of this woman and his mind. Whatever was happening to him was way out of his comfort zone and there was nothing he could do to stop it.

KARL – Present Day

Karl stared at the four new paintings that now covered the walls of his bedroom. In the first, the trees were menacing, full of shadows and the howling of wolves. One of them was stalking round the base of a tree, looking upwards as though its prey was hiding in the branches.

In the second, a blackbird was singing in snowy darkness, trying to sew the leaves of a tree together to create a screen which would hide them all.

In a third, a man figure lurked in a forest. Thin and unkempt, his eyes were full of loathing. He was playing with something round his neck which gleamed in his hand as though fired by a sun that nobody else could see.

Thankful that he had not painted anything else, Karl closed his eyes, but as soon as the darkness hit his retinas he found himself hurtling downwards. It was like being propelled through space: round and round, in and out, spiralling and yet falling.

By the time he landed, he was so disorientated that it took him a long moment to decide what was up and what was down. Then he realised that he was in some sort of a cave. On the walls were ancient paintings of animals, activities and people. He recognised them all as though somehow, he had painted these, too.

On the floor in the corner lay a ragged figure he had not seen before. She seemed to be asleep, although her eyes were open. Unable to stand any longer, he sank to his knees. At the same time, the woman morphed into the red-haired girl he had drawn so many times before.

Terrified, he reached up his arms as if he could fly out of the cave and back into his bedroom, but disjointed words and phrases were filling the air like bats, pinning him down.

Something inside him screamed and flew out of him.

The link was broken.

<

Kenaz – light

Chapter Eleven

circa 2000 B.C.E.

The day was to be taken up with preparation for the Ordeal. Several sheep, pigs and an ox were butchered for the feast, and smells of roasting meat filled the village as the Folk prepared to send the warriors into the cold of the night. Each of the four contenders were to go into a different part of the forest and stay alone until dawn to prove bravery and initiative, a challenge that would precede the trials of more physical strength.

When the sun was high in the sky, everyone met in the central space of the village. Heavy, squat pots decorated with thick rims and flat bases were brought out filled with food and offerings. Usually used for storing dry foods, they were now representative of collective wealth so that the warriors would feel pride in the quest they were about to undertake. The huge central fire had been stoked high and there should have been much merriment as the feasting began, but everyone knew this was a sham. Now Hogan was gone, Mevin was the strongest among them. He was bound to win and all their lives would inexorably change.

As the sun began to dull, the villagers stood to clear the space for the dance of the Ordeal.

To everyone's surprise, Mevin was absent. This shocked many but gave heart to some. Lanalla should have waited for him to appear but instead took the opportunity to begin the ceremony, hoping that if he did not attend, he would forfeit his chance to compete.

Silence fell as hands were joined around the fire. The sound of a loud drum split the air and the people began to sway without moving their feet. The drum was huge, its reverberations deep and compelling. Made from deerskin stretched over a hollowed piece of wood, it was painted with animals and plants. A woman joined in with another, smaller drum, also beautifully decorated, and added a faster rhythm to intensify the dance. As one, people stepped to the left, then right, moving in time as a different group of women started to sing. Long streams of notes began to join together in rangy tunes, up and down, in and out, weaving through the air like a rushing river.

Lanalla waited for a lone bird to sing from nearby before she clapped her hands high in the air, causing all movement and sound to stop. Then she nodded to Seela. The girl reached for her small harp and began to run her fingers across the strings. With her red hair floating around her face and down her back, her white skin glowed orange in the firelight as she pulled light from the air. Larna breathed a sigh of relief. This was the women's part of the ceremony and must not be defiled by men.

But then Riadd raised the flute to his lips and joined Seela's music. Lanalla glared at him, trying to signal to him to stop, but Riadd ignored her, instead locking eyes with Seela as together they began a musical dance.

231

Unseen by them all, Mevin was limping through the forest, the bite on his leg beginning to fester. Aware that the Ordeal would already be underway, he knew he did not have much time. As soon as he arrived at the place he was looking for, he put his fingers to his mouth and whistled. After a worryingly long time, the signal was answered and an old man came into view. Mevin couldn't help staring. Hogan had aged years since his banishment into the forest.

Hogan stared back, his face thin and pale. "What are you doing here, White Hair?"

Clenching his jaw against the name, Mevin took the bag from his back and held up his hands, open-palmed, to prove he was not holding any weapons. "I have come to help you," he said curtly. "I've brought you food and some implements."

Suspicious, Hogan moved forward. Then he snatched the pack and ripped it open. Grabbing the bread and cheese, he crammed as much as he could fit into his mouth. "Have you come to gloat, White Hair?" he asked, his mouth so full that the words were barely intelligible.

"No. The Stone is raised, and the Ordeal has started."

"What?" Hogan swallowed hard. "Am I dismissed so soon?"

"We need a new Leader."

"I am your Leader."

"Lanalla thinks you are dead."

Hogan spat on the ground.

"But I knew you wouldn't be," said Mevin slyly. "I have come to help you. You will not last out here on your own for much longer. Already you look half dead."

Hogan glared furiously at him. "What is your price?"

"If you help me to become the new Leader in tonight's Ordeal," said Mevin, shifting weight onto his uninjured leg, "I will make sure that you do not die."

"Are you hurt, White Hair?"

Mevin shorted. "It's nothing. Riadd's filthy cur bit me."

Hogan laughed. "Riadd shows much promise. Although he is already too tall to be strong, he will be useful one day." He stuffed some more cheese into his mouth. "Have you got a plan, White Hair?"

Mevin nodded. "Come back with me now. Once the ceremony is finished, we will take the village by force while everyone sleeps and the other contenders are out in the forest. We will overthrow Lanalla and throw out The Mother for the last time."

"And what will I do once you are Leader?"

"You will be my second."

"Your second?"

"Yes. And two New Bloods have arrived in the village. I shall take the older one. You can have the younger."

"Well," drawled Hogan, "you have worked it all out, haven't you?"

Mevin was about to nod when Hogan lunged for his wounded leg. Fortunately he had foreseen such an action so he was prepared and pulled out his knife. In moments it was against Hogan's neck. "Do you wish to die or are you with me?"

Hogan tried to smile. "Calm down, Mevin. I thought you had come here to help me? Look, it is cold here. I have lit a fire. Let's go and warm ourselves."

Mevin didn't trust him. "There is no time. We must go back now."

"Then loosen your hold and we will make a plan."

Frowning, Mevin put the knife back in his belt and stepped backwards.

"That's better," said Hogan, rubbing at the tiny nick on his neck. "Who are the other contenders for the Ordeal?"

"The idiots Kurt and Bannan. The boy Riadd has even put himself forward."

"The priestess wanted Alanis and Fellana to enter, but Alanis is dead, killed while raising the stone."

Hogan's lip curled. "What a waste. Alanis was one of the few strong women we have left."

"There is still Fallana," said Mevin.

Hogan shook his head. "Fallana is not strong enough to enter the Ordeal. She is a woman."

"But, Lanalla says..."

"Pah," hissed Hogan. "Lanalla says this. Lanalla says that. I've had enough of her. Let her rot."

"Then we agree. You will help me, then?"

"I will consider your plan," Hogan said as he reached for his bag and thrust his hand inside.

"What are you doing?" asked Mevin suspiciously, once again reaching for the knife in his belt.

"If you want me to come now, then I need to check my belongings."

"You have nothing to check."

"I have this," said Hogan, holding out his closed fist. Then he turned over his hand and opened his palm.

Mevin gasped. "What have you got there?"

"Lanalla's precious Amulet."

Mevin gasped and stepped backwards. "The Amulet that the SeeSayer uses? But men are forbidden to touch it."

Hogan grinned, exposing two black teeth at the front of his mouth. "I thought you said you wanted to get rid of the priestess?" He stepped towards Mevin, forcing the white-haired man to retreat.

"I do, but..." He tried to steady himself. "Where did you find it?"

"I took it from Mana, the SeeSayer."

Mevin blanched.

"Before I killed her." Without warning, Hogan pushed the Amulet into Mevin's face.

"No," whimpered Mevin.

"Call yourself the next Leader?"

Mevin felt the ground beneath his feet slurp under him as though it was preparing itself for a meal.

"Let's go, White Hair," Hogan said very quietly. "We attack tonight."

MARCUS – Present Day

In his flat, Marcus woke sweating, feeling as though he was about to lose everything he had ever worked for. The nightmare had felt so real. He felt sick, and there was a strange taste in his mouth like dank forest leaves. He could feel the ground slipping under his feet even though he was lying down. Moreover, his leg throbbed. If anything, it was hurting even more than last night.

As he remembered the evening, he groaned. Had he really walked out on his mother, leaving her to pay the bill in *Chez Nous*? But she had deserved it. Her behaviour had been outrageous. Fancy ordering his food for him as though he was still a little boy, deliberately choosing something that she knew he hated. Nevertheless, if he were not very careful, she would find a way to make him pay.

The truth was that he should never have agreed to see her in the first place. Now he would have to be careful and make sure that he never saw her again.

HESTER – Present Day

Hester woke, still livid. How dare Marcus walk out on her and leave her to pay the bill? She had told him the financial position of *Frattons*. He should have been more considerate. She would find a way of making him pay if it was the last thing she did. She only wished she could see his face when he went to the field and saw that it had been ploughed up.

Now on a roll, she decided that it was about time that the Avery woman was moved on. As she carefully dressed, she wondered whether the vicar had managed to frighten her off. If not, then she would take it upon herself to contact the relevant authorities today and have the ghastly boat removed.

It was only when she had washed her hands several times that she realised her skin was bleeding. At the sight of the blood, a picture of Selena came into her mind. Yet another pitiful excuse for a human being. With a shudder, she dried her hands, but this time she didn't have enough plasters to cover the wounds.

By the time she heard the bell pull on the front door, she had wound herself up into such a state of fury that she decided not to answer it. However, when she looked out of the upstairs window and saw Selena's red hair, she changed her mind. The manor was crawling with insects and desperately needed a clean. Stomping down the stairs, she opened the front door. "Exterminate them," she spat. "There are bugs everywhere."

Selena shook her head. "I haven't come here to work."

Hester frowned. "What do you mean?"

"I've come here to collect what you owe me."

"I told you, I'll pay you at the end of the month."

"I won't be coming back."

Disappointment flared inside Hester. "But we had an agreement."

"Which you broke."

"I did not. I said I'd…"

"I know what you said. I came to tell you that I have another job."

"You're cleaning for someone else?"

"No."

"What kind of work then?"

"That's none of your business."

"It is, if you want your money."

The girl looked as if she would choke. "Very well, I'm helping someone with research."

"What kind of research?"

"As I said before, that's none of your…"

"Don't use that tone of voice with me, young lady. I don't think you realise quite who I am," spat Hester.

For a moment, they glared at each other. Hester was just thinking how much she was enjoying playing with the redhead, when the woman slowly and very deliberately reached up to her eyepatch and pulled it off.

Hester gasped. The luminous eye looked like a pearl. There was no iris, only a black pupil staring right into her as though it could see right to her core. Rooted to the spot, she was unable to look away.

"Now," said Selena. "Pay me what you owe me."

Hester began to panic, heat rising upwards from her belly until it reached her face. As tiny droplets of sweat erupted on her nose like a teenager's pimples, she tried to loosen her collar, but she was wearing the damned blouse with the high buttons and couldn't get them undone. Mortified, she tore away from the hideous gaze and turned, almost running to the cold tap in the kitchen, where she filled a glass of water and downed it in one. It wasn't enough. She was halfway through drinking a third glass when the heat finally subsided.

Half hoping and half dreading that Selena had followed her, she turned to see Selena looking at her, eyepatch firmly back in place. Breathing a sigh of relief, she motioned to one of the chairs. "You'd better sit down."

"I'd rather stand."

Unsure how to respond, she put the half-full glass down on the table between them. Then, suddenly feeling as cold as she had felt hot, she shivered and accidentally knocked it over. The water went flying, most of it landing on Selena's coat. The spillage was the shock she needed. "Oh for God's sake, the water will make a mess all over the floor. Give me your coat. I'll hang it up in the utility room. It can drip quite safely in there."

"No," said Selena, more uncertain now. "Just give me a cloth. I'll…"

"I said give me your coat."

"But…"

"For Christ's sake, give me your coat!"

Shocked, Selena obeyed.

"Good. Now, the money is upstairs. You can mop up all this mess while I'm gone."

Without giving Selena a chance to reply, Hester strode out of the kitchen. Once in the utility room, she hung up the coat on the back of the door and buried her nose in it. The scent of the woman was intoxicating. Just as suddenly, she sprang away, horrified at herself.

With a shiver of disgust, she reached out to smooth down the coat and rid it of any drips. She tried not to linger on the contours of the fabric but her hand snagged on a bulge in one of the pockets. Quickly, she snatched her hand away. Then she cursed herself for being jumpy. What was the matter with her? She hated the woman and that was that. Curious, she reached into the pocket to see what could be inside and her fingers closed around a soggy brown paper package. Wrinkling her nose with distaste, she drew out the mushy object and placed it on the draining board. Intrigued, she peered closer. The back of her neck started to tingle. As she reached out to touch it again, her hands began to buzz.

Taking a corner of the pulpy paper, she began to peel it back. Inside was a chain. It was partly shiny and partly dull, at once new and old, equally beautiful and ugly and so expensive to look at that it must be cheap. Both horrified and mesmerised, she dropped it. As it landed on the floor, the chain slithered like a serpent before lying still. She stared transfixed. On the top lay a stone pendant with an X carved into it. The amber bead above was stunning but the white wand underneath stared at her as if it were Selena's pearly eye come to life.

She was about to return it to Selena's pocket when she had an idea. Holding it away from her, she ran as silently as she could up the back stairs to her bedroom and opened the wardrobe. With one hand still clutching the chain, she rifled through a jumble of boxes with the other. Once she had located a hideous piece of costume jewellery that one of the villagers had given her, she dropped Selena's chain in her jewellery box. Then she looked in the back of a drawer and found a pile of £20 notes that she'd hidden away. Peeling off three and then adding another for good measure, she crept back downstairs to the utility room. She wrapped the ghastly piece of jewellery in some clean brown paper and put it in Selena's coat pocket. Then she took a deep breath, picked up the coat, and re-entered the kitchen.

"Here you are," she said calmly, holding out the notes. "There is a little extra there to thank you for your time."

Surprised, Selena took the bundle from Hester's outstretched hand and counted the money. "Thank you," she murmured in obvious surprise.

Hester smiled. "And here's your coat. I've managed to remove most of the water."

She waited for Selena to take it before gesturing towards the door with her hand, giving the redhead permission to leave.

As soon as she was alone, Hester ran back upstairs and retrieved the chain from her jewellery box. Holding it up to the light so she could examine it, she marvelled at the multiple stone pendants that jingled seductively like a bracelet. When she touched the crystals at the bottom, her skin began to tingle again. The surge of power made her feel dizzy. She became very cold. The amber seemed to be calling to her, so she brought it up nearer to her face.

What she saw this time made her cry out loud. An insect was caught inside the crystal. Horrified, she hurled the chain onto the bed. As her legs buckled, she sank onto the ground. A buzzing was droning in her head. It was the loathsome thing calling to her. Begging her to reach out. Touch it. To release it from its prison.

She was about to scream when her vision began to blur. At the same time, her heart started to pump hard and she began to sweat as a powerful current of energy surged through her. Turning on her side, she looked at the chain. Tentatively, she reached out her hand and touched the metal. When nothing happened, she moved her hand down towards the amber with its trapped insect inside. She didn't see the two men lurking behind a tree, waiting to pounce.

circa 2000 B.C.E.

Hogan reached into his pack and threw Mevin some honeysuckle twine. "Quick!" When Mevin didn't move, he pulled the Amulet out from under his skins and held it up, his face full of menace. "Riadd and the other men will be back at daybreak. Get into those huts, or I will throttle you with this."

Mevin didn't need to be told twice. After Hogan had tucked the Amulet back into his furs, they made their way stealthily into the nearest huts. In moments, children and adults had been gagged, bound with the twine, and deposited outside by the central fire, unable to move or call for help.

Eager for revenge, Hogan ran to the priestess's hut. He could hear her snoring even from outside. With a grin, he pushed his way through the door flap and ran to her side. Then he kicked her in the head, stopping her scream short by tying a coarse gag brutally over her mouth. He was about to drag her outside when Mevin reappeared.

Hogan then saw the girls hiding in the shadows. The older one had her petrified sister on her hip and was preparing to flee. Hogan grabbed the smaller girl, pulled her away from her sister and thrust her into Mevin's arms, where she began to wail in terror. Then he turned back to the older girl. Pulling her forward into the light, he grabbed her hair, wrenching her head back so that he could scrutinise her face.

"I told you Hogan, she is mine," growled Mevin. "She's the New Blood I told you about."

"You mean that Lanalla's stone is actually working?"

"No, of course not. She arrived before the Stone was erected."

Hogan laughed unpleasantly. "Then I will take her for myself when I am reinstated as Leader."

"No, you won't," Mevin protested angrily. "We made a deal. I am going to become Leader. Here, you can have this one instead."

Before Hogan could react, Mevin had wrenched the older girl away from him and thrust the younger one into the space that was left. Disgusted, Hogan lowered his voice so it was menacingly quiet. "I am not interested in cripples, White Hair, New Blood or not."

Mevin took an instinctive step away. "You wanted sport, remember?"

"With your redhead, yes. With this creature, no." Hogan dropped the child onto the floor. "That should stop her wailing."

"But ..."

Hogan's eyes narrowed dangerously. "Do you want me to strangle you with the Amulet?" He looked down at the ground where the older girl had run to her sister and was cradling her in her arms. Before Mevin could stop him, he snatched up the redhead in a grip so tight that she could not move. "Go and hammer in two more stakes. Then tie them both up, one on either side of the priestess. It's time we had some fun."

Hogan half dragged and half carried the struggling girl outside to the fire. As soon as Mevin had erected the stakes, he tied her onto the one on the right hand side of the priestess whose head was lolling as though she was still asleep. "Go and fetch the younger one," he barked.

Mevin hesitated. Then, as though he had remembered the threat of the Amulet, he disappeared into Lanalla's hut and brought out the child.

In moments the girls and the priestess were all tied to the stakes in front of the fire. The smaller girl was still crying. "Gag her," Hogan ordered.

Mevin's jaw clenched furiously in the light of the fire, but again he obeyed.

"Good. Leave the other one. I want to hear her squeal."

"Untie my sister at once," the redhead protested. "Let her go. She is ill. You'll hurt her."

Hogan stood back on his heels and grinned.

"Remember, she is mine," warned Mevin.

Hogan laughed.

"You promised," Mevin snarled. "You said we would do this together. That you would help me become Leader and be my second."

Hogan flexed his fingers. "And you believed me?" He turned away and surveyed his handiwork. On the other side of the flames, the remaining villagers were trussed up like animals waiting for slaughter. He turned to them. "Who wants to challenge me now? If anybody wishes to fight me for the leadership, make it clear. I will kill you right here."

Mevin went to protest but Hogan pulled out his knife and jabbed it into the white-haired man's side, drawing blood. Once he had yanked it out again, Mevin sank to his knees, clutching the wound.

Next, Hogan pulled the Amulet from his bag and held it up for everyone to see. There was a stifled gasp. He walked over to one of the older men and ripped off his gag. "Do you accept me as your Leader?" he demanded. When the man failed to answer, Hogan hit him hard and sent him sprawling onto the ground.

He was just about to reach for a woman and child, when the redhead cried out. "Stop it. Leave them alone. The men will be back at any moment from the Ordeal."

Hogan's hand dropped to his side in surprise. Then he slowly walked towards the fire and grabbed her hair, yanking her head backwards painfully. "Who are you to question me, girl?"

"I am the new SeeSayer," she spluttered.

Hogan roared. "The new SeeSayer?" Without releasing her, he turned to face the villagers. "Do you hear this? Lanalla has already chosen a new SeeSayer. She has wasted no time, I see." He turned back to Seela and spat in her face. "Do you know what happened to the last girl who called herself the SeeSayer?"

Seela desperately tried to pull back from the stench of his breath, but there was no room for her to move.

"Shall I show you?"

Mevin forced himself to his feet. "No, let her go!"

Hogan put his fingers to his lips and let out a long, high-pitched whistle.

Kurt immediately appeared from the shadow, grabbed Mevin's arms, tied them up, shoved him onto the ground, and put his foot on his back.

"You fool, Mevin," Hogan cried. "Did you think you were the only one I spoke with? Kurt is cleverer than you: he never wanted to be Leader." Spinning round to face Seela again, he thrust the Amulet towards her face. "I expect the priestess told you that no man can touch this. That only women can hold it. Well, she lied. I am a man, and it is now mine." He turned back to face the crowd. "There is no woman's magic here. There never has been. You need a man to lead you, not a woman. Worshipping The Mother has only turned our children into weaklings. It is a man's seed that makes a strong child. In order to survive, we need the strength of men, not the vague promises of women." He walked back over to the man he had sent sprawling to the ground and yanked him up to his feet. "Now, I ask you again, do you accept me as your Leader?"

This time the man whimpered a yes.

"That's better." He looked up. "And the rest of you?"

More nodded.

"Good. Be thankful that it is me who has given you this lesson and not another clan. I have saved you from certain death."

With a nod to Kurt to guard the Folk, he walked back over

to Seela, untied her bonds and flung her to the ground. "Now, let me show you how I dealt with the last SeeSayer."

Ignoring Mevin's cries he loosened the thongs on his trousers.

He didn't notice the wasp that had started to circle leisurely around his head.

SELENA – Present Day

"Larna?" I call out anxiously. There is no sign of her in the living area of the boat so I walk through to the bathroom, but that, too, is empty. Then I hear a little moan coming from behind a closed door. She is lying collapsed on her bed, clutching her head in pain, her face a ghastly yellow colour and her eyes screwed tightly shut.

"Larna," I try again. "What is it? What's the matter?"

Her only answer is a moan. I put my hand on her shoulder but she flinches away, so I run back into the snug. Bertie's number is written in big letters on the back of the phone receiver. Quickly, I press them into the pad and call him. The ringing tone seems to go on forever. "Come on," I mutter under my breath, but he doesn't answer so I leave a message for him to come immediately. Then I key 999 into the pad and wait. Someone is just starting to speak when the line suddenly goes dead.

I'm starting to sweat so I rip off my coat, fling it onto the floor and run back to the bedroom. Larna's face is a ghastly colour. Reaching out, I put my hand on hers. Although she has shown no sign that she even knows that I am there, she grabs my fingers and clings on as though I am a lifeline. Sinking down onto the bed beside her, I start to murmur to her as though she were a child.

Then I find myself thinking of Seela. I feel a dragging sensation as I am pulled backwards into her life. Two men are staring at me. One has white hair. The other I have never seen before.

Or have I?

Suddenly I am terrified.

BERTIE – Present Day

When Bertie knocked at the door of the boat, the only response was Buddy's frantic barking. Without waiting, he opened the door and went into the kitchen. In the snug, Selena's coat was lying abandoned on the floor. Ignoring the tilt of the boat, he ran, passing through the meditation area and the bathroom into the main bedroom beyond.

Both women were collapsed on the floor. Quickly, he felt for Larna's pulse. It was rapid but strong. When he put his fingers around Selena's wrist, he had to stop himself from flinching backwards. She was as cold as a cadaver. Horrified, he felt for her pulse. It took him a while to locate it. Even then, it was weak and erratic. Swiftly, he put Larna into the recovery position and covered her up in a blanket.

He had just lifted Selena onto the bed when Larna opened her eyes and sat up. "What happened?" he cried. "Are you all right? Selena phoned me in a panic. I got here as soon as I could."

She put her hand up to her head. "I have no idea," she groaned.

"Have you been attacked?" he said, full of concern.

"No, a blinding, hideous headache."

"Oh, thank God."

"Seela, she was…" She looked as though she was about to pass out again. "I couldn't help her. Oh God, what have I done?"

Bewildered, he frowned. "Dear girl, what are you talking about?"

She ran her hand through her hair and blinked rapidly. "It must have been the dream."

"The dream? What do you mean, the dream?"

"I saw her, Bertie." She shuddered. "Selena was someone else and yet her as well."

Bertie took one look at the woman on the bed. She was very pale and her breathing was shallow. Carefully he wrapped her up in the duvet. "I think we should call an ambulance." He pulled his phone from his pocket, but there was no signal.

"Try the landline," Larna suggested.

He ran back out to the snug and grabbed it where it lay on the table.

That, too, was dead.

SELENA – Present Day

A man and a woman are peering down at me, alarm on their faces. Cringing away from them, I try to disappear, but I don't know where to go. *The necklace*, I call. *Come back to me.*

"Selena, love, are you all right?" It is the priestess. I want to trust her, but she betrayed Riadd, didn't she?

"Selena?"

It is the man. I recognise him too. He's gone off to prepare for the Ordeal with Riadd. Does this mean that they have come back? That they can save us now? I try to reach up to him, but I can't move. *The necklace. You've got to take it back from Hogan.*

"What are you saying?" they both cry together. "Speak to us."

I want to save myself, to save my sister, but it's too late. My throat is parched. I try to say something, but my voice died long ago. Now the necklace is all that is left and Hogan is brandishing it over me as though he's claimed a great victory. He's ripped my body apart and shattered my mind. I want to curl up and die, but now I know we never die. We simply go on and on and on, dragging the past behind us like a stony wraith that's ready to strangle us whenever we weaken.

Waves of grief drown me, churning me around in great somersaults until I no longer know where is up or down or sideways. At first I resist the buffeting and try to swim, but the current is too strong and so I grasp the pain as though it's a raft. As I try to stay alive, the waves wash and rub and scour me clean until I am lost and everything has gone. There is no longer any past, present or future, only a trussing up, like an animal ready to be sacrificed. I sink downwards, my arms and legs dragging behind as though they no longer belong to me. Nothing is left but surrender and the letting go of everything I thought was myself. I am gone. The necklace has gone. My heart beat has gone. There are no more songs.

I land on the seabed and sink into the sand. It is soft under my bones which clank together and then fall apart. All falls to silence as the world disappears.

"She's gone in too deep," says a man. "We've got to find a way of bringing her round."

"She keeps murmuring something about a necklace" says a woman. "What do you think she means?"

"I'll look in the caravan to see if there's something in there," says a man.

When he returns, there's silence until he says: "Nothing, but I nearly tripped over this again. It was lying on the floor in the snug."

"That's Selena's coat."

"I'll check the pockets, just in case anything is in there that might help."

There's a great sucking sound as though a cork is pulled from a bottle, and I come rushing up towards the surface. I expect to see Lanalla and Bannan. Instead, my pearly eye opens onto a strange looking parcel, all brown paper and creases, being pulled out of my coat. I try to raise my hand to reach for it but my arm refuses to work.

"What's that?" the woman asks.

"No idea. Let's have a look."

My heart rushes up into my throat as I wait to see the necklace again, but as he peels off the paper, all he reveals is a gaudy piece of costume jewellery. He puts it down on a nearby table and reaches into another pocket. His eyebrows rise in surprise. "It's cash." He counts it. Then he frowns. "£80. I thought she didn't have any money?"

"Perhaps your sister paid her at last. That's where she went, wasn't it? To clean the manor?"

"Not to clean. To tell Hester that she wouldn't be coming back now she's got another job."

I manage to force my green eye open.

"Oh thank God. She's coming round. Selena, love, are you all right?"

It takes a long moment before I can focus but then I see them. Larna? Bertie? The Bronze Age ghosts have disappeared.

"Oh God, I thought you would never come back. I was terrified. I..."

"It's all right, old girl. She's okay now, aren't you, Selena?"

"Where's the necklace?" I croak desperately. As I look at the ghastly object on the table, the blood rushes back into my veins. Silently, I scream for Riadd to come and save me, but all I can see is the water dripping off my coat in the manor.

Hogan.

Hester Knebworth.

I'm going to be sick.

Kenaz reversed – arrogance

Chapter Twelve

HESTER – Present Day

The necklace was glowing against the white throw of the bed. Hester was just about to scoop it up and throw it into a drawer when the doorbell rang. Her first thought was that Selena had discovered the theft and come back to demand she give the necklace back. A feeling of dread mixed with triumph overcame her, and she found herself unable to move. Only when the doorbell rang for a second and then a third time did curiosity get the better of her and force her to her feet.

It was the postman with a special delivery letter for Alan. After she had signed for it, she closed the door. Curious, she reached for her reading glasses on the hall table. The silver letter opener glinted like a dagger as she sliced open the envelope. After a few moments, her face changed from red to white and back to red again. Hands shaking and legs weak, she sat down, reached for the telephone and dialled her husband's work number.

"*Frattons*. How may I help you?" Alan Knebworth answered after a moment.

"How dare you," she croaked, in a voice so stricken it was barely audible.

"Hester?"

"I've just received a letter from the bank. It says that if we don't pay our overdraft in the next seven days, then they're going to take the manor. The manor is *my* house, Alan. *Mine.*"

"Yes Hester, I…"

"How dare you use it for collateral? The manor has been the Fratton family home for generations. You took my company when we married. Wasn't that enough? My house was never part of the deal. You knew that. *You knew it*!"

"But…"

"Don't try to wriggle out of this one, Alan. Fourteen days ago, the bank was demanding £100,000 as the excess on the overdraft. I told you, they cannot, and will not, have the manor as well."

Silence. He did not even try to answer this time.

She slammed down the phone. What was she going to do? She would need a fortune to save the manor as well as herself. She had lost everything. There would be nothing left. She had wasted her life on idiots. She felt dirty as though their weakness had rubbed off on her and stuck like slime to her skin.

Suddenly desperate to be clean, she ran upstairs to run a bath. The water was so hot she scalded her skin but she barely felt the heat as she scrubbed at herself with a brush meant for cleaning the basin. It was only when she accidentally rubbed off one of the scabs on her hand that the pain hit her. She wanted to howl her despair out into the world like a wolf who had lost its pack and knew it would starve.

Back in the bedroom, her eyes fell on the necklace. The wasp was looking at her from deep inside its resin prison. If she didn't get it out of the light soon it would surely free itself and sting her. Screwing up her face as though she was about to pick up a snake, she lifted up a tiny part of the chain and held it as far away from her as she could.

The touch was magic. In moments, her panic began to subside and her breathing to slow down. The selenite started to glow as though it was sucking the life out of the amber, ensuring that the wasp was dead. Mindlessly she began to stroke the chain and its pendants. When she arrived at the stone with its X at the bottom, it seemed to sigh with relief, as though it had been searching for her all of its life.

What was this piece of junk that Selena has so carelessly allowed her to steal?

And if it really did have a power of its own, might she be able to sell it and save herself after all?

Draping it carefully over one arm, she went downstairs to the telephone, dialled directory enquiries, and found the number for Christie's Auction House in London. After she had described the necklace to several different people, she was eventually put through to a man who dealt with archaeological antiquities. He seemed surprised at her description but wouldn't give her any more information as to its potential value over the phone, saying only that he must see it first.

Excited by his response, she booked an appointment to show it to him and ended the call. Then she climbed back up the stairs to her bedroom. The man had sounded keen, very keen, in fact. Intrigued, she lay down on the bed and looked at it afresh. There was a power in it that made her feel she could achieve anything.

Moreover, the wasp inside the amber had fallen asleep.

For the moment, she was safe.

SELENA – Present Day

Eventually I manage to persuade Larna and Bertie that I have recovered. I do not show them that my dislike of Hester Knebworth has turned to terror. It's easier to be angry that the vile woman has stolen the necklace. I will force her to give it back and confront her about what she has done to me.

About what she did to Seela.

And so I do the one thing that is guaranteed to make me feel sick to my stomach. I start walking to the manor. It doesn't take me long to cross the footbridge into Little Stenning or to stride up the drive. I don't bother to use the bell pull. Instead, I hammer the front door as though I'm trying to cave it in.

Hester Knebworth appears quickly, as though she has been waiting for me.

"I believe this is yours," I growl, holding up the cheap piece of costume jewellery.

"Good Lord," she says, feigning dramatic surprise, "how ghastly. What dreadful taste you have."

I throw it at her. It lands at her feet. Without glancing at it, she hooks the point of her shoe around it and kicks it back into my hands. She should have been a footballer. "You stole my necklace," I shriek. "*Give it back!*"

The look she gives me drains all the energy from my body. Her eyes are devouring me as though she wants to climb inside me and take me apart, organ by organ, bone by bone. I feel myself being sucked into her until my heart is no longer mine. Until I barely exist anymore.

Until I am Seela.

There's a noise behind me. A man is lurching into the drive on a bicycle. At the same time, the front door squeaks. Realising that the odious woman is about to slam the door shut in my face, I rekindle the fury and jam my shoe firmly in the doorframe. "I'm not leaving until you return my property to me," I hiss.

Her expression suddenly changes from gloating to annoyance and then dislike as the man on the bicycle dismounts and approaches us. "What are you doing here, Karl?" she snarls in a voice so contemptuous that it threatens to kill the air itself. "Why aren't you at the office?"

This must be the artist. In his early thirties, he has large protruding eyes and a balding head. Karl Knebworth is no picture and looks more like a frightened frog than a brilliant artist who hides his sketches under his bed. Suddenly, I realise that he is staring at me as though he is looking at a ghost.

"For God's sake, Karl, stop gawping. This… this *girl* is just leaving." She jabs the sharp toe point of her stiletto shoe into my knee.

I fall backwards and Hester drags Karl inside before slamming the door shut in my face.

KARL – Present Day

"For God's sake, why are you here?" rasped Hester venomously.

Karl stared at the back of the door as though he was trying to see through it.

"Wh … who was th … that at the d … d …?"

"You don't want to know."

"Wh … why d … d … d … id you s … slam the d … d … d … oor in her f … f …? Wh … who w … w … was she? T … t … ell m …. m …"

"Oh for God's sake, go back to the hole you were born in and leave me alone."

"B … b … b …"

He watched her raise her eyes to the ceiling in extravagant

contempt. "If you have to know, she used to be my cleaner, but she was so hopeless that I sacked her. She just came here to make trouble, that's all."

"W ... w ... w ... hat's her n ... n ..."

"What is this, twenty questions?"

"W ... w ...w ... hat's her n ... n ..." he tried again.

"Does it really matter?"

"Y ...Y ... es. Te ... tell me," he forced.

"No, you tell me why you are here. It's the middle of the day."

There were no words to answer her with, not when he had just seen his drawings come to life.

Her face turned puce. "Have you gone deaf or something, Karl? I asked you why you are here."

He forced himself to remember why he had left the office. "F ... F ... Father's w ... w ... worried."

"Your father's worried? Don't be a fool. He's never been worried about me in his life. Go back to work. I'm sick of both of you."

But instead of leaving the manor, Karl fled to his room. He had to check what he thought he had seen. Sinking to his knees, he pulled his sketchbooks out from under his bed. And there she was, the girl just as he'd seen in his mind and now at the door: red hair, finely chiselled face, dimpled chin and those green eyes. He had known they were green even though he had only used charcoal. Even though the woman at the door had been wearing an eye patch, in both of them he'd had the impression of fire, ice, hurt and fury all at the same time.

Hands trembling, he turned to the sketch of the tall youth with long, black hair. There was no doubt about this figure either. It was a younger version of the man who was working with his brother at the dig.

It didn't take long for the now familiar compulsion to draw to overtake him. He tried to dismiss it but before he could stop himself, he snatched up a pencil and turned to a fresh sheet of paper. At first, he drew a necklace hung with scraggy shapes. Then it was the girl. Next, it was the girl again but this time with a little bird on her shoulder. Carefully, he tore out the pages and laid them adjacent to the sketch of the boy.

What he drew next, however, made him flinch back in horror. A man who looked unmistakably like his father was lying sprawled on his back in a pool of blood, a knife through his chest. Filled with a feeling of foreboding so strong that his pencil dropped to the floor, he wondered if he would ever draw again.

Then the telephone rang downstairs.

When his mother didn't pick it up, his blood ran cold. He tried to ignore the sound, telling himself that it would surely stop soon. But it didn't. Instead it rang on and on and on until he had no choice but to tiptoe down the stairs, praying that his mother wouldn't look in his room while he was gone.

He hated telephones; it was difficult enough to speak in front of someone, speaking into a receiver was impossible. "H ... hello?" he managed, to his surprise.

"Mr Knebworth?"

"Y... yes."

"Is your mother there?"

At last, his voice stuck in his throat.

"This is the John Radcliffe Hospital," the person continued. "I'm afraid your father has had a heart attack. Could you come in?"

At first, the words passed over him as though they were in a foreign language. Then he remembered that he had just drawn his father lying bleeding on the ground.

"Mr Knebworth, are you still there?"

"Y ... y ... y ..."

"You need to come now. Do you understand what I am saying?"

He had nodded several times before he realised that the woman couldn't see him. Desolate, he pressed the red button on the telephone.

Oh God, was all this his fault? Had he somehow caused his father to fall ill by drawing him? "M ... M ...other?" he tried to call, but his voice only came out as a squeak. He went in search of her, but she wasn't downstairs and he dare not go up to her bedroom. He would have to tell someone else instead. But who? Gingerly, he crept back downstairs to the telephone again. On a pad at the side, Marcus's number was scribbled.

Heart in mouth, he pressed the buttons on the keypad but got them all wrong. He tried again. Then again. Eventually, there was a ringing tone and a voice answered.

"Hello?"

Karl choked. "I ... i ... it's ..."

A long silence.

"K ... K ... K ..."

"*Karl?*"

Nothing.

"What the fuck are you phoning me for?"

"H ... h ... hos ... hospit ..."

"Hospital? What are you talking about?"

"F ... F ... Fath ..."

"Father's in hospital? Is that what you're trying to say?"

Silence.

"I'm on my way."

SELENA – Present Day

"She kicked me!" I cry as soon as I am back on the boat. "She is a vicious, lying..."

"Did she give you back your necklace?" asks Bertie.

"Did she heck," I spit, hurling the unwanted baubles onto the table.

"And she's definitely got it?" asks Larna.

"Definitely," I growl.

"Calm down dear girl," Bertie says. "Why is this necklace so important to you?"

It's a question I have been expecting. It would be easy to say that it has sentimental value, that Mum gave it to me, or my sister, but I am in too deep for that. Raff knows about it and Marcus has seen it. The secret is out. And yet I am scared to speak Seela's name out loud. What if that makes her even more real?

I have just decided to change the subject when an image of Seela being impaled by Hogan ravages my vision. My knees start to fold and it's only Bertie's grasp of my arm that stops me from collapsing altogether. They half carry, half drag me through the beaded curtain into the snug and sit me in the chair by the window.

"I think it's time you told us about the dreams, love," Larna says gently, kneeling at my feet.

She sounds so much like Mum that I think my heart will break all over again. How am I supposed to reveal what has been happening and not have them dismiss me as mad? And yet if I don't then Seela's grief will destroy me and I will stop being myself altogether. "They're about a girl who needs help," I confess, trying to expand my lungs and get more air into them but there's a great weight on my chest.

"What have dreams got to do with the necklace?" Bertie asks.

I take as deep a breath as I can. "I started to dream after I had dug up the necklace at the bottom of Stenning Hill on the first day I was here. Raff seems to think that it might have something to do with the dig."

"Raff is an archaeologist," Larna explains to Bertie. "He's working on the dig at the foot of Stone Clump."

"Marcus's dig?" asks Bertie.

She nods.

"He likes restoring things," I continue, "so I let him keep the necklace for a night. He's worked wonders on it. I wish you could see it. It's all bronze, gold and stone. There are even two crystals embedded into it: amber and selenite."

"Crystals?" he says in surprise. "Is this necklace valuable then?"

"Selena," says Larna, "it doesn't matter about value. Continue with the story of the dreams."

I stare at them both, unsure how to begin. "There are two sisters, Seela and Duna. Duna is only about six or so, while Seela is about eleven. Because Duna is disabled and looks strange, her own people have threatened to kill her. In an attempt to get her to safety, Seela takes her away, but it is the middle of winter and they are not equipped to survive the freezing temperatures."

Bertie holds up his hand. "Dear child, go slower."

"Sorry," I apologise. Now I have started I cannot stop and the story begins to pour out of me like milk from a jug. "One night, when they are walking through a forest looking for shelter, they are followed by a wolf. They climb a tree to escape it but it scratches Duna's leg, leaving her with a nasty gash.

"The next day they come across a settlement. The two most important people there seem to be the priestess and a man called Mevin. They are arguing about the future. Apparently, they haven't had any visitors for a while and the inbred babies are all being born weak.

"As part of her power, the priestess has what she calls a SeeSayer, a girl who can see into the future and warn them of any trouble ahead. This girl has just been murdered by a man called Hogan who, apparently was the Leader. As a result of his crime, the priestess has banished him from the settlement.

"Mevin wants to replace him as Leader but he refuses to recognise the power of the priestess. This is a matriarchal society that worships a goddess figure they call The Mother and, as far as I can tell, women have been in charge for a long time. However, the community is dying and in order to survive, they must find a way of strengthening the gene pool."

Only now does Bertie hold up his hand to stop me. "For a moment you had me. I thought you were talking about real history." He shakes his head. "Shame about the gene pool."

"They didn't call it that, of course," I tell him, "but they did realise that their children were being born weak because no new people had come to their settlement in a long time. They called these new people New Bloods and there were plans afoot to persuade some of them to join them."

"Hang on a minute," he says. "I thought this was meant to be a dream. It sounds more like a history lesson."

"I think I'm dreaming about what happened here in the Stennings."

Larna grows rather pale. "Go on, love."

"Mevin discovers the girls and threatens to take Seela for himself," I continue. "He goes looking for Hogan in the forest in the hope that the banished man will help him to become the new leader. What he doesn't know is that Hogan has stolen the Amulet."

"What's the Amulet?" asks Bertie.

I look at him for a long time before I reply. "The necklace," I whisper, my voice now trembling. "The Amulet, as they call it, is the heart of their spiritual tradition. Without it, the priestess has no power."

"Dear God …"

"As soon as Mevin realises that Hogan has stolen it, the tables are turned. Hogan wants to reclaim the Leadership for himself. He doesn't believe that the priestess's idea of erecting a Stone monument on top of the hill to attract New Blood will work. He would rather raid other settlements and steal their women."

There's a long silence while they both try to digest what I am saying.

"Surely you're not talking about Stone Clump?" Bertie asked, incredulous.

Larna moans. "Oh God, this is not a dream. It's a nightmare."

I turn to Larna who looks as though she is about to cry. "I'm so sorry you had to see the dream with me," I say to her gently. "I had no idea that was going to happen."

"What do you mean?" asks Bertie. "How could Larna have seen your dream?"

"Somehow we shared it." I confess. "That's why you found us both passed out in Larna's room."

He turns to Larna. "Is that true?"

She nods, her eyes full of tears. "I had a really bad headache. Selena was holding my hand and I started to dream. She must have somehow transferred it to me." Her face starts to crumble. "It was beyond hideous."

"Hogan and Mevin attacked the settlement," I continue. "After they had tied up all the villagers, they made an example of the priestess, Seela and Duna by binding them to stakes in front of the communal fire."

"Why didn't anyone stop them?" Bertie demands.

"Because all the strong ones were out of the settlement for the Ordeal."

"The Ordeal?"

"It's what they did to choose a new Leader." I wait for another question but Bertie says no more. Trying not to clench my jaw, I speak the words I never wanted to hear myself say. "Hogan raped Seela and hurt her really badly. Then he threatened to sacrifice the little girl Duna at the foot of the Stone."

"Selena, my dear girl," says Bertie, "you should have been a novelist. However did you think up such a story?"

"I promise you that I didn't make any of it up."

He looks confused. "Are you trying to tell me that you dug up a necklace and started seeing what happened here, in the Stennings?"

I can do nothing but nod.

He's quiet for a long time. Then without warning, his confusion disappears to be replaced by excitement. "My God, this is going to make my new book sensational! If we can prove that these dreams really are the story of what happened here thousands of years ago, then I have a best seller on my hands. My agent will love it." Eyes sparkling, he looks at me. "Do you really think that the necklace is responsible for the dreams?"

"Partly," I reply.

He does not give me a chance to explain. "Then what are we waiting for? We must get it back from my sister. It is essential evidence. Moreover, when you have it again, Selena, you'll be able to dream the rest of the story."

"Actually," I confess, "I don't always need the necklace to have the dreams. When I was at your place doing the experiment, I dreamed then, too, but Raff was restoring it that night."

Guts clenching, I pull the eyepatch off and look unblinkingly from one to the other with both eyes. "I think it might be my pearly eye. I'm not blind. I just see differently with this one. My green eye has normal vision. This pearly one sees inside rather than outside. The necklace might be helping but I think it is my eye that is showing me the dreams." I put the eyepatch back in place and wait for a response.

"Larna, dear girl," Bertie says faintly after a long time. "I think we need some tea. And cake. Lots of it."

At last, some of the fear leaves Larna's face. Standing up shakily, she briefly holds onto the back of the chair for support. Then, without a word, she walks towards the kitchen. Buddy follows her. I've completely forgotten him. Poor dog must need to go out.

Once they have left, I turn to Bertie. "I'm sorry, but I can't allow you to use my dreams for the book. I only told you about them to explain why it is important for us to get the necklace back from your sister."

Bertie is stroking his chin thoughtfully as though by doing so he can release a genie from a bottle. "Is this necklace worth anything financially, do you think?" He asks, sounding strong again.

"Why do you ask?"

"The rumour is that *Frattons* is in deep trouble. If the necklace is valuable then she may have stolen it so she can sell it."

"Sell it? But she can't!" I protest.

"Unless she agrees to give it back to you, you won't be able to stop her."

"But Raff says…"

He starts to pace, making the boat feel very small. "Do you think we could talk to this Raff chap and ask him his opinion about the necklace? Not only is he an archaeologist, but if he's started to restore it, he might have some ideas."

I nod.

"Where will we find him?"

Out of the window, the light is already fading. "At the farmhouse, I would imagine."

"Wonderful. Then let's go, we'll have to forget the cake."

MARCUS – Present Day

"Follow me."

The night nurse led Marcus to a side room where his father lay attached to a monitor. He had not seen his father in years and the sight of him now made his knees go weak. Gone was the severe, rather distant man he remembered to be replaced by a much smaller man whose breathing was shallow, his face grey under the oxygen mask.

Shocked to see how much his father had changed, Marcus felt a stab of guilt. He had been angry for so long that he had created a devil in his mind. But the man he now saw lying so helplessly in bed was no monster. He reached out to touch the still hand. Perhaps he should say something. But what? He'd always had such a formal relationship with his father. Hadn't called him Dad in years. Hadn't even thanked him for giving him the job of excavating the field.

As his eyes began to prickle, he bit down on his lip. The nurse had put a chair by the side of the bed, so he sat there for a while, stupefied by his own response. It was his mother he was angry with, not this man.

He had no idea how long he sat there, only that he began to feel very tired. Knowing he needed to sleep, he stood up, bent down and dared to murmur the unfamiliar words, "Thanks, Dad," half hoping that this would produce a miracle; that his father would suddenly open his eyes and smile, telling him that everything was going to be all right.

When there was no response, he pulled himself together and left the room. Outside the hospital, he found a text on his phone from Karl asking him to call round on his way home. Shit. All he wanted was his bed. Nevertheless, he decided not to ignore the message and drove rather faster than he should have done to the manor.

It was well after midnight by the time he pulled into the drive. Karl was not only waiting for him but hurried out to the car, opened the passenger door and climbed in. It was years since they had seen each other. Marcus stared at Karl's nearly bald pate in surprise while Karl stared at Marcus's white hair. Then Karl's lip quivered. Embarrassed by the show of emotion, Marcus looked away.

"H ... h ... h ... ow is ... ?"

"Still unconscious. He's on oxygen," Marcus said.

"W ... w ... would you m ... m ... m ..."

"For God's sake, Karl, can't this wait until morning? I need to get some sleep."

Karl opened his mouth, looking distraught. "H ... h ... hospital," he forced. "D ... d ... drive me ..."

"What?"

"D ... d ... drive ..."

"Yes, I heard you. I'll take you there tomorrow. Now please get out and let me get to bed."

"Now," Karl said surprisingly clearly.

Marcus raised his eyebrows, surprised at the single, forceful word. "Now?" he repeated, not sure if he had heard him correctly. "You've got to be joking. I've got work early tomorrow morning, or rather this morning. Mother can take you."

Karl tried to speak, but while his mouth worked, no words came out. Desperate, he pulled some paper and a pencil out of his pocket and wrote: Mother's in no fit state to go.

Marcus frowned. "Why not? Has something happened?"

Karl shook his head and wrote: Something's wrong with her.

Marcus snatched the paper from him. "What do you mean?"

I don't know.

"But it's the middle of the bloody night," Marcus exclaimed irritably. I'll take you in my lunch break tomorrow."

Father shouldn't be left on his own.

"For God's sake, he's unconscious, Karl. He didn't even realise I was there."

You don't know that.

Marcus was about to rip the pieces of paper into shreds and toss them onto the driveway when something stopped him. What if Karl was right and his father had known he was there? What if he had heard him say 'Dad'? "Okay," he relented brusquely. "Put your seat belt on but I warn you, I'm going to drive fast."

SELENA – Present Day

By the time we arrive at the farmhouse, it is pitch black. Raff doesn't answer the door but his motorbike is round the back so he can't have gone far. My pearly eye prickles in warning, reminding me of the way I found him in the field when he called me Seela.

It doesn't take long to get to the dig. Since the attempted sabotage, a new security system has been put in place around the field, including a strong fence and bright lights. With each step, the sensation in my pearly eye gets stronger as though something is wrong and we're getting closer. Calling to Bertie and Larna to follow me, I lead us along the fence to the top where, thankfully, the gate beyond the Portakabin is unlocked. Holding a finger to my lips, I give Buddy's lead to Larna and gesture to them to stay. Then I make my way down to the workings.

At first, no one seems to be here but then I hear an indistinct moan from somewhere near the heavy, protective tarpaulin covering the top of the trench. One of the corners is askew so I lift it up. A girl is lying on top of a tall youth. Seela and Riadd. Mind flailing, I dig my nails into my hands. She disappears and I am left staring down at Raff. "Bertie, Larna," I cry. "Come quickly. He's here."

They attach Buddy's lead to the fence and roll up their sleeves. It is hard work unfastening the corners of the tarpaulin in the dark. Bertie is hardly dressed for physical toil in his immaculate suit, but to his credit, he ignores the mud and helps. Once the tarpaulin is free of its attachments, we heave it to the side and peer down into the cavernous hole, four thousand years deep. As I climb down the steps of earth that have been carefully carved into the mud and covered with mesh, the temperature drops even further.

In moments, I am crouching down by Raff's inert body. His pulse is weak and his forehead cool. "He's okay but very cold," I call upwards. "We need to get him out of here quickly."

As Bertie and Larna scrabble down the steps to join me, I wonder how on earth we are going to move him, tall as he is. It doesn't help that the cut-out steps up to the top of the trench are narrow. However, the effect of adrenalin in the blood is astonishing and little by little, we part-carry, part-drag him up to the surface.

As soon as we have laid him on the top, away from the workings, we all double up, our lungs bursting with effort. Once I have caught my breath, I kneel down beside him. "Raff, it's me, Selena. Are you okay?"

His eyes flicker open and then close again. He's begun to shiver violently.

"You're frozen. You need to get warm. Can you stand?"

We don't wait for a reply. Grabbing him under his arms, we drag him upright and somehow manage to get to the

Portakabin. Once he is in a chair, with Buddy by his feet, I find some blankets to lay over him while Larna fills the kettle and makes tea.

It's several minutes before his shivering decreases to infrequent shudders. When at last his eyes open, there's an expression of deep sadness in them. He opens his mouth to speak but no voice emerges. Finally he frowns, clears his throat and tries again. "Selena?"

The name is a relief. What would I have done if he'd called me Seela again? He has to make several more attempts before he can manage an entire sentence. "I…" He gulps. "I was in the farmhouse…" His voice trails away. He clears his throat and tries again. "I heard a call, pleading for help." He starts to pant as though he's been running. "She was under the tarpaulin. She looked so like you, Selena. I thought you had fallen in."

"It's all right, Raff; I'm safe."

"But then I saw that it wasn't you after all, but Seela. I don't remember any more."

Bertie is staring at him, trying to take in the torrent of words. "So you've seen the dreams, too," he whispers, "and Selena wasn't even touching you."

This isn't the time for explanations. They haven't even been introduced yet. When Larna puts a tray of hot tea on the table, I help Raff to sit up and sip it. "Raff, this is Bertie Fratton."

"Pleased to meet you, dear boy," Bertie says gently. "I am Marcus's uncle."

"And you remember Larna. I am staying with her in her caravan."

Raff nods.

"We came to ask you something," I tell him. "When you weren't at the farmhouse, I reckoned you might be here."

He closes his eyes briefly and then opens them again. "What did you want to ask me about?"

"The necklace," says Bertie.

Surprised, Raff frowns. "I thought you wanted the necklace kept a secret, Selena?"

"I did," I confess, "but things have changed. Since then, Larna has had a particularly nasty nightmare that, it seems, I transferred to her, and ..."

Bertie has his writer's face on again and is too keen to let me finish. "Dear boy, I understand that you had the necklace for a night. Did you dream anything while it was in your possession?"

If it is possible, Raff grows even paler. He nods.

"Yet you don't have it now and still you have dreamed again?"

Raff nods again.

"Perhaps holding the necklace, even once, is enough to unlock something," Bertie says frowning in concentration. He hesitates.

"Do you have any idea how old the necklace might be or whether it could be valuable?"

"I only had it for one night, but I suspect that it is old."

"How old?" Larna asks.

"That's impossible to say without verification, but as it seems to be showing us what happened here at the dig, I'd say it could be Bronze Age."

Bertie whistles through his teeth. "But wouldn't it have disintegrated by now if it were that old?"

"The gold mixed into the bronze may have helped it to survive in such a good condition," replies Raff. "Gold doesn't rust, you see. Touching it does harm it, however. Acid from skin causes corrosion." He pauses. "My advice would be to let me take it down to London to have it properly authenticated and dated."

"Sorry, I can't," I say.

"Why ever not?"

"It has been stolen, dear boy," Bertie confesses.

Raff looks horrified. "*Stolen?*"

"Yes, it would seem that my sister has taken it."

Raff looks back at me in alarm.

"Bertie is Hester Knebworth's brother," I remind him.

Stunned, he stares at me. "But why would Marcus's mother and your sister steal the necklace?"

I shrug. "We don't know."

"It's possible that she is in need of money," puts in Bertie. "That's why I wanted to ask you if the necklace could be valuable."

"It could be priceless."

"And can priceless artefacts be sold?"

"Absolutely."

"Then there we have it," Bertie groans. "Hester is never going to give it back. If I know her at all, she'll be driving down to London tomorrow to have it valued. Selling the necklace could help get her and the company out of a very deep hole."

HESTER – Present Day

Inside the manor, Hester lay in bed with her eyes open, clutching the necklace. She didn't dare close them in case she had another nightmare about insects. With a shudder, she thought of Alan lying in hospital. Of course, she should visit him, but she hated places of ill health. Yet what would the villagers think of her if they discovered she had refused? She was supposed to be a pillar of the community and a role model for all. Yet here she was, shirking her wifely duty in the most conspicuous way.

On the other hand, there was no love lost between her and Alan. Never had been, even in the early days. Her father had insisted she married him because he wanted a man to take over *Frattons*. She'd never forgiven him for that. She was twice as intelligent as Alan and several times more cunning. For a long time she had managed to rule silently from the inside but, after she had given birth, Alan had made some atrocious decisions and she had not been able to stop the company from sliding into this deplorable, shameful state.

Nevertheless, now Alan was no longer here, she surprised herself by realising how much she hated being alone. They'd had separate bedrooms for a long time and there was little contact or conversation between them, but at least he'd been here as a physical presence in the house. Now it was so dark and silent in the room that it felt as though the whole world had faded away and left her to be snuffed out.

She closed her eyes, hoping that sleep would give her the respite she so badly needed, but as soon as her mind began to drift, she saw the wasp trapped in amber trying to move. Mesmerised she imagined it pushing its way closer to the surface of the crystal. Then it was wriggling free. At any moment it would fly.

Terrified, she tried to open her eyes but couldn't. All she could hear now was the sound of buzzing. The wasp had escaped and now it was looking for a way to get inside her.

It was going to eat her from the inside out.

circa 2000 B.C.E.

Hogan swatted the wasp, wondering where it had come from in such cold weather. Retying his garments, he strode over to the stake where Lanalla was bound. "You are finished, priestess. As for your little SeeSayer, now she knows what will be expected of her in the future."

He was about to continue his mocking when someone suddenly jumped onto his back. He fought to keep his balance but a dog rushed at his leg and sunk in sharp teeth. "Kurt," he yelled. "Where are you?" He had no time to find out because he was having to lash out backwards, downwards, sideways as a second figure wrapped arms around his knees. A yank and he fell. He felt the man's hands move to his throat, find the chain and pull.

But the Amulet did not give way. The sensation of being strangled lit his rage and he managed to throw the man off balance and push him away. Moments later, someone else slammed him to the ground and sat on him. Head squashed to one side, his hands were tied behind his back and he was forced to watch Riadd throw a knife each to Fellana and Bannan so they could untie the villagers. Too late, Kurt appeared. For a moment Hogan thought he would be rescued, but as soon as he saw the fool untying Lanalla and Duna, he realised he had been betrayed.

When Riadd picked Seela gently up from the ground and carried her away, Hogan spat into the dust, ridding himself at the same time of two of his blackened teeth. Then Kurt released Mevin, who despite his injury, started to help Bannan guide the villagers back to their huts.

If they thought they were going to get away with this, they had another think coming.

He still had the Amulet and with it, he would get his revenge.

HESTER – Present Day

Hester woke, sweat pouring off her body and looked down at her hands. She was no longer holding the chain. Somehow it was round her neck, pulling tighter with each breath, as though it wanted to throttle her.

It was only when she felt something land on her leg that she leapt out of bed and switched on the light. There it was: the wasp. It really had escaped the amber. Shaking her leg violently, she tried to dislodge it, but it stayed clamped by its sting. Jabbing violently at it, she tried to throw it off, but the wasp began to climb higher. Terrified, she swatted at it again and this time managed to hurled it into the air.

Tearing off the necklace, she flung it into her handbag and fled from the room, down the stairs and out of the manor. Outside it was pouring. Sheltering her hair from the rain, she ran outside to look for her car but couldn't find it. She was just wondering where it was when she remembered that Alan had sold it. Instantly vindicated that she had not visited him, she decided to take his precious Silver Cloud instead. The Rolls was his pride and joy.

That would teach him.

Hurrying to the house, she found the keys to the Rolls and returned outside to open the garage. To her great relief, there was no sign of the wasp. With the stings on her leg throbbing, she opened the garage and ran to the driver's door. The maroon paintwork of the car was still in an immaculate condition despite the fact that it had been built in 1962. As a surge of resentment flared up in her, she thought about using the key to gouge out a scratch down the side, but she managed to stop herself. She would sell it while he was in hospital and take the money with her when she escaped.

First she needed to get to the auctioneer in London. With a smirk on her face, she threw her bag onto the passenger seat and climbed in. It was only the second time she had been inside the Silver Cloud and she had never driven it. Alan kept it for himself, preferring to go off on long drives at weekends without her. An unexpected wave of nausea rose up and she had to swallow down hard as the smell of leather and polish hit her. Refusing to give way to weakness, she pushed the key in the ignition. Then, glancing around her to make sure that the wasp hadn't reappeared, she started the engine.

As she jolted forward, another car came careering up the drive towards her. She didn't see it in time and the two vehicles collided, the impact jarring her arm so that she cried out in pain.

"What the hell do you think you're doing?" cried Marcus, as he leapt out of his Fiat. "You've dented the bumper. Father will go mental!"

Hester froze for a moment before she regained herself. "I was barely moving," she protested. "Stop fussing. I'll get it repaired."

"With what? You've got no money. Where's your Mercedes?"

"Being serviced," she lied.

"And Father's Volvo?"

"Still at the office."

He groaned and wiped at the rain on his face. "Look, I'm getting drenched out here. Why don't you go back into the house and get dressed? I'll reverse the Rolls back into the garage and then we'll work out what to do."

"No. I need to get to London."

"London? Why?"

"I've got an appointment with someone."

"Well, you can't go in your nightclothes."

Hester looked down at herself and gasped. Then she remembered the wasp. "I'm not going back in there." she refused.

"But …"

An image of all the people who had betrayed her rose up into her mind, giving her the energy she needed. "Move your car out of the way, Marcus. I don't want to be late. I can't afford to miss this appointment. You will have to take me."

Incredulous, he stared at her. "In case you haven't noticed, you've just ruined my car. It isn't going anywhere until it's been looked at."

"Then drive the Cloud."

Marcus almost choked. "I think not. It needs to go to the garage."

"You said there's only a little dent in the bumper. The engine is fine. Get in and drive."

"Father will have your guts for garters."

"He's in hospital. He doesn't have to find out." She threw him the keys.

Unable to stop himself, he reached out and caught them.

"Anyway, what is his is mine," she continued. "He has stolen the manor. I will steal his Rolls."

Marcus started to waiver as though he was remembering that driving the Rolls had been his dream. Hester watched his face turn from excitement to fear and back again. It didn't take long for the excitement to win. "How about I drive you to the hospital to see Father instead?" he suggested.

"I need to go to London," she insisted. "You could get the bumper repaired there while I'm at my appointment. That way, he need never know."

He didn't hesitate for long. "Oh, for God's sake," he swore. "Move over."

It was tricky shifting over across the gear stick but by the time she had managed it, he had moved his damaged Fiat to the side of the wide drive. Drenched with rain, he climbed into the driver's seat of the Silver Cloud and studied the dashboard. "Where are the wipers?"

"How should I know?"

"Then no wonder you hit me. You wouldn't have been able to see a thing in this deluge."

One by one, he went through the controls.

"Hurry up," she chided. "I'll be late."

Tentatively, he turned the key in the ignition. Then he gently pressed the accelerator and inched forward.

Hester gritted her teeth and waited.

There was still no sign of the wasp.

SELENA – Present Day

I'm exhausted by the time I return to the caravan. It's raining heavily now and threatening a storm. We have taken Raff back to the farmhouse to sleep and Bertie and Larna have shut themselves up in the boat with Buddy. I make up the bed and climb in, listening to the hammering of the rain on the roof. Without the necklace I feel naked, and there's a deep hurt inside me that throbs like a wound.

I close my eyes, praying that I will not dream. The idea of returning to that ghastly world again is almost beyond me. Seela has been split apart and spat out. I cannot imagine how she must be feeling. It doesn't take long for her to appear. I try to push her away so I can get some rest, but her pull is too strong and I begin to fall backwards like Alice tumbling down the rabbit hole.

circa 2000 B.C.E.

Seela couldn't stop crying. Lanalla had done all she could to staunch the flow of blood from where Hogan had so viciously torn her, but she could still feel the wetness between her legs and her belly was cramping painfully. She crawled over to Duna who was rocking back and forth, terrified and trembling violently from cold. When she put her hand on her sister's forehead, she felt burning. Collapsing by her side, Seela drew her close, trying to block out the sound of the savage fighting. At least everyone was against Hogan now. Kurt had changed sides. Even Mevin had ended up helping the villagers.

She must have drifted off to sleep because the next thing she knew, Riadd was standing in the doorway holding a wounded Bika in his arms. "Lanalla, look after him for me, will you? He's been badly kicked. I think one of his legs is broken."

"Put him down by the fire," Lanalla said, obvious relief that he was talking to her again briefly lighting her face. "What's happening out there now?"

"Hogan's gone mad," Riadd panted. "He's brandishing the Amulet and trying to claim leadership. He says there will be no more worship of The Mother and that you are no longer priestess. He reckons that Seela belongs to him and Duna is to be sacrificed at the Stone."

"But nobody else is on his side," she protested. "Why hasn't he been killed by now? The last time I saw him he was on the ground."

"With the Amulet in his hands, nobody will go near him."

She blanched. She would never forget the look on his face as he had brandished it at her. "Then we have to get it from him. But first we must help the girls to get away."

He looked across at the two girls who were lying huddled together. "How is Duna?"

Lanalla shook her head. "I can do no more for her."

He nodded his understanding. "What about Seela? Is she badly hurt?"

"She can just about walk but her shoulder was dislocated. I have put the joint back into place but she won't be able to bear weight on it for a while."

"Then she won't be able to carry Duna."

"I will go with them and carry Duna for her."

He looked wary. "Why should I trust you after you betrayed me? I will go with them instead of you."

"No," she flinched. "You are needed here, Riadd. You must become the new Leader. Find a way to overpower Hogan and kill him. Once you have retrieved the Amulet, everyone will follow you."

He paled.

"Now go. I need to help the girls to escape."

SELENA – Present Day

"No!" I cry.

"Selena, wake up."

I feel myself rising but something is choking me and I can't rise high enough to breathe.

"Open your eyes."

"Hogan," I sob. "He is too strong."

"Selena, love, it's a dream, that's all." She gathers me into her arms. "It's all right. I won't let you be hurt."

"But Hogan is going to kill Riadd," I choke, pushing her away. "I've got to warn him."

"Selena, you're here in the caravan. You're safe."

"You should never have made me SeeSayer. It's me who has to get the Amulet back, not Riadd. It's the only thing that will save him. Lanalla, please…"

"Selena, you're dreaming. I'm Larna…"

"You promised to keep us safe," I wail.

"Look," she tries, her voice cracking, "why don't you come back to the boat and eat some hot, nourishing food? That will do you the world of good."

"No, I've got to get the Amulet back," I roar. "I'm the SeeSayer now. I can use it to help him."

"You've got to forget about the Amulet, Selena."

"Never," I say, struggling to my feet. "I've got to go and find Riadd. I must save him. I must ..."

"But there's a storm brewing, love. Stay here where you're safe. I'll just go and fetch Bertie. He's in the boat. He'll know what to do."

I run to the door. Its pouring outside, the rain weeping a flood of tears from the sky.

Perhaps The Mother is grieving after all.

MARCUS – Present Day

"No!" Hester shrieks.

"What's the matter?" cried Marcus, feeling the steering wheel slide under his hands.

"The wasp is somewhere in the car. Get it out!"

"Oh, for God's sake, calm down. I need to concentrate. Besides, it's too cold for wasps. There's nothing in here apart from the two of us. It's in your imagination. Please be quiet. If I crash his car, you'll have to be the one to tell Father."

The wasp landed on her sleeve. "Go away!" she screamed.

Marcus felt the wheels skid underneath him. "Shut up!" he shouted, his heart thudding uncomfortably in his chest. "This storm is bad enough. You're making it worse."

Panic gripped her as the wasp suddenly reappeared and launched itself into the air, buzzing past her ear to land somewhere in the back. After what seemed like an age, they came to a halt with the engine still running.

"We're at the hospital, Mother." He tried to smile. "I bet they've never had a Rolls Royce in this car park before."

"The hospital? Why have we stopped at the hospital? I need to get to London."

"You need to see Father."

"I don't want to see him."

"For God's sake, he's just had a heart attack. Even you can't be that uncaring." Marcus tried to steady his breathing. "Look, when I saw him, he was unconscious. There's no way he'll realise we've driven his precious car. Let me drop you outside the front entrance so you don't get wet. You can wait there while I park. You'll be fine."

"Please ..."

He sighed. She'd never said 'please' to him in his life before. "Okay, okay. I'll park first and we'll go in together." He reached into his pocket for some coins for the car park. "Blast, I haven't got enough for the machine. And I haven't got my wallet with me. Have you got any change or a card we could use?"

"The wasp is in the back. What happens if it attacks again?"

"Oh, for fuck's sake. Forget the bloody wasp and look in your bag. You must have something."

"My purse isn't there," she whispered without looking.

"Of course it is. Why else would you have your handbag?

"Well. It isn't in it now."

He was stunned. "You mean you just expected me to pay for your nice, jaunty little trip down to London, just like you expected me to pay for dinner the other night?"

"I ..."

"Well, you got me wrong. We're going straight back to the manor, getting your purse and returning to this hospital, storm or no storm."

"But..."

"Don't say another bloody word. I've had enough of you

trying to trick me." Muttering another expletive under his breath, he put his foot on the accelerator and headed for the exit to the carpark.

Hester started to flap her hand. "The wasp is flying again. Look!"

Marcus swerved on the wet road.

She unclipped her seat belt, reached for the handbag on the floor by her feet, hauled it up onto her lap and started to rummage inside it.

"What the hell are you doing?" shouted Marcus, frantically trying to regain the steering. "Put your seat belt back on."

She barely heard him as she pulled something out of her bag.

Out of the corner of his eye, he could see something glinting. Quickly taking his eyes from the road, he looked over at her clutching hands. "Good God, isn't that Selena's artefact, the one she stole from my dig?"

SELENA – Present Day

I can't see Hogan and there's no sign of the Amulet. I'll just have to find Riadd and warn him. Wind and rain slam into my face as I start running. Half-blinded by rain, I tear across the grass towards the track that leads around the hill to the valley. Several times I slide on the drenched ground, but I pick myself up and continue running, rain and tears flooding my eyes.

I am just approaching the turning to the track that leads to the valley when I hear footsteps from behind. Someone is following me. Whipping round to look, I can't see anyone but I try to run faster. I only realise that I have missed the track when it is too late to turn back. The footsteps are close behind me now. With little visibility and no pavement, running along the road is tantamount to suicide. But I have no choice. I have to find Riadd and save him.

I cross to the right-hand side of the road in order to face the oncoming traffic, careful not to go too close to the stream that runs alongside. With the rain fierce in my face and the wind threatening to take me off my feet, I hug the edge of the road, mutter a silent prayer, and begin sprinting towards the farmhouse.

At first, the road seems empty of traffic as though the storm has scared everyone away from travelling, but when I am about half way along, a lorry begins to approach, flashing its headlights in warning. Almost too late, I jump onto the bank, only just keeping my balance as it hurtles through a deep puddle, drenching me in water. Wiping my face with my hand, I leap back onto the road.

Moments later, I am running again, the footsteps still chasing behind me. I am about to reach the valley when I see a big car approaching, throwing off spray in all directions. The white-haired driver is looking towards the passenger seat rather than the road. Staring at him, I will him to turn back to the windscreen so that he will notice me on the road, but as the car draws closer, I suddenly recognise the face of his passenger. My guts turn to water. No, *no*, No! It is Mevin and he's shouting at Hogan. Mevin must have changed sides again. They must be going to find Riadd, to kill him again, to…

There's a violent shove from behind as I am pushed sideways onto the grass verge. As a red-headed figure leaps out in front of the car, her raised hands empty, Mevin suddenly turns to the front and sees her in the headlights. Face opening with shock, he spins the wheel to swerve and miss her, but he's too late.

There is a hideous screech of tyres, and the car smashes into the far bank.

In the silence that follows, the world turns several times on its axis as though it is unsure where to settle. Giddy, I find myself lying on my back staring at the sky where a blackbird is flying overhead, tossed in the storm like sea drift. It must be Seela's blackbird, flown all the way through time to see me. When it turns towards me, its eyes are different colours. One is black whereas the other is white.

I try to stand so I can fly up to join it in the sky but the air in my lungs has vanished. My hand is flung outwards from me, my arm at an awkward angle, but there is no pain. At least I am not alone. There is a girl standing in the road, staring at something shiny on the ground by her feet. She bends down, picks it up and brings it to me. A wisp of her foetid breath drifts over me as she looks into my face, her green eyes etched with sorrow as her gaze locks with mine. Then she slowly stretches her hand out to me. It is the necklace, come back to me at last.

As if she is saying goodbye to the world, she bends again and puts it in my pocket, each of her joints creaking like the wood from a shipwreck.

"*Seela* …" I breathe, but my voice refuses to come out of my mind and she begins to drift away until, abandoned yet again, she turns into a mere shimmer in the air.

Gebo – a gift

Chapter Thirteen

LARNA AND BERTIE – Present Day

At any moment, the caravan looked as though it might fly up into the sky. *Water Haven* was swaying like a dancer, unsure which way she should pirouette across the stage. Somehow, *Marigold* hadn't moved. The wind shrieked like a banshee, a month's worth of rain falling in minutes. In the kitchen, crockery was falling off the draining board and smashing onto the floor as though the whole world was angry and lashing out in revenge.

While Larna and Bertie secured the boat with extra ropes, Buddy howled at the door, desperate to find the woman who had rescued him. For the first time since she'd bought *Water Haven*, Larna was truly frightened. She didn't fear for herself or Bertie or even the dog. It was the thought of Selena that terrified her. The girl had run off into the storm thinking she was Seela. She wondered if there had been a storm here thousands of years ago or whether the evening had been calm with nothing more than a breeze to scuff the clouds.

When there was nothing more they could do but baton down the hatches and wait, Larna tried to convince herself that the rain had brought Selena back into herself and that she had found somewhere dry to shelter. But there was no way of checking. The phone lines were down and there was no mobile signal. She asked Bertie if they could drive to the farmhouse to see if she had gone there but he persuaded her to stay inside.

The storm didn't lessen until just after 11pm when, with a roaring one minute and silence the next, it suddenly stopped. Once they were sure that the calm would continue, they each picked up a torch and went outside to investigate. This time, they couldn't keep Buddy inside. With a howl, he fled into the night. Larna called his name again and again desperate for him to return, but there was no answering bark. He had gone.

Bertie took Larna by the hand and pulled her across the field to inspect the damage. To his relief, *Marigold* was still untouched and the boat also seemed to have been spared. The caravan, however, had buckled at one end and seemingly been sprayed with bullets at the other. It had been rendered uninhabitable.

As though this was prophetic, Bertie put his arm round Larna and led her back inside the boat. Once he had sat her down in the snug and covered her with a blanket, he returned to the kitchen and made them both a mug of cocoa. They had only just finished drinking it when they were woken by a glare of lights as a vehicle bumped over the sodden field. As one, they both jumped up, rushed to the door and opened it. Buddy rushed in wagging his tail, while a man, propping up a groggy-looking Selena, walked towards the deck. With a shriek, Larna ran out to meet them. Bertie grabbed Buddy's collar and waited.

"I've brought your daughter back," said the man. "I'm a driver for the hospital. She's been in an accident and dislocated her shoulder, but apart from a touch of hypothermia she's otherwise unharmed."

"Oh God," shuddered Larna. "Thank you so much. We didn't know where she was." Her voice cracked. "We …"

He tried to smile reassuringly. "It was the dog that led me here. As soon as I saw him in the headlights he began to run here. Somehow, I knew he wanted me to follow him. Hardly protocol, but …" He stopped and looked at the boat. "Crikey, is this where you live? Is it safe being on the river in a storm?"

Bertie stepped forward, still holding buddy by his collar. "Thank you for your concern but, as you can see, *Water Haven* is very well tethered."

The driver shrugged uncertainly before looking at his watch. "Well, if you say so. Your daughter will need to keep warm, but she should make a full recovery. Now, I need to be getting back."

Larna held out her arms to Selena, who half fell, half staggered into them, her eyes barely open, the eyepatch no longer in place. Once they were back inside the boat, Bertie released Buddy and helped carry her into the spare room at the back of the boat. Selena whimpered several times as they peeled the damp clothes from her cold body but they did their best to avoid her shoulder. Once they had dressed her as best as they could in warm pyjamas, they laid her down in bed beside a hot water bottle and put two duvets on top of her.

"Fancy him thinking she was our daughter," Larna said as she stroked Selena's forehead. "She looks so tiny lying there. I'm sure she wasn't that small before."

Bertie glanced at her anxiously. "You really care for her, don't you?"

"She could have died out there tonight," Larna murmured, wiping a tear from her face.

"Well, be careful," he continued. "You can't afford to get too attached. Otherwise, when she returns home to Norfolk, you'll be bereaved all over again."

She bent to pick up the wet clothes that had been dropped onto the floor. Selena's coat was still wet so she hung it up on the back of the door to dry. The others would just have to be laundered. "I think I'll bring a chair in here and watch over her in case she wakes."

"You'll do no such thing," Bertie said gently. "She is safe now and her breathing is deep and regular. She just needs to sleep and so do you."

Tearing her eyes away, she looked over to him. "Thanks for staying with me."

"My pleasure, old girl."

"Bertie, it's far too late for you to be driving back now. Let me make up a bed in the snug for you. That way we can both be close if she wakes up and needs us."

"Are you sure?" he yawned.

"Of course," she said. "That's what friends are for, isn't it?"

KARL – Present Day

Alan Knebworth was lying propped up with an oxygen mask strapped to his face, his eyes closed. Slowly, Karl made his way to the chair at the side of the bed and reached for his father's hand. He didn't remember ever having held this warm but unresponsive flesh before.

"Is your mother on her way?" asked the nurse.

Unable to speak, Karl nodded. It was better to pretend she was coming than admit she didn't care.

"Good," the nurse acknowledged. "Now, I've put a chair on each side of the bed. Sit yourself down in one of them. Although he's unconscious, he'll know you're here."

Karl waited until she had left before he dared to gaze at his father's face. Alan Knebworth looked exactly as he had drawn him, except that here he was not lying in a pool of blood and there was no sign of a knife sticking out of his chest. The deep lines which grooved down the sides of his mouth, and the frown marks that cut into the skin above his nose, were testament to the anxiety which had ruled his life for most of his adult years.

Karl was flooded with guilt as he thought of the ways he had let his father down in the business. His speech impediment, timidity, and the restlessness that made him flit from one thing to another, had rendered him useless. The truth was that, apart from his art, he never alighted on anything for long enough to make any difference. Had he been more confident, perhaps he would have been able to save *Frattons* by getting more orders, but he doubted it. The business world was changing. His parents were not prepared to move with the times and he was not, and never could be, any sort of salesman.

The surprise was that his father had continued to believe in him, right up to the end. Not so his mother. He had been a colossal disappointment to her right from the start. She utterly misunderstood that he had the soul of an artist, whereas the man lying here had known that he was different from the rest of the family and had kept him employed, even when they were facing ruin.

Unable to stop his life flashing before his eyes, Karl wondered if he had given up too easily. If he had found the courage to stand up for himself and made a career out of his art, perhaps they would have been proud of him. If he had not developed such an incapacitating stammer, there was a chance he could have persuaded Marcus to stay and take some of the burdens from his father's shoulders. Perhaps then his father wouldn't be lying here now, dying in an anonymous hospital bed.

Mesmerised by his own failure, he watched as his father's head rose upwards with the effort of taking another breath, only to lapse back down again after completing the cycle. The next breath was slightly easier with less of an upward movement. Hope leapt inside Karl until he realised that it simply meant that his father was not breathing as deeply. Little by little, the breaths began to slow. As each pause became longer, his father's head shifted slightly to one side, only to fall back to its original position. Then suddenly, the colour drained from Alan Knebworth's face. There was one small sigh. After that, only silence as his father's colour drained away to a pasty shade of unbaked clay.

His father had gone.

SELENA – Present Day

Nursery songs babble in a language I used to understand as Mara smiles at me from a long way away. I try to touch her but she has been strapped into Dad's old car. Realising that there is still time to save them, I try to cry out a warning, but I am a blackbird with an injured wing and can't fly.

"Selena, love, it's all right. You are safe."

My shoulder screams along with my pearly eye as I try to move towards the voice. It is Mum and yet it is not. There's a loud crash and I am left staring at two tiny round windows covered by chintz curtains. Squeezing my eyes against the pain, I hear the sound of shouting. I try to cover my ears, but I can't move.

Then I see him: Riadd. For a split second, he looks at me before his head cracks backwards and he starts to fall.

Darkness descends and I am drawn backwards so fast that the world itself begins to tremble. There is a great howling from Bika. The sound goes on and on, like the roaring of a storm as it rips trees up from their roots and hurls them down onto the ground. It is only when Lanalla comes back into the hut that he falls silent. As soon as she faces me I know what she is going to say. I try to stop my ears but I cannot prevent my spine from going rigid.

"Riadd is dead," she confirms, the lines of her face turning into crevices which run with tears.

Unable to respond, I stare at her, still cradling Duna against me with my uninjured arm. She is shivering uncontrollably. I look down at her and wince at the fierce heat radiating from her skin.

We might no longer be hiding up the tree, but it seems that the wolf is finally about to get its prey.

circa 2000 B.C.E.

Hogan was standing astride Riadd's body like a lion over its kill.

"You have no men left to lead," Lanalla said. "You have destroyed everything."

He spat at her feet before suddenly flinching backwards. His fist slackened and began swatting at his neck as though something was biting him. "Go away!" he hissed.

At first, she thought he was talking to her but then she noticed that the fury in his eyes had turned to fear.

In moments he was clutching his neck and making a strange noise as though he was being strangled. Then he brought his hand forward to clutch the bottom pendant of the Amulet. Yelping with pain, he yanked the chain upwards off his neck and flung it at her.

Lanalla launched herself at the Amulet and scraped it up

from the ground. As she clutched it to her chest in relief, she felt The Mother enter her, turning her eyes into two flames. Power restored, she turned her face back towards him and gave him the full force of her deified glare. As though blinded, he fell to the ground.

The curse rose up in her like a wave. "You should never have returned, Hogan. You are not welcome here. You have been banished once. You are banished again and this time you will die." Then she pointed the bottom pendant of the Amulet down at him. "I curse you. You will walk the earth and only find pain. You will wander lost and never find comfort. You will never find love, only fear." Raising the Amulet up to the heavens with one hand, she pointed the other down to the earth as though she was making a connection.

Hogan raised his hands to his face trying to protect himself from the insect. "No!" he cried. "Get off me!"

"Mother," the priestess continued in a voice that was both hers and not hers. "Chase this man through time itself and show no mercy. Drive him to his knees until he can see what he has done. Punish him until he begs for mercy and rights the wrongs he has committed."

At last she saw the wasp. It was stinging him again and again and again, until his hands were a mass of reddened, painful lumps.

She smiled.

The curse was sealed.

Hogan was doomed.

FALALA AND RAFF – Present day

Falala arrived late for work the next morning because of a road block between the Stennings and Stone Clump. As she walked into the Portakabin, Raff stood to greet her, his face white with shock.

"Marcus has been hurt in a car accident," he said, holding out a note in his hand. "Karl stuck this to the door."

"Oh my God," she whispered as she read the note. "He's in hospital."

In two long strides, he was beside her and putting a comforting arm around her shoulders. "It's okay. He's a fighter. He'll be okay."

"You don't know that," she whimpered. "You don't understand. He ... We ..."

He pulled her closer. "It seems that he was with his mother."

"His mother? But he hates her."

"I know. It doesn't make any sense."

"And was she hurt too?"

"Apparently, she's even worse. I rang the hospital. They wouldn't tell me much because I'm not family but when I explained that I work with Marcus, they told me that he and his mother are both in a coma."

Fally sank onto the nearest chair, the note still in her hand. "It must have been that storm," she groaned. "It was ferocious. I've never heard anything like it. Roof tiles and trees are down everywhere." She looked up at him, her eyes wide with fear. "Oh, Raff, I was horrid to him after you left yesterday. He'd been so rude to Selena that I gave him a piece of my mind."

Raff nodded. "I wasn't too happy with him, either," he admitted.

"What are we going to do?"

Raff sat down beside her. "I don't know. I'm afraid that's not the only bad news. There was a second note." He handed that one to her as well. "Alan Knebworth has had a heart attack and died."

"Marcus's father?"

Raff nodded.

"Oh my God, that's terrible.""

Beyond words, they both sat.

Suddenly dizzy, Fally put her head between her knees.

"Are you okay?" he asked in concern.

It was several moments before she was able to raise her head. "We need to get to the hospital," she moaned.

"There's no point. Marcus is unconscious."

"Conscious or unconscious, we should still be with him. Besides, Karl will need our support too." She went to stand. "I'll get my keys."

He put out a hand to stop her. "You're in no fit state to drive, Fally. Besides, the road is blocked. Let's go on my motorbike. It will be quicker."

It still took a long time to arrive. Eventually they arrived at the hospital where they found Karl in the waiting area of Intensive Care, looking haggard and worn. Falala walked straight up to him. "Karl?"

He jumped at the sound but smiled weakly as soon as he recognised her.

"I'm sorry," she apologised, "I didn't mean to startle you. We got your notes. How's Marcus?"

Beyond speech, he pulled a notebook out of his pocket and wrote *Unconscious* in a shaky hand.

"And your mother?"

Same.

She took a deep breath. "I'm so sorry about your father. We both are." She took a step back and half-turned towards her companion. "Karl, this is Raff. You met him briefly at the dig."

Karl forced himself to look up at the tall man who looked so like the youth in his drawings. He waited for the shock to hit him, but he was too numb for it to register.

"Is there anything we can do?" asked Raff quietly.

Karl gave a little shake of his head.

"Have you eaten?"

Again, Karl shook his head.

"Come on, then," Raff said. "Let's get you some food. You'll feel better with something inside you."

SELENA – Present Day

I'm being rocked like a babe in arms. The motion is soothing and I wonder if Mum has come back to save me. It's only when I open my eyes that I find myself in a small, strangely shaped room. Apart from the single bed and a couple of chintz curtains, there's not much else. I try to lever myself up but pain in my shoulder makes me wince. Slowly, I manage to manoeuvre myself out of bed and open the door.

"Selena, you're awake."

As I wobble dangerously on my feet, I let Larna lead me to the armchair by the fire. Once Buddy has settled by my feet, she covers me with a blanket. Then she pulls up a chair so that she can sit beside me and hold my hand.

"What happened?" I ask. My brain feels all mushy and I cannot think.

"You were in an accident," she tells me. "You've dislocated your shoulder. An ambulance driver brought you back from the hospital and you've been here in the boat ever since." She tries to smile but looks as though she's going to cry. "The caravan has been battered by the storm. But don't worry, you can stay in the boat for as long as you like."

I want to say that I'll stay here forever if she asks me to, but instead I ask her about the accident. Images flit in and out of my mind. There's wind and rain and the sound of running footsteps, but then my mind goes blank again.

"You must be starving," she says. "I've made some thick soup. I'll just go and get some for you. You can have it on your lap."

She's right. I am ravenous but my stomach is tied in a knot and I'm not sure that I'll be able to eat. As Larna disappears into the kitchen, my mind returns to the memory of wind and rain, and my pearly eye starts to fizz as though it's trying to tell me something. There's an ache between my legs that shouldn't be there and I feel as though I've been torn and bruised.

But my eye won't let me rest. It shows me running to the farmhouse in a storm, trying to get to Raff to warn him about something. Except it wasn't Raff I was looking for, was it? It was Riadd. I needed to warn him about something. About someone.

Now a new face rises up in my mind. At first, it seems to be half man and half woman. The two sides don't fit each other as though they're parts of different jigsaws. But then I see the eyes. They are the same on both sides and they make me flinch. There's a chilling mixture of cruelty that seems to be directed right at me. My heart starts to hammer alarmingly and, suddenly frightened, I tear my gaze away.

To my relief, Larna returns with a tray in her hands and the image disappears.

"Here you are," she says brightly. "This will do you good and put some colour in your cheeks."

She places a large bowl of soup on a little table at my side and puts the tray on my lap. Tentatively, I try some soup but it sticks like ashes in my mouth. I put the spoon down.

The air between us thickens. "Oh dear," she says sadly, "don't you like it?"

I shrug helplessly with my one good shoulder. Ashes are floating down through me as though I am a fire that has died.

"Okay, you can eat later," she says gently. "Let's get you back to bed."

I let her remove the tray and lead me back to the tiny cabin. As though she were my mother, she tucks the duvet around me.

Once she has closed the door, my mind starts to topple again and I am plummeting backwards, past the crumpling of Dad's old car and into a forest of long ago. The trees are dark and menacing and full of shadows. I must land in a patch of light or I will be lost. My feet come to rest on a pile of long dead leaves that crunch beneath my weight as if telling me that they are alive and dead at the same time. As I look around, a wave of such utter loneliness hits me that I have to clutch at the trunk of the nearest tree to keep myself upright. The wood disintegrates under my fingers and I almost topple over.

Then I remember. I was searching for Riadd, wasn't I? He's the only person who can help me now but I have to warn him first.

A blackbird starts to sing in a nearby tree. Hope rekindles and the terror lifts. If I can find Riadd, then I will be safe.

But where is he?

I look around, searching for his hut. If I go there, then perhaps he'll tell me that everything will be all right.

I've got to be brave, that's all.

Stepping forward, I move backwards into the nightmare.

circa 2000 B.C.E.

Seela limped to Riadd's hut, before the priestess could get there. Lanalla had to be wrong. Perhaps Riadd had crawled there when Hogan had not been looking. Riadd was young. He was destined to be the next Leader. He could not be dead.

Careful not to jog her dislocated shoulder, she pushed her way through the door, trying to ignore the pain between her legs. Riadd was lying on the workbench, legs so long that they dangled awkwardly over the edge. Flooded with relief that he was only asleep, she slowly tiptoed towards him, careful not to make a sound and wake him. She reached across to smooth his skin and stroke his cheek so that he would realise he was not alone, but one touch and she snatched her hand away. He was as cold as stone.

Something inside her started to break as a great keening howl tore through the hut, shattering the silence. Numbness began to crawl up her like a worm, eating her from the inside out. The terror was beyond anything she had ever known. Lanalla could not be trusted and without Riadd there was no-one left to protect her and Duna. They were both prey to Hogan. He could do anything he liked with them.

Forcing herself to touch him again, Seela tried to ignore the pain screaming through her shoulder. As she peeled the torn clothes from his body, she gasped in horror at yet another example of Hogan's brutality. Great knife marks slashed the young skin in deep gouges of blood. Blackly swollen bruises rose up like hills on his bones. And there were scratches and bites as though finally, the wolf had come back to find her and torn apart the wrong person.

Tears poured down her face as she dipped a strip of woven cloth into a bucket of water and started to clean away the marks of his death. When he was as clean as she could make him, she smoothed back the long black hair and kissed his forehead. Then she stepped back. His tools and knives were stacked in the corner, the knife he had used to carve the animals standing a little further away from the rest. Walking over to it, she ran a finger over its hilt, imagining his warm fingers pressed into the wood. Lifting it to her nose to drink in its scent, she tried to conjure up the moment when he had last used it.

Stricken, she tucked the knife and its sheath into her waistband and went back out into the cold.

She would not die without a fight.

RAFF – Present Day

Raff searched the ground beneath his feet as though it might somehow give him some answers. Insects, voles and worms were busy in the warming soil. There was the vaguest hint of spring and fragments of life were on the move. Memories were stirring and water was flowing. The blood that had seeped into the ground during the past was coming alive again.

Yet he was falling apart. Something inside him felt dead as though part of him had been killed. It didn't help that his body ached all over. Of course it was all in his mind just as everything had been all in his mind ever since he had returned to the Stennings. He should leave but Fally's need for a friend kept him here, along with the shape that still lay hidden under the field. And of course, Selena. Try as he might, he could not put her out of his mind anymore than he could dismiss the girl with the red hair who was still pleading with him to rescue her.

As though he was saying goodbye to the field and all it contained, he felt his feet growing heavy and, closing his eyes, he felt himself being drawn down again into the mud, through the soil and stones into a layer that refused to recycle itself back into earth. The sad fact was that now the Knebworths had met with such disaster, the project was unlikely ever to be followed through. The girl would have to lie here for the rest of time, pleading into eternity to be released. So he tried to say goodbye to her, to tell her she should rest now and that he had done all he could to save her. That it was time for her to release him. But she refused to listen and set up a howling in his mind that made him clutch his head and sway with the pain.

When he could stand it no longer, he forced his eyes open and discovered that he had fallen onto his knees. As he pushed himself back onto his feet he ran his hands over his legs and found great lumps of bruises forming over his bones as though he had been attacked. Shocked, he began to walk back up the field but with each step he took he heard another cry, each of them tearing him apart until he felt he would fall down and never get up again.

As he approached the Portakabin, a different face imposed itself over the girl's. Also surrounded by a cloud of red hair, he surprised himself by wishing he could talk to Selena. Only then did he realise that he hadn't heard from her. Of course, there was no reason why he should except that they seemed to be linked by the dreams of Seela and Riadd, separated by four thousand years. He was mad to think there might be a future for them in the present.

Only just remembering to duck his head in time, he let himself into the Portakabin where he found Falala sitting at her laptop, completing the notes they had made on the finds.

"Would you like some tea?" he asked.

She had barely spoken since returning from the hospital. He understood that she was upset but there was something more. He just didn't know what. "Fally?" She looked up at him with an expression of such despair, that he flinched. "Tea?" he repeated.

After a brief nod, he filled the kettle from the jug of water and dropped the last two tea bags into mugs. "Fally, I know that now is not the right time but we're going to have to work out how we can continue here. With Marcus and his mother in the hospital, his father dead, and his brother dumbstruck, we've lost the Knebworth support."

It took her a long time to answer. "I know. Clem Hardwick will never take the project on now," she murmured.

"Do you think he would have done if the accident hadn't happened?

She shrugged. "I don't know. We have done a remarkable job considering the short amount of time we've been here, and that it's also the wrong season of the year. He was clearly impressed by what we've managed to find."

"But is that enough now that Marcus is no longer on the team?"

She spun round to face him. "Of course he's still on the team," she protested harshly. "He may be in hospital, but ..." Suddenly she deflated like a balloon that could no longer keep its shape. "Don't mind me. I'm just trying to take it all in, that's all."

He nodded and stirred the tea before giving her a mug. "Here you are. This should help."

She gave him a watery smile. "Raff, what are we going to do?"

"Well," he began slowly. "I've been thinking about that. In order to prove that there is a complete Bronze Age settlement here, it would help if we knew there was a burial ground. Of course we haven't been here long enough to do that, and we're digging at the wrong time of the year, but if we could find even the smallest evidence of one, then I don't think that Clem will be able to close the dig, Knebworths or no Knebworths."

She scratched her head thoughtfully. "A burial site? But how are we going to do that? There's no time left and the ground is still so hard."

Raff was about to say that he didn't know when something caught the edge of his mind. It was the red-headed girl, her green eyes flashing at him as though they were trying to communicate something. After a split second, an idea landed in his mind. At first it seemed preposterous but the notion refused to leave him. It was a long time since he had used dowsing rods. It was hardly a recognised technique in modern circles but he didn't know what else to try. It just might work.

"A penny for them," Falala said.

Raff bit his lip, unsure whether to say anything. Falala was an academic and unlikely to go for anything quite so unorthodox. And yet, behind the scenes at university, he had helped all the teams without ever telling them how he had done it. Now, perhaps, it was time to own up to his unusual method. "Actually, I was thinking about dowsing," he confessed, waiting for a scornful response. When she said nothing, he continued. "It's something I used to do at university. Dowsing is how I was able to come up with suggestions that, at the time seemed far out, but ended up saving us all a lot of time."

"And there I was just thinking that you were lucky."

"Luck wasn't involved. All my ideas were based on what I picked up."

She snorted. "Why haven't you told me this before?"

"Marcus would have laughed in my face."

She nodded. "And Marcus isn't here at the moment."

"Precisely." Raff put his fingers thoughtfully to his lips. "I don't wish to be disloyal to him but we have to do something. Then, when he wakes up ..."

"... we'll have some good news to give him," she finished for him. She clasped her hands in front of her. "Raff, do you really think it could work? Do you really think you could find the location of a burial site by dowsing?"

"It's worth a try."

She sat forward. "I don't know much about dowsing. How would you go about it?"

"I'd start with the map and then, if there were any clues, I'd go outside and dowse the land itself."

She reached for the OS map and handed it to him. "Here you are then. Do your worst. It can't hurt."

"Really?"

"Really. There's no time like the present."

He took the map. "I'll have to make the rods first. Are there a couple of biros I could use as well as a wire coat hanger?"

She managed to produce what he needed. In moments he had pulled the two biros apart and put the plastic shells on the table in front of him. Next he untwisted the hook from the metal coat hanger and cut it in half. Once he had bent the ends into a right angle, he fitted them into the biro holders. In just under ten minutes, he had created two freely moving dowsing rods.

Next he laid the map out on the table. Standing equally on both of his feet, he held the rods over the map. With the intention of finding the location of the burial ground he began to move them very slowly over the paper. It was a large map and showed the field, the brook and Stone Clump. He tried not to will the rods to cross over and give him a result but it was hard. In the end, he had to close his eyes and remove his thoughts.

When he felt the rods cross he had to stop himself from jumping. Carefully, he looked. They were poised over a hill but it wasn't Stone Clump. In fact it wasn't anywhere near the field. He searched his mind for an explanation but could make no sense of it. Burial grounds were located near a settlement, not on the far side of a river. So he moved the rods to a different location, watched them face the front, and closed his eyes again.

The next time they moved, he found that they had crossed over at exactly the same place. He tried a third time and a fourth, each time moving the rods further out until they were nowhere near the Stennings at all. But each time they crossed at the same place.

He turned to Falala who had come to stand beside him. "There's no doubt about it, Fally, the burial site we are looking for is at the foot of ..."

He was interrupted by the ringing of his phone. As he took the call his face grew ashen. "Is she hurt?" After a minute, he ended the call.

"What's the matter?" asked Falala.

"That was Larna, the woman Selena is staying with. She said that Selena was in the accident as well. That she was out walking in the storm when it happened."

They both stared at each other for a long moment.

"She wants me to go to the boat," he continued. "Apparently, Selena can't remember what happened and is having some kind of breakdown."

SELENA – Present Day

I'm standing on Birdinghall Spit, the lick of land that lies between marsh and ocean on the very top of the Norfolk coast. It is my favourite place in the world where the vast skies are washed by the wind and salt spray, and the smooth sand is silky. Here, I am one with everything. It doesn't matter which eye I am seeing through. Edges are blurring as everything that has happened is washed clean by the waves as they roll away from the shore.

And then I hear it. A howl. The wolf has returned at last then. We are far from the forest but somehow it has made its way to the shore. The sea is shattered into splinters and the waves into trees. Hurled back into the forest, I look frantically for a place to hide but there is nowhere safe in the rain which pours down in a demonic waterfall.

circa 2000 B.C.E.

Sweat mixed with rain as Bannan continued to dig. Every part of his body ached from his injuries. He needed to rest but Hogan wouldn't let him. He had changed sides at the last moment and this was his punishment.

As he stopped to wipe the rain from his face, he noticed a shadow between two of the trees he was about to fell. Straightening, he looked up to see the girl Seela approaching, her red hair plastered to her face, eyes darkly hollowed, and one arm strapped to her side. As soon as she was close enough to him, she held out a beaker with her good hand. Gratefully, he took it.

"So this is where he will be buried." she said, pointing to the inner ring of the circular ditch.

Exhausted, Bannan wiped the water from his eyes. "You came over the bridge then."

She nodded.

"That can't have been easy with only one hand to hold the rope." He watched the fear pass over her face. Turning his attention to the beaker, he drained it in one long gulp before giving it back to her. "The weather is likely to get worse. Look at the clouds."

Seela jumped when an enormous clap of thunder shattered the sky. He reached out to steady her, careful not to touch her arm, but she flinched away from him. "I am finished here," he said. "Let's go back together. I will help you over the bridge." Warily, he looked up at the clouds. "Hogan says that The Father lives up there, whereas The Mother lives in the earth beneath our feet. It seems that, from now on, we are to worship the weather." He looked back at the girl who was shivering uncontrollably, her face had drained of all colour. "Come on. I'll put these tools in the bag on my back. Let's return to the settlement."

SELENA – Present Day

I wake up with tears streaming down my face as though I, too, have been out in the drenching rain. I can still see the rickety bridge and feel the fear as its wooden struts threaten to give way under our weight. The man Bannan has been kind but my heart has caved in. Riadd is dead and will be put into the ground. According to Hogan, The Mother is dead too. She has been replaced by The Father as though She never existed. If He is anything like Hogan, then we are all doomed to rot.

In an attempt to rid myself of the ghastly feelings, I squeeze my eyes shut again but my pearly eye refuses to co-operate. Alive and hot, it is determined to show me faces I don't want to see. They hover just out of reach as though they would speak to me from far away and tell me what to do.

The wolf is there, just at the edge, still waiting to devour me. I need to escape but for that I must find somewhere to go.

It is time I decided what to do.

circa 2000 B.C.E.

Rain was dripping from Seela's hair and clothes as she let herself into Lanalla's hut.

"Thank The Mother that you are back," said the priestess. "Where have you been?"

"I went to see Riadd's grave. Bannan has nearly finished it."

"You're soaking, child. Take your clothes off and lay them by the fire. Dry yourself and put on some of mine. You know where they are."

It took a long time for Seela to change but Lanalla could not move to help her. Duna was sleeping fitfully on her lap, the child's face pale and her breathing fast and raggedy. Seela's dislocated shoulder throbbed painfully with every movement and it was as much as she could do not to give up and cry, but eventually she was dry and able to kneel down on the hard floor beside them both. Anxious, she laid her hand on her sister's forehead. "She burns with fever," she said. "Are there no more herbs you can give her?"

"I have done all I can. The Mother is preparing to take her."

Seela took the little girl's sweaty hand in her own. It seemed that the escape from their kin had not only failed but was about to kill the only person she loved.

"Where is the new burial ground?" asked Lanalla softly. "I heard that Hogan decreed it should be outside the settlement."

It was a while before Seela could answer. "Beyond the bridge, at the bottom of the second hill," she eventually replied. Despite the dry clothes, her teeth had begun to chatter again. "It is difficult to find."

Lanalla shook her head sadly. "Hogan is trying to separate us from our ancestors. If we lose connection with the earth then we will all die."

The blackbird that Seela had healed flew to her shoulder from its perch in the hut and squawked a warning into her ear. At the same time there was a shout from outside.

"The villagers are being called to the burial," croaked Lanalla. "We have to go."

"No," Seela protested. "Duna is too sick to move."

"You have no choice. If you do not go, Hogan will come and fetch you both."

Seela rose quickly to her feet. "Then we will just have to leave before he comes."

"But how?" said Lanalla. "You've just admitted that Duna is too ill to be moved."

Seela turned to her, green eyes enormous in the dim light of the hut. "I will not allow Hogan to take me as his mate and sacrifice Duna."

When there was another shout from outside, Lanalla reached round her neck and removed the Amulet, looking as though her heart would break. "Go if you must, Seela, but I cannot allow you to take Duna with you. She must stay with me." She held out the Amulet. "Take this instead. Put it around your neck. It will protect you. I promise that I will take care of your sister as though she is my own child. I will not let her be sacrificed. Remember, Hogan has been cursed. The curse will follow him wherever and whenever he goes. The Amulet is powerful, Seela. You have to trust it. You are the SeeSayer. You have the power. You must trust The Mother. And you must trust me."

"You want me to leave Duna with you?" said Seela in astonishment. "After what you did?"

"I had no other option," Lanalla said, crying openly now. "I had to make you the SeeSayer. It was the only way to save you."

Seela was incredulous. "You think that what Hogan did to me was saving me?"

"No, of course not, but …"

"Then help Duna and me to escape. It is the least you can do."

Lanalla stared at her in disbelief. "You cannot dismiss me like that."

"Yes I can," Seela retorted angrily. "I am the SeeSayer now, remember?"

"But I have done everything for you," Lanalla protested. "I have offered you my protection, fed you and kept you warm. Where do you think you would be now if I hadn't taken you in? The wolf's scratch would have killed your sister long before now. You cannot leave me. You are like my children. I have no-one else but the two of you."

"You should have thought of that before you betrayed Riadd."

The priestess bent her head, her tears dripping onto Duna's hot face. But the little girl did not stir.

Seela stroked the feathers of the blackbird on her shoulder and straightened. It was time for her to be brave and show Lanalla that she no longer needed her.

SELENA – Present Day

This time I wake up with my uninjured arm over my eyes as though I'm trying to protect myself. I've got to escape before it's too late. Painfully I push myself into a sitting position and try to swing my legs out of the bed, but I move too quickly and my head starts to swim.

Then I hear a bang. Horrified, I sink back down under the covers. What if Hogan has come to find me already? What if he's come to take Duna and sacrifice her? What if I can't save her?

The bang turns out to be a knock at the door. Larna pokes her head around, holding an excited Buddy by the collar. "It's Raff," she says, looking worried. "He's come to see you."

Raff? He's here? I stare at her, trying to halt the pictures flashing through my mind: Riadd trying to protect me, Hogan killing him, Bannan digging his grave. Determined to sit up, I ignore the pain in my shoulder. I'm about to ask Larna to help me get dressed when I stop myself. I am being too dependent on this woman. She is not my mother.

"I'll help you get dressed," she offers brightly.

"No need," I reply. "I can do it by myself."

Her face falls. "Are you sure? The sling will make it difficult."

"I'm fine," I lie, trying to ignore the way her hand reaches out to help me and then falls back down by her side. "I won't be long."

She hesitates. "Of course," she says flatly, before turning and leaving the room.

My heart starts to hammer as I swing my legs out of bed. Suddenly, the tiny cabin feels too small to contain my fear. It takes me ages to dress myself. Every time I jolt my shoulder pain shakes me as though I have been shot by a gun. In the end, I take so long that Larna returns to see if I am all right.

"Raff's waiting for you in the snug," she tells me. "I am going to make him some tea."

By now, my teeth are chattering. I can't seem to get warm. "Would you drape my coat around my shoulders, please?" I ask after she has helped me to pull on my socks.

She looks surprised. "You won't need it. I've lit the fire."

"I'd feel happier with my coat on," I tell her. I need as much protection as I can get.

"Okay," she says, fetching it from the back of the door.

Once it is over my shoulders, my eyepatch is in place and my hair brushed, I follow her out of the bedroom. I have taken so long to get ready that I wonder if he will still be there, but even before I enter the snug I can feel him. Just as I can still feel Riadd.

Buddy greets me enthusiastically before running back to

Raff, who is looking uncomfortable and far too tall for the boat. Larna takes the now empty mug from his hand. Once she has disappeared into the kitchen to make another pot, he sits down and I take my usual chair by the window.

It's several moments before he speaks. "Are you all right? Fally told me that you were in the accident."

"I dislocated my shoulder, that's all."

"Does it hurt?"

"Only if I knock it."

"That's a relief. What happened? What were you doing out on the road in the storm?"

I can hardly tell him that I'd thought he was Riadd and had been trying to warn him. "I don't remember," I say disingenuously.

He looks astounded and opens his mouth to question me further before he thinks better of it and shuts it again.

We fall into an uncomfortable silence which is only broken when Larna reappears with a tray of tea. "Is everything okay?" she asks.

I squirm, dislodging the coat. As I try to tug it back in place with my good hand, I accidentally brush against a bulge in the pocket. Without thinking, my hand slides inside. My breath snags.

"What's the matter?" asks Larna in concern. "Is it your…"

She doesn't get any further. There's a gasp of shock from them both as I pull out the necklace.

Larna looks as though she's going to be sick.

"It was in my pocket. It doesn't make any sense. Hester Knebworth stole it. How did it get there?"

"Well she can't have returned it," Raff says flatly. "She's in hospital."

I recoil. "What?"

"Raff, don't," Larna pleads.

He ignores her. "Hester Knebworth was in the car. Marcus was driving. He has a broken arm, a broken leg and he's unconscious. His mother is in a coma, covered in lacerations from going through the windscreen. For some reason, she wasn't wearing a seatbelt."

My blood runs cold. They are hurt because of me? Horrified, I think of the man with white hair at the dig and shudder. I might not like him, but I don't wish him any harm. And his mother might be awful and arrogant, but to be in a coma …

Underneath the eyepatch, my pearly eye swivels and a picture appears in my mind but it leaves me before I can work out what it is trying to tell me.

"Remind me where you dug up the necklace," Raff suddenly asks.

"In the woods at the foot of Stenning Hill."

His eyes widen and he shakes his head as though he does not believe what I am saying. "Exactly where in the woods?"

"By the big oak tree. Why do you want to know?"

He ignores the question. "When you are feeling better, will you show me exactly where?"

I nod, still staring at the necklace. It is glowing on my fingers as if it has just come home.

□

Wyrd – fate

Chapter Fourteen

SELENA AND RAFF – Present Day

It doesn't take me long to recover enough to take Raff to the bottom of Stenning Woods. Underneath the giant oak, the atmosphere is strangely thick and unmoving. Elsewhere, the leaves are ruffling in a gentle breeze but here they are as still as carvings.

There's no sign of the little mound where I buried the blackbird, but my pearly eye can still see its pained, frightened eyes looking at me as I tried to free it. Seela had been there too, a barefooted girl staring at a patch of earth that glinted in the sun. If I'd known then what I know now, I would have turned away and fled and not allowed myself to be drawn backwards into time.

"Is this where you found the necklace?" asks Raff, pointing to the roots at the bottom of the oak tree.

I nod, wondering what I have released into the world. As if the answer lies in the earth under my feet, I detect a faint scent of fire flames dancing here thousands of years ago. Raff crouches down to feel the earth with his fingers. Does he sense it too, the place where he once lay, his tall young body broken and limp?

"There's something here," he says, his head slightly cocking to one side as he listens. "It's the same voice I heard before, calling to me. "

My pearly eye begins to zing and we both spin around to see a girl with long red hair standing bare-foot on a patch of mud some distance away, her intense green gaze pinned to him as though he is the only one here. Looking at her is like looking in a mirror after insufficient sleep. The edges are blurry but everything else is clear enough. Unable to resist the reflection, I put my good hand up to my dislocated shoulder and imagine that I can feel the brush of feathers against my fingers.

"Seela?" Raff tries, once again on his feet, his voice little more than a croak. "Seela, is that you?"

My heart cracks and separates as though it has two heartbeats, rather than one.

"Seela," Raff pleads again, his voice breaking in his throat, "speak to me."

I want to ask her to look at me, but she only has eyes for Raff. When she opens her mouth to reply no sound comes out as though her voice has become tangled inside itself. Slowly, she begins to reach out to him with one of her hands. Her skin is both young and old at the same time, smooth as silk and yet wrinkled as old parchment that has been screwed up, discarded, and can no longer be read. Ridiculously, I am jealous.

Raff looks as though he is about to cry. His face has lit up with impossible hope and something that also looks like terror. Suddenly he seems more youth than man. As I look between her and him, me and him, her and me, the boundaries of person and time begin to merge until it is impossible to know who is, who was, or when we were or are.

By now, her look of longing at Raff is devastating. I can feel her pleading with him to rescue her from the fate that she has already endured. A ghastly pain shoots across my heart but I can't tell if it's her heart or mine. I try to warn him but already something like a shadow is breaking off from him and floating towards her.

It's only when I step forward between the two of them that she finally sees me.

You, she breathes into my mind in a strange, guttural language that I somehow understand.

I saw you in the tree.

Speechless, I nod.

Your eye.

Self-consciously, I put my hand up to my face.

I've been trying to look through it.

It's true. I can feel her now in my pearly eye, which bubbles in a way it never has before. At the same time, my green eye is beginning to smart as if I'm peeling onions so that, in seconds, tears are running down my face until I am truly blind. Then I am seeing her from the inside, all mottled and bruised like a bag that has been screwed up and thrown away. I gasp with the recognition of loss as she seems to float closer. It is like looking into myself and yet into someone else. I recognise her at a primal level although her heart beats more wildly and instinctively than mine. Rooted into the ground in a way that I have never been, she is like a sapling planted deep down from the very beginning.

There is only one thing I can do to help us both. Without looking away, I reach my hand into my pocket and feel for the necklace. Then, ridding it of the handkerchief so that I am skin-to-skin with the metal, I call in courage and wait for it to flow through us like a beam of light. "Take it," I whisper, holding it out to her. "Put it around your neck. It will keep you safe."

At first she looks frightened as though I am holding out

a snake, but then, as though she can see inside me too and realises that we are two parts of the same whole, she slowly reaches out to take it.

"No!" shouts Raff. His cry breaks the spell and her hand draws back.

I jump and let the necklace go so that it falls to the ground. For a long second, none of us moves. Then, as if in slow motion, Raff bends down to pick it up. Before he can touch it, Seela crouches down beside him and they gaze into each other's eyes as though all the years between have simply melted away. Her eyes are green and compelling. His are cavernous and so black that they might be holding the whole world's suffering inside them.

My pearly eye feels as though it's about to splinter. "He is not Riadd," I cry, concerned that she'll drag him into somewhere so deep inside himself that he will never be able to escape. "Step away."

Surprise and disappointment cloud her features as she looks up at me, her face cracked with grief. Bewildered, she reaches for the necklace. Our gazes lock and there is a kind of a sizzling between us until an even deeper connection is made. The pain in my pearly eye shifts and my sight clears.

For a moment I can see clearly through both eyes. I blink at the harshness of the unexpected light.

And she is gone.

KARL – Present Day

Karl walked into the room where his mother lay. Covered from head to toe in cream-coloured bandages, she looked more like an Egyptian mummy than a living human being. The lack of colour wasn't helped by the décor. The room in the hospital was stark. The machines were white, the sheets were white, the very air was white. Only the black screen of the monitor provided some sort of relief, telling him that she was still alive. As he sat down at the far side of the bed, a strong wave of love for her washed over him, threatening to undo him altogether. The doctors had told him that she didn't have much of a face left and, that if she survived, she would have to spend the rest of her life having skin grafts and plastic surgery.

He reached out to take her hand before realising that there was nothing to hold because of the bandages. Tears rose up, threatening to spill, but he kept them back. Although he wanted to weep and cling to her, telling her that he forgave the way she had treated him and that it was going to be all right, he knew he wouldn't be able to speak. He wanted to hug her, but that wasn't possible either. Bodies were dirty, she had always said. Besides, he had always disgusted her. He didn't think he'd been hugged since he was born.

He was trying to quell his emotions when, to his surprise, he heard a buzzing and, turning his head towards the sound, he saw a wasp land on the bandages which covered her body. Perplexed, he stared at it. What was a wasp doing in such a sterile environment, and when winter was only just deciding to slacken its grip? Nervously, he swished it away, but it only landed again on a different area of white. Suddenly, something in him revolted as though a deep-seated memory was stinging a dark part of his mind back into existence. At the same time, an image of his father's dead face began to swim in front of him. It was too much. He sprang to his feet and ran out of the room, forgetting to shut the door behind him.

As soon as he was back in the manor, he locked himself in his bedroom. There were drawings everywhere. In one, a red-headed girl dressed in skins was staring out into the distance, a look of longing on her face. In another, an over-tall, black-haired youth was carving a piece of wood with a dog at his feet. Next, a broad-shouldered man was striding through the forest with something shiny around his neck. Then there was a desperate-eyed woman standing with one palm down and the other pointing up to the sky. After that there were huts built into the forest, a track leading down to a river and an outside fire blazing next to three stakes jutting cruelly out of the hard ground. In the final picture, his father lay dead in a pool of long congealed blood.

In an attempt to make sense of them, he hung them on his walls one by one, not straight but crooked as if their edges might somehow stream into one another and give up their secrets. When they still made no sense, he tried rearranging them in an attempt to discover the story hidden in their lines. But they remained broken. The only thing that bound them together were the Xs at the edges.

And then, like a giant haphazard jigsaw coming together, he reminded himself that he recognised the faces. Somehow he had projected who he knew and who he didn't onto bodies from the ancient past. The girl was Selena, the woman he had met on the doorstep of the manor, while the tall youth was the man from the dig who had introduced himself as Raff at the hospital. The broad-shouldered man with white hair and grim determination in his eyes bore an uncanny resemblance to his brother. That left two characters. The woman in prayer had a watery quality to her which somehow floated in and out of focus. He didn't recognise her as anyone he knew, and yet she was familiar to him. Hatred poured off the remaining character like sweat. He had drawn only a profile and so couldn't see all the features clearly, but as he stared, the face seemed to turn.

As he recognised the face, the room started to crush him.

Unwilling to believe what he had seen, he fled downstairs, almost fell into his wellington boots, and ran away from the village to Stenning Woods, not stopping until he had reached the church on the top of the hill.

Panting hard, he let himself into the churchyard and closed the gate behind him. The extraordinary stained-glass window of Mary holding a lamb had been a refuge for him ever since he could remember. The image was art at its best: simple and stunningly beautiful, a magical combination of nature and the human need to understand the inexplicable. Looking at it from the outside always calmed him. But there was something different about the window today. Xs were scattered around the edges of the stained glass just as they were scattered around his paintings.

He rubbed his eyes in surprise. Surely they hadn't been there before? He closed his eyes and opened them again. Now they were even bigger. Heart thudding to the point of bursting, he clutched his chest in alarm. He knew this window as intimately as if he had created it himself.

Suddenly needing to escape the window and himself, he backed away towards the yew tree in the graveyard, out to the woods beyond and back down the hill.

SELENA, RAFF AND KARL – Present Day

A figure, pale and gaunt enough to be another wraith, is stepping out from between the trees, his throat working with the effort of trying to speak.

Raff straightens, pointing to the sky like a tree that has grown too tall for itself. "Karl?" he splutters. "Is that you?"

The two men stare at each other as though they have deep knowledge of one another and yet can't quite recognise who they are. Karl is the first to look away.

"Has something happened since we met you at the hospital?" Raff asks him.

Karl doesn't even try to speak. Instead, he pulls a notebook and pencil out of his pocket, writes something and hands it to Raff, who reads it before passing it to me.

I need your help. You are both in my sketchbooks. Will you come back with me to the manor and look at what I have drawn? I don't understand what the pictures mean.

Raff looks at me in surprise. I look back at him as if to say that we've just seen a four-thousand-year-old ghost so why should going to view some paintings be in any way peculiar?

We walk to the manor in silence. I have to force myself inside. Hester Knebworth might not be in here in person but I can feel her presence trying to crawl up my spine like one of her loathed insects. Karl leads us up into his bedroom. The walls are covered with haphazardly pinned-up sketches of me, Raff, his mother, Marcus and Larna, all dressed in skins from the Bronze Age settlement. There are far more pictures than there were before when I pulled his sketchbooks out from under his bed, and they are all scenes from the dreams. How can he have drawn these when he has not even touched the necklace? How can he see so clearly when both of his eyes are the same colour?

Pulling myself together, I set about arranging the pictures of Seela's story in chronological order. Karl and Raff both have to help me because I can only use one arm but it's a relief not to have to go through the scenes on my own. It is not long before we run out of space. We need longer walls and at least two of them. The narrowboat comes to mind so I suggest that we return there and ask Larna if we may use *Water Haven.*

Once we have gathered up the pictures, we carry them across the footbridge to the river. Bertie's car is once again parked by the boat. There is no time to turn away because

Buddy is already rushing out to greet us, closely followed by Larna. Behind her Bertie looks crushed, his immaculate suit creased, his face lined where before it was smooth.

"Karl?" he says, stepping forward, his mouth working as though he is about to cry. "Is that you?" When Karl only stares, he partially opens his arms. "It's me, old thing, your Uncle Bertie, a.k.a. Aunt Bee. I know it must be a surprise to see me like this, but it had to be done."

Karl's throat works. He is still beyond speech and now looking confused. When Bertie looks at me, I'm beyond speech too. I don't know what to say to him. My injury is so trivial compared with that of Marcus and his sister.

It is Raff who comes to the rescue. "Larna, we need your help," he says, grabbing Buddy's collar to stop him from jumping up at me. "Karl has done some sketches and paintings of the dreams but there isn't enough space in the manor for us to pin them up in the right order. May we use the long walls of your narrowboat to see if they show us what happened all those years ago?"

Shock registers on Larna's face before she slowly nods. We all disappear inside and suddenly *Water Haven* seems very small.

It doesn't take long to replace Larna's pictures with Karl's. It is an unsettling task and reminds me of all that I have dreamed. The sequence begins with a wolf stalking round the bottom of a tree, looking upwards to its prey hiding in the branches. Next a blackbird sings in snowy darkness, trying to sew the leaves of a tree together to create a screen to hide two exhausted girls. Then there is the oak tree where I found the necklace. After that is a magnificent painting of Riadd and his dog Bika, and several sketches of Seela, including one of her collecting water from the river. The priestess seems to be ever-present as do the huts of the settlement. So far, so good.

Next is an unkempt man lurking in the forest, his eyes full of loathing as he clutches something round his neck. Then a white-haired man is kneeling at the first man's feet, his hands out in front of him as though he is trying to shield himself from an unspeakable horror. The rape comes next, an almost unbearable depiction of pain and anguish. It is followed by the picture of a man I don't recognise lying on the ground in a pool of blood. Finally, the return of the Amulet and Lanalla's cursing of Hogan as she forges a sacred connection between earth and sky.

All of us are stunned into silence by the time we look at the final image. The thirteen paintings and assortment of sketches have turned Larna's boat into an extraordinary art gallery which brings Seela's story to life on paper. My similarity to Seela was never in doubt, or Raff's to Riadd, but seeing the likeness between Larna and the priestess is shocking. The pairs of Bertie and Bannan, Marcus and Mevin, and Karl and Kurt have become evident, while the resemblance between Hester Knebworth and Hogan, even though one is a woman and the other a man, is unmistakable. Finally, there seems little doubt that the Amulet and the necklace are one and the same. It is like looking at mirror versions stretched between ancient and modern.

Only one set of images is missing. "There's nothing to show that Seela has appeared in the present," I tell them.

"What do you mean, that she has appeared in the present?" asks Bertie.

"Selena and I saw her in the woods just now," Raff says. "And it's not the first time. I saw her several times when she was under the field, pleading with me to save her. And then, on the night I took the necklace back to the farmhouse to clean it up, I went for a ride on the motorbike. Seela was ahead of me in the road, as real as you and me. She forced me to swerve and I crashed the bike." Distractedly, he wiped his hand across his forehead. "I should have been hurt but somehow I escaped unscathed."

Now he takes off his glasses and holds them out in front of him as though they will somehow enable us to see something we have missed. "Something similar also happened to my colleague Fally in her car. A girl with bedraggled red hair flagged her down in a storm. She appeared to be hurt so Fally tried to take her to the hospital, but Seela jumped out of the car while it was moving. Fally searched, as I did, but there was no sign of her."

It's my turn to reveal the present day encounters. "I saw Seela at Oxford railway station," I admit. "She stopped me catching the train back to Norwich and, in the process, I lost my return ticket." I take a breath. "I've had other sightings, too. In the river at night in Oxford, by the oak tree in Stenning Woods where she showed me the location of the necklace, by the escarpment just before I hid in the cave to shelter from the storm, and in the churchyard after I'd dreamed about her in the church. I've touched her, too," I add. "Her skin feels like cold candle wax."

"She doesn't smell too good either," Raff says.

I nod, screwing up my face. "Like rotting talcum powder."

Larna, Bertie and Karl are staring at us. "Are you both suggesting that Seela has somehow come out of the past into the present?" asks Bertie, a combination of horror and fascination on his face.

Without warning, my memory clears like a series of stills being flicked forward into a film reel. I hear the sound of footsteps following me in pouring rain. "It was Seela who caused the accident."

His face turns to granite. "What are you saying?"

"I was trying to get to the farmhouse to see Raff. I wanted

to turn up the track but she started to chase me and forced me onto the road. When the Rolls appeared, it seemed to lose control and swerve towards me so she pushed me into a ditch." I blink rapidly. "She saved my life."

As my words sink in, speechlessness turns into silence. The only sound is the faint creaking of the boat as it rocks gently on the water and I wonder if any of us will ever speak again.

"We have to find a way of stopping her," says Raff after a long silence.

Karl starts to scribble a message and hands it to me to read out. "Do you think she is trying to tell us something?"

Larna nods. "We still don't know the rest of her story." It is the first thing she has said since we pinned the pictures up on her walls. "Perhaps she needs us to see what happened to her."

"Are you saying that she might rest if we allow her to die?" asks Bertie.

The idea of seeing what Hogan may have done to Seela and Duna makes me want to run away. I start to shake my head in refusal but Larna is right. If we are to stop Seela from appearing in the present and causing another accident, then we have to see her story through to the bitter end.

"What about if I borrowed some equipment so that I can document what happens?" Bertie suggests warily. "Some data would make Seela so much more believable to my readers."

Shocked that he should be thinking about his book, I baulk, but just as I am about to protest he looks at me with such longing in his face that I bite my tongue and nod instead.

It takes a couple of days for Bertie to borrow some portable equipment. When he returns to the boat, we are all there to meet him. Once again immaculately dressed, he perches his spectacles on the end of his nose, looks at each of us over the top of them, and collects us together like favourite chess pieces. I'm feeling sick and clutching the handkerchief-wrapped necklace in my lap.

"I've brought five recording devices," he explains, "a non-contact digital infrared thermometer, an EMF meter, a voice recorder and two video cameras. I also have my laptop so that we can run everything from a central station.

"The purpose of the thermometer is to detect any fluctuations in temperature because extreme cold indicates the presence of spirit and paranormal activity. It has a built-in laser pointer and a backlit digital display for viewing in dark locations so that instant temperature readings can be taken. The digital voice recorder will capture any sound. The EMF meter will help us to read the electromagnetic signature that all living things within our environment produce. As for the two video cameras on tripods, one is for you Selena, and the other is for the corner of the room so that we can have a broader view of anything that might happen." He bites his lip. "That's as much as I can cover outside a laboratory situation."

"What if Selena doesn't dream?" queries Raff.

"Then we will just have to try again another time," Bertie answers.

"And what if the experiment doesn't stop Seela from appearing in the present?" asks Larna.

Bertie rubs his chin thoughtfully. "Then we will have to try to find another way of stopping her." He looks briefly out at the river before turning back to face us again. "Selena, come and lie down."

Feeling as though I'm accepting an invitation to my own execution, I reluctantly settle myself on the cushions.

"Hold the necklace in your right hand. Raff, will you forgive Selena if she unwraps it from your handkerchief and touches it with her bare hands?"

Reluctantly, Raff nods.

"Good man. Now you take her left hand. Karl, you hold Selena's feet. I'll operate the equipment while you, Larna, give any necessary instructions."

Slowly, I unpeel the necklace from the cloth and clutch it tightly. Then I close my eyes. There is the sound of a candle being lit and Larna saying a prayer. Then, soothed by the gentle rocking of the boat, I let go, aware only of the fire crackling in the stove and the air coming in and out of my nostrils.

Finally, I dare to turn my pearly eye inward and descend into the darkness to meet my nemesis.

circa 2000 B.C.E.

"I am leaving," said Seela.

Larna stared at her as though her heart would break. "Very well, I'll come with you as far as the forest. Hogan will expect us all to be there for Riadd's burial. You will have your chance to escape when everyone walks to the hill for the sacrifice at the Stone."

"Have you got the Amulet?"

Seela touched the hidden place at her neck and nodded.

"And Riadd's knife?"

Before Seela could nod again, there was a sharp shout from outside commanding the remaining villagers to come out of their huts.

"Keep your head down and follow me," urged Lanalla. Pulling the fading Duna closer to her hip, she walked to the entrance of the hut.

With their heads down, they joined the last of the frightened villagers and began to trudge towards the flimsy bridge across the river. The river had subsided since the storm, but the water still lapped at their feet as they crossed.

Once everyone was gathered at the freshly created burial ground, Hogan began to speak. "Riadd has gone from us," he declared, now fully in charge. "He fought bravely and would have grown to be a powerful man had he lived. Let his death be a warning to all of you who would try to stand in my way. You need a strong Leader who is prepared to defend the land and your honour at any cost. I am the strongest amongst you, and in return for my protection and leadership, you will swear to obey me." Looking from one white face to another, he waited for a protest. When one of the villagers accidentally jostled Seela's injured shoulder, she cried out. Hogan saw her in the crowd and glared. Biting down hard on her lip, she looked away.

"In deference to our old way of life," he continued, "I will allow The Stone to work its magic for one of the moon's stretchings. If that does not bring New Blood, then we will raid other camps and bring women to us so that we can strengthen our breeding. But make no mistake. We worship The Father now and I am his representative. You will obey me or you will die." No-one moved. "Now, let us bury Riadd. I have instructed that this new burial ground be prepared here as a warning to you all. It is outside the protection of our village. Forget the ancestors. Anyone who defies me will have howling wolves as their only company." He waited for the words to sink in. Then he snapped his fingers. "Bannan, bring the body."

Bannan appeared with Riadd's body in his arms. As he stopped at the inner circle of the barrow ditch and laid the body on its right side in the deep central pit, Lanalla put her free hand over her mouth to stop a sob from escaping. When he began to drop twigs all around the body, Seela bit back her own howl of despair. Sweat rolled down Bannan's weakened body as he laboured to fill the central pit with gravel. Finally, he drove twelve pointed oak stakes into the top of the grave with an additional stake at the centre of the circle. Then he lit the kindling around the body and stood back.

It took a long time for the fire to blaze in the cold, damp air, but Hogan forced them all to watch until all they could see was smoke and flame. Then he spoke again. "Now, we will return to the settlement and climb up to The Stone. There I will sacrifice the girl-child called Duna, claim her sister Seela as my mate, and we will be strong once again."

As Hogan began to round up the villagers for the walk up to the place of sacrifice, Seela urged Lanalla into a tight clump of trees. "Give Duna to me," she whispered urgently.

"But you said I could keep her," uttered Lanalla in shock.

"I have changed my mind. She is my sister. You cannot have her."

"But what about your shoulder? You are not strong enough to carry her."

"I will find the strength."

Tears began to run down Lanalla's cheeks. "Then at least let me come with you," she pleaded.

"No. You must go with them and act as a cover for us. Now pass her over."

Weeping silently, Lanalla reluctantly released the sleeping child onto Seela's good arm, trying to ignore the way that the girl winced as she took her sister. "Are you sure you want to do this, Seela? It will be more difficult for the two of you to escape and she needs my care."

"I am sure."

Defeated, Lanalla briefly touched the Amulet at Seela's breast. "Then take The Mother's love with you. May she protect you and keep you safe." With a final look of love, she turned away and followed the villagers towards The Stone.

Once the last of them had disappeared, Seela stared out from behind the shelter of trees and shivered. The second hill was almost completely covered in snow, and she had no idea what lay beyond it. Cursing herself for not having asked Lanalla for more directions, she clenched her jaw. She had to be strong but it was as much as she could do to stop herself from weeping. Already her injured shoulder throbbed and the place between her legs still stung. Worst of all, there was no movement from Duna. She only hoped that it was because of the sleeping draught that Lanalla had given her to keep her quiet.

As another bout of shivering shook her, Seela looked longingly at the flames still dancing in the remains of Riadd's pyre. It would take everyone a while to clamber back over the bridge across the river and climb to the top of the hill with the Stone on top. Perhaps she could take this final chance to warm them both before Hogan discovered that she had gone. Riadd wouldn't mind. He'd be glad to be able to help them at last.

Holding the child close, she slowly stumbled out of the cover of the trees and down to the remains of the pyre. Flames still occasionally danced upwards, sending sparks into the air. Although the air was filled with a meaty stench that roiled her stomach, she drank in the heat as though it might save their lives.

As she began to warm up, the image of an eye appeared through her despair. It was a strange eye, white as though it was blind, yet able to see through into other worlds. She welcomed the vision. The pearly eye belonged to the woman who was helping her. The woman who watched. The woman who listened. The woman whose vision had been with her ever since the long night when they'd had to hide in the tree, terrified that the wolf would return and drag them down.

Now it was here again. She only hoped that it would show her how to escape.

Instinctively, she shifted the child's weight on her arm and grasped the pendant that lay over her heart. It was hot and sent sparks of flame into her hand, a glow of light pulsing around it as though it were alive. At the same time, she found everything surrounded by a milky glow as though she was looking through the woman's pale orb. There was the suggestion of a song, the one she had heard up in the tree, and suddenly an irrational sense of peace began to descend over her as though she were no longer in danger.

"It is time ..."

The woman's musical voice was calm and Seela felt her heart begin to slow. Briefly closing her eyes, she inhaled the warmth of the pyre, cuddling Duna close for comfort. If only she could sleep now and Duna was able to survive her fever, the woman with the pearly eye would surely help get them to safety. Then she would take them both home and they would see their mother again.

It was only when she realised that the little girl had stopped trembling that she opened her eyes. A touch to her forehead told her that the fever had indeed subsided. Filled with relief, she looked into the beloved face of her sister. The movement caused Duna's head to loll. Gently she pushed the child's face back into her shoulder but it fell backwards again. When she cradled the back of the tiny head with her hand, coolness bruised her palm. "Duna?" she whispered. The only response was the crackling of the dying flames. "Duna, wake up!" Horrified, she put her face next to the little girl's to seek her breath, but there was none. She put her hand on the tiny chest but there was no rhythm. "No!" she cried into the frigid air. She shook the tiny child, expecting her to cry out with pain but there was no response.

The face she adored was white, lifeless and already growing cold.

A terrible grief began to rise inside Seela, tearing her apart, filling her with despair and a fear so great that it threatened to overwhelm her completely. She wanted to shout and yell and scream her pain down to the earth, up into the sky, out to the stars. Where was the woman with the pearly eye? Why wasn't she taking her across worlds into safety? Why had she abandoned her when she needed her the most?

The only response was a man's voice. Eyes swollen with tears, she forced herself to look up to see Hogan running towards her, weaving angrily between the trees, bellowing her name. Slowly, she reached for the scabbard beneath her cloak, pulled out Riadd's knife and held it towards him.

"What are you doing there?" he yelled, his hair flying furiously around his head, his shoulders massive under the furs. "I need you both at the Stone."

She drew back at the stench of his rank breath. "No," she said, holding the knife up towards him. "We are not coming."

He made a growling sound in his throat and stepped closer.

She held the knife higher still. "You cannot have Duna for your sacrifice."

"I can and I will. Give her to me."

"I said no. She is dead," Seela moaned as she cradled her sister back into her body, swaying from side to side as though she was rocking her to sleep.

"It is of no importance," he said, gathering himself. "I'll find another child to sacrifice. Come to the Stone. You are New Blood and you must become my mate."

Ignoring the pain in her shoulder, she stood and looked directly into his eyes. "Never," she spat.

"You will do as I say. I am your Leader. Give me the knife."

Grasping the Amulet, she held it out towards him. The X on the pendant slithered towards him like a snake.

He had just taken two steps towards her when there was a blood-curdling yell from somewhere behind them. Neither of them had time to move before Lanalla ploughed into Hogan with an almighty crash. For a second, Priestess and Leader clung together in a grotesque parody of dance. Then they slowly toppled together into the flames.

The screams were terrible. Uncomprehending, Seela stared at the writhing bodies until they stilled. Then she heard the voice again.

"It is time."

Seela felt arms go around her. Then all the pain from her shoulder ceased. Gazing into the pearly white eye, she put the point of the blade to her heart, stepped forward and went home.

Epilogue

SELENA – Present Day

I awake the next day to the slight, soothing rock of the boat. Somehow, I feel calmer and more complete as though Seela is inside me, back where she belongs. Outside, a blackbird is warbling on the bank. This time the message is clear. *You must start singing again. Sing to Seela. Write your songs. Tell the world who you are and what you have seen.*

Wondering what the necklace would sound like if it too could make music, I wander outside, a water bottle clutched in my hand. The air is warm and balmy as I lower myself down onto one of the outside chairs that have been placed on the deck next to the little wrought iron table. Surprisingly, my injured shoulder no longer hurts as my mind starts to write words and notes and, for the first time since I left Highhill, I long to play my harp to bring the song to life.

I am just drinking some water when I see Raff striding over the field towards me. Somehow, he too looks different. There is new strength about him and the haunted expression on his face has been replaced with calm determination. As he reaches me he plucks the water bottle from my hand, raises it to his mouth and tips it backwards, his throat rising and falling as he drinks. A drop of water glistens on his lips as he removes the bottle and looks at me with all his vulnerability and strength shining in his eyes. I'm about to rise and go to him but I stop myself just in time in case this is Seela's response rather than mine. Overcome by pity for her and the boy who so desperately wanted to keep her safe, I force myself to stay seated.

"Are you all right?" he asks.

My pearly eye smiles. "I'm ready to start a new chapter," I say.

He nods slowly. "And what will you write?"

It's a good question and it's about time that I answered it. "Norfolk," I tell him. "I need to go back there and sort out the house."

He pales. "You're leaving?"

"I need to sell Highhill."

The muscles in his jaw start to work. "Does Larna know that you are going?" he says after a while.

I shake my head. "No."

"She'll be upset."

"Yes."

"And what about the experiment? Bertie won't want you to go either."

"He's got enough material to begin his book now," I say.

"What about Karl?" he tries. "Won't you stay and help him get his voice back?"

I don't move.

He looks out over the river where spring is painting the trees green at last, and there's a fragrance of flowers in the air. "You've made some good friends here. Please don't desert us all."

Tears push behind my eyes. I have to blink rapidly to chase them away.

He sinks into the chair next to me. "And what about you and me? Won't you give us a chance?"

The expression on his face nearly fells me. How can I bear to leave this gentle giant of a man who, four thousand years ago, tried so desperately to keep me safe and who is still trying to help me now? Something inside me starts to weep but I don't know whether it is Seela or me. "Would you like the necklace for the dig?" I offer, desperate to give him something. "You could put it in a museum where it is safe and can't harm anyone."

His face falls. "It will be a while before the dig has its own museum."

Unable to bear the disappointment in his face, I try to turn away but he takes my hand. I look down at the clasping. In some ways, he has never let me go in all the millennia we have known each other. An image of Seela's green eyes bubbles up into my mind. '*Dare to love him*,' she tells me. Her eyes flare. Then they fade and disappear.

"Is there anything I can do to persuade you to stay?" His thumb moves gently over my skin. Then he puts his hand under my chin and raises my face to his. "Can't we get to know each other as we are now, not as we once were?"

I don't know what to say. Caring means loss and I don't think I could bear any more of that.

"There are lots of people here for you, Selena. Please let us love you."

Deep inside me, Seela sighs. She has come home but what if there are other Seelas out there that need to be rescued?

"Please, Selena," he continues, his heart overflowing into his eyes. "Seela has been laid to rest. It's time for you to let her go."

Still I hesitate. Something inside me is holding me back. Whether it's Seela or my pearly eye I cannot say. All I know is that, before I can be loved, I have to accept every part of myself including the fragments that I have lost along the way.

As the blackbird begins to sing again, one of its feathers drifts down towards us. Raff reaches out and gracefully plucks it from the air. "Yours, I believe," he says, holding it out on his palm. "A gift. Take it. It is telling you to unwrap the present and leave the past behind."

My green eye blurs with a tear while deep inside, my pearly eye shivers as though it can see something unexpected. In my pocket, the necklace shifts slightly and I feel a renewed sense of courage.

With a smile, I take the feather.

For now, it will just have to be enough.

To be continued in *Amber Heart*

Author's Note

35 years ago, I moved to beautiful Oxfordshire after a violent marriage which left me with a serious injury. Ten years after that, I discovered the existence of an Anglo-Saxon grave which had been uncovered during excavations for a landfill site. Visits to each of the two bodies which had been separated and housed in different museums were overwhelming. A pall of sadness seemed to hover over each of them as though they were heart-broken that they were no longer together.

Although I had already had some children's poetry published, I decided to investigate trauma and ancient sadness by writing a novel. Over many years and my training in shamanic and sound healing, the novel began to explore soul loss. In an attempt to show why we behave as we do even when it makes no sense, the tale itself took on several different incarnations, eventually arriving at the form of a contemporary story which uncovers past lives, hidden relationships and behavioural patterns begun in the distant past.

After a visit to Norway and an introduction to runes, another divinatory layer was added and the idea for a trilogy began to form.

In the revelatory and powerfully cathartic process of writing, the reasons behind violent behaviour started to unravel and I began to understand that we all experience everything, good and bad, in order to grow and learn how to handle Free Will.

Compassion grew and the baddy I had begun with gradually morphed into the most sensitive character in the book.

In the first of the Rune Trilogy novels – *Pearly Eye* – Selena experiences the trauma of losing her family in a tragic accident. As she battles with living in the world with an eye that sees differently from other people, she is shown a previous life that she lived in the Bronze Age. Her story continues in the second and third novels when she travels back to lives lived in early Anglo-Saxon England and medieval Oxfordshire.

I hope you have enjoyed reading *Pearly Eye* as much as I have enjoyed writing it. It has been a privilege to have had the time to explore some of the reasons behind our complex human behaviour. We all have a pearly eye if only we will open it. My wish is that we will all learn to view things from the deeper, more compassionate perspective of internal viewing so that, at last, we can become kinder to ourselves, each other and the planet.

Acknowledgements

I could not have written all the versions without the support and patience of friends and family.

Thank you to Richard for his formidable editing skills at the beginning.

Also to my daughter Melinda who painstakingly edited large chunks of writing and pointed me in the right direction when I was getting lost.

Thank you also to Natasha and Sacha, my other two children, who, with Melinda, shine with such light, joy and reason to hope for the future.

Thank you to my soul sister Lynda Shaw who continues to support me whatever I do and also to her late and much loved mother, Joan Coates for wanting to read my book in its early stages.

Thank you to Deborah Bale and Roger Simmonds for reading middle drafts and having the courage to be honest.

I am also sincerely grateful to Basja Cengija who has shown such friendship and patience in reading my ideas over their many incarnations and for having such a brilliant grasp of the English language.

Thank you to Stephanie Hale, Writers' Coach, who helped me to believe in my writing.

Thank you also to Dee Nunan, Janet Britton and Jackie Jarvis who read an initial draft and gave huge encouragement.

Huge thanks to Jo Baldwin-Trott and Linda Aspey who read the first drafts of the entire trilogy and gave such invaluable feedback.

Thanks to Marilyn Messick especially for her invaluable guidance on the use of question marks, and to Donna Messick (no relation) for her brilliant editing skills and advice about the American Readers' market.

Thank you to Val Edson, Tara Shaw, Stephen Foster, Louisa Cox and Hilary Churchley for reading the final draft and loving it.

And to Vicki Morrison, writer extraordinaire, whose brave battle through cancer has turned her into an Amazing Wonder Woman. Thank you for your friendship and advice. It means the world.

Thank you to Sarah Houldcroft at Goldcrest Books for her kindness, encouragement, extraordinary patience and devoted love of animals.

Finally, to all my friends – you know who you are – including all the animals who have chosen to live their lives with me. I have loved you all. And now thanks to Pixie and Purrdey, present creatures of my heart – I adore you both.

I am hugely grateful to you all.

We are each of us angels with only one wing, and we can fly only by embracing each other.
Lucian de Crescenzo

About the Author

Laurelle began her career as a writer with poetry and has been published in several anthologies. Her love of music led her to train as a sound therapist and to write music for relaxation and to help in the healing process, some of which is available online via Spotify and other distributors.

All of her work touches on the spiritual nature of love, time, the universe, and our place within it. Laurelle has a B.A. Honours degree in Music and English, a PGCE teaching qualification, a Diploma in Sound Therapy – Dip ST – from the British Academy of Sound Therapy, and two certificates in Reiki. She has three children and lives in Shropshire with her dog Pixie and cat Purrdey.

www.laurellerond.com

Printed in Great Britain
by Amazon

37193141R00192